THE QUEERING

BROOKE SKIPSTONE

Skipst☀ne
PUBLISHING

ISBN (ebook): 978-1-7370064-5-9

ISBN (print): 978-1-7370064-6-6

Cover design by Cherie Chapman © ccbookdesign

First edition

"If you read this, you may understand that two women can truly love each other. And those who hate queers are a threat to everyone." — Taylor Baird

1

B&T

NO ONE in the world is *actually* named Brooke Skipstone.

Not for almost fifty years.

Taylor Baird MacKenzie, a long-term substitute teacher in Clear, Alaska, knew her secret had already begun to unravel. Brooke wrote novels about lesbian liberation, fierce coming-of-age stories full of high family drama. Her readers probably pictured an author in her thirties with tattoos and a gender-fluid appearance.

Certainly not a seventy-year-old grandmother with long, thick hair —still more brown than gray—wearing lined leggings and an oversized hoodie that covered her butt. And unhappily married to the same man for over forty years.

Much too old and too obviously straight to be writing such novels.

Soon, everyone would know the truth—*she* was the author Brooke Skipstone. How big would the shockwave be?

Taylor had long feared the repercussions and kept her pen name secret. What would her kids say? And her grandkids, who hardly knew her because she lived so far from them. And saw them even less than usual because of Covid. At times the thought of discovery had seared her guts, but the liberation of writing what she wanted, revealing the characters living in her mind and the love and pain in her heart, had become her main reason for existence.

While at her keyboard, Taylor lost herself in her secret world—vibrant, passionate, full of laughter and turmoil and utter joy. Not like her *real* world of silence and numbing isolation, where she couldn't talk about what mattered most to her.

Keeping the source of her greatest happiness a secret had suffocated her life.

Taylor stood at her classroom door before her last class of the day, while students thumbed phones and talked as they sat at a picnic table in the center of the Commons area. The same kind of table she and Brooke sat at in the spring of 1973.

Soon after Taylor's college roommate and fellow theatre major, Brooke Tobolovsky turned twenty-one, Brooke changed her last name. Though she didn't have the internet to check, she said she had never heard of anyone named Skipstone, so claimed it for herself. She thought it sounded cool. Much better for the stage and screen. Besides, she'd always hated the sound of Tobolovsky.

Regardless of her name, no one could ever forget her. Long, thick, cinnamon-colored hair; high forehead; deep-set blue eyes; and the biggest smile Taylor had ever seen. She could play Lady Macbeth just as easily as Juliet and belt out a song like a combination of Cher and Stevie Nicks. She was the natural lead, while Taylor was the utility player—competent actress, writer, composer, and organizational queen.

Once all the legal papers were complete, they celebrated with a pitcher of beer at The Hangout a few blocks from Southern Methodist University in Dallas, Texas. They sat at a picnic table under canvas stretched between oak trees, blocking the March sun. Brooke carved her new name on the bench as they pushed flip-flops through pea gravel and peanut shells.

"Does this mean I can't call you Tobo anymore?" Taylor laughed and snorted beer.

Brooke scoffed with a quick flash of her eyes, "I've put a curse on that name, as you can see. Say it at your peril." She cocked an eyebrow.

Taylor coughed this time, spewing beer on her shirt.

"I always knew you couldn't hold your liquor." Brooke wiped Taylor's chin with a napkin.

"That word will never cross my lips again."

"Which word?" Brooke teased. Her tongue peeked out the side of her mouth as she dabbed the snot from Taylor's upper lip. "Hmm?"

Flashing a smile, Taylor said, "From now on, you'll be BS to me. Nothing but BS."

Brooke narrowed her eyes and tightened her mouth. "You'd better be referring to Brooke Skipstone."

Taylor raised her hands and cocked her head in a perfect expression of amused innocence. "Certainly." She tried to swallow the guffaw rising from her gut. "That's exactly what I was thinking."

They stared at each other for three seconds, each holding her pose until Brooke broke into a smile. "That's BS and you know it."

Taylor's guffaw erupted, and in their laughter-filled haze, they both knocked their glasses to the ground. No matter. They drank from the pitcher and later started a burping contest. Taylor conceded when Brooke burped the chorus of "I Am Woman," earning a standing ovation from the crowd of hippie students and locals that had gathered around them. The girls walked home, Taylor's arm around her friend's neck; Brooke's around the other's waist.

They were known as B&T because they were inseparable. They'd shared the ground floor of a small rental house since sophomore year but spent most of their time acting, hanging lights, building sets, and running shows at the Owens Art Center. If one of them wasn't around the other, people would invariably ask, "Where's ___?" with a little frown and gasp.

Taylor wrote and directed plays and musicals mainly for teens, while Brooke snagged major acting roles every year. Taylor was involved in every one of Brooke's shows, while Brooke sang and acted in each of Taylor's studio productions.

They were two promising women, determined to make their own way in the world and support each other's careers in theatre—Brooke as an actress at the Oregon Shakespeare Festival in Ashland and Taylor as a drama teacher at a private school in a nearby city. After breaking up with their casual boyfriends and graduating in 1974, they headed west in a very used VW Camper Bus adorned with painted flowers to cover the rust.

They loved each other completely as friends and had only become lovers two days before Brooke's death.

At the end of the day, after all her students had left, Taylor walked to her classroom windows where five feet of snow pressed against the building up to the double-paned glass. Winter refused to let go, as always in March. The glaring sun could only force a glistening sheen on the white mounds before night formed a dull, frozen crust by morning. The sky yelled, "Spring," while the ground scoffed, "Maybe next month."

She shivered and hugged herself. No one else had touched her for years.

A knock on the door frame and a "You busy?" caused her to smile and turn around. "Never too busy for you." She had a special fondness for Grace. The girl had kept an eye on her house while Taylor and her husband taught in Native villages and kept the garden and flowers watered when they'd traveled in the summer. However, since her retirement and Covid, Taylor hadn't seen much of Grace. Taylor had missed their gossipy conversations and being able to teach her about gardening.

When the regular English teacher had to quit because of family illness in the Lower 48, Taylor happily volunteered to leave retirement.

She couldn't allow Grace to be taught by an aide or a P.E. teacher. The girl was an eager reader and writer, a rare combination in that school, and this was her senior year. She needed proper support so she could shine. "What's up?"

Grace walked toward her, sporting a wry smile, holding the book Taylor had given her last week. "Interesting name, Brooke Skipstone. I need to ask you something."

Taylor sucked in a breath. *She knows.*

Tall, slender, oval face framed by long, black hair and oversized glasses—Grace was considered hot by the boys but never seemed impressed by their attention. She held a copy of *Crystal's House of Queers* against her chest. "Loved it. Seriously. It's my new favorite. Will you sign it for me?"

Taylor's eyes jolted up to the girl's. "Sign it? Why would I sign it?"

Grace glanced at the door, looking for intruders. "Because you wrote it." Raising her brows, she said, "I know you did." The corners of her mouth stretched closer to her dimples.

Taylor could laugh and deny, and maybe her life would stay the same—alone, silent, immersed in a fantasy world she shared only with strangers—her readers. But she couldn't stand hiding anymore like she had something to be ashamed of. She had denied herself belonging to a community of writers and other . . . lesbians.

Should-have-been-lesbians.

She'd only realized this truth a few years ago when the agony of losing Brooke had once again clutched her throat, this time with fierce anger.

She'd been shamed into being straight. Without Brooke to help her, she couldn't summon the courage to be queer. So much heartache and fear followed her friend's death, and Taylor crumpled.

A tear oozed out of her left eye as she turned toward the window to hide her wipe. "The sun is so bright today."

"That's what we call changing the subject." Grace moved closer and laid the book on the sill.

Taylor couldn't stop her fingers from touching the cover and then tracing the continuous line drawing of a passionate kiss, precisely like the first between her and Brooke. Both of them were shocked, but they were drunk after a long party celebrating their last college production. What happened that night still echoed in Taylor's mind. The next morning was awkward, but they carried on as if nothing had happened. After all, they were trained actresses.

She'd been having flashbacks more frequently, especially at night. Sometimes she struggled to stay in the present. She'd look at something everyone else saw, but her mind ran a memory only she could see. She fought to leave the past and return to 2022.

After a deep breath, she said, "Why do you think I wrote it?"

Grace shimmied onto a desktop and held up one finger. "First, the town in your only book by Taylor Baird is named Anders Fork. In *Crystal's House*, it's Clear. But they're the same town with a river park and a shooting range. Both in Alaska." She held up two fingers. "The writing style is the same, though it's much more fluid in this one." Another finger. "Brooke Skipstone is not a real person. No social media, no photos of her anywhere. The only image is a silhouette of a girl with a ponytail, skipping over rocks."

"Maybe she doesn't like social media," Taylor said as her heart pounded.

Grace shook her head. "Okay, but I can Google your name and find a photo of you. Yet there's nothing for Brooke Skipstone. She simply doesn't exist."

Taylor's palms became sweaty. *The connection is so apparent. How has the secret lasted so long?* The answer was immediately clear— *because no one in this town would ever read Brooke's books.*

Grace raised another finger. "Crystal's house is like your house— two stories with a deck and a sunroom. Even the same location in town. The school in the book is identical to this one." She flipped out her thumb. "And last but not least, Ainsley, the girl who enters the story at the end after being beaten by her crazy, anti-government father, is me.

Including the big glasses. I like her name, by the way." She raised her brows and smiled. "Convince me I'm wrong."

Taylor never realized how tense she had been until her shoulders suddenly loosened like butter dropped in a hot pan. Her body felt instantly lighter. She closed her eyes and sighed. "Thank you."

Grace swung her legs. "You wanted me to figure it out. Didn't you?"

"Yes. I needed someone to talk to. I'm sorry I've put this burden on you, but . . . I thought you might be receptive to the themes." *You can tell me, Grace.*

They locked eyes.

Grace was the first to flinch. "Of three girls raising their dyke flag in Clear?"

"Yes. And not being afraid to shed their secrets."

Grace took a deep breath. "That would be hard to do by myself."

"Exactly."

Grace raised her brows. "Which is why you gave me the book."

Taylor nodded. "I figured the worst that could happen would be Principal Jackson firing me if you complained. Then I'd go home in disgrace and remain a recluse. The best that could happen would be us being able to talk freely about things we're afraid to mention elsewhere."

Grace laughed. "Yeah, I almost popped into his office this morning."

"Really?"

She frowned. "No. He's a creep."

Taylor tried to keep a straight face. "I cannot comment."

Grace grinned. "I hear you. So last week, when I came by after school, you'd put this book on your desk, knowing I'd be interested? Why?"

"Because I'd asked you what books you were reading a few days before that, and you answered romance. I said, 'You mean the ones with bare-chested men with bulging abs on the cover?'"

"And I said, 'Ick. No. I don't like those.' So you thought I'd like a book about queers."

Taylor leaned forward, pulled by the connection forming between them. "Did you?"

Grace's face glowed. "Very much."

"Were you shocked? Even a little?"

Grace blushed. "I have to admit that Crystal's sex dream on the first two pages was . . . let's say invigorating. You have a talent for writing steamy scenes without being explicit. And I've read plenty of explicit." She covered her mouth as she laughed. "Maybe I shouldn't tell you that."

Taylor grinned. "It's okay, Grace. Sex shouldn't be like Voldemort."

Grace took a deep breath. "Well, after I knew you wrote them, I reread all the hot scenes and thought, 'Wow! You are much more interesting than I ever imagined.'"

Taylor chuckled. "Because I'm so boring in real life?"

"No, you're not. But the author Brooke Skipstone is so obviously full of passion, wild, funny, and not shy about sex."

An image of Brooke playing Sally Bowles in *Cabaret* during their junior year—plunging neckline, bright red lips, bare legs—flashed through Taylor's mind. "Yes, she was."

Grace's green eyes bulged behind her glasses. "Brooke is real?"

Taylor's heart fluttered. "Until June 1974. And she was everything you describe. I know this sounds crazy, but when I write, I become her. I see the world through her eyes and live her emotions. I'm with her again."

Grace frowned. "What happened?"

"She died." Taylor shuddered and tried to ignore the memory of Brooke screaming her name as she fell.

"How?"

"I'm writing that story now."

Grace sucked in her lips and looked away, as if unsure what to say. "Can I read it?"

Taylor hesitated. She knew Grace would want to, but sharing a truth no one else knew left her so vulnerable. However, if the worst happened, as she feared, someone needed to know her story. "I'll give you the first few chapters."

"Cool. Your first book is good. It's won several awards. Why did you decide to use a pen name? Why not keep writing as Taylor Baird?"

Taylor sat down and sighed. "My family was not pleased with that book. They thought I had violated them by basing some of the plot on my daughter's life." Taylor gritted her teeth as her neck tightened. "My two sons and husband saw themselves in my characters and equated events in the story with their lives. They were outraged. They thought I had blamed them in front of the whole world."

"Did you?"

Taylor's sucked in a breath through pursed lips. "I wrote a story. Not a biography. Whatever blame they concocted revealed their own feelings of guilt."

Grace sat down facing Taylor. "What did your daughter think?"

Taylor balled her fists. "She died eleven years ago."

"I'm sorry. I didn't know."

"You were seven. We didn't know each other back then." Taylor's throat burned as she stared at her whitening knuckles. "Another victim of the patriarchy. Of course, my family blamed her for using drugs and alcohol. But the real story is the men in her life who manipulated her addictions for their own purposes." Taylor released a long, slow breath. "I'm sorry. I'm still very bitter."

Grace sighed. "So after writing your first book, you switched to Brooke Skipstone. Why?"

"Because the characters and events I wanted to write about would cause more family drama and disapproval, and I didn't want to deal with it." Taylor raised her brows and offered a tiny smile. "They think I've been working on a science fiction series for the past three years." She rubbed her hands. "The other reason I began to use her name is I feel closer to her when I write. I can live *her* stories rather than regret my own."

"Your family doesn't know about Brooke?"

Taylor inhaled deeply, trying to calm her swirling stomach. "No one knows about the real Brooke. I suspect my husband knows my pen name, but we haven't talked about it. Yet. He's not happy I'm an author. He complains I spend all my time on the computer and accuses me of having secret boyfriends."

Grace wiggled her brows and smiled. "Do you?"

"No. I have no friends." Her throat thickened. "Just beta readers and editors when I have something for them to read. Otherwise, I go months without any real conversation." Taylor leaned back and blew out a breath. "I've gotten used to living inside my mind."

Grace scrunched her forehead. "You're the same age as my grandmother, and besides Maddi, Gram's my best friend. Why can't we be friends?"

"We can. But friends need to be honest with each other." Taylor knew Grace was hiding a secret about her book. She gazed into the girl's eyes until Grace turned away.

She slumped. "My father gave me this book."

"I know."

Grace jerked her head back. "How?"

Taylor picked up the novel and pointed to the shout-out line at the top of the cover. "This isn't the book I gave you. My copy was printed a year ago with *Three senior girls in rural Alaska escape their abusive pasts by raising their dyke flag for themselves and their community*." She turned the book around and pointed to the line in red between two drawings. "A few months ago, *Publishers Weekly* reviewed the book, and I changed the line on the cover." Taylor turned the book around. "*This story of found family brims with high drama.* Whoever gave you this book ordered it recently."

Grace looked to the ceiling and clenched her jaw. "Dad gave me this copy this morning. He said, 'Ask Mrs. MacKenzie to sign this book. Tell her you know she wrote it. If you don't bring it back with her signature, I'll change the locks so you can't get into my house.' He didn't know you'd already given me a copy. Oh, and he warned me not to read the book. He said he'd know if I opened any pages. 'I see any evidence that you looked through this book, and I'll whip you.' I said, 'You can't whip me. I'm eighteen. I'll go to the troopers.' I stormed out of the house as he yelled, 'Get her signature!' The idiot doesn't know that anyone can read the first few chapters of any book online."

Taylor shook her head as her throat burned. *Why is my signature so important?* She knew Levi was loud and adamant about his politics but didn't know he was abusive to Grace. "What do you do when he threatens you like that?"

"Go to Gram's. She's the total opposite of him. What you said about the 'patriarchy' sounds just like her. Gram doesn't take any shit from him."

"His mother?"

"No. His mother won't have anything to do with him. Gram moved up here two years ago after Mom died of Covid." Grace's face turned red as she snapped her words. "You know, the disease Dad still calls a hoax."

My God, the man is crazy. Poor girl.

Grace held out a marker and raised her brows.

Taylor had never signed any of her books. Her family was too angry and ashamed to want her identified as the author of her first novel. She took the marker and carefully pulled the cover back to expose the title page. "I've never signed Brooke's name before. Let's see if I remember how she did it." Taylor scribed a large B with flourishes, then added an indecipherable squiggle. She did the same with the S, followed by a longer squiggle. Her hands shook as she replayed scenes of Brooke signing programs for her fans. "That's pretty close."

Grace took the book. "I'd already decided to tell Dad you laughed when I said you wrote this and signed it as a joke. 'Offer it on eBay,' you said. 'See if anyone will buy a signed copy. You don't have to say who signed it.'" Grace held the book against her chest and gazed at Taylor's face. "Did you love her?"

Taylor's skin tingled. "With all my heart."

Grace leaned closer and whispered. "Did you two . . . You know. It's cool with me if you did."

Taylor smiled. "You'll have to read this book to find out." Taylor pulled out her phone. "I'll airdrop it."

Grace fetched her phone. "Just text it to me. You should still have my number."

"Okay," Taylor said. "There it goes."

Grace's lips spread wide in a smile. "Cool. Since you texted me, I can text you back. Like real friends."

Taylor nodded. "Like real friends."

"Are you finished writing the book?"

"No. I'm still working on the ending."

Grace clicked on the pdf file. "Happy or sad or both, like *Crystal's House?*"

Taylor stood and slipped her phone into her hoodie's pouch. "I don't know. I'm a pantser, so I never plot out my books before writing. The story grows on its own. But this one is more complicated than the others because there's a comet headed toward Earth."

Grace frowned and stood. "Like in *Don't Look Up?*"

"No. A human comet." She hitched a breath and briefly closed her eyes. "My brother was released from prison a month ago, and I think he wants to find me."

Grace frowned and tilted her head. "Is he dangerous?"

"Possibly. But that's part of the ending. I'll have to wait and see." She shook her head to eliminate any images of Austin threatening to fill her mind. Taylor changed the topic. "When will parents learn that forbidding their children to do something ensures they'll do it? And then learn to lie and keep secrets. Reading a book shouldn't be a crime."

Grace looked back at the door, then turned toward Taylor with a mischievous grin. "I set a goal two months ago to read every banned book. I have *Gender Queer* and *The Bluest Eye* on my phone right now. If idiot parents and politicians hadn't called them porn, I wouldn't have known about them."

Taylor coughed a laugh. "Good for you."

Grace opened the cover and smiled at the signature. "Even though he ordered me to get this, I'll always cherish it."

"Why do you think your father wanted me to sign the book?" Taylor asked.

Grace spit out her words. "So he can *prove* you wrote it and then *condemn* you. So he can stir up *outrage* like he always does. So he can *pretend* to be somebody important." She shook her head. "How did he know you wrote this?"

"I'm sure my husband told him. He and Levi have become great friends recently."

Grace's lips flattened against her teeth. "I hate him. I can't wait to get out of that house."

"Can you live with Gram?"

"She wants me to."

"Then follow your heart and find the courage. The shit's about to hit the fan."

Grace nodded. "Thank you for sharing and trusting me." She grabbed Taylor's hand.

"That was easy. The next part is the killer."

Grace squeezed then let go. "Bring it on." Her face lit up with a smile. "Bye."

"Hey, before you go. Where's the copy I gave you?"

"With Gram. She wanted to read it."

Taylor sucked in her lips.

"Don't worry," Grace said. "She's cool. You two would like each other."

The girl scampered out of the room, clutching the book. Taylor couldn't help but smile even as the quiver grew in her stomach. Grace's father and most of the town would consider *Crystal's House* pornographic because queer sex is perverse by definition. She'd heard such comments many times on Levi's podcast. They would claim Taylor had given Grace "inappropriate" material to read to groom her because all queers are pedophiles.

She and Grace had shared secrets and planned to share more.

Everything about this interaction was wrong, according to the outraged.

Those who ban and condemn and restrict and shame.

Who see scandal everywhere.

The same crowd she had succumbed to long ago.

Not anymore.

As Grace had said—*Bring it on.*

2

THE ONE-OFF

Grace walked through the Commons area toward her locker, staring at her phone. The title page loaded on her phone screen—*The Life and Death of Brooke Skipstone* by Brooke Skipstone. Other students walked by her, muttering hellos, but she didn't respond. She couldn't wait any longer to read.

Chapter One

"Open the frigging door," begged my roommate Brooke. "I need to pee." She squeezed her legs together and leaned against the wall.

We'd just come home from the cast party of *Twelfth Night*, our last college production before graduation in May 1974. Staggering on our dark back porch, I tried to focus my drunken eyes and aim the key toward the lock. "I keep missing the damn hole."

"Yeah, that was Jacob's problem too."

I choked on a laugh. "What?"

"We were smashed in the back of his car. Dark as shit, and he's humping my leg, the seat, and my stomach, grunting louder and louder."

The key scraped against the lock and into the wood as I doubled over with a howl. "What happened?"

"I said, 'Jacob! Don't you know where to put it?' He whimpered, 'I can't find it.' So I grabbed him," she said as she found my hand to guide the key into the lock, "then pushed him in." She tried to push the key into the hole. "Taylor, that's the wrong key. It's too big."

I snorted. "Like Jacob?"

"Normally, yes, but tonight he went limp and crashed. I left him snoring in his car."

Grace shrieked in laughter and slid down the lockers until she sat on the floor.

Allison, a teacher's aide and volunteer who led cooking classes for middle school students, opened the kitchen door and found Grace cackling. "Don't you need to get home?" she barked. Her dyed black hair was ratted up and heavily sprayed.

Grace rolled her eyes, stood up, and opened her locker. "I'll just be a minute."

Allison huffed, shot her an icy stare through heavily lined lids, and returned to the kitchen, leaving the door ajar.

Grace continued reading.

I tried to push the key into the lock. "That's the opposite problem I have with Charles. I never know whether he's inside me or not. His dick is maybe two inches long."

Brooke touched my cheek. "Poor baby! Why do you stay with him?" She took my key ring.

"I'm not. I broke up with him tonight."

She moved her face close to mine. "Good for you." Brooke held up one key. "This is for your car." She held up another as she moved even closer, her lips nearly brushing mine. "This is for our house." She held up her middle finger. "And this is for two inadequate men who will not be allowed to ruin our evening." She moved the key to the lock while brushing her arm against my breasts. After she unlocked the door and flicked on the lights, she ran through the kitchen. "I've got the bathroom."

Grace cackled. "Oh my God, Taylor. Not even two pages and we have tiny, limp dicks and a guy humping a car seat. I love it."

Allison burst out of the kitchen and scowled. "What did you say?"

"Nothing." Grace grabbed her jacket and slammed her locker. "On my way." She trotted down the hall and out of the building. She walked carefully through the icy parking lot until she reached her old Ford Ranger. After climbing inside and turning on the motor, she continued reading.

I wet a towel by the sink and wiped my face and neck, trying to calm myself. I'd almost kissed her. For the past two weeks, I had sat on the downstage right corner of the Bob Hope Theatre stage, playing the harpsichord while Brooke performed an amazing Viola. Disguised as a beautiful boy, she turned Olivia into a lovesick, horny woman while trying to hide her own attraction to Duke Orsino. At one point in the play, Olivia loved a girl, Orsino loved a boy, and Antonio loved Viola's brother. And then, with the excuse of mistaken identities, these loves were returned to "normal," meaning heterosexual.

I could understand Olivia's infatuation. Indeed, I'd begun to root for her. Why couldn't it be possible? I had watched Brooke rehearse and perform that role for the past month and found my affection for her growing daily. We'd been roommates and theatre junkies for the past three years, done everything together, even had sex with boyfriends at the same time in our house—she in the bedroom, me in the living room—but had never crossed the line with each other.

Except for a few times in my dreams and that night during the final scene when I lost myself in her face and almost missed my cue to play the last number. After the show, we went to the director's house and danced, got drunk, swam naked in his pool with half the cast, then disappeared in our boyfriends' cars for a passionless, obligatory interlude.

Brooke opened the bathroom door, wearing only a t-shirt, holding both hands behind her back. She'd pulled her cinnamon hair into a ponytail. Her tongue peeked between her freshly painted lips as she slinked toward me like an intoxicating wolf.

I couldn't breathe.

She stopped when our breasts pressed together. Her deep-set blue eyes possessed mine, pulling me closer until she flicked my lip with her tongue. I gasped and pressed my lips to hers. She gently bit my lower lip and sucked it into her mouth, tugging moans from my throat. My hands touched her cheeks as our tongues urgently explored each other. My fingers pushed through her hair and pulled her face hard against mine. I wanted her so.

She leaned back and flashed the most seductive smile I'd ever seen. Her hands emerged from behind her back, holding a rubber dildo and a Magic Wand vibrator. My eyes bulged as I clasped my mouth. "Where did you get those?"

She touched the dildo to my lips. "At a back room in a head shop. Bet you'd feel that inside you," she purred. She pushed the wand against my breast. "The muscle relaxer was on sale at Macy's."

"Relaxer?" My heart raced.

"Depends on where you put it." She pressed it against my shoulder. "I think this would be relaxing." She pushed it down between our crotches and undulated against it. "Maybe down there, not so much."

I moaned and reached for her hips, pulling them closer.

Brooke kissed my cheek and whispered in my ear, "This was our last college show. I expected to get laid and go to bed exhausted and satisfied. Jacob and Charles were a bust, so how about you and me?"

I hitched a breath as every nerve sparked. "My bed or yours?"

"Mine." She held out the wand's cord. "There's a plug exactly where it needs to be." She backed away. "Meet me there in two minutes with fewer clothes on."

Warmth surged through my skin. "Is none too many?"

"None is perfect."

After two hours of grunting, laughing, begging, and moaning, we collapsed against each other. Wasted. Drenched in sweat and our own juices.

As Taylor walked to her Subaru Outback, Grace half-opened her door to tell her how much she liked the book. Then the memory of her father's plan slipped into her mind—maybe she shouldn't bring any more attention to her . . . But when Taylor looked over at the truck, Grace couldn't resist. She jumped outside and half-skidded over the ice toward the woman.

"I love this. Really love it." Grace flung her arms around Taylor and squeezed.

Taylor laughed and said, "My my . . . where are you in the story?"

"You and Brooke just had two hours of sex." *Just like Maddi and me.* Grace released the woman as Allison exited the main entrance, throwing a scowl their way. "But I'm worried about Brooke. I think I'm going to cry soon."

"Crying shows you care about others. It's the people who don't cry we have to worry about."

"I'll finish it tonight." Allison watched them, shaking her head. "Now, that's a lady who wouldn't shed a tear for anyone. I'll see you tomorrow." She turned and hurried back to her truck, where she resumed reading.

I awoke to the smell of coffee and Brooke humming in the kitchen. I buried my face in her pillow and inhaled her scent to make it permanent in my brain—sweet lemons, sweat, butter. Something I could always summon when I wanted it.

Emerging naked from her bed, I nearly ran into the kitchen to hold her but hesitated. What if she had dressed? What would she think? After slipping on a t-shirt, I moved to the bathroom, washed my face, and fluffed my hair before sucking in a breath and opening the door.

Brooke wore shorts and a t-shirt as she fried bacon. She didn't look up.

I walked toward her with wobbly legs but tried to act confident and sexy. "Maybe I should have stayed in bed so you could serve me." I leaned toward her and kissed her cheek, noting no reaction, just continued humming. My chest burned. Resting my chin on her shoulder and wrapping my arms around her stomach, I whispered, "Are we going to pretend nothing happened?"

She stared at the stove. "Something very pleasurable happened."

My stomach dropped. She hadn't touched my hands. "But it's a one-off?"

She hesitated. "For now."

My throat knotted as I backed away. She lifted bacon strips out of the pan, dropped them onto a plate, flipped off the gas, and pushed the skillet to the back burner.

She turned around and raised her hands to my face. "Taylor, I love you as my best friend. I don't want that to change."

"Why would it?"

"Right now, we totally trust each other. No jealousy. We're free to be with whomever we want. I think that would change if we . . ." She swallowed and looked away.

"Kept having the best sex either of us has ever had?"

"Yeah." She touched her forehead to mine. "The best."

My fingers found her stomach. "What we do in our house is private. Outside, we just act normal."

"That can't last. I don't want to have to act around you. Besides, you were hired as a good little straight theatre teacher at a Christian school. Not a gay teacher. The only reason we've never been accused of being lesbians is because of our periodic boyfriends."

"Who never meant anything to either of us," I said.

"No. Which worries me because I also don't feel a desire to be with a guy right now."

I played with her hair. "Okay, last night was a one-off, and I'll keep my hands off you." I traced her mouth with my finger. "But if you ever kiss me on the lips again, I am not responsible for what happens next."

"Deal."

I took a step backward. "I'm going to take a shower. For some reason, I feel sticky, and I smell." I turned around and started walking toward the bathroom, making an extra effort to swing my hips as I raised my arms to stretch.

"Your shirt is a little short."

I reached back and exposed my butt. "Must have shrunk in the wash." I felt her eyes burning my skin.

"Maybe you should lock the door."

I turned around. "Otherwise, you'll barge in and attack me?" I tried my best to flash her a sexy smile. "In that case, I won't even close the door." I turned again and pulled off my shirt as I walked away. "You're the great actress. Just act like you don't want me."

She blurted, "I'll go for a walk." Then rushed out the back door.

"Coward!"

After my shower, I wrapped a towel around my head and put on clothes. I found her sitting on the porch, her arms draped on the rails, panting. I leaned against a post, my belly knotting. "I'm sorry. It won't happen again."

She groaned. "I had to walk around the block three times."

"Only three?" I dropped down next to her with a heavy sigh.

Brooke cleared her throat. "I won't kiss you, and you won't flash me."

"Promise. What about your toys?"

"I'll hide them. Give me a few minutes to clean up, then we should go to the laundromat. I can't sleep in those sheets as long as they smell like you."

"I don't ever want to wash those sheets, but I'll strip the beds."

She turned her face toward me, her eyes pleading. "We can't talk about last night. At least for a while. Okay?"

A knot grew in my throat. "Promise."

We stood. She reached for the door and pulled it open. With her back toward me, she said, "Taylor, you . . . I . . ."

Tears welled in my eyes. "I know, Brooke. I feel the same. Go take a shower."

She walked into the house as I wiped my eyes. I swore to myself I would do everything to maintain our friendship and do nothing to threaten our lives together. We would be best friends and nothing more, though I could never quell my passion for her.

Grace tightened her jaw and tried to swallow. Tears flowed down her cheeks. Brooke was going to die soon. Why? How did Taylor live through that? Why did she marry Marshall and have children?

Because life sucks.

Evil people try to tear you down. Or force you to live their way and agree with their beliefs.

Like her father. The man glorified the protection of personal freedoms and speech, but only what he agreed with. There was no right to read queer books or discuss gender identities in school. No right to discuss racism or suggest it still exists.

When he was home, she had the right to remain silent or nod at everything he said. Which is why she went to her house only when he was away. She backed the truck and exited the parking lot, heading home.

This had been a heavy snow year, which in some ways was good because all the dead cars and yard junk lay hidden under insanely white snow. The melting would start in two weeks, and the snow would blur into a muddy fuzz of drunken monoliths.

She turned down D Street, where the house on the corner had collapsed that winter. A few guys lived in a very old motorhome nearby with a flue angled out a window to vent the small wood stove inside. They had pirated wood and insulation from the nearby house until the snow load collapsed the roof. Only a few sheets of plywood still stood erect.

People did what they had to do to stay warm during the winter, even if it meant scavenging wood from their own houses.

The same thing had happened to her family. Two years ago, her mother and brother had still lived with Grace and Dad. When Covid arrived, Mom quit her job. She was a diabetic and asthmatic and feared the disease. Chase, a senior at the time, and Grace had been sent home from school for remote learning.

Grace's dad, Levi, had always been far right in his politics, but Covid pushed him over the edge. It was a hoax invented by Dr. Fauci to push Trump out of office, after all. He had railed at everyone in the house and refused to take precautions. No one could wear a mask in his presence. He'd drunk and played poker with his friends while Mom had begged him to think of her safety.

Levi seemed to thrive on outrage, and his family's supposed weakness fed his fire. The more he screamed about the radical left online and with his friends, the more respect he gained outside his home. He started a podcast and blog and even a call-in show.

In April 2020, he caught a cold and went berserk when his son and daughter refused to let him into the house without wearing a mask. "It's just a cold, damnit!" he yelled before pushing his way inside. Despite keeping Mom isolated in her room wearing a mask while Chase and Grace wore theirs, Mom became sick and was rushed to the hospital in Fairbanks.

When the doctor delivered the Covid diagnosis to Levi, he lost it.

"Just another damn lying liberal!" He would have punched the man if his children hadn't intervened.

Mom died of Covid two months later. According to Dad, her death was caused by heart failure, diabetes, and obesity. He claimed as others did at the time that deaths were being blamed on Covid because of media hype, all designed to make Trump lose the election. The fact that Levi recovered from his "cold" proved him right.

Chase and Dad fought all the time after that. Her brother finally moved to Fairbanks and joined the pipefitter's union. When vaccines were available the following year, Chase returned to Clear to take Grace to get her shot. Of course, Dad refused, even threatening to shoot his son if he "trespassed" again.

By then, Gram had moved to town to "protect" her granddaughter from the man who'd killed her daughter. As soon as Grace turned eighteen, they'd secretly driven to Healy for her vaccine.

At the end of D Street, Grace slowed her truck as she passed Fourth Avenue, where Taylor lived down the road. She'd always thought Taylor and Marshall were a happy couple, but she'd mainly spent her time with Taylor and rarely seen them together. Then she remembered in Taylor's first book that the father and mother argued about how to respond to their daughter's drug use. Maybe that part was real.

She turned the corner onto Center Drive toward her house while thinking of all the secrets she knew about families in her town—the gossip kids told about their parents and the things kids hid from them.

She'd kept her secret about her relationship with Maddi from everyone for years until Gram moved to town. When Grace introduced Maddi to Gram, her grandmother knew they were girlfriends. A woman whose face quickly revealed all of her thoughts and emotions could also read everyone else's. "No secrets in my house," she'd said. "I'd rather you love a girl anyway. No chance of getting pregnant. Use the back bedroom whenever."

So they did.

But no one else knew, though evidently, Taylor had suspected.

Until she'd read *Crystal's House*, Grace would never have thought to share her sexual identity with Taylor.

Grace parked her truck and entered her house, where she made a beeline for her father's office door, leading to his secret room in the basement no one ever saw. He recorded his podcasts down there with the door to the stairs locked from the inside. Dad claimed the room contained expensive equipment and soundproofing that he didn't want to be damaged.

But he had to have been hiding something else.

She lifted the combination lock and took a photo of the numbered dials to ensure she returned them to their original position before she left. She'd tried every birthday combination she could think of, every special date she knew, but none had worked. Now she went through random numbers systematically using a chart of the 10,000 possible combinations of four numbers, checking them off one by one. Every day she'd try twenty, sometimes more.

She worried that he changed the code sometimes. He must have suspected her because each time she'd seen him open the door, he'd always stare at the dials for a few seconds before spinning them.

What would she do when the lock clicked open?

Look inside and photograph everything. Because he constantly railed against the decline of western culture and the rise of the queer agenda, she suspected he was hiding porn. Maybe even gay porn. Wouldn't that be ironic as hell?

She remained in his house to find out. To nail him. To reveal to the world that, once again, someone who condemned the behavior of others was frequently guilty of the same.

It bothered her that many in Clear loved him. A giant of a man with a long beard hanging straight down from his chin, quick to smile and laugh outside his family, he had opened an abandoned church and held services on Sundays and game nights on Tuesdays.

"All are invited! Come as you are!" As long as they weren't queer, or liberals, or Trump haters, or trying to indoctrinate children with CRT and LGBTQ nonsense. Or intent on confiscating everybody's guns. If there was a town in the state with none of the above, it was Clear, Alaska. Or they kept their heads down like Grace and Maddi.

Grace had promised Gram she'd leave town with her after graduation—along with Maddi. Gram had a house in Homer, which was far more tolerant of "lefties" than Clear. They even held Pride Marches. Gram called it a drinking village with a fishing problem.

After twenty tries, Grace called it quits. She wrote a note to her father about Taylor laughing at her request to sign the book, which she left on the kitchen table.

She hurried to her room to grab some clothes because she intended to spend the night at Gram's and with Maddi. Since she'd turned eighteen, her walls were covered with photos of Biden and Harris and AOC and the Squad, various rock stars—including Lil Nas X and Phoebe Bridgers—Bernie, Black Lives Matter posters, and more. What Grace did not display, however, were Pride Flags. She couldn't summon the courage to do it because she feared her father would crucify her during his podcasts and tell the world she was queer.

Crystal, Haley, and Payton in *Crystal's House of Queers* didn't care what others thought, which was why she admired them so much. If only she could summon the same courage.

When her Dad had seen her newly decorated room, he'd fumed and threatened to kick her out. She had expected him to destroy her property and slap her around even as she said she'd call the troopers. But surprisingly, he didn't.

He'd merely stomped off and never entered her room again, as far as she could tell.

Why? She had no idea.

So she stayed with him—though she spent more and more time at Gram's—and redoubled her efforts to break his combo. She had only two months left.

She grabbed some chips to snack on as she drove to Gram's, one half of a vinyl-sided, two-bedroom duplex rental on F Street. She saw Maddi's car in the driveway, squealed in excitement, parked her truck, and bolted through the door.

The two girls crushed each other with hugs and kisses as Gram sat at the table reading *Crystal's House of Queers*.

"I didn't expect you until later," Grace said, breathless, pushing her fingers through Maddi's red-haired pixie. She'd graduated last year and now worked at the Blue Sky Lodge a few miles from town. Resembling an anime character with huge green eyes and a button nose, she looked younger than she was.

"The restaurant was dead," Maddi replied in her distinctive husky voice, "and I'd already finished wrapping the silverware, so I cut out."

Grace rubbed the girl's nose with her own. "I met another lesbian today," she teased.

Maddi's eyes bulged. "Who?"

Gram stood, a large, handsome woman with a buzz cut she did herself. "Taylor Baird MacKenzie. Your teacher," she said with her soothing, mezzo-soprano voice. She dropped Grace's copy of *Crystal's House* onto the table and removed her reading glasses to hang on the lanyard around her neck. "AKA, Brooke Skipstone."

"Your teacher is a lesbian?" Maddi asked. "Cool."

Grace had shared her suspicions about Taylor's pen name before giving Gram the book the night before. "Did you finish?" Grace asked.

"Just now. I love the ending." She blew her big nose into a tissue. "A time to blow strawberries, a time to love, and a time to fight. Such a heartwarming romance, even if everyone is gay." She chuckled, revealing her lovely smile. "Imagine a house of queers in Clear. Your father would blow it up."

"No," Grace said, "he'd rant about it on his podcast until the town did it for him."

Maddi pulled on Grace's arm. "Come. Take a bath with me. I'm tired of smelling like cigarettes and grilled meat."

"Okay. But wait a second." She turned back to Gram. "Taylor loved a woman in college. Guess what her name was."

Gram smiled and scratched her ear. "Brooke Skipstone?"

"Yes!" Grace held out her phone for Gram and opened the chapters Taylor had given her. "Read this."

Gram took the phone. "By Taylor?"

"Yes. The story of her and Brooke in college before Brooke died."

Gram frowned and pursed her lips. "She died? Why did she give this to you?"

"I asked her to. No one in her family knows about the real Brooke."

"No one?"

Grace shook her head.

Maddi looked at the phone in Gram's hand. "Will you read it to me later?"

"Yes," Grace said. "After our bath." She pulled Maddi to her.

Gram put on her glasses. "Someone so important to her, and yet no one knows?"

"Except me," Grace said.

Gram plopped into her wingback chair. "She's kept a secret for so long, and now she's writing a book about it. Why now?"

"She said her brother was just released from prison and wants to find her."

"Why?"

"Come on, Grace," Maddi urged.

"I think he wants to hurt her. She turned pale when she mentioned him."

Gram blew out a long breath as she raised her glasses to her eyes. "Prison, huh. I wonder what for."

Maddi squealed when she finally pulled Grace from the room.

3

THE SOUND OF FALLING WATER

Having just climbed into her car, Taylor watched Allison glare at Grace as the girl walked back to her truck. Allison moved toward her just as Taylor was about to close her car door.

"That girl is a wild one," grumbled Allison. "I'm surprised her father allows it."

Taylor looked up at the angry face and flashed a smile. "I don't think he has a choice. Good night." Taylor wasn't sure if Allison had heard the "two hours of sex" line or not, but she was sure about her witnessing the hug. She gently pulled her door closed, avoiding more conversation.

So far, the only news Levi could spread was that Taylor wrote obscene fiction. No one knew she had given books to Grace. But that would come out eventually.

Perhaps her husband told Levi by accident, possibly blurting it out without thinking of the consequences. Or did he have his own plan?

She'd find out in an hour when he came home from work.

As she drove down Fourth Avenue toward her house, she noticed tiny catkins emerging from willows next to her garage. Snow covered her yard for seven months of the year. When the temperature finally broke forty degrees, and the first buds formed on the most spindly limbs, Taylor allowed herself to believe in rebirth and change.

And color.

She parked her car and stepped slowly onto the ice covering her gravel driveway. She stared at her empty iron hanging baskets and imagined them full of multi-colored calibrachoa spilling over the sides of coconut fiber inserts. And the delphiniums, which returned every summer to grow higher than the window, thick with light purple and dark blue petals.

Would she see them bloom this year?

She'd been so busy writing during the past weeks she hadn't bothered to order seeds to plant under her grow lights in the back bedroom. This would not be a normal spring-to-summer transition—transferring seedlings into larger and larger pots until a joyous planting on the first of June in the outside beds.

This year, there was no scenario she could imagine permitting that sequence. One way or another, she'd be gone.

She opened the door and again missed the excited scraping of claws on the floor and the unrestrained tail wagging as Sunny greeted her. The big Golden Retriever had always welcomed her as if she'd been gone for days rather than hours or even minutes. Coming home to that love and excitement had been the highlight of her day. But Sunny had died of cancer during their last year teaching in a village. Not able to withstand another loss, Taylor had opted to forgo pets, thereby ensuring her remaining life of no physical affection, no unbridled joy, and no absolute, non-judgmental empathy for her.

The joy of being loved seemed never enough to stand the pain of its loss.

Once inside, she removed her computer from her satchel and opened it on her desk. She wanted to record what had happened that day with Grace.

Slipping on her headphones and starting her ten-minute continual loop of the sound of waterfalls, she escaped into the persona of Brooke Skipstone—talented, kind, extroverted, romantic, sexy. Taylor's own mundane existence, devoid of love or passion, was inadequate to create the stories and characters she wanted. Only through Brooke could her heart and mind soar. Her office disappeared, and her fingers found the keys automatically as she replayed the day's events.

Two hours later, the time on her computer screen indicated six o'clock. Marshall was late. She rose and walked the length of her house to the sunroom, her favorite area because of all the windows, but now six-foot berms of snow loomed over the deck, blocking the view on two sides. The third side faced the driveway, which gleamed under the sun shining along the path through the trees.

Above her hung etched baleen from a Bowhead whale caught by the father of one of her students in the village of Kaktovik some years ago. Tied to some hair strands were fossilized tusk ivory from walrus and bear claws. She had witnessed the village celebrate twenty-seven whale harvests during the years she and her husband taught the Iñupiat, the last time she felt part of a community. She had been beloved, and she had loved in return.

But in the confines of their house on stilts next to the school, Marshall and Taylor had drawn farther apart. Their daughter, Heather, had gone to rehab twice and used drugs both times immediately after release. She had become pregnant and had a miscarriage. Once, she was clean for a few months and had become a popular motivational speaker at 12-Step meetings, but a former boyfriend hooked up with her, and she'd used again.

Heather had called them infrequently, mostly asking for money to fix a crisis of one kind or another. Marshall refused to send anything and wanted to change their phone numbers. He'd had enough.

Taylor wanted to fly down to Oregon to be with her, even if it meant losing her job.

Then one evening, Heather called and complained that her boyfriend had hit her, and one of his friends had come by, threatening to kill him. She'd fired a shotgun in the friend's direction to get him to leave.

Taylor asked if she'd come to visit. Would she agree to leave her boyfriend and live with them? They could start over if she promised to stay with her parents for at least six months. Heather promised.

Marshall argued against the idea. He and Taylor fought, but she bought all the tickets anyway. Her daughter would arrive the next day.

Taylor couldn't sleep from anticipation and worry and happiness, but when Heather exited the plane holding an underweight, crying toddler, Taylor couldn't stop her tears as she ran to grasp her daughter and grandchild. Heather had never mentioned a baby.

"You had a baby?" Taylor asked. "Why didn't you tell us?"

Heather took her daughter out of her mother's arms and shot her a cold glance. "Like you would care."

Taylor gasped, her legs almost buckling.

As soon as they entered their house, Heather asked, "Do you have any vodka?"

"No," Marshall answered in disbelief. "This is a dry village."

Heather scoffed, "I met a guy on the plane who said he could get me some. Do you want me to call him?"

Taylor prepared food for Sierra, who ate everything and asked for more. Then the phone calls began. Her boyfriend wanted her back.

Taylor begged her daughter to stay while Marshall threatened to break her phone. Heather demanded money to fly back. She and Marshall screamed at each other while Taylor tried to distract Sierra.

The boyfriend announced his mother had given him money to fly Heather home. She left the next day after the village police questioned Marshall about his threats against his daughter and the kidnapping charge she'd levied against him, claiming he had refused to let her leave the house. All lies, of course, intended to make her parents want her to leave.

Seven months later after no contact, Taylor answered an early morning phone call from Heather's boyfriend. Heather had died of a seizure. The young man said he was very sorry and hung up. Taylor screamed uncontrollably, waking up Marshall, who couldn't understand why his wife was acting insane.

Despite their repeated attempts to talk to Heather's boyfriend, they never heard from him again.

During the next five years, husband and wife barely spoke to each other. Taylor spent more time at the school—teaching music, preparing the kids for talent shows, organizing the student store, and more.

But nothing could fill the hole in her heart, which gaped wider and deeper when she started dreaming about Brooke. After all the intervening years, Taylor had managed to lock her memories of Brooke into a dead section of her brain. But after Heather died, it burst open. Two women had been stolen from her life. She'd been able to bury thoughts of Brooke behind family obligations and the natural progression of her children's lives, but when Heather died, the façade of her world shattered.

The beautiful, passionate, engrossing life she'd lived with Brooke began to insinuate itself into every empty, insipid moment of her existence. What she'd had then and what she'd been condemned to since mocked her every day.

One night Taylor broke down wailing and couldn't stop. When Marshall asked what was wrong, Taylor whimpered, "I miss Heather." Which was true, but Brooke had forced the tears.

He sat next to her, filling her nose with his aftershave lotion. "She wasn't herself since high school. The person we met here a year ago was someone else."

Taylor choked on her tears. "Still . . ." She'd never told him about Brooke. He tried to hold her, but she shuddered and couldn't even pretend.

The only embrace she wanted to feel was Brooke's, and she was gone forever.

Again.

They retired from teaching and moved back to Clear. Marshall fixed up their house and built elevated planters and flowerbeds, while Taylor nurtured seedlings and began to write a story loosely based on her daughter's life.

For a year, she was able to distract her mind and lose herself in the all-consuming rush of creation. She enjoyed her sons' and families' visits to Alaska, fishing, hiking, and gardening. But the long winters became increasingly cold and lonely, especially after her family's response to her first book.

Until she found refuge in Brooke Skipstone and wrote *her* stories.

A pickup truck turned onto Fourth Avenue. Not Marshall's.

Levi's. Marshall rode shotgun.

Her heart thumped against her chest. She hadn't expected to deal with both of them.

She hurried to fetch her coat and stood on the deck when Levi parked.

Both men emerged with tight lips.

Marshall wore a Carhartt knit cap, hiding his still-thick, whitening hair. He'd always been a handsome man and had aged well. When they met, he was a little taller. Seventy-two years and some back problems had pushed him down to a little over six feet. Still strong with just a hint of a beer belly, he worked part-time at the bowling alley on the nearby air base.

"Where's your truck?" Taylor asked.

"Being towed to Nenana," Marshall answered. "We couldn't get it started."

"I think the alternator's bad," Levi said, hooking his thumbs on his overalls, pushing back his jean jacket.

There was a pause as both men scrutinized her.

Taylor smiled. "Your daughter asked me to do the strangest thing today." Levi's eyes tightened. She didn't think he expected her to mention it.

"What's that?" he asked.

Taylor smiled. "Sign a book. Something she'd been reading. She said she'd never had a signed copy before and wondered whether I'd oblige." Her heart pounded, but she managed to appear calm and bemused.

Marshall's jaw tightened. "Did you sign it?"

"Sure I did. Why not? I told her she could sell it on eBay as a genuine signed copy." Taylor winked. "Just don't mention who signed it."

Both men's mouths dropped open.

Taylor couldn't help but puff out her chest. "I told her to bring me any other books she wanted to be signed. I hope that's okay with you, Levi."

"I'll have a talk with her," Levi grumbled.

"No need. No one's ever asked me to sign anything, so it made me feel special." She wasn't lying. She knew Grace loved having a signed copy of her book.

Levi pursed his lips. "Marshall, you need a ride tomorrow?"

"Nope. I won't be going to the Base. Thanks anyway."

"Okay." Levi nodded toward Taylor. "I'll be seeing you, Taylor."

"I'm sure you will," Taylor said with as much innuendo as she could muster. "Thanks for bringing my husband home."

Marshall didn't take his eyes off his wife, even as Levi turned around and drove off.

Taylor waved vigorously, then looked over at Marshall. "We need to talk." She opened the door and walked inside until she reached the kitchen. She heard Marshall's slow footsteps behind her as her anger grew.

Marshall folded his arms and leaned against the kitchen table. Taylor leaned back against the sink. A granite-covered island stood between them.

"Do you have something to say to me?" Taylor asked, slinging a hard stare at her husband. "Or do you just talk to Levi about your discoveries?"

Marshall rolled his eyes and shuffled his feet. "You're something else, Taylor. You're the one keeping secrets for three years."

"What secret have you kept for two weeks after I turned off my screensaver? You were able to read my computer screen when I wasn't around." She searched his eyes.

Marshall scrunched his forehead. "You wanted me to see what you wrote?"

"Duh. It never dawned on you that suddenly my screen was always on when it had been dark for months?"

Marshall sucked in breaths as he flattened his lips against his teeth.

Taylor smirked. "You always snoop around my computer when I'm away from it. You try to guess my passwords, then leave the screen in a different position than where I'd left it. I decided to make it easy for you. And then see what you'd do with your discovery."

Marshall balled his hands into fists and muttered.

"I think I just heard 'bitch' or maybe 'shit,'" Taylor snapped. Her body vibrated in anger as her neck throbbed. "What I never heard was, 'Taylor, we need to talk about your books and your pen name. I want to understand what you've been writing and why.' No, what you decided to do was tell your secret to the biggest right-wing asshole in town! For what purpose, Marshall? So he can destroy me on his podcast?"

Marshall stared back at her, his chin thrust out. "You've been writing filthy books about queers, Taylor. Seems to me you're the one at fault here. Why were you hiding it if you didn't think what you were doing was wrong? Why haven't you told our sons?" His eyes were wide as he paused. "Because you don't want them to know you're writing queer porn."

Her stomach hardened. "Porn? Have you read any of my books? They've all won awards. My latest received a Kirkus Starred Review, which is pretty damn hard to get. Lots of people have left heartfelt reviews. They've cried and laughed and loved my characters."

He shoved his hands into his pockets. "Yeah, well, there are millions of people out there. You can always find a few who'll like anything."

The air between them sparked with hatred. Taylor had long since deadened her feelings for him and sworn to herself he would never hurt her again, but no shield was impervious all the time.

"And you know what's worse?" Marshall asked, his nostrils flaring. "You're promoting a perverse lifestyle in which gays and transgenders and 'I'll have sex with anyone or anything' are normal. Something to teach about in kindergarten. There's movies and books and TV shows everywhere, full of these people. It's gotten to the point where being straight and normal—"

"Is dull and boring!" Taylor mimicked his voice. "You've got to be queer or trans to be cool nowadays. Says your great friend, Levi Mitchell, almost every day."

Marshall stabbed the air. "Well, it's true. It's all part of *The Queering of America*. If we don't stamp it out now, there'll be no normal males or females in this country or the world. Everyone can choose to be whatever they want."

Taylor tightened her eyes. "Define 'stamp it out,' Marshall."

"Stop it!" he shouted, his upper lip curled back. "Stop publishing books like yours. Get rid of queer media."

"Just 'Don't say gay.'"

"Exactly!"

"And 'Don't ask, don't tell.'"

"Exactly!"

Taylor shook her head and blew out a breath. "What will you do if one of our grandkids comes out as gay?"

He folded his arms and scowled. "That will never happen."

"Really? What if one or more of them does?"

Marshall cocked his head. "I'm sure Gene and George will know what to do."

"Which is what? Throw them out? Or maybe the kids will be so scared of consequences they'll hide who they are and be miserable for the rest of their lives." Heat surged through her neck. "And then get married to someone you never really loved because you were afraid to tell anyone you're a lesbian? Because your girlfriend was killed by a homophobic piece of shit!"

Marshall's mouth dropped open. "Who are you talking about?"

"Brooke Skipstone."

He grimaced. "You're Brooke Skipstone."

"I wish I was." Taylor wiped tears from her face. "More than anything." She strode toward her office, Marshall stomping close behind. "I'm going to send Gene and George copies of all my books and links to my reviews." She sat at her desk and lifted her computer lid.

"No, you will not!" He slammed the computer lid down.

Taylor yanked her fingers out just in time. "Are you resorting to violence, Marshall?" She pulled out her phone. "I'm recording everything, starting now." She punched her camera button. "So what do you have to say after slamming my computer lid?"

Marshall growled and raised his fists to his head. "Sometimes, Taylor, sometimes—"

"I want to kill you? I wish I'd never married you? I wish you'd drop dead? All of the above?" His face turned purple on her screen.

Marshall took several deep breaths before speaking. "If you don't agree to stop writing books and remove the ones you've already published forever, Levi will share your secret with everyone in town and his thousands of listeners. He's waiting for my call."

Taylor's stomach balled up as she stared at her husband's smirk.

"Think hard about this, Taylor. You'll be crucified in this town. Is that what you want?"

She shook her head, stopped recording, and tried to keep from laughing. "That's not what *you* want, obviously. My embarrassment would spill over onto you, which you couldn't stand. I have another proposal since we're bargaining over my life." She leaned back in her chair. "I'll keep writing and doing what I want without interference from you *or* Levi, and in return, I won't bring my books to school for anyone who wants to read them. And I won't post links on the community Facebook page to download free ebooks." She watched Marshall's eyes widen in fear. "What do you say to that? Do we have a deal?"

Marshall swallowed and cleared his throat. "You wouldn't."

"I would. No doubt about it."

"What about our sons?"

She sat upright and opened her computer. "I probably won't have time to send them anything tonight. I'm trying to finish a new book."

He harrumphed. "What's this one about?"

"The life and death of Brooke Skipstone." She watched his right eye twitch. "You'll read it someday."

He shook his head. "Don't think I will."

"We'll see." Her eyes perused his face, noting the strong nose, chin, and still-full lips he had since they first met. And blue eyes, which had faded only a little. She spoke softly, "When did you become such a hateful homophobe? You didn't use to be this way."

He sneered. "When did you turn gay?"

Taylor sucked in breaths, trying to decide if she'd admit what she'd kept hidden for over forty years. "I was always gay. Just too scared to admit it." Angry at herself for holding back for so long, she clenched her jaw. "I loved one woman with my entire soul and might have found another to love, but I fell into a trap."

His upper lip curled. "By marrying me."

"Yes." Her voice shook. "The kids at your father's school thought we were cute together, the youngest teachers by far on campus. Eddie and Leo and Anna played matchmaker." Their cute faces flashed in her mind. "Every day was full of giggles and whispers until they screamed in delight when you told them we were getting married. Neither of us wanted to disappoint them. I loved those kids."

Marshall's face drooped. He asked quietly, "Did you ever love me?"

"I thought I did." He dropped his gaze. "At best, our marriage has been rocky, Marshall. I know you've had regrets, and I don't blame you. I can't pretend anymore."

The muscles in his jaw tightened. He spat out his words. "You need to stop this nonsense."

"I am." Her gaze fixed on his for several seconds before she said, "Go call Levi. I've got work to do."

He started to turn then stopped and mumbled, "Dinner?"

She offered a thin smile. "If I don't cook, you won't have to clean. There are leftovers and lunchmeat. Figure it out." She slipped on her headphones. "I'll send you a copy later."

She didn't notice his leaving.

In years past, she had cried and screamed after such fights, but she had become numb to them. Days would go by with nothing more than casual, meaningless comments. One day she'd kept track of how many words she'd said to him. Twenty-three. Then the inevitable flare-up, like an unpredictable geyser, would drown the day with hate and accusations and anger. Always the same words but in different arrangements.

She'd learned it was better to stay silent, to ignore him, and escape into her writing.

Closing her eyes, she focused on the roaring sound in her ears and remembered standing with Brooke under a gushing showerhead at a KOA Campground near Carlsbad during their drive to Oregon. They'd both entered separate stalls, but as soon as two mothers and kids left the bathroom, Brooke had knocked on Taylor's door.

They'd dropped their towels and stared. Soon, Brooke hugged Taylor and walked her into the shower.

They'd stood under the warm water—nose to nose, breast to breast, thigh to thigh—and watched the streams trickle over their skin as they'd stared into each other's eyes. The rest of the world had disappeared except for them.

Taylor had never felt so completely happy and relaxed in her life. When she started writing as Brooke Skipstone, she immersed herself in the same sound of falling water.

After several minutes, she opened her eyes to find a text from Grace.

Are you busy?

Taylor picked up the phone and hesitated. Should she respond? Technically she shouldn't be texting a student unless it related to classwork. She decided to be brief—*Writing more chapters.*

Do you listen to my father's podcasts?

Taylor's heart skipped a beat. *Sometimes.*

He's talking about your book without mentioning your name. He even read some sections. He said he'll reveal more on future shows.

An uneasy combination of fear, excitement, and relief swept through her mind, swirling her thoughts—*He couldn't control himself. Marshall told him* No, *but Levi still couldn't resist. Everyone in town would be hanging onto his every word. Marshall must be petrified.*

Very interesting, Taylor replied.

Grace texted. *Gram wants to meet you. She has sugar cookies and scrumptious Samovar tea. Can you visit?*

Taylor took a deep breath. She had to get out of the house. She didn't want to deflect another torrent of rage from Marshall. What harm could there be in meeting a student's grandparent? *I'd love to. Sounds yummy. Where?*

F Street, between 2nd and 3rd, on the left, duplex. My truck's out front. Left unit.

Taylor's scalp tingled. She couldn't remember the last time she visited another house or sat down for a conversation. *Five minutes.*

Taylor slipped her computer into her bag and walked into the kitchen. She couldn't see Marshall in the den or sunroom. Maybe he was upstairs, hiding.

She opened the door, peeked outside, and gasped at the rippled, pink and magenta clouds glowing in the western sky. "Such a beautiful sunset!" If Marshall asked where she'd gone, she'd say, "To watch the sunset in the park." Hell, she'd tell the truth. Why not? She'd already told him she was gay.

As she drove, she realized she hadn't felt *real* anticipation or excitement since . . . when? Outside her books' characters, she often felt numb, almost emotionless.

It was nice to feel something real within herself at long last.

4

THE GAY SCENE

After their bath, Grace and Maddi climbed into bed, wearing t-shirts and propping themselves against various-sized cushions while they read Taylor's book. Grace reread Chapter One out loud to Maddi, who could read but lacked fluency and loved to hear Grace's expressive voice. Maddi couldn't stop laughing after the porch scene. "I want to see the movie!" she screamed.

After finishing Taylor's next chapter about meeting Brooke for the first time in college, they walked to the kitchen to grab something to eat.

Maddi hooked Grace's arm. "Brooke and Taylor are cool together. Almost as good as us." She kissed Grace's cheek.

"Yeah," Grace said. "But we know she's going to die. Each chapter makes me more and more nervous."

They found Gram sitting in her chair, reading her iPad.

"Where are you?" Grace asked.

"About to finish Chapter Four." Gram removed her glasses and rubbed her eyes.

"Don't tell us," Maddi said.

She sucked in a breath. "I won't."

Her heart skipping, Grace asked, "Is it bad yet?"

"Not bad, but the plot thickens. There's a pot of homemade chicken soup on the stove. Help yourselves."

"Yum!" Maddi shouted. The girls found bowls to fill then sat down to eat.

Grace slurped a big spoonful into her mouth then Maddi slurped longer and louder. Soon they were snorting and cackling.

Gram laughed. "I love to have you girls in my house. You provide such interesting sounds. Whether you're eating or bathing or . . . whatever you do at night."

Grace's face heated. "Can you hear us?"

"Certainly. I'm not deaf."

"Do you mind?" Maddi asked, hiding her face.

Gram chuckled. "Heavens, no. It reminds me of when Pete and our friends used to get together."

"Friends?" Grace blurted. "You and Grandpa were swingers?"

"We experimented," Gram said with a twinkle in her eyes. "But only after your mother and uncle had moved out of the house."

Both girls stared open-mouthed at the old woman.

Gram put her hands on her hips. "Why do young people think the elderly aren't interested in sex? Pete and I enjoyed each other for many years before we decided to try something different."

"Did you have sex with a woman?" Grace whispered, her chest about to burst.

Gram nodded. "Clara and I were great friends."

"Even after Grandpa died?"

"Yes. But her husband got a brain tumor, so they moved to Seattle for treatment. Then your mother died, and I moved up here. When Clara's husband passed away, she moved even farther away to be closer to her children." Gram wiped her eyes. "So much tragedy happened at once."

Grace's chest ached as she hugged Gram. "I'm sorry you've been stuck in this shithole town without your friends because of me."

Gram squeezed her granddaughter. "I'd rather be with you any day." She held out an arm. "And Maddi."

Maddi joined the hug.

Gram kissed both girls' heads. "Does your mother know you'll be leaving soon?"

"I hardly see her," Maddi answered. "She spends most of her time with her asshole boyfriend. I'm either alone at my house or over here."

"Well, you can stay here as much as you like."

"Really?" Maddi kissed Gram's cheek.

"Sure thing. You're like my second granddaughter." She released them both and fetched an Amazon box from the counter. "I got this today. It's a noise machine. You can set it to white noise, ocean waves, rain, or a waterfall. Whatever you want. Turn it up loud when you two are wrestling with each other. My neighbor has called to complain about the noise a few times. The wall between us is not soundproof." Gram lifted her brows twice. "She wonders what's going on."

Tingles swept up the back of Grace's neck. "What do you say?"

"You're watching movies."

Both girls grinned.

Grace laughed. "Now all the movies will be about lesbians doing it on the beach."

Maddi's eyes widened. "Or inside a tent in the rain forest. We can think of all kinds of scenarios. This will be fun. Thanks, Gram."

Gram chuckled. "Just make sure it's loud."

The girls carried the box to their bedroom and climbed back into the bed. Maddie pulled out her phone. "Ready for Chapter Three?"

Maddi snuggled against Grace's arm. "Let's do it."

Grace started reading.

Chapter Three

After our one-off encounter in April, Brooke and I had restrained from sexual behavior or innuendo. We'd been busy preparing for the next chapter in our lives.

The summer of 1974 was the first time I'd come back to San

Antonio in two years. Typically, Brooke entertained at a dinner theatre while I worked theatre camps for middle and high school students.

Brooke's parents wanted her to stay near Fort Worth, where they lived. Why couldn't she work in Dallas? But Brooke wanted a change of scenery. She'd never been outside Texas in her life.

Brooke was offered several job opportunities, but the one she accepted was because I found a position in nearby Medford. She'd join the Oregon Shakespeare Festival in Ashland—well-known with many famous alumni—and I'd teach at a private school that had just built a new theatre.

We skipped graduation ceremonies, sold our furniture, bought a hippie van, and headed to San Antonio to say goodbye to my family and pilfer the camping gear they would never use again. Brooke and I planned to stop at national parks and rest stops along the way to Oregon.

My last project to earn my teaching certificate was to direct a high school play. I had written a musical version of *Midsummer Night's Dream* the previous semester and decided it would be perfect for the kids I'd been teaching. Brooke helped me as a singing coach and choreographer. The auditorium was packed both nights, and the show was a great success. However, Mom and Dad had to attend a business conference that weekend, so they'd missed it.

Soon after Brooke and I arrived at their house, we decided to give them a quick version. I played piano for Brooke during the songs, and we acted all the parts in the living room while Mom and Dad sat on the sofa, laughing and applauding.

Puck, a girl in my version, was singing "The Power of the Flower"—she uses a magical flower to make people fall in love with each other—when my brother entered the house. He had never met Brooke or seen any of our shows in Dallas. A year younger than I, Austin had shown no previous interest in my plays or songs, but when he heard Brooke's voice and saw her sing, he stood transfixed in the foyer as if Puck had squeezed the flower on him.

The power's in the flower
Your eyes will spin around
The magic's in the color
To take resistance down

When you hold your lover close
And feel your fever soar
And put your lips together
You will ache to your core

Let the power of love
Make a fool out of you
Make your heart stop beating
And take the breath out of you

When you fall in love
You revert to a child
Sophistication leaves you
Your emotions they go wild

Brooke was an expert at playing to her audience. She noticed Austin's response and zeroed in with all her charm.

In my version, Bottom and his crew entertain the nobles with an upbeat, crazy version of Romeo and Juliet, where the Montagues and Capulets are like a comical version of the Jets and Sharks in *West Side Story*. When Romeo finds Juliet "dead," he stabs himself dramatically a hundred times while squirting himself with ketchup. Then Juliet awakens because "the pills of deadly poison were really only laxatives." She finds bloody Romeo and asks the crowd to

Say Romeo Say Romeo, rise up and take a bow

Say Romeo Say Romeo, we want you standing
now

Brooke pleaded with our audience to chant and clap. Even Austin got into it, standing shoulder to shoulder with Brooke, repeating the chant over and over.

Maddie stood up on the bed. "I like this version of *Midsummer* better than the one I had to read last year. I can't believe Taylor wrote this." She juked her hips as she chanted, "'Say Romeo Say Romeo, rise up and take a bow. Say Romeo Say Romeo . . .' What was the rest?"

Grace laughed. "'We want you standing now.'"

"That's right. 'We want you standing now!'" Maddi repeated the chant as she twerked her butt in Grace's face. "Do you think this would make Romeo . . . 'rise up?'"

Grace slapped Maddi's ass. "First his boner, then the rest of him."

Maddi squealed and plopped back next to Grace, who continued reading.

I hammed up my rebirth until Austin bent over laughing. Brooke ran back to my side, and we both kissed the air between us. Then Romeo said,

Alive again with Juliet on midsummer's eve
You did it with the power of love and a little
make-believe
Now all the actors are at hand to take a bow
or two

Thank you all for clapping. We had fun,
didn't you?

We bowed to great applause and described the next action. All the actors and nobles paired up, feigning sleepiness when actually all they wanted to do was find a room to make out with their lovers. Left alone onstage, Puck (still played by Brooke) complained about how she'd helped everyone else to find a lover, but she's left with nobody. "Always Miss Nice. Always Miss Chump."

Then Titania (me) came onstage, still affected by the flower Oberon had squeezed into her eyes. She saw Puck and was immediately love-struck. "You're so gorgeous. So beautiful!" Titania lunged at her.

Puck backed away. "Look, Titania. I'm a woman, and you're a woman. It doesn't make sense to love me. Listen to reason."

Titania replied, "Love and reason keep little company nowadays. Now let me run my fingers through your hair."

I lunged at Brooke, who ran around the piano squealing until I tackled her, put my hand over her mouth, and repeatedly smooched the back of my hand, full of exaggerated lust, while she struggled and fake screamed. Mom and Dad howled in laughter while Austin stopped clapping and shook his head.

When Brooke and I got off the floor, he said, "That ending's kinda sick, don't you think?"

Brooke and I frowned and looked at each other before I said, "It's a silly comedy, Austin." I shook my head. "Brooke, meet my brother, Austin, the killjoy."

Brooke nodded.

Hurriedly, Austin said, "I thought what I saw of the play was really good, and I can't believe you both acted all the parts. I just questioned the ending."

"I think the whole play was amazing, Taylor," Mom said, beaming. "And you wrote it."

I smiled. "With a little help from Shakespeare."

"Great performance, girls," Dad said. "Brooke, you have a helluva voice."

"Thanks, Ken."

"How did the audience respond?" Dad asked.

"Standing ovations both nights," I said. "The kids did a great job and had a lot of fun."

Austin frowned. "No one complained about the gay scene at the end?"

"The gay scene?" I scrubbed my hand across my face and thought my head would explode. "Maybe someone did, but I never heard about it."

"In Taylor's play," Brooke said so sweetly, looking directly at Austin, "Puck runs off stage, chased by Titania, so there's no actual kissing. Taylor and I ad-libbed a few minutes ago. We like to have fun together, and sometimes we're a little crazy." She threw her arm around my neck and pulled me close, her cheek against my head. "Next time she tries to tackle and kiss me, I won't let her, but she's so cute. Has anyone noticed how much you two look alike?"

"Eww!" I said too loudly and drew back from her.

Brooke smiled. "It's true. You two could easily play Viola and Sebastian."

"Who are they?" Austin asked.

"Says the geology major," I scoffed.

"You were so good as Viola," Mom said.

"Thanks, Pat," Brooke said.

I grabbed Brooke's hand. "We're going upstairs for a bit. She hasn't seen my room." I led her to the stairs. As soon as we entered my room, I shut the door. "That was brilliant! Now he thinks you called him cute."

"Yup." Brooke's eyes twinkled. "Now his male ego can swell and distract him from gay bashing. Why is he so sensitive to gay humor?"

"I have no idea. Since I left for college, we've hardly seen each other. He thinks acting and theatre are nothing but,"—I air-quoted—"playing dress-up. He's into rocks and finding oil, you know,"—I air-quoted again—"real things that people need. He wants to be a petroleum engineer."

Brooke rolled her eyes. "Sounds exhilarating." She walked around the room. "So this is where little Taylor grew up. It's a little more girly than I'd imagined. White furniture, a four-poster bed with a lace canopy. A desk that looks like a make-up table."

I straightened the bow on one of the bedposts. "Mom chose everything when I was too young to argue."

Brooke cocked a brow. "Any boys been up here?"

"Yeah. One. My brother."

"Really?" Brooke asked. "That sounds yucky but interesting."

I sat on the bed. "Yucky because of him. But interesting because of Julie."

Brooke leaned against the dresser. "Ooo, tell me."

"I was a cheerleader, and one night after a game, I had the other four girls spend the night. Austin played basketball. All the girls thought he was hot. He dropped by my room wearing gym shorts and a t-shirt. We'd already changed into pajamas. They got him to play *Truth or Dare*. Before long, three of the girls followed him to his room."

"Why didn't the fourth girl go?"

"She wasn't into Austin, I guess. I said, 'Gross. How can they like Austin?' after the girls left. Julie said, 'I agree,' and jumped into bed next to me. We talked for a while on our backs, laughing and giggling. Then she propped herself up on her elbow and put her hand on my knee. She said, 'Do you think Susan will let him touch her knee?' I laughed and said, 'Maybe Mary.' Julie moved her hand up to my thigh. 'Do you think Mary will let him go this far?' I got a little nervous but said, 'I think she'd let him reach higher.' Julie moved her hand slowly up to my panties. 'Up to here?'

"By then, my head was spinning, and I couldn't catch my breath.

She moved her fingers around. 'Would your brother do this to her?' I looked her in the eye and tried to swallow. She pushed harder. Then I said, 'I don't know, but you can to me.'"

Brooke sat down next to me and put her hand on my thigh. "How far did you two go?"

"Just as I was about to cum, Susan and Mary opened the door. Julie flopped over on her side and pretended to be asleep. Susan said, 'What are you two doing? Hmm?' I sat up, trying to calm the butterflies in my stomach. 'Trying not to barf about what you and my brother were doing. Where's Alice?' They laughed. 'I swore not to tell,' Mary said. They climbed into their sleeping bags, giggling and whispering."

Brooke put her arm around me and pulled me close. "What happened between you and Julie?"

"Nothing. Neither of us ever talked about what happened."

Brooke kissed my head. "Another one-off."

I couldn't help moving my lips toward her neck, but Austin knocked on the door, and we both jerked around.

"Can I come in?" he asked.

I stood and opened the door. "Checking to see if we're making out?" I snapped.

He sucked in his lips and pushed his hands into his pockets. "Hey, I'm sorry. I shouldn't have made such a big deal about it."

I folded my arms across my chest. "Okay."

He stepped into the room and focused on Brooke. "And to make it up to you, I'm inviting you both to join me and some friends to go bar hopping tonight."

"No thanks," I said. "We need to finish packing the van so we can head out tomorrow."

"Head out where?"

"We're driving to Oregon," Brooke said with a smile.

Austin jerked his head back. "Oregon? Why?"

"Did Mom and Dad tell you nothing?" I asked. "We have jobs in

Ashland. We'll camp in our van, see the Grand Canyon, Lake Tahoe, the Redwood Forest, and then head up the coast."

He sucked in a deep breath. "You leave tomorrow?"

"That's our plan."

He leaned against the door jamb. "You two by yourselves? Where will you stay?"

Brooke stood. "Campgrounds. Rest areas. Wherever we want."

He frowned and put his hands on his hips. "That's crazy. Two girls by themselves driving across the country?"

I barked a laugh. "Girls aren't allowed to do that?"

"They're allowed," Austin replied, "but I don't think it's very wise."

"Why?" Brooke asked.

Austin shook his head. "Because there's lots of bad people out there."

My muscles tensed. "Guys, you mean." I snapped, "They'll see two hot girls by themselves and think we're looking for trouble."

"Basically," Austin said. "Look, I don't make the rules, but that's what some guys will think."

Brooke tightened her lips. "But you *are* making the rules by saying women can't be without a man for protection. Men repeat it to women over and over until they're scared to do anything on their own."

Austin tilted his head. "I should've known you're a women's libber." A bemused smile covered his face. "What will you do when a couple of bikers give you a hard time?"

Brooke's lips stretched thin as she stared at him for two seconds. I covered my mouth because I knew what was coming. Then before he could blink, she reached for the knife in her boot and held the point against his temple.

Austin stiffened. "Whoa."

I laughed. "Your eyes nearly jumped out of your head."

"Mr. Biker," Brooke purred. "Would you kindly leave us alone?"

Austin's face was still pale. "You carry a knife in your boot?"

"Duh." She slipped the knife back into its sheath. "So does Taylor when we think we might need it. Stage combat was one of our favorite classes."

I held the door open for Austin to leave. "Have fun drinking with your buds tonight. Be sure to look for girls without guys. They're the easiest prey. And make sure they're not wearing boots."

"Yeah. Very funny," Austin said as he walked out the door. "I still think you're asking for trouble."

I closed the door behind him and leaped at Brooke for a hug. "That was so badass. You were like lightning."

She hugged me back. "Do you think we're making a mistake? Stage combat is fun and games. A real biker would throw me to the ground and stomp my head."

I leaned back and searched her eyes. "What do you want to do?"

"Maybe buy a shotgun."

We'd had this conversation before. "I'm scared of guns. Besides, neither of us has ever fired one. We'd have to practice."

Brooke sat on the bed and pushed her hair back. "It would just be for show, like my knife. We've never been in a real fight. People will stay away from us if we act like we know what we're doing."

I sat next to her. "Or come at us harder. We'll be on the road for just ten days. We can have fun and be safe without having a gun hanging in the rear window above our bed." I grabbed her hands. "Mom and Dad want us to show them where we're going."

We walked downstairs. Austin had already left the house.

While Mom made dinner, we examined maps with Dad at the kitchen table. He was excited about our plans and kept recalling special moments from our family trips, laughing about minor mishaps, and describing amazing sights to Brooke. I was fortunate to have parents who loved to take their kids all over the country during the summer.

But the trips stopped when I entered college. I couldn't afford to take weeks off between semesters. I had to gain experience and figure out what I wanted to do in theatre. I realized early that I didn't have the mega talent to be a star. I wasn't Brooke Skipstone. When I worked my first theatre camp, I knew my future. I liked teaching teens. My songs and plays wouldn't be staged on Broadway, but they were perfect for middle and high school productions.

After the summer of 1970, Mom and Dad stopped their RV journeys and flew to theme parks and Europe.

"I wish I could drive with you," Dad said. "I miss our trips."

"Do you want to be seen driving a hippie van?" I asked. "We could make you some tie-dye shirts, and you can wear a leather strap around your forehead. And grow a beard!"

Mom laughed. "I'd pay to see that, Ken."

"I'll bet." He scratched his face. "Beards itch." He sighed. "I don't think I can drive all day like I used to. But I'd go if for no other reason than to keep you two safe."

Brooke and I exchanged glances. I wondered whether Austin had talked to him.

He opened a folded paper with a list of Dos and Don'ts. "Maybe if you were ugly, I wouldn't have to worry so much, but you are both beautiful."

Mom turned around and rolled her eyes. "Ken, please. Bad men don't care what women look like."

"The main rule," Dad said, "is to never be isolated. If a rest area isn't crowded, don't stop. And always park near a light. Same with choosing campgrounds. Find a crowd. Don't hike a trail unless others are hiking nearby. Don't stop at shitty gas stations late at night. Don't get anywhere near bikers. And never pick up hitchhikers."

"I think that's a good list, Ken," Brooke said.

"Are your parents okay with this trip?"

"Yes, because they believe we're staying at hotels each night. They never saw the camper bus." She turned red and covered her face.

"You never told me that," I blurted.

Brooke shrugged her shoulders. "I knew what they'd say if I told them the truth."

Mom brought dishes to the table. "These girls will be fine, Ken. They're smart and independent. They'll have the time of their lives."

After dinner, Dad helped Brooke and me pack the camping equipment in the van.

Before we went upstairs to my room, Brooke sang a medley of songs from various musicals while I played piano. Dad filmed the performance with his Super 8 camera.

I never saw the film.

Months later, I asked them to send it to me, but they wouldn't. They had disowned me by then.

Since our one night of sex weeks ago, Brooke and I had slept in our separate twin beds. I'd been thinking about us sleeping together in my double bed and even closer in the van, wondering if she'd done the same.

We climbed into my bed. I knew Brooke moved around during her sleep, so we would inevitably touch. "Do you want me to sleep on the floor?" I asked as we faced each other in the middle of the mattress.

"What are you worried about?" She moved her nose closer to mine. "Our bed is smaller than this in the van."

My pulse raced. "I'm worried about another one-off."

She touched my lips with her thumb. "Okay, we'll make some rules, at least until we move into our house or apartment or whatever it will be. No kissing on the lips. No fondling. No sex. But we can touch and hug and stay warm." She followed the curves of my ear with her fingertips. "Will that work?"

I swallowed and tried to calm my pounding heart. "What happens when one of us breaks a rule?"

An evil smile spread across her face. "You get a spanking, of course." She moved her hand behind my butt and swatted.

I gasped. Maybe the thought of us sleeping together *had* filled her dreams like mine. "I don't think that will deter me." I touched her lips and cheek.

"Taylor," she said in feigned shock, "I never knew you were kinky."

I held my wrists together in front of her face. "Did you bring the handcuffs?"

She squealed, grabbed my wrists, got on top of me, and pushed my arms above my head. "Do you want me to punish you?"

"Yes. Please punish me." I pretended to struggle. "Please, mistress."

She laughed then bent down until our lips were almost touching. "I wouldn't hurt you for anything. You're the absolute best friend I could ever hope for." She lifted up a little and searched my eyes with hers. "I love you, Taylor Baird. Don't ever leave me."

"I love you too, Tobo. Oops, I forgot!"

She growled, and we wrestled until I was on top of her. "I love you, Brooke Skipstone, and I will never ever leave you." We stared at each other with tiny smiles.

"We'd better sleep," Brooke whispered. "Let me spoon you."

I turned on my side. Brooke snuggled up behind me, moving her hand under my shirt to hold my stomach. I felt her breath on my neck as our heads lay on one pillow.

A few hours later, I awoke to a bumping sound in the bathroom which was behind the wall against my headboard. The clock said 2:30. Austin grunted, "Shit!" Brooke was still asleep, snoring softly. I crawled out from her embrace, put on a robe, and entered the hallway outside the bathroom. After knocking quietly, I asked, "Austin, are you all right?"

After a few seconds, he opened the door. His face and hair were wet. His shirt was thrown on the floor, and bloody scrapes and bruises covered his right hand. He caught my glance and whipped his hand behind his back. He wobbled and breathed rapidly.

"You're drunk," I said. "What happened to your hand?"

His words slurred against slack lips. "I had to fight a Mexican and defend a woman's honor."

"So you're racist *and* homophobic? Since when?"

He blew out a breath and shook his head.

"Which woman?" I asked.

"Doesn't matter. It was just a short fight. No big deal." He rubbed a towel over his face and hair. "Look, I've been thinking about you two driving alone. I can't let you do that. I'm coming with you."

My neck stiffened. "*What?*"

"I'll go with you, then fly back here. I'm sure Dad will agree."

Cold filled my belly. "We already talked to Dad. He gave us a list of rules, and we're good to go."

"Yeah, well, I'll talk to him tomorrow morning." He gasped more breaths, and fear twitched in his eyes. "I need to go."

"You *need* to go? Why?"

"Because I couldn't live with myself if I let you two go by yourselves."

My head hurt. I couldn't believe he was saying this. "We barely have room in the bus for the two of us. And where would you sleep?"

"I'll bring a tent. I can strap it on the roof. All my crap can go on the roof. You two won't have to worry as much with me there."

"Because you'll beat everyone up?"

"If I have to. That crap with the knife won't stop anyone. Please. I need to go with you."

My stomach turned into a rock. Something was wrong, but I couldn't figure it out. "We'll talk in the morning." My brain swirled as I quietly opened my door. After I closed it and turned around, I found Brooke sitting on the edge of the bed, panting. I moved closer, and she clutched my waist, pushing her face into my stomach.

"I had a nightmare," she whispered. "I woke up alone in the middle of nowhere, and you weren't there." She gulped breaths.

I stroked her hair and softly said, "I'll never leave you."

Her eyes were wide open. "Where were you just now?"

"In the bathroom. Just for a minute."

"Okay."

She obviously hadn't heard Austin. "Here. Lie down and I'll spoon you."

Still tense, she rolled onto her side. I pressed as much of my skin to hers as I could and rubbed her tummy. I kissed her neck and shoulders. She shuddered, and I pulled her hard against me.

"I love you, Brooke. I love you more than anything. I'll never leave you."

A few minutes later, her breathing steadied and she slept.

Why does he need to go with us?

"Wow," Maddi said. "What do you think's wrong with Austin?"

"I don't know, but he's an asshole," Grace replied. "Want me to read more?"

Levi's voice drifted in from the living room. Gram had turned on his podcast.

Climbing out of bed, Grace said, "I think we should hear this."

They both left the bedroom.

5

THE QUEER AGENDA

Taylor parked next to Grace's truck and checked her face in the visor mirror. She stroked her lips with chapstick. *When's the last time I did this?* She hadn't worn makeup in years or felt the need to spend time on her appearance, but tonight she felt an itch and had to scratch just a little. She left her computer bag in the car, walked to the door, took a deep breath, and knocked.

A girl with long, curly blonde hair and false eyelashes pulled the door open and offered a big, glossy-pink smile. "Hey, are you Taylor?"

Her skin tingled. "Yes, I am."

"Come on in." The beautiful girl beamed, grabbed her hand, and pulled her inside. "I love your book. You and Brooke are so dope. Is everything true?"

"Yes." *So much joy and enthusiasm from this girl.* Her stomach stopped churning, and she breathed easily.

Grace appeared. "Hey, Taylor. I see you've met my girlfriend, Maddi." Grace fluffed Maddi's ringlets. "Don't you love her hair?"

"Yes, I do."

"How about her real hair?" Grace yanked off Maddi's wig with a laugh.

Taylor's hand flew to her chest as her mouth dropped open.

Maddi squealed and grabbed it back, positioning it on her head. "I like to glam out when I stay over here. Do you have any photos of Brooke? She sounds hot."

"She was. Very much. I have them in a book at my house. I'll be sure to bring it next time."

"We just finished chapter three," Grace said. "Was that time with Julie your first?"

A surge of heat rushed to Taylor's face. "Yes."

"My first was when Maddi attacked me in the school bathroom without warning," Grace exclaimed.

"You were staring at my boobs!" Maddi laughed.

"Because you purposely bent over and jiggled them," Grace said.

"I was brushing my teeth. Please show me how to brush your teeth without shaking your boobs."

Taylor caught her breath as Gram approached with a kind smile. She wore an embroidered tunic over leggings and a hint of rouge on her high cheekbones. But what made Taylor gasp was her eyes—deep-set and piercing blue, like Brooke's.

"Hello, Taylor." She held out her hand. "I'm Shannon. Aren't these girls a hoot?"

Taylor shook Shannon's hand—firm, yet pleasantly soft. "They're lucky to be with someone who gives them the freedom to be who they are."

Shannon covered Taylor's hand with hers. "Everyone is free to say and do what they want in this house."

Taylor caught her gentle look and couldn't move her eyes away. "I can't imagine what that must be like."

"Yes, you do. You and Brooke had that relationship."

Taylor's stomach fluttered. "Grace gave you the chapters?"

"Yes. They're beautiful and painful at the same time. To love someone so much and have to hide it in your house or bedroom must have been gutting."

Grace squealed as Maddi chased her into their bedroom.

Taylor craned her neck to watch the girls, remembering what that happiness felt like. "It's the same restriction those two girls live with. After fifty years, what's changed?" She looked back at Shannon. "At least they don't have to hide from you."

"Or from you."

Taylor realized she'd been holding Shannon's hand all that time. She cleared her throat and pulled her hand back to scratch her cheek. "Because I took the chance to share my story with Grace."

"Do you plan to publish it?"

Taylor exhaled. "Yes, but I don't think many others will respond to it like the girls have . . . and you."

Shannon raised her brows. "You might be surprised. Anyway, I've got tea and cookies on the table."

"I'd love some." Taylor followed Shannon, gazing at the few photos hanging on the walls. One showed a younger Shannon standing by a tall, bearded man with a beak of a nose, his hand on a young boy's shoulder. Shannon's left arm draped around a young girl's neck, holding her close. They all stood in front of a log cabin. "Is this your family?"

The two girls entered the kitchen and grabbed cookies.

"Yes. That's my husband, Pete, when we lived at the fishery across the bay in Homer. Emma was Grace's mother. Ethan is a wildlife biologist. Pete died three years ago of a heart attack."

"I'm sorry."

Shannon carried a kettle from the stove. Two ceramic cups waited on the table. "He was a good man. We had many good times."

The girls exchanged smiles.

"Some *really* good times," Grace teased. "You should tell her, Gram."

Shannon stopped pouring tea and pursed her half-smiling lips.

"Tell me what?" Taylor asked.

Shannon tilted her head as she looked at Taylor. "Pete and I experimented with swinging during our later years. They're shocked because old people aren't supposed to be sexual. But you're evidence to the contrary, Taylor. Though you look like you're in your late forties, maybe early fifties, you are about seventy. And you certainly are sexual." Shannon sent a tiny wink.

Taylor's cheeks heated, and she knew she was blushing. She wanted to say she wasn't sexual at all except in her memories and imagination since she and Marshall had slept in separate rooms for years. The last time they'd tried to be intimate seemed a lifetime ago.

"I definitely don't look fifty but thank you. I've always worried about how much sexuality to include in my novels, not because girls don't dream about sex or enjoy it, but because of what the prudes will say, especially about queer sex. For some, two girls being intimate is the most perverse kind. Even the suggestion of it."

"Like the *gay scene* at the end of your play," Grace said. "Did your brother know about you and Brooke?"

A cold breeze seemed to chill Taylor's skin. She tried not to shiver. "You'll have to read to find out."

Shannon moved a cup near a chair. "Your husband told Levi about Brooke Skipstone?"

Taylor sat down and lifted the tea. "Yes."

"He's not a fan of your writing?"

"To put it mildly." She sipped while her nose tingled at the aroma. "Oh, this is so good."

Shannon smiled. "It's Samovar tea from a shop in Anchorage. Orange peels, cinnamon, clove, black tea, lemon peel. I love it. Why did your husband talk to Levi?"

Taylor clenched her jaw. "Because he wants me to stop writing and unpublish my books."

"No," Maddi said. "You can't."

"How cruel is that?" Grace exclaimed. "I write poems and stories all the time. I couldn't just stop. Does he know anything about writing?"

"Only that it embarrasses him." Taylor sipped again. Despite the tea's warmth, she felt a chill. "What did Levi say tonight?"

Shannon sighed. "I can't bear to listen to the whole thing again. I'll play the highlights." She sat down and lifted her iPad. "Here he is." Shannon adjusted the volume.

We are under attack in America. The mainstream liberal media keeps hyping what's happening to the Ukrainians, so they can hide what's happening to everyday Americans. An evil walks among us in plain sight, yet most of us don't see it. Why? Because it hides within our institutions—the schools, the media, even Disney. The LGBTQIA2S and LMNOP crowd—their acronym keeps getting longer every day. Soon they'll run out of letters, make up their own extended alphabet, and force everyone to adopt it. That crowd of perverts wants to queer America. We have tapes of Disney executives saying they want half of the characters in future movies to be queer.

"That would be great," Maddi said.

Shannon stopped the podcast. "I heard some are demanding that movies issue warnings about containing queer content and characters."

"The next thing they'll want to know," Grace said, "is the sexual orientation of all the actors."

Taylor smiled at them, but inside, her guts were churning. She knew Levi would tear her apart, but hearing his actual words and tone of disgust hit her hard.

Shannon clicked *Play*.

Some of you may have trouble believing in a worldwide conspiracy to turn all of us into queers, but it's true. There truly is an international queer cabal. We have an example here in the little town of Clear, Alaska. Even in this town of Christians and conservatives and responsible gun owners and veterans right next to an air base with one of the most powerful radar systems to detect foreign intruders, a queer has slipped in among us. Right here under our very noses.

"More than one, fool," Maddie added.

And not just any queer, but a writer of books so foul and so perverse whose intent is to spread the glory of queerness and to depict ordinary, straight, cisgender Americans as evil. Cisgender. Ever hear that word? That's woke talk for normal males or females. The queers made up a new name for normal!

So who is this pervert living in our community? Her name is Brooke Skipstone.

You don't believe me? I've got one of her books right here in my hand. It's called Crystal's House of Queers. *You heard that right, folks. The story is about a lesbian who turns her house into a haven for queers. While her grandparents are in Fairbanks at the hospital, no less. While they're dying, she fills their house with queers.*

Here's the first sentence: "Crystal lies naked on her back, watching Haley remove three wet fingers from between her plump lips then slowly insert them into Crystal's mouth." That's the FIRST sentence, folks. It goes downhill from there.

Here's another line: "Girl sex is more honest and fun for everyone involved." This whole book is like an advertisement for gay sex.

"Girl sex rocks!" Maddi said, high-fiving Grace.

And here's a description of two girls enjoying each other: "Crystal moves her knee back as she slides her tongue down Haley's stomach, twirling into her navel, meandering to her pubis, then down.

"He sounds like he's about to cum," Grace said.

The scent spanks every cell inside her nose and pushes deep into her throat—salty, rich, intoxicatingly pungent. Her tongue . . ." You know, folks, I might get arrested if I read what comes next. It's explicit and filthy.

Now I am well aware that many people like to read romance novels. And some are very explicit, depicting sex between a MALE and a FEMALE. As in NORMAL sex. But Brooke Skipstone wants our teens, our children, to read her queer erotica. Why? To make queer sex seem normal. See, everyone's doing it. There's no shame. It sounds really great in that paragraph with Crystal and Haley. Go try it yourself!

Throughout the book are nude drawings. Crystal can't read very well, but she can draw and go down on a girl with the best of 'em. Three girls raise their supposed dyke flag in Clear, Alaska. In CLEAR, ALASKA, folks.

The queer agenda has come right here to our town.

Shannon stopped the podcast. "That man is such an ass."

"He's exaggerating about the drawings," Grace said. "There are only two nudes. All the others are portraits."

Taylor sucked in a breath. The fact that the girls ridiculed Levi calmed her nerves. "It sounds like he enjoyed reading the book," Taylor said. "At least the racy parts, like he skimmed the book looking for his version of filth. But he sounds more excited about it than offended."

Shannon clicked *Play.*

Who is Brooke Skipstone? She is a woman living under our very noses. But you say you've never heard of anyone named Brooke Skipstone. Exactly. Because the real author is hiding her true identity. The Queering of America slithers in the back alleys, hides itself in textbooks, tries to replace education with indoctrination, tries to slip into the minds of your children and turn them against the very system that has made our country great, the best in the world. They want to replace the American flag with a Gay Pride flag. That's the dream of every Democrat, every liberal and socialist, and every queer. To see a Gay Pride flag flying above our post office. Above our school! Above the Capitol Building in Washington, D.C.

But I think we should replace these queer books and queer ideas instead. And queer authors. I refuse to let them replace us! The queers will not replace us!

Tomorrow I'll reveal more information about this Brooke Skipstone. Until then, keep your children safe.

Taylor's heart pounded in her chest. At first, she was nervous and couldn't help pangs of fear squeezing her stomach, but the more Levi spoke, the more determined she became. He was making a fool of *himself*, not of *her*.

"It was worse the second time around," Shannon grumbled.

"Hey, I want that book," Maddi said. "Is it on Audible?"

"Yes," Taylor said. "I can send you a promo code. Would you grab my satchel from my car?"

"Yup." Maddi ran to the door.

"Dad thinks everyone will condemn your book," Grace said, "but a lot of people are going to buy it now." She laughed. "Kids and teachers and even Allison will be staring at their phones all day tomorrow."

"Don't they do that every day?" Shannon asked.

"Yes, but they'll be using one thumb to scroll, not two to text or play a game."

Maddi ran inside and gave Taylor the bag. She opened her computer and checked her author's account.

"Any sales?" Maddi asked.

Taylor guffawed. "So far, twenty-two ebooks and four paperbacks. That's for *Crystal's House*. Five copies of *The Moonstone Girls* were also bought. Those numbers will likely increase because the sales don't always register immediately."

After a few more clicks, Taylor found and copied an Audible promo code. "What's your email address, Maddi?"

Maddi told her.

"Okay," Taylor said. "Just sent it."

Shannon reached out and held Taylor's hand. "Are you all right?"

Taylor's pulse quickened as she found the woman's blue eyes. "My stomach turned over several times initially, but I'm fine now."

"How do you think Levi intends to replace you?" Shannon asked.

Taylor smiled. "Maybe surround my house with chanting crazies carrying pitchforks and torches. I don't know. Marshall told Levi to not talk about the book, but Levi couldn't resist the scoop. What will he say tomorrow if he doesn't reveal my name?"

Shannon squeezed Taylor's hand before releasing it and picking up her cup. "More readings, perhaps. But don't you think some will figure it out even without Levi's help?"

Taylor's heart skipped. "Yes, I do. Tomorrow will be interesting, but it's the last day before Spring Break, so I won't have to endure it for long."

Maddi punched up the volume on her phone as the narrator said,

Chapter One

Crystal lies naked on her back, watching Haley remove three wet fingers from between her plump lips then slowly insert them into Crystal's mouth.

"Get them wet. Very wet," Haley purrs as her green eyes fix on Crystal's browns. Haley lies against Crystal's left side, propping her head on her right arm.

"Oooh. I love the narrator's voice," Maddi said.

Taylor's phone rang. She pulled it out and stared at the screen. "It's my husband. Probably wondering where I am."

Gram signaled Maddi to stop her audio, then put her finger to her lips.

Taylor swiped to accept. "What's up?"

"Where are you?" Marshall barked.

Shannon shook her head and held her hands like they gripped a steering wheel. Taylor answered, "I drove out to the park to watch the sunset. Is anything wrong?"

Marshall sneered, "One of your boyfriends called."

Taylor gasped and dropped the phone on the table. Her stomach turned to stone. Her mind filled with fog.

Shannon took the phone, signaled the girls to keep quiet, and then punched the speaker button.

"Are you there?" Marshall shouted. "I said one of your boyfriends called."

Shannon placed the phone on the table and held Taylor's hand. She touched Taylor's cheek until their eyes met. Shannon mouthed, "You can do this."

Taylor nodded and cleared her throat. "I don't have any boyfriends. What are you talking about?" Her chest heaved.

"Some guy named Austin claimed he's your brother. I said you don't have any brothers, at least none I've ever heard of. He laughed and said, 'Really? Taylor never told you about me?' I said, 'I've never heard of anyone named Austin.' He said he's been trying to find you and wanted directions. I told him to go to hell and hung up. Who the hell is he?"

Taylor's body shook. *How did he find me?* She felt Shannon squeeze her hand harder. Taylor held Shannon's arm.

"I said, *who is he?*"

Taylor took a breath and closed her eyes. "He's my brother. I'll be home soon." She ended the call and sat back in her chair, watching the pained expressions on the girls' faces. She had to show strength and not let her new friends become afraid for her.

"Would you like a drink?" Shannon asked.

"Yes, please."

"I have vodka and whiskey. And some Diet Coke."

"Either one on ice with Coke."

Shannon released her hand, stood, and found a glass.

"Is Austin going to hurt you?" Grace asked.

Taylor rubbed her face. "He swore he would."

Maddi stood, spitting her words, "We'll protect you. I can bring a shotgun tomorrow."

"You can stay with us," Grace added. "Hardly anyone knows where Gram lives."

Shannon put the drink in front of Taylor, who grabbed it and guzzled half its contents.

Taylor set the glass on the table. "How'd Austin get my phone number?"

"He probably Googled it," Shannon said.

"But he doesn't know my last name."

Grace thumbed her phone as she spoke. "He knows Taylor Baird. He Googled her and found the name of your first book. He went to Amazon . . . which lists your website address . . . where . . . he found your home phone number on the Contact page." Grace held her screen for Taylor to see.

"Shit," Taylor muttered. "I'd forgotten about the number. I haven't looked at that website in years."

Shannon poured herself a drink and sat down. "Maybe he can't find your address without knowing your married name."

Grace still searched through web pages. "It's just a matter of time. He'll find it."

Taylor finished her drink. "I need to do some writing tonight." She pushed back her chair and stood.

"What will you tell your husband?" Shannon asked.

"I plan to give him my book about Brooke and me. He can read it if he cares enough. I don't have time to explain things to him. I have to finish soon."

"Can you send us more chapters?" Grace asked.

"Yes." Taylor opened her screen and sent a file. "This is what I have now. Shannon, what's your number?"

Shannon held her contact info up for Grace to see.

"Will you be in school tomorrow?" Shannon asked as her phone dinged with Taylor's message.

Taylor rubbed the back of her neck. "Yes. Otherwise, I'd be home all day with Marshall." *Silence, followed by obvious disdain, then endless questions. No thanks.*

Shannon stood and held Taylor's arm. "Maybe you should stay over here for a few days. I can sleep on that sofa. It would be no problem at all. Bring a bag of clothes with you to school. Leave your car parked in the lot and catch a ride with Grace."

"Please, Taylor," begged Grace. "Otherwise, Maddi and I will have to guard your house all day and all night. We'd be happy to do it, but you'd be safer here."

The intensity in Grace's eyes confirmed her commitment. "Thank you all. I'll stay here."

Maddi hugged Taylor. "Cool."

Grace hugged them both.

Taylor released the girls. "A week ago, I was very alone and nervous. Then Grace came by and took my book. I hoped you'd like it and we could talk, but I wasn't sure. And now I have three friends I can be open with." Tears welled in her eyes. "Thank you."

Shannon handed Taylor a tissue. "You can message me anytime. You're an amazing writer and a very strong woman. You need to be with those who appreciate you."

Taylor gave Shannon a quick hug, smelling a hint of earthy, sweet patchouli. "I'm glad I met you." She turned to Grace. "I'll see you tomorrow morning." She tousled Maddi's hair. "I do love your hair. Both versions." She breathed deeply. "Okay. Off I go." She gathered her satchel and walked to the door.

"Send us a text later," Shannon said, "so we know you're okay."

"I will." Taylor exited the house and climbed into her car. Soon, she was driving down Fourth Avenue toward her home. She remembered when they first saw the house in April 2004. Overgrown, naked alders leaned over a narrow road, flooded with spring melting. The parking area was mainly mud, and the house needed paint, but it was one of the few two-story houses in town with two bathrooms. She and Marshall envisioned frequent trips from their kids and grandkids (though none had arrived by then), so they wanted a big house. But the school's expected enrollment increase never materialized. The district hired them both when they actually needed just one. After two years, Taylor and Marshall took jobs in the villages where they earned more money but saw their house only during the summer and Christmas holidays.

They'd made many improvements inside and out over the years, creating a beautiful anomaly in a town comprised mainly of transported prefab base housing, Quonset huts, A-frames, and mobile homes attached to homemade extensions.

Few moved to Clear. Houses stayed on the market for years. Marshall and Taylor were stuck living there, especially since housing costs had skyrocketed everywhere else.

As soon as Taylor parked and opened her door, Marshall marched outside.

"Where have you been?" he barked.

"I told you." She shouldered her satchel and walked toward the house. Her entries were always met with either silence or anger.

"You must have stopped somewhere."

"I did. At the park." She opened the door and walked inside. "I have a lot on my mind, Marshall. I needed to get out of the house and think."

He followed. "Why didn't you tell me you had a brother?"

She dropped her satchel onto her office chair. "Well, he was in jail for murder at the time. I didn't feel like talking about him."

"Murder?" he blurted. "Who?"

"I'll send you something to read to explain that."

"Don't you ever learn?" he screeched. "Your filthy plays are what forced us to go to Alaska. And now they'll kick us out because of your books."

Taylor barked a laugh. "Oh, here we go again." She put fists on her hips. "We'll never know how inappropriate my last play really was because when Board members, staff, and parents saw it, half of them had already read your salacious emails to your administrative assistant. The school settled a lawsuit because of what *you* did, not me."

Marshall shook his head. "I'd had complaints from parents for three years about your plays. The only reason you weren't fired for them was because of me."

Taylor grabbed a Diet Coke out of the refrigerator. "Then we were both fired because while I wrote about supposedly inappropriate topics, you lived them."

"However you want to spin the truth, you're in trouble again for writing more filth. Did you hear Levi tonight?"

She twisted off the cap. "Yes, but only part of his ranting. You couldn't keep him quiet, could you?"

"No. He said this information was too important to keep hidden. He wants to call a community meeting at the church on Saturday."

Taylor laughed. "Great! We should all go. I'll do a book signing in the lobby."

Marshall paced around the kitchen, shaking his head. "I can't believe you wrote what he read tonight."

"Why? Because it's so perverse?"

"Yes!"

"Because it's about lesbians and gay boys."

"Yes! Why do you write that shit?"

"Do you think the queers wouldn't exist if I didn't write about them? We're everywhere, Marshall. Even in Clear. Why shouldn't our stories be told and shared?"

"*We're* everywhere?" He slapped the counter. "*Our* stories?"

"*My* stories. There's always a little truth in what I write, even if it's hidden on the edges." She pulled out her phone. "But this story I'm sending you right now is all true. *Every* laugh. *Every* tear. *Every* intimacy. *Every* heartbreak. *Everything* is true. You can read this story or not. It's your choice. It's not quite finished because the ending depends on what you and others decide to do." She punched the send arrow. "It's in your hands. If you read it and want to talk—not yell or accuse—then we can talk. Otherwise, I want you to leave me alone. I have too much work to do."

She walked into her office and closed the door.

Once she opened her computer, she rubbed her hands to keep them from shaking. Her fingers stabbed at the keyboard until she told her sons about her books and her pen name. Now that Austin knew where she was, she had to tell her children the truth.

She added this note before she attached her unfinished copy of *The Life and Death of Brooke Skipstone*. "Before you respond with shock and accusations, please read the book I've attached. It tells the story of the woman I loved in college—Brooke Skipstone. Everything in this book is true. Please read all of it before you cast judgment. I haven't written the last chapter yet because I don't know whether I will live or die."

She clicked "send" and felt a little less weight on her shoulders and a little more hope in her heart.

After slipping on her headphones and hearing the waterfall, she began to type the ending she feared and the one she hoped for, knowing that the actual event would remain out of her control.

6

MY BROTHER'S KEEPER

After Grace finished some homework and helped Gram clean the kitchen, she sent Taylor a message. *How's it going? Are you ok??*

Taylor replied. *Yes. I miss all of you already. I have locked myself in my office to write.*

Marshall?

I gave him the book. Maybe he's reading it.

We're here for you if you need us.

Grace sat at the table, staring at her phone, imagining Taylor alone and unprotected in her house. Her guts churned with hatred for her father. Once again, he had threatened someone she cared about. She'd blamed herself for not standing up stronger to Dad when Mom was alive. Both she and Chase were angry with themselves for not doing more to save their mother. And now it was happening again with Austin and her father. She had to do more this time.

While Maddi sat in the beanbag chair, listening to *Crystal's House*, Gram read Taylor's book. Gram's iPad dinged. Her expression changed from a smile to steely determination as she read a message. After she typed a reply, she turned the iPad to Grace.

From Taylor: *I hope you don't mind me sending you this, but I have no one else to talk to. My mind has been racing. My fingers can hardly keep up with my thoughts. When I reached out to Grace (some will think that inappropriate, but I couldn't think of another option. I suspected she was lesbian.) I had no idea you existed—someone so supportive of those girls. Such a kind soul, you truly are.*

Months ago, I was contacted about my brother's release in February. I panicked. I worried I would die without warning, and no one would understand why when it happened. I had lived such a secret and lonely life. I decided to write about Brooke and me so that when the inevitable occurred, at least my family would understand.

But now I realize that Austin represents more than vengeance against me. He is Levi and all the hateful anti-LGBTQ+ crowd, many of whom would cheer Austin on. We thought we had made some progress during the past few years. But now the tide has turned and threatens to push us into another Gilead.

I don't want to live in fear of Austin's bullet. I want to stand tall and face him down and others like him. I don't have Brooke to give me strength, and I can't do it alone. I would welcome your help.

Gram replied: *I am here for you. Whatever you need. And the girls are too. But you have plenty of strength, Taylor. Throughout your book, it is clear to me that you were the rock of B&T. You were the one to push boundaries, challenge the norm, to not buckle under pressure. Brooke would be so proud of you, as all of us are. We stand with you.*

"Would you like to add anything?" Gram asked.

Grace took deep breaths as a surge of hope left her skin tingling. "Yes." Grace typed: *This is Grace. I knew you'd like Gram! As I told you earlier today, Bring it on!*

The tablet lit up as Taylor's response appeared on the screen. *Thank you! For one of the few times in my life, I feel seen and known. Now, back to writing. See you all tomorrow.*

Gram gazed at Grace before holding her hands across the table. "You are an amazing young woman. I'm very proud of you."

Grace squeezed back, her cheeks warm. "Unlike every other student at school, I don't have to hide or keep secrets from an adult. I could always be miserable and nervous at home, trying to sneak out at 2:00 am like Laura and Paige to meet their boyfriends. But I don't have to with you. I wish I could feel that way outside this house with Maddi."

Gram pushed her shoulders back. "That's what we have to fight for."

Grace nodded, her jaw set. "I'll do what I can."

"I know you will. Are you going to read more of Taylor's book?"

"Yes. Right now." Grace walked over to Maddi, who pulled out her earbuds. "You want to read Chapter Four with me?"

Maddi stood. "Yes. For such a little thing, Crystal is such a badass."

Grace cocked a brow. "Wait till you meet Payton."

They climbed into bed, Maddi curled inside her girlfriend's arm, and Grace started reading.

Chapter Four

I awoke the following day to the sound of Dad's voice. "Girls, are you awake? I'd like to talk to you."

I tried to speak, but only a croak emerged from my mouth. I cleared my throat and whispered, "Brooke. Wake up." Her head lay on my right breast, her arm on my stomach and left leg draped over mine. I kissed her forehead.

Dad knocked. "Girls. Get up, please."

"Hang on, Dad. Give us a second."

Brooke yawned and stretched.

I whispered, "Dad's at the door. He wants to talk."

We got out of bed, slipped on shorts and a shirt, and ran our fingers through our hair. I reached for the door.

"Wait," Brooke said. She moved very close to me and picked away an eye booger. "Okay. Now you're perfect."

I opened the door and found Dad wearing khakis and an open dress shirt over his wife-beater t-shirt, chest hair, as always, protruding from the neck scoop. "Why so early, Dad? It's Saturday morning."

His face was grim. "I need to talk to you about something."

I remembered our early-morning encounter. *It's about Austin.*

He moved into the room. "Why don't you both sit on the bed, and I'll sit in this chair."

We did as he asked. Brooke frowned at me as in *What the hell?*

Dad leaned forward, elbows on his knees, and rubbed his face. "I'm sorry. I didn't get much sleep last night."

"Because of Austin?" I asked.

He blew out a breath and sat up. "Yeah. Yesterday, he talked with me after he talked with you two about how dangerous driving by yourselves across the country would be. He said he'd go with you, but he had a job starting next week. He really wanted to, though."

I didn't believe him. I turned to Brooke. "Austin was drunk in the bathroom last night at about 2:30, making a lot of noise." I leaned forward. "He told me he beat up a Mexican over a woman's honor. When did he become a racist?"

Dad furrowed his brow. "Why is he a racist?"

"Because he had to add the man's ethnicity. He wouldn't have said he beat up a white guy. Like saying Mexican would make his act more excusable."

Dad shook his head. "I think that's over-analyzing his words. The point is this guy kept bothering Austin and his friends, even out to the parking lot. They ended up fighting."

"How many friends?" I asked.

"Three. Austin was with Tony and Phillip."

My neck tightened. "Three against one. How badly was the man beaten?"

Dad sighed. "I don't know. Austin said Tony was the main one fighting. They all ran off when someone started yelling at them."

"Did you see Austin's right hand?" I asked. "Last night, it was bloody and bruised. Maybe Austin was the main one fighting."

"I didn't notice his hand." He looked away.

"So he's in big trouble and wants to leave town."

Dad waved his hand. "He's not in big trouble. Just a fight outside a bar. How many of those happen each night?"

"So if it's no big deal, why does Austin need to go with us?"

Dad rubbed his face and took a deep breath. "Because someone shot Phillip early this morning."

Brooke and I gasped. "Is he okay?" I asked.

"He's alive. He called Austin this morning from the Emergency Room. He said he's going to be okay."

My stomach hardened. "Austin's not worried about the police. He's worried about the guy's friends. Was he a gang member?"

Dad covered his face. "I don't know."

"Austin's not telling the whole story. He's hiding something."

"He probably is," Dad said. "He's a young buck who went bar hopping with his friends and got into trouble. I did the same thing. Most guys do at that age. He fucked up, okay? But he doesn't deserve to be shot. So take him with you. You'll be out of Texas tonight, and he'll be gone for over a week. Your mother and I would feel a whole lot better if you two weren't driving by yourselves anyway."

"We're safer if he's with us?" I scoffed. "He's dangerous. What if they follow him and shoot all of us?"

Dad rolled his eyes. "No one knows you're leaving town in a hippie van today. How could anyone follow you?"

My head ached. Didn't he realize what he was asking us to do? "What would you do if we weren't here?" I asked.

"I don't know. Probably fly him to my parents in Amarillo."

"Then do that."

He squeezed his hands. "The shooters might be checking the airport or the bus station. That's what they would expect us to do. But no one's checking on you."

I turned away.

"Look, Austin is pretty scared," Dad said. "But he hides it behind his cocksure attitude. I see it in his eyes." Dad's face drooped, and he sighed. "Taylor, he's your brother. He'd do the same for you."

"Really?" I shook my head and looked at the floor. "We hardly know each other anymore. I've barely seen him for the past four years."

"Then this trip will be good for both of you." He paused and swallowed. "Please? He's already packed and strapping his gear to the roof."

My face burned. "Then why bother asking us? Look, Brooke and I need to talk."

Dad stood and cleared his throat. "I know you're paying for this trip. You haven't asked us for any money, which I'm very proud of. But you weren't expecting another person, so I'll give you something extra." He reached into his pocket and pulled out a wad of fifties. "I think $300 should cover him." He reached out his hand, expecting me to take the money.

I knew it was a trap. If I had taken it, I'd already agreed to bring him with us, so I didn't.

He put the bills on the dresser. "You two talk and let me know."

"What does Mom think?"

He swallowed hard and pursed his lips. "She's been crying all morning. She wants you to get him out of here."

My throat tightened. I didn't like the idea of my mother in pain.

He quickly wiped his hand across an eye, pushed his hands into his pockets, and left the room. I watched him walk down the hall and turn the corner before I closed the door.

"Austin's not telling the truth," I hissed. "And I think Dad knows more than he's saying."

Brooke stood. "Of course. Your dad was acting a little to persuade us. For all we know, Austin and his friends killed that man." She wrung her hands, and creases lined her brow. "But he is your brother. If we don't take him, and something happens to him, we'll regret it forever. And your parents will never forgive you."

My head was spinning with all the reasons not to take him—we'd have no privacy, the gang following us, dealing with his homophobic and racist attitudes, and more. If Brooke had been angry and refused to be with him, I would have gladly screamed *No* to my parents and brother and peeled out of the driveway. "So you want to take him?" The words echoed in my head like doom.

"I'd rather not, but I think we have no choice. If he causes a problem, we'll drop him off at an airport. Then your Dad can fly him to Amarillo." She picked up the cash. "Besides, $300 is a lot of money."

"Which is why he gave so much." I shook my head. "I know we should do it, but I feel very nervous about this. My gut is screaming at me to say no."

She hugged me. "We can still have fun. Let him play macho man and protect the fragile females."

"Playing macho man is what got him into this mess." I leaned back so she could see my face. "He's not sleeping in the van. Ever. I don't care if it rains cats and dogs, and he has to set up the tent in a parking lot, he's staying in the tent. If he doesn't agree to that, I won't take him."

Brooke stroked my hair. "Fair enough. I'm sure he snores and he'll start to stink quickly. We're used to each other."

I hugged her back. "I love your stink."

"Do you?" She wiggled her brows and smiled. "I wasn't aware I ever stunk."

"And your snoring. It sounds like a cat purring in my ear. I love it."

"We have a little sink in the bus, so we can take bird baths." She licked her top lip. "That could be fun."

My neck tingled. "Wouldn't that be breaking the rules? Someone would get spanked."

She rubbed her nose against mine. "That could be fun too."

I searched her eyes. "Do you remember your nightmare last night?"

She pulled me close. "No. I just remember the fear, like I was falling. But you caught me. You always catch me."

But that wasn't true.

Maddi sat up. "What would you do if Chase had done what Austin did? Would you take him with us?"

"I would hope not, but Taylor didn't know he was a threat to Brooke." Grace's skin filled with goosebumps. "I don't see how Taylor can write this, knowing how it ends. All the signs were there. Even the thirty pieces of silver."

Maddi sat up and frowned. "What?"

"Her father gave her $300 like Judas took thirty pieces to betray Jesus. Except, in this case, they're betraying themselves and selling out."

Maddi shook her head. "How do you figure out this stuff?"

"Don't know." Grace casually twirled her fingers in Maddi's hair. "Just seems obvious. I bet Taylor's dad gave her some other amount, but Taylor changed it for the symbol. That's what authors do."

"If you say so." She smiled and pushed her fingers under Grace's waistband. "Do you want to try out our new sound machine?"

Grace pulled Maddi's hand out. "Yes, I do, but I want to read more."

"That could be our new code word. One of us will say, 'sound machine,' and the other will start stripping. No one will know what we're talking about." She giggled.

Grace harrumphed. "Or you could say nothing and just strip."

"Okay." Maddi started to pull off her pants.

"Not now! Don't you want to know what happens?"

Maddi pulled up her pants and frowned. "I do, but I don't. It's going to hurt." She snuggled up to Grace, who started reading again.

Mom put a platter of pancakes on the table as we entered the kitchen. Her face was puffy. She wiped her nose with a tissue. Outside the windows, a shirtless Austin tied a plastic tarp over a duffle bag, sitting on the van's roof.

"Eat up, girls," Mom said. "I've also packed sandwiches and snacks."

"Thanks, Mom. Brooke, go ahead. I need to see Austin." I went into the garage from the kitchen. He climbed down a step ladder. "We need to talk."

He wiped sweat from his forehead with his hand as he came toward me. He was hairy-chested, like Dad. And he'd obviously been lifting weights because he was ripped. Handsome, tall—a girl's dream come true, he thought of himself. He'd always worn a cocky grin like he knew he was a stud.

"Who shot Phillip?" I asked.

"He said a car raced by his driveway just as he opened the door to his truck. He saw an arm sticking out the window, holding a gun. He ducked. Two shots were fired. One hit his window where his chest would've been, and the other hit his arm."

I gasped. "How'd they know where he lived?"

"I guess someone saw his license plate when we took off. We rode in his truck last night."

My throat tightened. "Is someone going to drive by our house and shoot at Mom or Dad?"

"Dad's hired a security guard. He's supposed to be here soon."

I searched his eyes. "Austin, I think you're lying about what happened last night, and I really don't want to get involved by bringing you with us, but . . . I guess I don't want you shot. However, you have to agree to some rules first."

He folded his arms across his chest. "Such as?"

"You always sleep in the tent. We're in the van."

"That's why I brought my gear."

"This will be Brooke's first time outside of Texas," I said. "She's picked out what she wants to do, so no arguments about routes or places to stop."

He nodded.

"She and I are driving. You sit in the back without making shitty comments and no complaints about our choice of music. We are not playing Led Zeppelin, Black Sabbath, AC/DC, etc."

He sighed. "Okay." He snickered. "Are you two married or something?"

I sucked in a breath. *Of course, you have to make a gay reference.* "We're best friends. We've lived together in the same house for three years."

He cocked an eyebrow and snickered. "Really?"

My muscles tensed. "What the fuck, Austin? We've had lots of boyfriends."

He held his palms up and grinned. "Hey, I was just making a joke."

"Great joke. We're going out on our own and thought it would be good to support each other for at least a year. You need to be pleasant and helpful without being patronizing. I want her to have fun on this trip. Can you do all that?"

He nodded. "Yeah, I can do that." He looked straight at me without a hint of cockiness and said, "Thanks, Taylor." He held out his hand.

I shook it, feeling the sweat and dirt. "Can you clean up before riding in our bus? And please wear a shirt. I don't want you sweating on our seat covers. We spent a lot of time decorating our hippie home."

"Yes, Mother." He chuckled and scratched his ear. "Are you going to talk to me like this all the way to Oregon?"

I grinned. "I'm your big sister. How else would I talk to you?" I went back to the kitchen and sat down between Brooke and Dad. "Austin's taking a shower before we go."

Dad threw his arm around me. "Thank you." He kissed my head. "Please try to call us collect once a day."

"You hired security?" I asked. "For how long?"

"For the next few days."

I stabbed a couple of pancakes and dropped them onto my plate. "What sucks is you can't go to the police."

Dad sipped his coffee. "What good would they do? They're not going to put a patrol car on our curb all day and night. Look, if Austin causes any problems, you let me know. I'll talk to him, and if he doesn't shape up, you can drop him off at an airport, and I'll take care of him."

"I'd already thought of that," Brooke said with a little smile. "I figure we'll know by Albuquerque whether to boot him out or not."

Twenty minutes later, we gathered by the van, waiting for Austin. Brooke wore her signature cut-off jean short shorts—frayed, cheeky, and loose. She'd had the same pair ever since I'd known her. She'd opened the side door and was leaning inside the van, her butt in full view. When Austin trotted out the front door carrying a small pack, he stopped and stared with mouth agape. Brooke stood up and turned around with a bag of Hershey's kisses she'd retrieved from a cabinet under the sink. She saw Austin's dazed look and frowned, eyes narrowed.

We went through another round of hugs and kisses with Mom and Dad before moving into our seats.

"Austin," Dad commanded, "keep these girls safe."

"Yes, sir," Austin replied with a mock salute before climbing into the bench seat and setting an ice chest on the floor.

I planned to drive for the first several hours. After pushing the stick into reverse, we all waved at Mom and Dad as I backed into our street and headed toward the access road to IH10. Just before the stop sign, Brooke lifted her bare feet onto the dash where she usually kept them while I drove.

"Whoa, that's a lot of leg!" exclaimed Austin.

Brooke side-glanced me and put her feet on the floor.

"Hey, Austin," I said, "pretend you're not a caveman."

I eyed him in the rearview mirror and realized we'd have to deal with his body comments and stares for the next ten days. *Shit!* Why did guys always think girls dressed for them and posed for them and wanted to look pretty and sexy for them? In their minds, the only reason girls did anything was to attract their favor.

I realized the only time Brooke and I could act normal on that trip was when he was in the tent or bathroom.

Brooke popped in a cassette tape with our favorite mix—"Cat's in the Cradle," a variety of James Taylor, Roberta Flack, Diana Ross, "Annie's Song," "Country Roads," a bunch by Elton John, Joni Mitchell's "Help Me," "Both Sides Now" and more. Brooke had also made tapes with her favorite show tunes. We'd made enough cassettes to keep us singing and awake for at least ten hours of driving before we had to repeat anything.

But the first song Austin heard us sing was "You've got a Friend" by Carole King. I harmonized on the chorus.

Austin's eyes nearly popped out of his head when Brooke started, but I soon saw his fingers tapping on the seat. His head started juking when we lit into "I Feel the Earth Move Under my Feet."

"No, we're not doing this for your entertainment," I said. "We like to sing when we drive."

"Fine with me," he said. "You guys sound good."

The traffic on the highway started to slow down close to Boerne. We had to merge left. "Must be a wreck," I said. *Teach Your Children* had just started when we saw the ambulance's flashing lights.

"It's a bad one," Brooke said as we crawled along the road.

Austin leaned forward, squinting his eyes. A red truck with bright yellow and orange flames painted on the side had crashed into the metal railings at an exit. What looked like bullet holes were in the driver's window.

"Shit!" Austin screamed. "That's Tony's truck. I'm getting out. Pull off on the shoulder when you can. I'll find you."

My stomach jumped up my chest. "Austin, you can't—"

He opened the side door, stepped onto the road, and ran across the lane toward the grass.

"Who's Tony?" Brooke asked, looking out the window.

"Remember? He was with Phillip and Austin last night. Can you see him?"

Brooke leaned out the window. "He's running toward the ambulance."

As soon as the right lane was available, I moved into it and found a place to park on the shoulder. My heart pounded in my ears.

"What the hell happened last night?" Brooke asked. "What did they do?"

"Something bad. Phillip was shot this morning, and now Tony."

Brooke hoisted her feet onto the dash and hugged herself. "What did we get ourselves into?"

After another five minutes, Brooke said, "I see him." She pointed. "He sees us, and he's running." Brooke turned toward me. "He's crying, Taylor."

I couldn't think. Should we go back home or get the hell back on the highway? My pulse raced as I checked traffic to see when I could move back on the road.

Austin yanked the door open, jumped inside, slammed it shut, and yelled, "Get outta here!"

I spun my tires and leaped into a gap between cars, trying to keep my eyes on the road instead of looking at him through the mirror.

Austin was bawling. "Goddamnit! They killed Tony! Shit! They killed him!" He held his head in his hands, weeping and coughing.

My face was on fire. I bit my lip as tears streamed down my cheeks.

Brooke got out of her seat and sat next to him. She pulled him into her. Our tearing eyes met in the rearview mirror. I turned down the music and drove as fast as possible, my breath bursting in and out of my lungs.

Maybe twenty minutes later, Austin had crashed. Brooke carefully slid away and laid him across the bench. Then climbed back into her seat.

I grabbed the thermos of coffee I'd stashed in my door and offered it to her. Her hands shook as she unscrewed the lid and poured. She closed her eyes and tried to slow her breathing before she drank.

"What are we going to do?" I asked.

"Get out of Texas, then find a phone." She drank again. "Three boys beat up one guy at a bar, and two of them have been shot. That doesn't make sense. I think they killed the guy." She offered me the cup.

I took it and kept checking my mirror for somebody driving up next to me with a gun pointing out the window. Or someone crashing into the van to run us off the road. I tried to drink, but my teeth chattered on the rim.

Both of us stared out the windshield, trying to keep from screaming.

DRAG QUEEN

"You're not stopping, are you?" Maddi asked.

"For just a second," Grace said. "I need to catch my breath." She lifted her arm from around Maddi and sat up, breathing heavily. "This story wipes me out. What are they going to do?"

"I'd speed until a cop stopped me and turn him in."

"Really? What if the fight wasn't Austin's fault?" Grace stood, her stomach gurgling with worry. "I mean, right now, Brooke and Taylor don't know what really happened."

Maddi jumped out of bed and fluffed her ringlets. "Austin said he beat up a guy. Three against one in a parking lot."

Grace rolled her eyes. "If the guy has friends to shoot Phillip and Tony, why is he fighting alone against them in the parking lot? That doesn't make sense."

"Okay. So . . ."

"How do you turn in your brother when you don't know what he did?"

"Because everyone else in his group has been shot, and he's next."

"Yeah," Grace said, "except Phillip and Tony were either in or by their own trucks when they were shot. Someone can match license plates and addresses and names for this gang. How can they find Austin if he's in that van?"

"But as long as he's in the van, Brooke and Taylor are in danger."

"True," Grace said then sighed. "I'm going to check on Gram. Do you want something to drink?"

"I'll go with you and make some tea. I want to try it with cream."

They entered the kitchen and found Gram holding her head over the table on her elbows. Grace ran over.

"Gram? What's wrong?"

She sat back, revealing red, watery eyes. "If anyone in this town gives Taylor any trouble, I think I'll bite off their heads."

A lump formed in Grace's throat. "Is Brooke dead yet?"

"Where are you?"

"Just finished Chapter Four. Tony was shot."

Gram sighed and nodded. "You should read the next chapter."

Maddi was heating water and filling the strainer with tea. "It's hard to believe the girl in that story is now living in this little town at age seventy. How the hell did that happen?"

Gram steepled her hands. "There are three kinds of people in Alaska. Those born here, like you girls, who don't have any idea how special this place is because you've never been anywhere else. And then there are the Outsiders, who are either running toward a dream or fleeing from a nightmare. Or both, like Taylor."

Grace wrinkled her brow. "Now the nightmare is coming to find her."

Gram pursed her lips. "Evidently."

"Here, try this. It's good." Maddi brought her cup to Grace, who took a sip.

"Yummy. Are you going to share, or do I have to get my own?"

Maddi sipped and offered the cup to Grace. "I always share drinks with you. It's how we kiss in public."

Grace's chest filled with warmth. She took a sip and moved her lips down toward Maddi's. Her girlfriend opened her mouth and accepted the tea Grace pushed onto her tongue. "That's how we kiss in private."

Maddi grinned. "Mmm. Now that's especially yummy." She kissed Grace's lips. "Gram, do you want to try this?" She held out the cup.

Gram chuckled and stood. "I'll get my own cup, thanks. You girls are such a hoot."

A few minutes later, the girls sat in bed, shoulder to shoulder, Maddi sipping the tea as Grace started reading.

Chapter Five

Austin had turned over a few minutes earlier, his face against the seat back. Otherwise, he hadn't moved for the past hundred miles. Traffic had been light, and I'd stopped twitching every time a car or pickup moved to pass us. Brooke and I had not spoken to each other for over an hour. James Taylor sang "Fire and Rain" to us as Brooke held two Hershey's kisses in her hand. I checked on Austin in the mirror and held her hand for a few seconds before taking the chocolates. We'd always loved singing that song but now only mouthed the words.

Yesterday, Brooke and I had driven down IH35 from Dallas, singing, laughing, and dancing in our seats, so looking forward to our grand adventure.

Now we were hunted.

"We should stop for gas in Junction," I said softly. "Dad said the gas prices will be higher down the road."

Brooke frowned and half shook her head. "You sure?"

"We have to buy gas at some point."

"Should we call your parents?"

"Maybe."

I turned to exit and headed toward the Texaco station.

"Should we wake him?" Brooke asked.

"Why?"

She looked back at him. "Maybe he has to pee."

"Guys can pee anywhere. Do you have to go?"

She glanced down at her crossed legs. "I wouldn't mind."

"Wait 'till we fill up, and we'll both go." I stopped by a pump. We both got out of the van and felt the stiffness in our necks and butts. We stretched and shook our legs. Brooke bent over, pulling her head to her knees.

We heard a whistle then, "That's impressive."

She jerked up and turned to see a convertible approach on the other side of the island. She rolled her eyes and moved to the pump. I met her coming around the other side.

Two boys—young, with tank top shirts and cargo shorts, one with windblown blond hair and the other with a crew cut—jumped out of their car and walked toward us. "That's a cool van," the blond said, smacking his gum. "I'm Stewart and that's Bobby."

Usually, both of us could've handled them with smiles and flirty talk, but our stomachs twisted into knots. We couldn't say anything as I fumbled with the gas cap, and Brooke banged the nozzle on the edge of the tube. Our eyes met. Hers were damp and bright, her lips tight. My legs shook.

I gritted my teeth and pushed my fears aside like I'd done a hundred times before entering a stage. I whispered, "Showtime."

"Where are you girls headed?" Crew Cut asked.

I put as much sarcasm into my voice as I could muster. "Away from here."

"Ooh. Tough girl." Crew Cut laughed and licked his lips.

"Are you girls by yourselves?" Blond asked, his eyes moving up and down Brooke's legs.

"I bet they're going to California," Crew Cut said. "In a hippie van. All by themselves."

Blond puffed out his chest. "That could be dangerous."

Shit! I thought. *Why is this happening?*

Brooke folded her arms and cocked a brow, her face pale. "I think we can handle it."

"Really?" Blond laughed and moved closer. "Think you can handle me?"

The side door burst open, and Austin strode toward them. "Anyone can handle you," his deep voice boomed. He stopped inches in front of them, a head taller and fifty pounds heavier than either one. "Get lost," he growled.

They backed away. "Just getting some gas, man," Blond sputtered.

"I see lots of other pumps. Use one of them."

They scrambled back into their car and drove out of the station.

"Why didn't you wake me up?" Austin complained as he eyed the boys' car until it disappeared.

"Because we thought you needed to sleep," I said. My legs wobbled as I reached for Brooke. She covered her face and leaned into me.

"What's wrong?" Austin asked.

"Nothing, Austin," I snapped. "We've been driving for over an hour, worried about someone shooting us. Normally, we could have handled those punks, but we've been nervous as hell."

Austin took a deep breath. "Okay. I'm sorry."

Brooke stood up straight. "If he'd moved any closer, I was going to kick him in the nuts. Thanks for waking up when you did. I've staged-kicked guys many times, but never for real."

"Thanks for holding me when I cried like a fucking baby." He looked down. "I can't remember ever blubbering like that."

"Did you see Tony?" I asked.

He shook his head. "He was already in the ambulance. I talked to a guy he was riding with."

"Did he see it happen?" Brooke asked.

"No. He said they were driving and talking and then—boom! Tony fell over and they crashed."

"So he didn't see the type of car they shot from?" I asked.

"Nope." Austin removed the nozzle with shaking hands and screwed on the cap. "You got the key?"

"Yes," I said.

"Then lock the doors and let's go inside. I need to pee."

Five minutes later, we were back on the highway. We'd decided to call home that evening. Austin rummaged through the ice chest and pulled out a can of Coke. "Either of you want a drink?"

Brooke held out her hand for the can. She popped the lid, took a sip, and handed it to me.

"We have plenty of cans," Austin said. "Taylor, do you want your own?"

"No, we always share," I said.

I saw Austin scrunch his brows. "Really? Why?"

"Just something we do," Brooke said as she took the can back. "It's cheaper. Less sugar."

"And it keeps us from poisoning each other's drink," I said.

Brooke coughed a laugh and sprayed some Coke.

"Gotcha!" I jeered. "It's been like two hours since any of us laughed."

Brooke handed back the can, her fingers lingering against mine. "Thanks, Taylor. I needed that."

"We all needed that," I said.

"There's a rest area up ahead," Austin said. "Let's stop and eat these sandwiches."

Soon we sat at a concrete table protected from the wind by brick walls. All the fear and excitement had made us hungry. None of us spoke as we devoured Mom's Italian hoagies and bags of chips and cookies. When Brooke and I were full, Austin ate all our scraps.

Brooke's eyes widened at the human waste disposal. "Maybe $300 wasn't enough."

"Funny, funny," Austin said. "Dad gave me money too. I'll buy dinner tonight."

I glanced at Brooke and mouthed, "We need to know."

She nodded.

"When will you tell us what really happened last night?" I asked.

He stood up, avoiding looking at our eyes, and gathered the trash. "When we get back on the road." He took a deep breath and sucked in his lips. "Where are we stopping?"

"The Carlsbad KOA," I answered. "We've stayed there before."

"I remember," he said as he tossed the trash into a container.

"But I don't know what we're doing tomorrow or where we're staying," I said, walking back to the van.

"Why?" he asked.

I stopped, my muscles tightening up. "Are you kidding me? Do you really think it's a good idea to go sightseeing right now? Or hiking? Or get to Oregon as quickly as we can? Or stay on back roads or go faster on the Interstates?"

He nodded and hooked his thumbs in his pockets. "I hear you. Let's see what Dad says tonight."

We climbed into the van, and soon I was merging onto an empty highway. Austin threw his arms across the top of the seat, his legs spread wide. He tilted his head back and looked at the roof. I glanced at Brooke, who lifted her feet to the dash, then dropped them back to the floor.

"So what happened?" I asked.

He hunched forward, put his elbows on his knees, and picked at the scab on his right hand. After blowing out a breath, he said, "Fuck it. By the time we walked into this club, we were already drunk. I don't even remember the name of the place. We had to pay five bucks each to get in because there was entertainment. We went to the bar, ordered beers, and watched the show, which was a small band and a female singer. She was beautiful, and her voice was something else."

He cleared his throat, sucked his lips, and rubbed his hands. "Tony was mesmerized. He took his beer and walked toward the stage. The girl saw him staring at her, and she directed all her attention to him. Phillip laughed and said, 'Tony's going to cum in his pants.' At the end of her last song, she kissed his cheek and slinked off the stage. He followed.

"He was gone for fifteen or twenty minutes. We were about to go looking for him when he bolted from the back toward the bar in a panic. He said, 'We have to go!'

"I said, 'Okay, but we have to pay our tab.'

"He yelled, 'Now!' and almost ran to the exit.

"Phillip and I got up and followed. The bartender yelled after us. A bouncer stepped in front of us when we got to the door. Tony was already outside, so I slugged the guy, and we split. We heard people yelling after us, but we didn't stop until we barely got into Tony's truck. He was already moving. Once we were out of downtown and on the highway, he started crying."

Austin's chest was heaving, his eyes staring at a movie only he could see. "The singer took him to her dressing room, where they kissed. Then she gave him a blow job. Tony reached up her dress and felt a boner. The singer was in drag. Tony freaked. He punched the guy and threw him against a sink. And kept punching him until blood gushed everywhere. That's when he ran to get us." Austin rubbed his face. "Phillip said, 'You killed him? Why didn't you just leave the room?'

"Tony kept saying, 'I killed a fag. He was a fucking fag! Who cares?' Tony was crazy. I mean, freaking crazy. When he took us back to our trucks, he said, 'You tell anyone, and I'll swear one of you did it.' He saw my hand and said, 'Austin killed her.' He held out his hands which didn't have a mark on them and laughed. 'You guys better say nothing to no one.' Then he left us. Phillip and I decided to keep quiet, but we were scared. We didn't think anyone from the bar could recognize us because the place was dark, but we were worried about Tony. What would he say?"

Brooke frowned at me and barely shook her head.

I stared at my brother in the mirror, my stomach in knots. "Tony killed a drag queen. Just Tony."

"That's what I said," he snapped.

"You told me you needed to go with us because you were scared of Tony?"

Austin's face reddened. "You didn't see the way he freaked out. The guy was acting insane."

Alarms were blaring in my head. He was lying. "Austin, if what you're saying is true—"

"*If* what I'm saying is true? *If?*" he snarled.

"What I mean is, the only one who did anything wrong was Tony, and he's dead. You didn't pay for a few beers and slugged a bouncer. Why didn't you and Phillip go to the police?"

He panted. "We talked about it after Tony took off but hadn't made up our minds. Then Phillip got shot this morning."

"So did Tony," Brooke said. "They got their murderer. This should be over."

"Except they don't know which of us killed the queer."

"Goddamnit, Austin!" I shouted. "You sound like Tony. The man was an entertainer who dressed in drag. All of you thought he was a beautiful woman and a great singer. Why did he deserve to die?"

He sucked in a breath. "I didn't say he deserved to die. But the asshole tricked Tony into having sex with a queer."

Brooke turned toward Austin and spoke in her kindest voice, "Is it possible you didn't realize you walked into a drag bar? Maybe everyone else in there knew he was a drag queen, so when Tony showed interest, the singer thought Tony knew what he was. Maybe he wasn't tricking him. Some guys like sex with drag queens."

He wrinkled his nose and half-bared his teeth. "Jesus. How would you know?"

Brooke blinked her eyelashes quickly. I knew she was pretending to be friendly even though she was scared.

She continued, "Taylor and I know lots of gay guys in the theatre, music, and dance departments. Some of them perform at drag bars for extra money."

He narrowed his eyes. "You've seen this?"

"Sure we have," I said, copying her tone. "They're our friends. We saw their shows. They'd come to see Brooke perform at the dinner theatre in the summer. A few came to see my high school play. We all supported each other."

Austin shook his head and looked to the roof. He sat back in his seat and folded his arms.

"Does Dad know?" I asked.

"Not what I just told you."

"Will you tell him?"

"I guess I'll have to when I call him later. Look, I don't want to talk about this anymore." He lay down on the seat with his back to us.

Brooke looked at me with wide eyes, her breaths shallow and quick. She mouthed, "I think he did it."

The same thought had been hammering the inside of my skull.

What if my brother was a murderer?

Grace asked, "Is there any tea left?"

Maddi handed her the cup. "Some. Do you think Austin did it?"

Grace drank and nodded. "Duh. Maybe he got so angry with the drag queen because he enjoyed the sex. Maybe Austin didn't start the violence when he grabbed the penis."

Maddi's eyes widened. "Yeah. He couldn't stand the thought that he liked gay sex, so he killed the evidence."

"Maybe." Grace realized her hands were sweaty and rubbed them on her shirt. Then her whole body turned to goosebumps. "Brooke and Taylor must have been so scared. What do you think they should've done?"

Maddi shrugged. "Easy. Stop for gas, send the bastard inside to buy something, then leave."

Grace pulled Maddi to her and squeezed. "Remind me to always take you on my road trips."

"Where else would I be?" She curled against her girlfriend.

Grace picked up her phone. "A train wreck is coming. We just don't know when. Ready?"

"Yes."

Grace continued reading.

We drove for hours. In Fort Stockton, we switched to Highway 285 and veered north toward New Mexico. Brooke and I did not speak. Every so often, one of us would reach out our hand to pass nuts or candy, and we'd hook fingers, like prisoners reaching through bars in separate cells.

My head and butt hurt. The scenery was boring as hell. We should have been singing and recalling funny events, but all we could do was drive through our unease of knowing enough to make us edgy but not enough to make us choose a definitive plan.

I needed time alone with Brooke to talk about options. If Austin did murder the queen, what would we do? Turn him in? My own brother? How?

Then a thought hit me in the gut—were Brooke and I aiding and abetting a criminal? Could we be charged with a crime?

Shit. We could say we didn't know he was a murderer, but we knew he was involved.

We could deny we suspected him, but did we want to face an investigation?

What if the police were looking for him? If a cop stopped us and saw we were transporting Austin, we'd all be arrested.

I slowed down, making sure I stayed five miles an hour below the speed limit.

I looked over at Brooke. She leaned against the door with her feet on the seat, using her legs to support a pad of paper. She was writing me a note.

After another few minutes, she glanced back at Austin and handed me the pad.

We are possibly transporting a murderer. I know he's your brother, but if he killed someone, we're in deep shit. Now that we suspect what he did, we're helping him escape. I don't want to go to jail for him.

I handed the pad back and mouthed, "Neither do I."

Brooke wrote quickly and gave me the pad.

Keep acting friendly. Don't push him. He has a short fuse and

*might turn on us if he feels cornered. Try to tell your parents the truth
and see what they say.*

I nodded and gave her the pad. She ripped the page, stuffed it
into her pack, and reached out her hand. I held it for several minutes.

An hour later, we entered the town of Carlsbad.

"Hey, Austin," I said. "Wake up. We have to get gas."

He groaned and pushed himself upright. "Where are we?"

"Carlsbad."

"Really?"

"Yeah, you missed some beautiful scenery," I snapped.

"Bullshit." He stretched, pushing his hands against the roof.
"Last semester, one of my geology classes drove out to Carlsbad and
the Guadalupe Mountains, which were great. But the drive after
Junction was horrible." He peered out the windshield and pointed.
"Head for that Shell station."

Once I parked, he opened his door. "You guys fill it up. I'm going
inside to get some beer and ice. Do y'all want anything? Maybe some
wine?"

Brooke opened her door. "Sure," she said with a big smile.
"Something white and sweet. Thanks, Austin," she gushed.

"Got it. I'll pay for the gas." He strode toward the convenience
store.

I'd already started the gas when Brooke came close and whispered. "Don't start the pump."

"What? I already did." I stopped the pump. We both saw
numbers on the gauge.

"Shit! We can leave him. Just go." Her eyes bulged as she looked
at me, then the store, then back. "Please, Taylor."

Her pleading made my heart ache. I felt guilty for putting her in
that situation, and I almost pulled out the nozzle. But my brain
stopped me. "If we leave now, they'll call the cops for not paying."

"Okay," she rasped. "Fill the tank, wait until he's at the counter,
and then leave."

My stomach dropped as I restarted the pump. Her arms shook. "Hey, calm down."

"I don't want him with us anymore. He's going to drink tonight. Who knows what he'll do?"

I held her sweating hands and wanted to pull her into me. "We can always drive away from the campground when he's in his tent with his gear. Anytime we want to leave, we can do it at night."

Her eyes filled with tears. "You promise?"

My stomach twisted into knots. I couldn't bear seeing her pain. "Yes. When you want to go, we'll go."

"Okay." She leaned back against the van, her chest heaving. She closed her eyes and slowly calmed down.

The pump kicked off. I screwed on the cap and replaced the nozzle. We both watched the store. Sweat trickled from my armpits. Soon, Austin backed through the doors, carrying a twelve-pack of beer, two bottles of wine, and a bag of ice.

Brooke ran toward him. "Let me help you." She grabbed the wine and walked back to the van with a big smile. "Look what Austin bought us!" She held up the wine. "A Riesling and a Moscato."

Austin hoisted the ice onto his shoulder. "The guy said they're sweet."

"They're perfect," Brooke said as she sat in her seat.

Austin removed the ice chest and drained it behind the van.

I climbed through the side door and squatted next to Brooke, leaning against her arm. "Are you okay?"

"No. I could guzzle this bottle in ten seconds. I can't stop shaking."

I so wanted to hold her, but every nerve stood on guard at Austin's return. "We're about fifteen minutes from the KOA. Just a little longer."

She touched my cheek and moved her face an inch from mine, staring at my lips. Then her eyes darted away, and she pushed back. "He's coming," she whispered.

I moved to my seat just as Austin heaved the ice chest inside. He climbed in and closed the door.

"The man said there's a Church's Chicken down the road a bit. We could get a bucket and take it with us."

Brooke turned in her seat. "Sounds great, Austin. Thanks for taking care of us."

I started the van, angry that my brother had no idea how much we wanted him to disappear. That it took all our effort to pretend in his presence.

"Wait!" Brooke blurted.

I stopped.

"I just realized I'm out of Texas for the first time in my life."

Austin popped the cap from a bottle of Budweiser and offered it to Brooke. "Then have a beer to celebrate."

"Why, thank you!" She took the bottle.

He opened another, sat back in his seat, spread his legs, and chugged half the bottle. After a raucous burp, he scoffed, "You'll have to wait for yours, Taylor." He lifted his bottle and drained it. "Think I'll have another."

As he bent over the ice chest, Brooke's eyes met mine and then squeezed shut.

8

TAKE IT OR LEAVE IT

Taylor closed her computer lid with a sigh. She had written about half of her last chapter and wanted to finish, but her mind kept wandering, and she had to teach the next day.

Possibly for the last time.

Before working at the school, she'd write until one or two in the morning and wake by ten. She had never been an early riser except when forced to be.

Her sons had sent no emails, and Marshall had disappeared since Taylor had sent him her book. His bedroom was upstairs with a TV and a small refrigerator. She had slept downstairs for the past three years with the excuse she couldn't cope with his snoring. But her actual reason was she no longer wanted to perpetuate a façade in a loveless marriage.

Since then, he'd made snide comments about her wanting time alone on her computer with her boyfriends. According to him, that was the real reason she'd moved downstairs. Maybe after their argument that night, he'd accuse her of searching for girlfriends.

She thought about taking a shower but didn't want to look at her naked self. She'd gained weight from drinking and snacking before going to bed.

And not caring about her actual life outside of her writing.

Her throat felt thick, and the familiar emptiness gaped inside her chest. These were the most lonely hours of her day. Shut off from her characters, from her family, from everyone.

She checked her phone. No messages. She tapped on Shannon's last note and almost typed something, but decided it was too late even though she knew Shannon wouldn't mind. Maybe in the next few days, Taylor would feel more comfortable starting a conversation with her at any hour.

Taylor reached into the cabinet to the left of the dishwasher and grabbed her half-empty bottle of Jameson. She poured two shots of whiskey over ice, sipped, and then chewed on a handful of cashews. Her goal was to fall immediately asleep when her head touched the pillow. Otherwise, images of her past would swarm her mind and lead to lucid, exhausting dreams. Sometimes terrifying.

A good night was sleeping like the dead until just before the alarm sounded. A typical night was having to pee three times and repeatedly watch a dream play behind closed eyelids, even as she stumbled to the bathroom. Sometimes the dream seemed to last all night.

She drank another glass and ate more nuts. Soon she lay in bed, though her thoughts hadn't slowed. *I should have downed another shot.*

She heard a ringing. *Is that the house phone?* She jerked her head toward the handset. Who would call this late?

Her skin erupted in goosebumps. She knew who.

"Hello?" She tried not to sound frightened.

"Taylor Baird MacKenzie," Austin teased, almost in a sing-song voice. "I'd apologize for the late call, but since you answered, I'm not sorry at all." His voice was deeper and raspier than she'd remembered it.

Taylor clenched her jaw, trying to keep him from hearing the screams in her mind. Sweat oozed from her hands and forehead. After hitching a few breaths, she managed to say, "You never felt sorry about anything, Austin."

"Not true, Taylor." His voice was cold and taunting. "I'm sorry I didn't kill you when I had the chance. Before you stole most of my life."

"You did it to yourself."

"Really? If you hadn't testified against me, would I have spent forty-eight years in jail? Don't think so. But Karma is a bitch. You'll get yours."

Her heart thundered in her chest. "Thanks so much for the heads up. When my husband told me you'd called, I wasn't sure whether to plan a party or load my guns."

Austin chuckled. "Husband, huh? Does he know you're a queer?"

"And you're still a loathsome human being. Let me guess. You joined the Aryan Brotherhood in prison."

He breathed hard into the phone. "I had to stay alive to fulfill my promise to you."

Marshall turned on the hall light and stood outside her room, frowning.

Taylor glanced at Marshall before speaking. "Why are you calling me, Austin?"

"Just wanted to check an address. 143 West 4th Avenue."

Taylor shivered. "That's correct. Go to the end of D Street and take a right. Just so you know, I have an AR 15 in my bedroom with five 40-round clips. We also have a 12 gauge pump shotgun, a hunting rifle, and another shotgun, plus a .44 Magnum pistol. I've shot many animals, Austin, all of which were more intimidating than you."

He laughed. "Be sure to check your six. See you soon." He ended the call.

Taylor closed her eyes and took deep breaths, remembering the glare he'd shot her after she'd finished testifying at his trial.

"He wants to kill you?" Marshall asked.

"Has for forty-eight years." She opened her eyes.

"Why?"

"Because I told the truth at his trial."

"What can I do?"

"Would you hand me my robe?"

He reached around the door and passed it to her. "I mean about your brother. Shouldn't I call the police?"

"You can do what you want, Marshall." She wrapped the robe around her shoulders and stood. Her husband was between her and the door. "I need to get to the kitchen."

Marshall backed up. She walked past him toward the liquor cabinet.

He followed her. "Do you know where he is?"

She poured whiskey into a glass and added ice. "I have no idea." She drank two gulps and barely felt any burn. "He was released from prison in Texas a month ago. He could be anywhere between there and here."

He cleared his throat in disapproval. "I thought you drank that with Coke."

"I did. It was too easy to drink, so I started sipping it straight, thinking I wouldn't drink as much. But that hasn't worked." She finished the glass and tried to relax her neck.

"Shouldn't we leave the house?"

"I think *I* should. He wants to kill me, not you." She swirled the ice around the glass.

"We could go to Fairbanks."

"What would we do in town? Get a motel room, watch a movie, eat out? All in total silence? I'd rather deal with Austin."

He sucked in his lips and gazed at a wall.

"He called tonight to scare me," Taylor said. "He could be here tomorrow or a month from now, which is more likely. He has his own six to watch."

Marshall shook his head and snorted. "Meaning?"

"He needs to watch *his* back. Did you read the book?"

He scratched his neck and looked away. "I started to . . . but . . . it's hard, Taylor. Your relationship with Brooke . . . is difficult for me to read."

"Why? Because you're jealous? Or because I'm queer?"

Marshall raked his fingers through his hair. "How can you be a queer? You had children with me."

Taylor blew out a long breath. "I shouldn't have."

He stared at her for a few seconds, then looked away, shaking his head.

"If you want to understand why my brother wants to kill me," Taylor said, "you need to finish the book. I don't want to relive those events by telling you. It nearly killed me to write them." She crossed her arms. "I'll be staying someplace else for a few days."

He threw out his arms. "With who?"

"I won't tell you. If Austin comes here, you can honestly say you don't know where I am."

"I should be the one protecting you!" he barked, pointing his finger at her.

"Really?" Taylor almost laughed. "Is that why you told Levi about my books? To protect me? I'd rather be with friends who actually care about me and want to keep me safe. Not because of some manly duty you feel you have to follow. The truth is, if Austin killed me, the only reason you'd care is if your reputation were harmed because you couldn't stop him."

Marshall started to speak but could only grit his teeth and pull in raspy breaths.

She spread her arms along the counter behind her. "If he kills me while I'm out of this house, you're free. If he doesn't, then Levi will give you plenty of good reasons to leave me. So either way, your future is golden."

He flattened his lips against his teeth. "What are you going to do now? Drink, like always?"

"*Yes, I am.* Until I can't think about him or you . . ." Her eyes flooded with tears. "Or Brooke." She turned away from him, her throat knotting in pain. "Please go upstairs," she gasped.

After a few seconds, he left the kitchen.

Taylor's chest convulsed in sobs. *Except I'll never stop thinking about you, Brooke. No matter what.*

She poured another drink.

When her alarm rang, Taylor was dreaming of the night she first met Brooke. New undergraduate and graduate students to the theatre department traditionally performed audition pieces for their peers at the start of each school year. Most freshmen were outstanding, having won trophies at regional and state speech contests. Even among them, Brooke stood out.

Holding a full-length cape around herself, she performed Ophelia's tragic "Oh, what a noble mind" speech. Immediately afterward, she threw off the cloak to reveal a skimpy, sequined cocktail waitress' costume for a musical number, then donned a skirt and belted out Barbara Streisand's "My Man" from *Funny Girl*. The crowd went wild. Taylor thought Brooke was dazzling and brilliant and beyond beautiful.

Taylor had to follow her act. She pushed out an upright piano and performed funny scenes from her own one-act plays, which included her singing and playing the piano. The audience laughed and gave her a good round of applause.

After the auditions, a crowd of guys gathered around Brooke, full of smiles and compliments. When she saw Taylor come from backstage and head toward the apron stairs, she called, "Hey, Taylor. You were great!"

Taylor stopped in shock and looked back at the beautiful girl with a gorgeous smile. "Thank you."

Brooke broke away from her fans, quick-walked to a disbelieving Taylor, and grabbed both of her hands. "You wrote those songs?"

Taylor's skin flushed with heat. "Yes."

"How many do you have?" Her smile was so warm and genuine.

"Tons," Taylor said. Her heart raced as every nerve tingled. "That's what I do. Write songs and plays and try a little acting."

Still holding Taylor's hands, Brooke gushed, "I thought you were excellent! So funny! And I love your music."

"Thank you." She squeezed Brooke's hands. "That's high praise from the most talented young actress I've ever seen. Your voice is amazing."

Brooke's cheeks blushed a rose red. "I just sing other people's songs. You write them. Can you play some for me?"

"Sure." Taylor's heart fluttered. "We can find an empty practice studio."

"Cool." Brooke let go of her hands. "Lead the way."

They worked together for two more hours before they broke for food. From that moment on, they were B&T.

Taylor slapped the alarm and gazed at the ceiling. She could be fired, even killed, but unlike in previous days, she wouldn't be alone. With a gulp of air, she arose, changed her clothes, and opened a suitcase on her bed. The first thing she retrieved from her drawers was an album of Brooke's college photos. A few showed them together, but most were shots from all her shows.

She lifted the cover as her heart skipped beats but closed her eyes and the album. She had too much to do and didn't want to start the day in tears.

After packing, she went to the kitchen to make coffee, fry two eggs, and cook toast. Usually, Marshall would be downstairs by then, but he hadn't appeared.

Taylor gazed out the kitchen window toward her backyard. Four-foot-high raised garden beds were still smothered under mounds of snow like graves for giants. Long, gnarly fingers of ice reached down from the roof, sparkling in the morning sun outside the glass.

Taylor rubbed her knuckles, a few knotted with arthritis. Not enough to affect her typing or piano playing. Yet. She couldn't imagine living without being able to do both.

Of course, if Austin shot her, arthritis wouldn't matter. She decided to call the trooper station in the nearby town of Nenana. Surprisingly, a man answered the phone after the first ring with no intervening "our phone options have changed" message.

"Officer Barnes, Nenana Station. How can I help you?"

Taylor gave her name, address, and phone number before stating her purpose. "My brother, Austin Baird, was just released from prison after forty-eight years for several murders, but he blames me for being caught and not lying to keep him out of jail. He promised to kill me when he got out. Last night he called my house phone and told me my address. He said, 'I'm sorry I didn't kill you when I had the chance.' And 'Karma is a bitch. You'll get yours.' I don't know where he is, but it's clear to me he's coming here to shoot me. What are my options, Officer?"

"Do you know what he looks like?"

"I haven't seen him for decades and don't have any photos. What if you had his picture? What could you do?"

"If one of the officers sees him, he could be questioned, but we can't do anything until he says or does something more threatening. He said Karma will get you, not necessarily him. I know that's not what you want to hear, but he'll deny making a threat. We can't pick him up for that."

"That's what I thought. Thank you." She sucked in her lips and shook her head in frustration. There were many benefits to living in a tiny town on the edge of the wilderness, but services were limited. People depended on themselves or friends to fix anything around the house. A real doctor was eighty miles away, and troopers were few and far between. Maybe twice she had seen an officer patrolling the town without being called.

What chance did she have against Austin? The end seemed inevitable. The question was whether only she died or one of her new friends. She couldn't stand being responsible for one of them being hurt.

After a few minutes, the sound of Marshall's footsteps on the stairs competed with the sputtering of the coffee machine. She plopped two over-easy eggs onto buttered toast just as he entered the kitchen.

He glugged his orange juice; she chewed her breakfast. She poured coffee, added cream, and sipped. He did the same.

She looked out the back window. He looked out the front.

The silence was thick, their movements an awkward dance of never touch and never look. Hide and seek without the seek.

Taylor rinsed her plate and fork, then put them in the dishwasher. She went to her office, slipped her computer into her satchel, and zipped it up. After retrieving her rifle from her bedroom, she headed toward the mud room.

Before she pulled the door open, Marshall said, "When will you be home?"

She turned around. "I don't know. Does it matter?"

"I read through Chapter Five." He paused, lips pressed tight, eyes averted.

Do you want me to say thank you?

He shuffled his feet. "Sounds like that was a harrowing road trip."

"It was, but there were some good parts."

His shoulders slumped. "Am I in the book?"

"Yes."

He grimaced. "Are you planning to publish it?"

She opened the door. "I'm planning to give it to everyone in this town."

Cords flexed in his neck. "Why?" he rasped.

Her stomach gurgled. "Because maybe a miracle will happen." Taylor slipped on her boots in the mud room and exited the house. She hid the rifle under a blanket in the back of the car then turned to fetch her suitcase. Marshall banged her bag against the porch railing as he wedged himself through the door.

"Is this everything?" he asked.

"Yes. Thank you." She opened the back hatch of her car, then closed it after he pushed the bag inside.

"What does this Austin fella look like?" Marshall asked.

"I haven't seen him in forty-eight years. He was over six feet, with thick dark hair, which must be grayish by now. Or he shaved his head since he's a white supremacist. It used to be obvious we were brother and sister. Brown eyes, big ears."

He stood up taller and jutted his chin. "If he comes here looking for trouble, I'll give it to him."

Taylor almost laughed at his fake bravado. "If you kill him, let me know." She got into her car, pushed the start button, and backed up until she could turn into the road.

Neither waved.

As she drove toward the school, she kept an eye out for anything different—a car parked where it shouldn't be, a stranger, or an open door in one of the many abandoned houses along her route. When she crossed Second Avenue, she noticed the city steamer truck was working on a sewer line two blocks away. And the Williams brothers were burning trash. Again. She parked in her usual spot and took a deep breath to calm her nerves. Today would be different than usual. Someone would say something about her books. Someone would have guessed she wrote them.

Maybe someone would be kind.

She exited her car and trudged toward the front entrance. Grace was waiting in the lobby for her and pushed the door open.

"Hey, Taylor." She looked over her shoulder then back. "Maddi and I read up through Chapter Five. Your brother was an asshole."

Taylor walked inside, trying to keep her composure. "He still is. He called me last night. He knows my name and address."

Grace's eyes bulged then tightened. "You're coming over after school?"

"I want to, but I'm afraid of putting you in danger."

She raised her brows and grinned. "*He'll* be the one in danger. I'll bring one of my father's guns."

"I don't think he's in Alaska yet." Taylor looked down the hall toward the table in the Commons. "Has anyone said anything about Brooke Skipstone?"

Grace laughed. "Yes. I've walked around peeking at everyone's phone. Two of the guys were looking at the drawings of Crystal's breasts. Paige and Laura are definitely reading the book. I heard Allison whisper to Megan in the office, 'This is about our town and our school.' Have you checked your book sales?"

"Not since last night at your house."

Grace opened Amazon and typed *Crystal's House of Queers.* "It's number two in LGBTQ + Mystery."

Taylor smiled. *At least if I die, my bank account will be fatter.* "Be sure to thank your father for me. Have you heard anyone guessing who Brooke is?"

"Not yet. But I'm sure if you announced who she is, a lot of kids would want your autograph."

"Or want to throw stones at me."

As they walked through the Commons and into her classroom, Taylor looked for any glances her way or whispers as she approached, but everyone stared at their screens.

She opened her satchel, put her computer on her desk, and sat in her chair. She held her hands to hide their shaking. "How's your grandmother this morning?"

"Her eyes were red and puffy at breakfast. I think she stayed up reading most of the night." Grace opened her pack and pulled out a bag and an envelope. "She wanted me to give these to you."

Inside the bag was a large, fresh banana nut muffin. Taylor inhaled its aroma and exhaled a moan. "Smells delicious." Her entire body relaxed.

"Gram makes great muffins. Maddi and I pigged out and ate six this morning."

Taylor opened the envelope and read the note.

Dear Taylor,

I couldn't stop reading your book last night. It is the most beautiful and tragic story I've ever read. I cannot understand how you survived and persisted. I know you have more love and beauty to share with the world. The girls and I will make sure you do.

Love,

Shannon

Taylor squeezed her eyes shut, leaving tiny tears along her eyelashes. She slipped the note inside the envelope and tucked it into her satchel.

"Mrs. MacKenzie?" Principal Jackson knocked on her door jamb, his ample belly pressing against a *Go Grizzlies* t-shirt. "Do you have a few moments?"

Taylor touched her throat, trying to catch her squeal before it escaped. She smiled and took a deep breath. "Certainly."

"Grace, would you mind?" His gestures and voice were entirely neutral, devoid of any genuine emotion as if he wanted others to wonder what he really thought.

Grace shot a glance at Taylor before hurrying out.

The Principal closed the door and walked toward Taylor with an enigmatic smile underneath rimless bifocals. "Do you have any plans for Spring Break?"

Other than living through it? She shook her head. "Do you?"

He leaned back on a student desk. "I think I'll take the missus to Fairbanks to see the ice sculptures."

Taylor smiled. "That should be fun. I haven't been in ages."

He tilted his head and half-grinned. "The kids have enjoyed being in your classes these past three months."

Her chest froze. *I'm being fired.* "Well, I've enjoyed teaching them."

"As you know, we listed this position in December to find a permanent replacement. We received several applications, all interested in starting next fall. But the wife of a recent transfer to the Air Base is available to start after the break. I hired her a few days ago. She and her husband are moving to Clear next week."

Her shoulders relaxed. "Well, that's wonderful," Taylor said and meant it. She wasn't being let go for her books. Plus, she'd worried about being at school every day, possibly endangering her students as long as Austin was on the loose. "I'd be happy to meet with her during the break."

"That's great. I know she'd appreciate your help." He stood and cleared his throat. "Have you heard about this Brooke Skipstone business?"

Her chest felt hollow and cold. "Yes, I have. I listened to part of Levi's podcast yesterday. The whole thing is very intriguing, don't you think?" She cocked a brow. *The ball's in your court.*

He stroked his chin. "You wrote a book some years ago, didn't you?"

Her stomach tightened. *He knows.* "Yes. I did."

His mouth curled up slightly in the corners. "I can't believe a town this size would have more than one prize-winning author."

She steepled her fingers, trying to hide their trembling. "That would be unusual."

"I started *The Moonstone Girls* last night." His eyes twinkled. "It's excellent."

Every nerve tingled. "Why, thank you." She'd always been irritated by his ambiguous demeanor, but this message was clear—he approved. She breathed deeply.

He raised his brows and folded his arms. "Do you plan to say anything to your students?"

"No. I think Levi will take care of that this evening or tomorrow at his community meeting."

The Principal pursed his lips. "He's calling a meeting?"

"That's what my husband tells me," Taylor said. "Have you had any angry parents call today?"

"No." He chuckled. "But Allison is pretty steamed up. She claims you're the author because the house in the book is yours."

Taylor stood and grinned. "When is Allison not steamed up? Do you think she'd be as upset if Levi had mentioned *Moonstone* rather than *Crystal's House?*"

He shrugged. "Probably not. It sounds like *Crystal's House* is more . . . racy, so there's more to object to. Plus, she wouldn't have guessed you're the author of *Moonstone*."

"Exactly. Which is why I led my husband to tell Levi about *Crystal's House*."

He raised his brows and pulled his ear. "You *wanted* this to happen?"

"I felt I had no choice," Taylor said. "I'll explain why on Saturday."

A buzzer sounded. Some students opened Taylor's door and found their seats.

The Principal nodded, said, "Have a good day," and made his way through a swarm of kids pouring into the classroom.

Once the second buzzer sounded and her students settled down, Taylor asked, "How is everyone progressing on their book reports? Remember, they're due a week after Spring Break."

Amanda, an eager girl wearing blue lipstick, raised her hand. "Can I change my book?"

"To what?" Taylor asked, knowing the answer.

"*Crystal's House of Queers*. I love it."

Christopher, shaggy-haired with a new beard, bellowed from the back row, "You want to read a book about queers?"

Amanda's face reddened. "It's well written and set in this town. Whether it's about queers or not doesn't matter."

Christopher scoffed. "Really? That's disgusting."

"You're disgusting!" Amanda shouted.

Typically, Taylor would have stepped in to stop the shouting, but she worried someone would accuse her of being the author. Maybe if she said nothing, they'd forget she was there.

After the uproar subsided, Taylor said, "Your book reports must be from the district's list of approved books. But I can give you extra credit if you want to read another book and write a report."

After class, Taylor checked her phone. She'd received messages from her sons. After sucking in a few breaths to calm her nerves, she tapped Gene's. *I'm not sure what to say, Mom. Finding out my mother was a lesbian in college is a slug to the gut. There's too much going on in our house right now, and I don't have time to deal with this. Audrey and I decided it would be best to hold off on sending the kids to visit this summer. Maybe we can talk about this in a couple of weeks.*

Taylor hitched a breath and clutched her phone. George's note was similar. "Shocked." "No visit." "Talk some other time." Their responses were what she'd expected, but they still hurt. What was the point of family if she couldn't be honest without fear of disdain? She had suffocated, hiding inside her skin for so long that living had become theatre. The self she now exposed was an easy target, but whether it was damaged or not was up to her.

And to Austin.

And her friends.

Writing her book had said, "This is who I am. Take or leave it." She desperately wanted someone in her family to accept and love her for her true self. To make her realize her hiding had been a mistake.

Students in her next class dribbled in except for Grace, who strode up to Taylor and whispered, "I want to start your next chapter, so please don't call on me this period."

"Okay. What about Maddi? I thought you read to her."

"I gave her a copy of the book. She knows how to activate the text-to-speech control. She's listening while she works."

"By the way," Taylor said, "Principal Jackson is not as much of a creep as you believe. He's reading *The Moonstone Girls* and likes it."

Grace's face broke into a wide smile. "Cool. See, you have more supporters than you thought."

A glimmer of warmth stirred in her chest. "Maybe."

9

SEX NOW, WINE LATER

Grace found an empty seat in the back row by the window. She opened her school-issued computer and AirDropped Taylor's book from her phone, so she could read and pretend to be working on an assignment.

Grace scrolled to the next chapter.

Chapter Six

As soon as I parked to check in with the campground manager, Austin leaped out of the van and headed for the bathrooms. He had already downed three beers of his own and finished Brooke's bottle. We had to pay for two sites—a short pull-thru and a separate tent area—putting some distance between him and us. Meaning it would be easier to get away with leaving him behind.

The campground was close to the highway, so road noise would be constant. Starting our van in the middle of the night wouldn't be noticed as easily.

We didn't need a plug-in or a sewer connection. Technically, we didn't need to be there, but the bathrooms and showers were decent, and Dad had made us promise to stay in KOA campgrounds if one was in the area. They were safe, full of families, and had pay phones.

We didn't wait for Austin. "He'll finish all twelve bottles tonight," Brooke said.

"I had no idea he drank so much," I said while driving through the entrance lane toward the sites. "He also had two mini liquor bottles in his back pockets."

"Let's try to spend time away from him," Brooke said. "We can walk around the sites and talk. Take a long shower. Go to bed early. I feel talk deprived."

"And song deprived. Should we press him for more information?" I asked.

"No. Maybe wait to see how the conversation with your parents goes."

I parked the van to block the sun from our picnic table.

"Are you hungry?" I asked.

"Yes. Being tense and nervous all day eats up calories."

We set out the chicken, plates, and utensils. Brooke opened the wine and filled a large plastic cup with ice.

We heard Austin trotting toward us before he slowed to a walk near the van.

"Why were you running?" I asked. "Afraid we'd eat all the chicken?"

He was still panting. "I thought y'all had dumped me."

Brooke and I shared a glance. She closed her eyes and bit her lip. "Really?" I asked, realizing we had missed a perfect opportunity. "We figured you could find us."

Brooke sat at the table. "Did you honestly think we'd left you? Who else would buy us chicken and wine and protect us from shitholes at gas stations?" She grabbed a wing and took a bite.

He sat across from her and pulled out a breast from the bucket.

"Are you worried about us leaving you?" I asked. "Seriously?"

Shit! Now he'll be looking for any signs and cling to us to make sure we don't go.

"I guess I'm getting paranoid. Seems like everyone's turning against me." He took a bite of chicken and stood up. "You forgot the beer." He quick-walked around the van and rummaged in the ice chest.

I sat next to Brooke and poured the wine as I mumbled, "Should have, would have, could have." She spread her legs and touched her knee to mine under the table.

Brooke whispered, "Everyone's turning against him? Where's that coming from?"

Austin came back with two open beers, drinking one as he walked. He sat down and hunched over his plate, devouring the chicken with his mouth open.

"I see you graduated with honors from the Emily Post School of Etiquette," I teased.

"Fuck that shit." He grabbed a thigh and kept eating.

Brooke and I ate a little more before she tapped me with her elbow and jerked her head toward the rest of the campground. "Think we're going to take a walk, Austin." She and I shared the rest of the wine in the glass and moved away from the table. I kept waiting for him to say, "Hey, I'll go with you." But he didn't.

We turned toward the playground on a lane filled with motorhomes before we checked whether he could see us. "I think we're clear," I said.

"Can I scream yet?" Brooke said. "He's turning psycho on us. If he's afraid we'll leave him, he'll make sure we don't."

"How?"

"Disconnect something in the van. Take our keys."

I stuck my hand in my pocket to make sure I had my key. "Where's yours?"

"Hidden in my pack."

A Cocker Spaniel pulled against his chain and barked at us. A woman sitting under an awning shushed him. "Sorry."

"No problem," I said. "Cute dog."

We walked toward the playground, where a few kids tried the swings. Someone was burning hamburgers on a grill.

"Let's look at this situation from his point of view," I said. "Like he's a character we have to play. Use our Method training."

"Hmmm," Brooke said. "What incident in my life can I use to substitute for killing a drag queen who just gave me a blow job. That's a hard one."

My pulse quickened as my brain raced. "It would feel like an assault. At first, you think the guy is hot and making you feel good, but then he grabs your neck and slams your face on the bed. You'd fight back."

"Sure, but the queen didn't do that, according to Tony, AKA your brother. Austin wasn't being raped." Brooke stopped and faced me. "Austin was angry at our gay scene yesterday, so he already dislikes queers. Why? What would make a man want to kill the queen?"

"Because he's a witness to Austin enjoying gay sex?"

Brooke grabbed my shoulders. "Exactly. He felt the boner and wanted it. Your brother hates queers because he hates himself. The queen made him see what he really is, and he couldn't stand the view."

A rush of tingles swept up my neck. "The bit dog barks the loudest."

"And hits the hardest."

We walked over to the now vacant swings and sat down. Could my brother feel disgust toward gays because he's also fascinated by them? I tried to imagine how I would feel if the girl who turned me on had a dick. Would that make me angry? No. I'd had sex with guys. Maybe I'd feel disappointed if the girl was a guy, but not angry.

What would Austin have felt? I couldn't imagine him throwing punches immediately after discovering the boner. I think he'd be fascinated like I felt when I realized what Julie was doing to me. Part of my brain told me to flee, but my body pushed against her fingers.

As I drew closer to an orgasm, my panic increased until the other girls opened my door. Then shame slugged me.

Did someone open the queen's door? Or knock?

Or call Austin's name?

I gasped.

Austin told us he and Phillip almost went looking for Tony but didn't. What if they had? What if Austin heard their voices? He'd panic and kill. Maybe his friends saw the body.

Brooke pushed back on the swing and let go.

I followed her. "When's the last time you rode a swing?"

"At the Old San Francisco Steak House in Dallas. I was the girl in the red swing during the summer before college." She swung higher. "I wore fishnet stockings and a skimpy red velvet costume, and I kicked the bell hanging from the ceiling before I sang some songs. It was good money."

"And lots of dates?"

She slowed down. "I was asked a lot, but I didn't accept many. I liked entertaining but not what came after."

"What was that?"

She dug her feet in the sand and stopped. "Having to deal with a bunch of fawning, horny guys. That seems like ages ago. So much has happened since."

"I know. Everything before we met seems like a different lifetime."

Brooke stood up. "Well, I've come full circle—from showing off my legs to men in suits at a fancy restaurant to showing them to teenagers at a trailer park in the desert." She looked across the road to shirtless boys waving at us.

We turned and walked out the back of the play area. She hooked my arm for a few steps and then unhooked it. "This fucking sucks."

I touched her elbow. "What would you like to do?"

She faced me and raised her brows. "Hold your hand. Put my arm across your shoulders and walk around saying *Hi* to everyone." She hugged herself and walked a few more steps before stopping. "I feel so sorry for that drag queen. A man thought he was beautiful and sexy and then killed him."

"I had a thought a few minutes ago," I said. "What if Tony and Phillip went looking for Austin and either called his name or even opened the door?"

"Wow. That would cause Austin to flip out."

"Or Tony. Maybe we shouldn't be so quick to accuse Austin. What's wrong with Austin's story?"

She walked backward in front of me. "He told you last night he needed to get out of town and come with us. You assumed he was afraid of the guy's friends, but he told us today it was because of Tony—that *he* threatened them."

"Which doesn't make sense because Tony was killed," I said. "How'd they find him anyway?"

Brooke shrugged. "Matching a license plate to its owner. Someone saw Tony's truck leave from the bar—" She stopped mid-sentence, tightening her eyes.

A memory flashed in my head. "Tony's truck or Phillip's?"

"Shit!" Brooke blurted. "I remember now. Your dad said Phillip got shot because it was his truck in the parking lot."

My stomach fluttered. "If it was Tony's, they couldn't know about Phillip. If Phillip's, then no Tony. Yet both were shot."

We looked at each other with wide eyes and had the same thought simultaneously. I blurted first. "Because Austin called someone at the bar last night or this morning—"

"And told them where to find Tony and Phillip."

"Otherwise," I said, trying to suck in breaths, "why didn't anyone come by my house this morning to shoot Austin when he was working on the van?"

Brooke's face reddened. "But the people in the bar saw three guys run out. Who did Austin tell them was the third guy?"

"Maybe no one," I said. "Maybe someone else he knows."

We stared at each other, our breathing fast and shallow.

"Who else was shot today?" Brooke asked.

We started walking again, my brain racing, looking for answers. "Why did he call the bar about Phillip and Tony?" I asked.

"Because they were witnesses. If they're gone, who will know Austin did anything?"

"Just us," I said as a chill flushed my chest. *We're in danger.* The realization flooded my mind and froze my gut.

Shoes slapping gravel stopped behind us. Brooke gasped.

"Hey," Austin said. "Are you two lost?"

We both yelped. "Shit, Austin!" I barked. "Did you have to do that?"

He shrugged, his head wobbling a little on his neck. "What'd I do? You were gone for a while, so I've been trying to find you."

Brooke pushed a smile onto her face. "We weren't lost. We were just now heading back."

Austin scoffed. "You two looked terrified. Did any boys bother you?"

"No," I answered. "We're fine."

We walked quickly along the road toward the front of the camp-ground, now loud with the rumbling of generators.

I shuddered. "Did you clean the table or leave it for the women-folk?" I glanced over at him, looking for any hint of suspicion.

"I cleaned everything and set up my tent."

"Have you called Mom and Dad yet?" I asked.

He sighed. "No. I guess I should do that now."

We found a phone booth outside the camp store. He inserted a dime and dialed zero for the operator.

Brooke walked away from the booth while Austin gave instruc-tions for the long-distance call. I followed her.

"What's wrong?" I whispered.

"We can't make him suspect we think he did it," Brooke said. "His story is the truth. Otherwise, he might do something to us."

"Phillip is still alive. I sure would've liked to hear their conversa-tion this morning."

We walked back to the booth.

"Yeah," Austin said into the phone. "We're at the KOA in Carlsbad. Everything's fine with us."

Brooke and I heard Dad's muffled voice until Austin pressed the handset more firmly against his ear.

"Oh, no," Austin said. "We had no idea. Where did this happen?" He pushed the door closed and faced the phone, turning his back to us.

"Where did what happen?" Brooke asked, her eyelids blinking rapidly.

"Maybe Dad heard about Tony being killed," I whispered. "And Austin's pretending he didn't know."

"But he spoke to someone at the scene," Brooke said. "He won't get away with that."

We stood outside the booth for ten minutes before Austin opened the door.

Austin wiped his face and sucked in a breath. "Phillip is dead. Somebody killed him in a bathroom at the hospital."

Brooke grabbed my arm and sagged against me. My head spun as I closed my eyes. When I opened them, I saw Austin's face bending over mine.

"Taylor, can you hear me?" Austin pleaded.

He'd sat us on a nearby bench. Brooke leaned into my shoulder, whimpering.

"Yes," I answered. I peered into the eyes of my brother. The man who had killed three people in less than a day. "Did you tell him about Tony and what happened at the club?"

He sucked in his lips and blinked rapidly. "Yeah. He'd already heard about Tony being shot." Austin sat in front of the bench, clasping his knees, his head hanging down. "His father called Dad an hour ago."

Probably asking why the fuck his son was dead, I thought. Maybe Tony told his dad what had happened last night. And Phillip had done the same. I stared at Austin, who must have realized he couldn't eliminate all the loose ends. Someone would start looking for him.

I pulled Brooke closer to me. "Has anyone asked Dad where you are?"

"Yeah," Austin said, his gaze still toward the ground.

"Police?"

"No."

"What did Dad tell them?"

He lifted his head and looked to the sky. "That he didn't know."

So Dad will lie for you and expect the same from me.

Brooke sniffed. "How long can that last?" She leaned back against the bench.

Austin shook his head.

"What does he want you to do?" I asked.

He looked at me, working his mouth before speaking. "Get you two to Oregon as soon as possible, then decide what to do."

I nodded. "That makes sense." I pulled my arm from behind Brooke. "We should try to get going early tomorrow."

He nodded and pushed himself up. "Think I'll take a shower. Might be my last chance for a few days." He aimed a wary look at us. "What are y'all going to do?"

Brooke stood. "A shower sounds good to me."

I stood. "Me too."

As Austin ducked inside his tent, we walked back to the van, where I raised the "pop-up" roof with the canvas sides. An accordion board with a two-inch mattress could be stretched across the opening for a single bed, but we planned to put our bags up there at night so we'd have room to sleep below.

Brooke flattened the bench seat, and we reached for the pile of duffles at the back and pulled them forward.

"Close the door," I said.

Brooke pulled it shut.

I opened my bag and looked for a change of clothes. "We should wear jeans and boots for the rest of this trip."

"I was going to tell you the same thing. Where's your knife?"

"Under the floor mat," I answered.

"Do you think he told your father about the drag queen?" Brooke asked.

"I don't know, but I want to call tonight and find out."

Brooke rolled up her sweatpants. "My guess is Austin won't want you to call."

"He can't keep you from calling *your* parents."

"True. I'll pretend to be talking to them if he catches us. So we're going to haul ass to Oregon."

I stuffed clothes in a pack. "That's fine with me. I know you wanted to see the Grand Canyon and Zion, but they're hot and dusty. I'd rather get to mountains and trees. We'll have time this summer to see the redwoods and the coast."

Her eyes met mine. "If we make it that far."

I touched her cheek. "We will."

She held my hand. "Okay, we will. Then what will he do?"

"If I were him, I'd drive to Canada and get lost."

Someone banged on the door. We both yelped. Austin stood outside, his hand cupped to the window to see inside.

Brooke opened the door.

He pointed to the roof. "The top pops up? Is that another bed?"

My stomach dropped. "It could be, but we're using it as storage for our bags at night." I pointed to the pile of luggage on the main bed.

He came inside and stuck his head through the opening. "That's pretty cool. I want to keep the ice chest in my tent tonight, so if you want anything, you'd better grab it now."

"It's all yours," I said.

"How about some ice?" He opened the chest and lifted cubes with his hands.

"In the sink is fine," I said.

"Thank you, Austin," Brooke said with a smile.

He dropped them in the tiny sink behind the driver's seat and pulled the chest outside.

After he moved away from the van, I asked, "Why can I tell you're acting, but he's oblivious?"

She smirked. "Most men are oblivious around women unless we tell them what we really think. Even then, they often miss the message."

"Which is?"

"That they're self-centered, narcissistic brutes." She cocked a brow. "Are you ready?"

I grabbed my toiletry bag and my pack. "Lead the way."

After locking all the doors, we headed for the bathroom, where we found two women fussing at their kids to finish brushing their teeth.

"We'll be out in a jiffy," said one with a towel wrapped around her head. "Then you'll have it all to yourselves."

"No problem," I said. "Your kids are cute."

"Cute little devils," the other woman said with a chuckle.

Brooke and I moved to the shower stalls and claimed two next to each other. I undressed, turned on the water, and arranged my soap and shampoo. I heard Brooke doing the same.

"Are they gone?" Brooke asked as she opened her faucets.

I listened and heard only water running. I peeked out my door to be sure. "They're gone."

"Are you naked yet?"

I laughed. "Entirely. Aren't you, or are you worried about me peeking?"

My stall door rattled. "Open the door, Taylor."

I held a towel to my neck and flipped the lock. Brooke opened the door and stepped through, a towel around her chest. "Yes?" My heart pounded.

Brooke licked her lips. "On three," she said. "One, two, three." She pulled her towel open as I dropped mine. Our eyes locked. Then she stared at my breasts.

I panted. "I thought we weren't supposed to flash each other."

"Rules change." She pressed her body to mine and walked me

back into the shower. "I can't stand the thought of dying without touching you again."

I wrapped my arms around her. "No one is going to die." The restraint I had forced upon my body and mind dissolved in her embrace. Desire surged through me until I whimpered, "Oh, Brooke."

She touched her lips to mine. "Shhh. We need to be quiet."

We stood under the water, pressing every bit of skin together we could find. We held out our tongues and fed each other drops.

"Can we leave him tonight?" Brooke asked.

"Yes."

She took a step back and raised her brows. "Wash me."

I twirled the soap bar in my hands and swirled suds around her skin, moving the bar between her butt cheeks and legs.

She held out her hands. "Now you."

I gave her the soap and stepped back from the water. Her hands moved slower than mine, forcing shuddering moans to escape from my mouth.

"Turn around," she ordered.

I did.

Her breasts brushed against my back as one hand reached around to wash my stomach and below while her other caressed my butt. I could barely stand.

"You have the sexiest ass," she said.

"It's big, that's for sure."

"It's luscious." She rubbed herself down my left butt cheek before we heard voices.

In a second, she had left my stall and entered hers. I locked my door and tossed her towel over the divider just as two women entered the bathroom. I washed my hair as fast as possible and rinsed as they talked.

"You about done, Brooke?" I asked, my heart still racing, frustrated once more that we had to hide our affections.

"Just now," she said.

The women entered the other two stalls as we opened ours. When I turned toward the sinks to brush my teeth, Brooke grabbed my right butt cheek through my sweatpants. I tried to stifle my squeal, which Brooke covered with a laugh.

As we squeezed toothpaste on our brushes, I whispered, "I'll get you back."

"You'd better."

I opened the bathroom door. "Let's go around this way." We walked past the office and the back of the store toward the phone booth, which wasn't visible from Austin's campsite. I darted into the booth. "Keep a lookout."

Brooke put her back against the glass as I talked to the operator. Then I heard Dad's voice. "Taylor?" he said.

"Dad, I didn't get to talk to you earlier. Did Austin tell you what really happened at the club?"

He sighed. "Yes."

"About Tony and the drag queen?"

"Yes, he did." His words were bitter. "They shouldn't have been anywhere near that place."

My skin quivered, and I had to catch my breath. "You told me and Brooke this morning that the boys rode in Phillip's truck, and someone must have seen his license plate. But Austin told us they left the club in Tony's truck."

"Okay," he grumbled. "So maybe it was Tony's. What's the big deal?"

"If it was Tony's license plate, how did anyone find Phillip? If it was Phillip's truck, how did they find Tony?"

"Shit, I don't know. These bastards probably have informants everywhere."

He couldn't see the obvious, and I wasn't sure I should tell him. "Austin said you want us to get to Oregon ASAP. Then what?"

"What do you mean, then what?"

My head was pounding. "What's Austin going to do once we're there?"

"I don't know, but he can't come back here. Two officers stopped by since he called me, asking questions about Austin. I told them I didn't know where he went."

"You know that makes you an accessory."

"To what?" he snapped. "Not paying for two beers? I should sue that place for hiring a predator queer! Look, I'm sorry Austin got himself into a mess, but he'll do his job of making sure you get to Oregon safely. Try not to be too hard on him. He's under a lot of stress right now."

I fucking wanted to *scream* at him, but I bit my tongue. "Okay, Dad. Whatever you say."

Brooke whispered, "I think someone's coming."

"Got to go, Dad. Bye." I ended the call and gave Brooke the handset.

Without hesitation, Brooke said, "And you'll be happy to know that Taylor's brother, Austin, is accompanying us, so we'll be safe." She paused and nodded her head.

Austin emerged from the shadows, a scowl on his face.

"Yes, he's a big, handsome guy," she said, smiling at Austin. "He bought us a bucket of chicken and some wine. We both feel much safer now." She nodded, following her mother's imagined words. "Well, we better go. We have a long day ahead of us."

"Wait," I said and grabbed the handset from Brooke. "Hey, Francis. I love you! Good night."

Brooke laughed as she took the phone back, listened, and said, "She loves you back. Bye, Mom." She hung up the phone. "Mom is thrilled you're with us."

Austin nodded and tightened his eyes. "I wondered where you were."

"We had to wait for showers," I said, "and then had to wait for the phone. Brooke had promised her parents she'd call them tonight."

As we returned to the van, I noticed Austin's movements seemed looser than usual. He'd been drinking. When we reached his tent, he sat down on the ice chest.

"There's something I need to tell you."

A chill spread across my skin.

Austin cleared his throat. "When his father discovered Phillip in the bathroom, he was still alive, bleeding from a stab wound. Phillip said a guy in a mask came out of a stall and held a knife to his neck. He wanted my name and address. He wouldn't hurt him if he told him, but he stabbed Phillip anyway. Before my shower, I called our neighbor's house. This morning when Mr. Singleton came out to get his paper, he saw me working on your van. He asked what I was doing, and I told him I was escorting you to Oregon. This was before I'd heard about Phillip. This afternoon he said a very friendly guy knocked on his door who said he was trying to return a watch to Austin Baird, but he didn't have a house number, so he was knocking on doors until he found me. Henry told him I lived next door but had left in a hippie camper van, heading to Oregon. He laughed and said bluebonnets were painted on the back panel and bumpers. He told the man he could leave the watch with my parents." Austin looked directly at us. "So now these bastards know what car I'm in and where I'm headed. Think about that when you consider driving off tonight. Whether I'm in the van or not, someone bad is looking for it. I swore to Dad I'd get you both safely to Oregon, and I will."

I held my breath, searching his eyes, looking for any sign of deceit. How could I believe anything coming out of his mouth?

"We know you will, Austin," Brooke said with her kindest voice. "We have no intention of leaving you. I don't know where that's coming from other than all the trauma you've experienced. Besides, my parents are counting on you. Just make sure you don't dump *us*." She laughed.

"What time do you want to get up?" I asked, shoving my clenched fists into my pockets.

"No later than six."

"Okay. I'll set my alarm. See you in the morning." We moved to our van, unlocked the door, and got inside. I whispered, "Let's wait before talking." We pushed the curtains we had made all the way around the windows, including the windshield. I cleared the bed while Brooke added ice to a cup before filling it with wine.

We pulled off our sweats, leaving us in tank tops and panties.

Brooke drank, her teeth chattering on the cup. "Do you think that story is as much bullshit as I do?" she asked.

I took a long drink, hoping the wine would slow my racing heart. "Yes, but it could be true, which is why he told us. Dad said some cops came by the house, looking for Austin. Where'd they get his name?" I passed the cup back.

"Maybe from Tony or Phillip's parents. I'm sure they both blame Austin for the deaths of their sons. Or the guy with the watch. I wonder if the cops know about our van."

We drained the glass and passed the bottle.

As Brooke opened the other bottle, she said, "Maybe we shouldn't leave tonight. He'll be expecting it." She poured wine into her mouth and passed me the bottle.

"If someone is following the van, maybe it's better he's with us. At least for another day." I pulled a long drink, finally forcing my nerves to calm. The alcohol had pushed Austin and Tony and Phillip far away.

"So we're staying tonight." She took a sip. "How drunk do you want to get before we have sex?"

My heart quaked. "We're having sex?"

She licked her top lip while staring at me. "You're damn right. I love you, Taylor Baird. I can't pretend otherwise anymore. No more one-offs."

I leaned over to kiss her lips, tasting the wine she'd just drunk. "I love you, Brooke Skipstone. I vote for sex now and wine later."

She put the cup by the sink. "Agreed. Sex now and wine later, then more sex." She pulled off her shirt, then her panties, and hissed, "Take off your fucking clothes." She crouched over me as she dragged her tongue up my leg. "And spread your legs."

I scrambled back with a stifled squeal. She attacked while my head was still inside my top.

When the buzzer rang, Grace closed her computer and looked outside, replaying scenes she'd just read. How could Brooke and Taylor have managed the danger and tension? Because they could depend on each other just like she and Maddi did. And no matter how bad things got, Maddi could still giggle and pull her to their tub or bed. Grace smiled, gathered her stuff, and walked to the front of the room to speak with Taylor. Beaming and breathless, she said, "You and Brooke were like me and Maddi."

Taylor lifted her hand and almost touched Grace's cheek. "Yes, we were. For a few days."

10

SORRY FOR THE DISTURBANCE

Grace laughed and trotted out of the room toward her locker, where she opened a chewy bar and drank from a thermos of coffee. Two other senior girls stood nearby.

Laura, her auburn hair in box braids, told Paige, "The house in this book is definitely Mrs. MacKenzie's. She has a pond and a bridge in her backyard, just like Crystal."

Paige, short with a curly mop of light brown hair framing her round face, leaned closer, their foreheads almost touching. "So you think she's the author?"

"Who else?" Laura just then seemed to notice Grace standing behind them. She sucked in a breath. "Hey, Grace. Have you read the book?"

"Yes." Grace forced herself to keep a straight face.

"Who do you think wrote it?"

"Probably MacKenzie," Grace said.

Laura leaned closer. "Do you think she's gay? I mean, how can anyone write the sex scenes without being gay?"

Grace bit her lip. The same thought had come to her when she'd read the book but decided it couldn't be true. And yet it was, and these girls had shared their suspicions with wonder, not disgust.

Paige's eyes turned to saucers. "I watched Allison and Megan reading. Their faces looked like they'd sucked lemons."

Laura snorted a laugh. "Must've been when Crystal was sucking Haley."

Paige bumped against her, laughing. "Which time?"

"See ya, Grace," Laura said as they walked away.

A glimmer of a thought touched Grace's brain. *They seem to be enjoying the sex scenes as much as I did. Could they be gay?*

Grace gobbled the rest of her bar and drank more coffee. Maybe there was more hope in this town than she'd realized. Allison's crinkled face appeared just as Grace flung her locker door closed. She couldn't help but shriek a little. "Allison, you scared the crap out of me."

Allison moved closer, her ratted-up hair bouncing on her head. "What were you and Taylor talking about in the parking lot yesterday?"

"What?"

The woman narrowed her eyes and pursed her thin lips. "When I opened the door, I heard the word *sex*. Then you stopped hugging her. What was that about?"

Grace tried to slow her whirling brain and think. Should she laugh it off or be angry? "You heard the word *sex*? What have *you* been thinking about lately?" she teased. "Hmmm? What I said was, 'Thanks for the text.' I took a test yesterday in her class, and she texted me my grade."

Allison shook her head and narrowed her eyes to slits. "You lie, young lady. I think you were talking about that book."

"Which book?"

"That *queer* book," she snarled.

"Did you read it?"

Allison's face turned red as she spat her words. "I read some of it. It's the filthiest book I've ever come across."

Grace chuckled. "You need to get out more. There are thousands of books that make *Crystal's House* seem modest. We couldn't have been talking about that book because my dear daddy hadn't revealed it to the world yet. Now I think half the town's reading it, including me." Grace backed away. "Excuse me, but I need to get to class. I'll tell Mr. Banks you wanted to talk about the book, and that's why I'm late."

"You'd better not," she snapped.

"But that's the truth," Grace teased. "And Daddy always taught me to tell the truth."

Allison took a fierce step toward her with a clenched fist. Grace squealed and ran down the hall, laughing. It was amazing how the same book could elicit so many reactions—anger, hatred, joy, courage.

Once in her history class, she found a seat in the back row and opened her computer. Banks was showing a video about the Cuban Missile Crisis. Grace needed to know about Taylor and Brooke's crisis and why Taylor had kept her love secret all these years.

Chapter Seven

Brooke moaned and snuggled closer to me. We were still naked, Brooke lying on top, covering most of my skin with her own. I stroked her arm and shoulder with my fingertips as I replayed what had happened between us. What started as unbridled fun to give and experience orgasms morphed into an intimacy neither of us had ever felt before—a profound warmth and tenderness where a simple touch or kiss was no longer a prelude to a more manic ecstasy but the core itself.

I had always adored Brooke, but now I knew Brooke felt the same for me.

To love and be loved in return. To know someone as deeply as I knew myself. To shudder at my love's casual caress. To hear her say, "The only real love I will ever know is what I feel for you now and always. I want to be with you forever. I don't want to hide anymore." That night had changed my life.

Brooke fell asleep kissing my neck.

For a while, I drifted with my love, floating in silken clouds barely pushed by warm breezes, watching stars twinkle, imagining each as a beautiful moment in our future.

A car drove slowly nearby. A door opened and closed. Heavy footsteps crushed the gravel. How could I hear it so clearly?

We left a window open! Somebody heard us! My insides quivered. Without disturbing Brooke, I reached for the curtain and pulled it away from the side of the van. The louvered glass window revealed half-inch gaps between the panes.

I saw a flashlight glowing through the back curtains. "Brooke," I whispered. "We have to get up. Someone's outside."

She moaned.

"Brooke, please." I pushed her body to the side and tried to sit up. "We need to get dressed."

My head spun as I scrambled to find our clothes. Her sweats were on the floor by the sink. I tossed them to her and pulled on my pants. My shirt was near her head. I slipped it on. "Brooke. Get up. Get up."

Someone tapped the glass of the side door. "I'm the Deputy Sheriff. I need to talk to whoever's in this van."

Fuck! I gulped breaths. *We're going to be arrested.*

Brooke jerked up, eyes wide. "Who?"

I pulled her shirt over her head. "Put your arms in."

She lifted her shaking limbs as I pulled the sleeves over them. "Put on the pants." I waited until she covered her butt before I switched on a light above the sink. I slowly pulled the curtain back until I saw him holding his ID against the window.

I stuffed my feet into flip-flops and opened the door.

He pointed his flashlight to my face. "Is there anyone else?"

I reached out my hand to Brooke. "Just me and Brooke."

She clutched my wrist and took two steps, her face strained and pale.

"Why are you here? It's three o'clock in the morning," I complained.

His voice was stern, and his eyes were dark and hard, peering from underneath a wide-brimmed hat. "Someone called in a complaint . . . about the noise."

"Noise? We were sleeping."

"I need to see your IDs, please."

I scrambled to the front seats and pulled my license from my bag. My fingers trembled. "Brooke. Where's yours?"

She tried to speak but croaked. After clearing her throat, she said, "Inside my pack. Zippered compartment in the front."

I found her license and gave them both to the officer. "What noise?" I barked.

"Someone called and complained that two women were having very loud sex in their van." His eyes darted to each of us. "For well over an hour."

Brooke gasped.

I shot him my best glare. "You have no proof that what this person said is true."

"Well, actually, I do." He inhaled deeply. "This van stinks of sex." He tightened his eyes at me. "Illegal sex."

My eyes flinched from his toward Brooke, who had covered her face.

He shone his light on our IDs. "Even though that kind of behavior is considered sodomy in this state, that's not why I'm here. The woman mentioned a hippie van with painted bluebonnets. We received an APB yesterday afternoon to be on the lookout for such a van. I see you are Taylor Baird. Any relation to Austin Baird?"

I hitched a breath and glanced at Brooke. "That's my brother."

"Do you have any idea where he is?"

My heart skipped beats. I could point toward his tent and then be accused of being an accessory to whatever he did or claim I didn't know and try to get to Oregon so Brooke and I could live our lives.

"Miss Baird?"

I swallowed. "He was with us until he saw his friend's truck just outside of San Antonio. He wanted to see what had happened. We pulled over to let him out. Then we drove on."

"Did he want you to leave him?"

I shook my head. "No, he told us to wait."

"Then why did you leave?"

I hoped Brooke would ad-lib something, but all she did was shake and wring her hands. My brain raced. "Because that was the second friend of his to be shot. We were afraid someone would come after us with him in our van."

He flicked his flashlight between us. "Were you two helping him leave town to avoid arrest?"

I gave him my best shrug of disbelief. "Arrest for what? He planned to accompany us to Oregon because girls aren't supposed to travel alone. My father forced us to take him. He was supposed to keep us safe."

He tilted his head like he was trying to find what I was hiding. "A man was killed at a bar. Your brother and his friends are suspects, but both his friends were killed, so we're interested in talking to Austin."

I tried not to flinch. "We know nothing about a man killed in a bar. Look, Brooke and I just graduated from college. We both have jobs in Oregon. We just want to get there as quickly as we can. Whatever he did or didn't do is no business of ours."

He pursed his lips. "Mind if I look inside your van?"

"Go ahead."

I stepped aside as he pulled himself through the door, flashing his light to the front and back. He lifted the bed pad. "Any secret compartments?"

I grimaced. "Do you think we hid him in the van while we had sex?"

He turned his flashlight to my face. "Why not? You're already perverts. Why would that be beyond your limits." He stood on the bed to look into the pop top.

Brooke grabbed my arm and whispered, "Don't provoke him."

He stepped down and flashed his light around again. "So you left him in Texas. Just ran off and left your brother on the side of the road."

"Yes, sir," I said. "We were pretty scared."

"What'd you do with his stuff?"

"Some of what you saw up top is his. We'll mail it after we get to Oregon." *Please don't open any bags.* My insides churned.

He looked hard at both of us, then gave us a card. "If you hear from him or hear anything about him, you can call this number."

I took the card. "Thank you, Sheriff. Are you through with our IDs?"

"Yes, I am." He returned both cards to me. "Where are you headed tomorrow?"

I didn't want him to stop me tomorrow and find Austin in the van. "We'd planned to see the caverns, but we're not sure now. Either head to Albuquerque and IH40 or El Paso and use IH10."

"Good night, ladies." He walked around the van to his patrol car and after a few minutes, drove away.

We locked the door and drew our curtains, then sat together at the end of our bed, holding hands, breathing loud and fast for over a minute.

"Maybe you should have pointed to the tent," Brooke said.

"I thought about it, but I was afraid we'd all be arrested."

Brooke squeezed my fingers. "Everyone's looking for this van. We need to cover up the flowers."

"Yeah. We can buy some paint tomorrow. And Austin needs to cram his gear in here. If that sheriff sees us with a tent tied to our roof, he'll know we were lying."

"Good idea. Is there any wine left?"

I reached for the almost full bottle by the sink. "Yeah. Lots."

She covered her face. "People heard us for over an hour. I wonder who ratted on us."

I poured wine into our glass. "We'll know tomorrow by the

glares." I took a few sips and passed the cup to her. "We need to sleep." I took off my clothes and scooted back onto our bed.

She drank and crawled onto the bed to give me the glass. "I seem to remember screaming once or twice. Guess we'll have to wait until we find a house." She pulled off her clothes.

"We can scream later," I said. "But we can love now. I just want to hold you."

She snuggled against my neck and chest. "Do you think Austin heard the sheriff?"

"No. I'm sure he drank everything he had, so he's unconscious. He'll buy more tomorrow and probably drink all day."

"Are you going to tell him about the sheriff?"

"Not unless I have to." I took another sip of wine and set the cup in a recessed compartment. I pulled her closer, noting the now stale aroma of our love-making, what I had smelled on her sheets weeks ago—sweet lemons, sweat, butter.

She pushed her leg across my pelvis and cupped my breast. "Do you mind me draped on top? I feel like I'm always smothering you."

"You do the opposite." I kissed her forehead. "We form our own cocoon, and for a little while, we become entirely one." I pulled her closer and listened to her breathing, trying to match mine to hers.

I knew tomorrow would be worse than today. We had to get rid of Austin.

Just before the alarm rang next to my ear, I pressed the button and listened to doors opening and closing. One engine started. The campground was coming to life.

I looked at Brooke's face and debated again which version was her most beautiful—asleep or after orgasm. Both had their merits, but the face I saw then was pure Brooke, unaware of my gaze, vulnerable, in perfect peace. I kissed her lips. "Hey, Brooke. Time to rise."

She moaned then puckered. "More, please."

I flicked my tongue across her mouth.

She squirmed. "Mmm. Why don't I pretend to be asleep, and you spend all morning trying to wake me up?"

"Because we have to drive my asshole brother to Oregon to get rid of him. Then we can spend all day kissing and screaming."

She propped herself on her elbow. "Oh, yeah. Have you checked outside for pitchforks and torches?"

"No, I thought we'd get dressed first."

She sat up. "Remember, jeans and boots and knives."

I pulled down bags from the pop-top area and handed them to Brooke, who tossed them onto our bed. We rummaged through our clothes until we found our outfits for the day, then shoved the bags toward the back window.

Standing naked before each other, we let our eyes roam.

Brooke cocked a brow and said, "Mr. Sheriff told us we smelled like sex, so . . ." She grabbed a washcloth. "We should wash."

"I'd love to, but we need to get on the road." I pulled out a can of Glade from under the sink and sprayed until we both gagged. "As soon as we dump Austin, we'll toss this can."

After a few more minutes, we were dressed.

"What will we say about the noise if anyone mentions it?" Brooke asked.

"We love each other. Sorry, we disturbed you."

"Your brother won't be happy."

"I'll remind him I lied to the sheriff."

We took deep breaths before pulling back the curtains, hoping no one was waiting for us.

As I opened the side door, one of the women we saw last night in the bathroom brushed her daughter's hair two slots away from us. She glared as she wrapped a rubber band around the girl's ponytail.

I smiled back and headed toward Austin's tent. Brooke carried our Coleman stove around the van to the table.

"Austin," I said, squatting in front of his tent door. "Time to get up."

He groaned.

"Brooke's making coffee and oatmeal. You have time to make a bathroom run." I heard movement.

He cleared his throat. "Okay. I'll be out in a second."

I joined Brooke at the table with bowls, spoons, instant coffee, sugar, cinnamon, and instant oatmeal. She had boiled water in a kettle and was adding coffee powder to all the cups.

Austin stumbled toward us in a t-shirt and boxers, puffy-eyed with swollen face and lips, carrying a shaving kit. "Any coffee ready?"

Brooke lifted the kettle. "It's probably hot enough." She poured the water. "Would you like sugar or cream?"

"Just sugar." He shifted his stance and snorted.

"It looks like you had a rough night," I said, searching for any sign of anger toward us.

Brooke handed him his cup.

He mumbled, "Bad dreams," took a sip of coffee, and walked away.

I called after him, "You need to hurry, Austin."

We ate our oatmeal and drank coffee in silence as we watched others in the camp pack up. So far, no one else had looked our way. We kept the water simmering while we finished straightening up inside.

"Taylor," Brooke said. "I need to pee."

"Okay." I locked up the van. We headed toward the bathrooms and saw Austin talking to a man outside the store. As we moved closer, Austin glared at us. The man followed his gaze, tightened his eyes, and said something to Austin.

Shit! Now he knows everything.

When Brooke and I entered the bathroom, the two women with kids we had seen last night hustled their kids outside. Another woman brushing her teeth scowled at us as we entered two stalls.

My ears burned and my neck throbbed. The last time I felt such embarrassment was during seventh grade when I'd made a presentation to the class. For some reason, the kids started laughing, and I almost ran back to my seat. But I continued, causing more laughter. Soon I realized they thought I was funny, so I kept going until they all applauded. I'd never been embarrassed since—until then.

The lady spit water out of her mouth and tightened her eyes at me. "What's your problem?" I barked.

Her face reddened. "You two shouldn't be allowed in here."

I wouldn't have said anything else if she'd just glared and left, but my anger overcame my embarrassment. "And why is that?"

Her body tensed. "We didn't appreciate hearing you two queering off last night. It was disgusting."

Brooke exited her stall.

"Really?" I scoffed. "I think you're just jealous because you heard for the first time what great sex really sounds like."

The lady's mouth dropped open, and she scrambled to gather her things.

Brooke took a step forward. "Taylor and I love each other. We're sorry we disturbed you." She turned around to me and said quietly, "Which was what we were supposed to say."

The lady kicked the door open and stomped away.

"I'm sorry," I told Brooke, "but now we have the bathroom to ourselves."

Soon after we both started brushing our teeth, someone banged on the door and shouted, "You two need to leave this campground!"

We spit and rinsed and moved to the door, fully expecting to see a lynch mob gathered on the porch. We found the office manager we had paid yesterday and several men and women standing at a distance with tight lips and folded arms.

"We're sorry for the disturbance," I said with a slight smile. "We'll be gone in ten minutes." I clutched Brooke's hand as we walked at normal speed toward our van, refusing to let their evil looks goad us into running.

Austin was taking down his tent as we passed. "The Sheriff was here?"

I stopped and faced him. "Yes, but we'll talk about it later. You have five minutes to get your shit in the van, or we're leaving without you. Not on top. Shove it behind your seat."

We went to the table, grabbed our stuff, and took it inside the van. After a few minutes of stowing everything, we climbed into our seats, and I started the engine.

Austin's head snapped up at the sound. He snarled at us, but he hustled nevertheless. Soon he was at the side door, tossing in his tent and bag and lifting the ice chest inside. "What the fuck happened last night?" He slammed the door shut and sat down.

"Wait until we're on the road." I drove the van slowly, waving and smiling at everyone as they glared daggers at us until we exited the campground and turned toward the highway.

"You two are *queers*?" Austin shouted.

I glanced at Brooke as my gut struggled between fear and anger. He wouldn't believe a denial, so I opted for unabashed honesty. "We love each other," I said. "We've always loved each other as best friends, but we've realized recently we're more than friends." I reached for Brooke's hand. She clasped mine, and we shared a look. A tear rolled down her cheek. I wished I could pull over and dump the bastard out more than anything. "We didn't know we'd left a window cracked open last night while we made love. We were asleep when the Sheriff arrived." I merged into traffic, heading north on 285 toward Albuquerque.

Holding his head in his hands, he asked, "Do Mom and Dad know?"

"No," I said.

Brooke turned in her seat toward Austin. "I think Taylor and I have known for a while, but we were afraid to admit it . . . until last night."

Austin growled in frustration. "After all that's happened to me, after I was assaulted by a queer and my friends murdered, you decided you *had* to screw each other last night? Unbelievable!"

I glanced at Brooke, who'd also caught what he'd just said. *After I was assaulted.* I spoke gently. "I can understand how frustrated you were after being tricked by the drag queen, but what happened between Brooke and me last night has been building up for weeks."

"Don't try to put some romantic spin on this. You two are fucking queers, and queers are ruining my life."

"How are Brooke and I ruining your life?" I snapped. "We saved your ass last night! I could easily have told the sheriff you were sleeping in the tent. The police are looking for this van. He came to the KOA only because the lady mentioned a van with bluebonnets."

"Which wouldn't have happened if you two could have controlled yourselves! Now everyone knows where this van is." A vein engorged across his forehead.

I gripped the steering wheel. "Some other cop would've seen this van on the road today regardless of what happened last night. At least now they know you aren't in it."

"But I *am* in it!" He slapped the seat. "Stuck in here with queers. My own fucking sister is a queer!"

My vision clouded with rage. "What are you going to do about it, Austin? Beat us up, bash our heads against a sink like you did the drag queen?"

Our eyes met in the mirror, his crazed and bloodshot. Panting like a dog, he pleaded, "That's what Tony did. Not me."

"Then who was the queer who assaulted you?"

He turned his eyes away and kept panting. I could see the cords stretch in his neck. "I said the queer assaulted *Tony.*"

"No, you just said after all that's happened to *you*, after *you* were assaulted . . ."

He stood up, fists clenched. "Fuck you, bitch!"

I braked and pulled onto the shoulder, causing the car behind me to swerve and honk.

"What are you doing?" he yelled.

I stopped the van and turned around in my seat. "You can't stand being around queers, so get out. Take your shit and leave."

He sneered. "You'd like that, wouldn't you? Then you two could fuck all you want and tell the sheriff where I am."

"I would like that very much," I said. "But remember one thing. I lied to the sheriff last night."

"Why?"

"Because I didn't want him arresting us for helping you escape. We want to get to Oregon and never see you again. But if you keep acting like a maniac, I will stop at the next sheriff's office I see and turn you in." If looks could kill, I would have died that instant, but I stared right back until he looked away.

Brooke cringed in her seat, holding her knees to her chest.

I took a deep breath and touched her arm. She grabbed my hand. "At the next town," I said, "we're going to find a paint store or a Ben Franklin and buy the stuff we need to cover the bluebonnets. Then we're going to find a safe place to do the job. After that, we'll buy gas and some food while you stay in the van. You can't be seen by anyone outside this van. When you have to crap or pee, you'll do it in a rest area, wearing a hoodie. Got it?"

"Maybe. But if I see you ratting on me, I'll—"

"You'll be too late because we won't care what happens to us as long as you're gone. The only reason I don't turn you in now is so Brooke and I can get to Oregon without having to answer for you. Then you'll be Mom and Dad's problem, not ours."

His lips were a white slash on his face, and I had never seen such hate-filled, flinty eyes. Something seemed to snap inside him. No longer my little brother, he had become a dangerous murderer.

He sat down. "Okay," he said with a hard edge. "Let's get the paint. And we all better watch our sixes."

"Grace," Mr. Banks said from the front of his empty classroom. Short, bearded, wearing sandals and cargo pants, he pursed his lips. "Class is over."

Grace clutched her computer, staring at Austin's last words. Evil and hate could jump out at any time without warning. How could anyone live in a world like that? Was it best to stay hidden? Or find a friend you could trust who'd help you fight back? She knew Brooke's end was close. Her stomach gurgled and her chest ached.

"Earth to Grace!"

She jerked her eyes toward Banks. "Yes?"

"Did you see any of the video?" he asked.

"Sure."

"Are you reading that Skipstone book everyone seems obsessed with?"

Her brain struggled to leave the van and come back to school. She stood, confused, shut her eyes and breathed, but couldn't stop her recurring thought—*Austin had reason to kill both of them. Why did Taylor survive?*

She took steps toward the door, then realized she hadn't answered his question. "No, not that one. Another one."

He harrumphed. "This whole thing is a scam. Whoever Skipstone is paid your father for the advertisement." He smiled knowingly. "She's laughing all the way to the bank."

She scowled at the cocky little man. "No, Mr. Banks. She's scared to death, but this time she has friends to protect her." Grace left the room, desperate to know what had happened to Brooke, hoping for an easy mistake she and others could avoid. Worried that nothing could have stopped Austin.

What would stop him now?

11

LOOKING AT NOTHING

Grace found the table in the Commons crowded with her math class students, most staring at their phones or computers. "What's up?"

Paige's head popped up. "Ms. Kelly left early, so we're supposed to stay here." She ducked her head behind her computer screen, sharing a laugh with Laura.

Grace looked through the glass windows of Megan's office to see if she was watching the Commons. When the secretary got up to file a folder, Grace headed to Taylor's room, where she found three middle school students sitting around a curved table, reading to their smiling teacher.

Grace waited for a pause in their conversation before saying, "Ms. Kelly is gone for the day. I'm starting Chapter Eight. I wanted to be here."

Taylor's smile sagged before she gave a grim nod.

Grace sat in the back by the window, opened her lid with trembling hands, and started reading.

Chapter Eight

Brooke slipped in a John Denver tape and tried to hum to "Take Me Home, Country Roads." After a minute, she lost interest. "Mr. Denver would never have written that song if he'd lived here. When do we see real trees instead of mesquite and scrub brush?"

"Northern California," I answered.

Brooke groaned. "I want my money back."

I laughed. "Wait till you see Nevada. You'll have fond memories of this beautiful stretch of road."

I glanced in the rearview mirror. Austin's chin sagged on his slumped chest as he snored. My brother, the murderer. When he told *Tony's* story, I remembered being startled by his line, "And kept punching him until blood gushed everywhere." Tony told Phillip and Austin this? That didn't make sense. Austin had to have seen the blood.

When did he become such a hothead? The only time I saw him angry was during sports contests in high school. Otherwise, he was always Mr. Stud, looking for admirers. But what really frightened me was his casual proxy murder of Tony and Phillip because they'd known the truth.

And now he knew we did.

Was his breakdown at seeing what happened to Tony real? It had to have been. Like seeing the broken skull of the drag queen and realizing what he'd done, he saw what his simple phone call had done to his friend.

His crying and fear of abandonment at the campground yesterday signaled he still felt some human emotion, even if it was self-hate. He hadn't turned completely psycho on us, but I thought he was nearing the edge.

A large red sedan approached quickly from behind me, then jockeyed into the left lane to pass. Maybe it was a Cadillac, something like that. As it moved beside us, my pulse raced. I glanced to my left and saw a young man with black hair and dark skin, his brown eyes fixed on me. Then he moved his head out the window as if trying to see past me.

"Austin," I yelled, trying not to move my lips. "Get on the floor. Now!"

He jerked his head up. "What?"

"Get on the floor. There's a guy trying to see who's inside." I looked to my left as the car inched ahead, the man craning his neck back at us. *He's looking for Austin!* I smiled at him.

Austin rolled onto the floor just as the Cadillac moved into my lane. After another minute, the Cadillac sped ahead.

"Okay, he's gone."

Austin climbed back into his seat, breathing heavily.

"You need to pull the curtains up to our seats on both sides," I said. "We're a few minutes outside of Roswell. Before we stop for gas, you should pop your seat flat and hide behind the bags."

"Why?"

I tapped my fingers on the steering wheel. "The troopers know the van with bluebonnets only carries two girls, but others didn't get the message. Who do you think that Cadillac is looking for?"

Austin sat back, his fingers laced behind his head, staring at the ceiling. "We wouldn't have this problem if you two hadn't—"

"Don't go there, Austin," I barked.

He shook his head and snarled.

"There's a big Shell station up there," Brooke said. "They should know where to buy paint."

"I want three six-packs of Bud and a fifth of Jack Daniels," Austin said.

"I'm not paying for your booze," I said. "Give me a twenty, and we'll buy it. And you need to hide. I'm about to exit."

Austin pulled a bill out of his wallet, flipped it toward me then flattened his seat. He climbed onto the bed and dragged bags forward until he had an empty pocket to lie inside. "Don't forget ice!"

I parked by a pump and jumped out the door with my day pack. Brooke opened the side door and pulled out the ice chest.

As I pumped gas, the red Cadillac parked at a pump on the other side of the store. Two men got out and walked inside, neither glancing our way.

After filling the tank, we walked toward the store. "The Cadillac guys are inside," I said.

Brooke stopped. "Maybe we should wait."

"If we'd really dumped Austin yesterday, why would we be worried about them? Just act normal."

We entered the store and headed toward the cooler section in the back. "I'll get the beer," I said. "Pick out whatever wine you want. And some Coke."

Brooke veered toward the wine aisle.

I opened one of the glass doors, pulled out two six-packs of Bud, and set them on the floor before reaching for another.

A man chuckled behind me. "You two must like to drink beer." His voice was deep and smooth with a heavy accent.

I tried to swallow my gasp as I hooked my fingers through the cardboard handle. I knew who stood behind me. Turning around with a smile, I said, "I'm driving, so this is for my friend. But I'll catch up to her tonight."

The man who'd looked at me from the Cadillac smiled, revealing a silver front tooth. "Or maybe it's for your brother." His voice turned cold. "After what he did, he probably needs to stay drunk to keep the nightmares away."

My stomach quivered. "We left him just outside San Antonio."

He shook his head very slowly. "No. A friend of mine saw him get back into your van." He tilted his head, focusing his dark eyes on mine. "Do you know what he did to my little brother?"

"No." My hands trembled. *Austin murdered his brother?*

"He bashed his face onto the sink and faucets a dozen times. Most of his teeth were shattered. Every bone in his face was broken. His eyes were mush. Not even my mother could recognize him. Did he tell you that?"

I could only shake my head. My eyes locked onto his, searching for any sign of deceit, but all I saw was anguish and rage. Another man opened a cooler door behind me and grabbed some beer before leaving.

The man with the silver tooth sneered. "Your brother is an animal. Why are you protecting him?"

I tried to swallow. I couldn't breathe.

"We didn't know," Brooke said from behind. She put her arm around me and squeezed. "Her father wanted Austin to accompany us on our trip to Oregon. Austin said he got into a fight but blamed his friends. Taylor and I just want to start a new life together. We had nothing to do with this and don't want to be involved."

He tightened his eyes, scrutinizing both of us then nodded. "Okay. I'll believe you. Where are you stopping tonight?"

I cleared my throat. "I don't know. We'll drive as far as we can, then find a rest area."

"Does he sleep in the van?"

I glanced at Brooke. "He has a tent." *Did I just condemn my brother? Did I care?*

He tilted his head and licked his lips. "I have no quarrel with you unless you get in my way."

"Thank you," I whispered and grabbed my hands to stop their shaking.

"And keep the police out of this."

I nodded, unable to pull my gaze from his.

"We'll wait here until you're gone."

I stood frozen until Brooke pulled my arm. Then I picked up the other six-packs and hurried to the register. I tried to calm down, but all my movements were rushed and awkward.

Brooke held my hand. "We'll be fine. Showtime."

We set everything on the counter and asked for a bag of ice.

"Hey there," Brooke said to the young man behind the counter. "Do you know where we can get some paint?" She flashed her beautiful smile.

He looked at her face and stared.

"Paint?" Brooke asked.

He blew out a breath. "What kind of paint?"

"We want to add more decorations to our van."

"Yeah, there's a hardware store on College. Take a right. Go two blocks. It's on the left."

"Thank you so much," Brooke said.

The young man just stared at her. I understood what had happened to his brain because I had felt it many times.

I paid our bill and realized we didn't need paint. Now that the drag queen's brother knew Austin was in our van, covering the blue-bonnets wouldn't help us. But Austin didn't know that, and Brooke and I needed privacy to talk.

We gathered everything and walked toward the door. Before she opened it, Brooke said, "All smiles. I just told you a joke." We laughed all the way back to the van, where we filled the ice chest with beer, Coke, and one bottle of wine. I opened the side door, and both of us lifted the chest inside. "Don't move yet, Austin," I whispered to the murdering animal. It would take all my acting abilities to hide my disgust and rage from him.

In another two minutes, we pulled out of the station.

"What took so fucking long?" Austin complained as he lurched forward to grab a beer.

"I had trouble picking out wine," Brooke said, "and the counter guy had to ask someone else where we could buy paint. And then they had to argue about directions like guys do." She opened a can of Coke, took a sip, and handed it to me.

I couldn't stop thinking about the queen's brother and was unable to look at Austin in the mirror. I knew all I'd see was the bloody, broken face of the man he'd slaughtered.

I parked at the store and bolted toward the entrance. Brooke hurried after, barely slipping inside before the door closed behind me.

After we found the paint section, I asked, "How much did you hear?"

"Everything after his broken face."

I sucked in a breath. "I can't believe Austin did that." My skin burned.

"I can see it in his eyes, especially after he drinks. He can snap any second and turn into a monster."

"What should we do?"

"We have three options," Brooke said as we sat on the floor, putting tubes of acrylic paint into our basket. "One, we say and do nothing and see what happens tonight."

"Then Austin is likely killed, which he deserves."

"Two, we tell Austin what happened, so he's on guard. Maybe *he* kills *them*."

"Or not," I said. "Maybe he sets up his tent as a decoy and stays in the van. Then we're off the brother's nice list, and the guy comes after all of us."

"Three, we tell the store manager to call the cops to pick up Austin because we just found out what he did."

I looked toward the front of the store. "Then Austin claims we knew everything already, and we lied to the sheriff last night."

Brooke shrugged. "Take your pick."

"What do you think?"

She pursed her lips. "Say nothing, then drive away at two or three in the morning after we're sure he's drunk and unconscious."

"Okay." We stood up and started to walk toward the cash register when I saw a *Keys Duplicated* sign. I held my van key out to a man behind a counter. "Can you make a copy of this?"

"Sure," he said. "Give me two minutes."

Brooke hooked my arm. "Good idea."

"He's going to want our keys. How else would he keep us from driving away? Our paint job can be quick. Its only purpose is to convince Austin we're trying to keep him from being caught."

The man gave me both keys. "Try it out. If there's a problem, bring it back."

"Thanks." When I got back into the van, I tried the new key. It worked, and I dropped it into my boot. After five minutes, we found a shaded area to park. Austin chased his whiskey with beer, as we transformed every flower into a tree. Twenty minutes later, we tossed our brushes and paints in the trash and started the van.

"Find a Dairy Queen or a drive-thru," Austin said. "I'm hungry."

After one more stop for burgers and a refill of our coffee thermos, we were on our way.

For a few hours, I kept checking for the red Cadillac, but weariness numbed my sense of caution. I had experienced so much emotion during the past twenty-four hours. My nerves were raw and needed a break.

We traveled west on IH40, one of hundreds of vehicles. I had seen this view from a plane—bugs crawling slowly along an endless track. So pointless from the air, even more so from the road.

Hour after hour, the dry desert rock shimmered in the heat.

"Drink." Brooke held out a cup of coffee. "Your eyes are drooping."

"Sorry." I took a few sips.

"Do you want me to drive?"

"No, I'd rather hear you hum and sing." I looked in the mirror and saw Austin on his back, his arms and legs splayed over the bags. "Our protector."

Did I care what happened to my brother? I'd been asking myself that question. If he were a stranger and we knew what he'd done, I'd throw him out and never look back. But because he carried that label —brother—I wasn't sure. I wanted to believe there was more to the story between him and the queen.

But why? To justify what he'd done?

What possible information could explain Austin's behavior? Somehow Austin justified his crime by labeling his victim. A drag queen. A predator queer. A Mexican.

But that man was a brother too, who even Austin admitted was a great singer. Captivating. Talented.

How powerful labels could be. All of his abilities and potential were hidden behind the word queer.

The same could happen to Brooke and me. All of our creativity and skill were vanquished by *dyke* and *lesbian*.

However, names we could deal with. Broken bones at the hands of a monster . . . we could not.

The inevitable would happen that night. I had no doubt those men would track us and attempt to kill Austin, the murderer in a drunken stupor, now fouling the bed where Brooke and I became lovers.

We had to escape this storyline and write our own. We'd be in Oregon in two more days.

An hour later, Austin woke up and peered out the windshield. "Stop up here," he ordered.

"Where?" I asked.

"At the historical marker turnout."

What the fuck? "Okay." I moved over to exit and glanced at Brooke. She shrugged.

"Pull up real close," he said.

Once I stopped, he slid open the side door, stepped onto the pavement, unzipped, and peed onto the marker. "I always hated history."

"Austin!" I yelled. Then realized he didn't want to leave the van at the next rest area.

Brooke jerked her body around so she wouldn't see him through her mirror.

"Move up to the trash can," he said.

"You are not going to crap in the can," I shouted.

"Nope. But I am tossing these empty bottles."

Which he did.

Just outside of Flagstaff, we found a rest stop.

"You girls go ahead," Austin said. "I'll stay here." He lay back on the bed.

Brooke and I hurried to the restrooms.

"Maybe he'll drive off," Brooke said.

"I wish. He's worried about us leaving him, which is why he pulled that stunt at the turnout."

"He has to shit sometime," Brooke said.

"Maybe he's doing that now in the van."

"Ugh!"

When we exited the bathroom, a State Trooper's car turned into a parking spot fifty feet from us. We both gasped and grabbed each other's arms.

"Do you think Austin can see the car?" Brooke asked.

My heart raced as I craned my neck to look back toward where we parked. "I can't see the van, so he can't see us. Maybe the trooper will come over here."

We stared at the car, squeezing each other's arms.

"C'mon," I muttered. "Get the fuck out of your car."

I was about to move toward the trooper when someone draped his arms around our shoulders. We both flinched then froze when his mouth came between our ears, "Time to leave, girls."

Austin!

He turned us around.

Brooke squealed but recovered quickly, throwing her arms around Austin's waist. "Thank you, Austin. We came out of the bathroom, saw him, and froze. We didn't know what to do."

I turned my head to look back at the trooper.

"Taylor, don't you dare," Austin barked.

"What's wrong with you? I wasn't going to go over," I spat out. "Just checking to see if he's following us."

"Which is what you want, isn't it?" He jerked my arm. "Just get inside."

"If we'd wanted to turn you in," I said, "we would've walked over to him." I pulled my arm away. "Do you want to make a big scene right now? Attract his attention?"

Austin turned toward me, balling up his fists.

Brooke slowly hooked her arms into ours and walked us to the van. "Let's all calm down. We're tired from driving all day."

We drove past the empty Trooper car and exited onto the highway. Austin thought we would turn him in, but I wasn't sure. If Austin hadn't surprised us, would we?

At midnight, I decided I couldn't drive any farther and saw a sign for a rest stop ten miles ahead. "We're stopping in ten minutes."

"Fine by me," Austin said as he sat up and stretched.

"Must have been a hard day for you, huh?" I taunted. "Sleeping and drinking all day. And more of the same tonight."

"Fuck off, Taylor."

Brooke turned toward me, clenched her jaw, and barely shook her head.

I tried to stifle my frustration. Of course, Brooke was right. He was ready to snap.

I pulled into the rest area and found a concrete, enclosed picnic table away from lights and everyone else, though a distance to the bathrooms.

Brooke and I grabbed our day packs and scrambled out of the van.

"Where are you going?" Austin barked.

"To the bathrooms," I snapped. "Is that allowed?"

"Depends on what else you're going to do." He glared at us, then pulled a whiskey bottle from his back pocket.

I pointed to the pay phone between the restrooms. "There's the phone. Maybe you should stand guard."

He took a drink and screwed the cap back onto the bottle. "I might do that."

"Great." I hooked Brooke's arm and took a few steps.

"One of you should wait here."

Brooke stopped, her mouth and eyes open in a silent scream.

I pulled her arm. "Fuck you, Austin." As we walked away, I waited for his big hands to grab our shoulders. I freed up my right hand to grab my knife if he did.

The bathroom was dingy, with painted cinder block walls and steel mirrors that needed polishing. No soap or paper towels. One roll of tissue paper. Fortunately, we carried a hand towel and a bar of Dove in a plastic container.

"He's going to demand our keys when we get back," Brooke said, wiping soap on her face.

"Let him. We could keep the top down and just pile the bags on the floor so we could leave in seconds when we decided to."

Brooke handed me the bar. "Then he'll know we're leaving and wonder how since he has our keys. No, let's do everything like normal."

We both wiped our bodies under our clothes with wet washcloths.

"Did you ever see the red Cadillac again?" Brooke asked.

"Maybe. Something red passed us an hour ago. I was half asleep, so I don't know."

"I hope we can leave before they show up."

We exited the bathroom and half-trotted across the rest of the lot back to our van.

Austin had set up his tent and threw his clothes bag inside. He folded his arms and glared at us as we jumped inside the van. Silently, Brooke and I readied our bed and stowed our bags up top. I found our cup and leaned out the side door. Austin was drinking a beer at the table. "Are you sharing ice tonight?"

"Sure. Come help yourself."

Brooke and I walked over to him.

As I started to open the lid, he laid his arm across the ice chest, palm open. "I need your keys first."

"You *need* them?" I asked, my pulse beating in my neck.

"As insurance. So you don't drive off tonight."

I reached into my pocket. "You have unresolved separation issues, Austin. You should get that checked out." I dropped my key into his hand.

He glowered at Brooke. "Both sets, or are you going to lie and say you only have one key?"

She tried to smile, but her lips quivered. She dug her key from her pocket and gave it to him.

His sleeping bag lay on the bench behind us. "Are you sleeping out here?"

"I'm thinking about it. I need to keep an eye on things."

"You have our keys," I said. "What else are you worried about?"

"The guys who killed Phillip and Tony."

I shook my head slowly. "How do you think this ends?"

He drained his beer and opened another. "I'm not going to jail because of a bunch of queers."

The back of my neck burned. "Bunch? Besides the one you slammed onto a sink a dozen times, who else?"

Brooke placed her hand on my back and moved her fingers back and forth, saying, "Don't."

"That's what Tony did." He pulled a drink from his bottle. "The rest of the bunch is looking at me. You two just had to fuck each other and bring out the sheriff."

"We got rid of the bluebonnets," I barked. "No cop has shown any interest in us."

"Doesn't matter." He finished the bottle. "That sheriff reported that this van was spotted in Carlsbad."

"Without you in it," Brooke said. "We told the sheriff we left you—"

He laughed. "Maybe the cops believe that shit, but not the shooters. The location of the van was identified. We're headed to Oregon. How many ways could we go? But I'll be ready for them." He pulled a pistol from behind his back.

Brooke shrieked and jumped back. Adrenaline surged through my body. I crouched and almost pulled my knife.

Austin laughed. "It's just Dad's pistol." He pointed it to the sky, letting moonlight reflect off the stainless steel barrel. "A Colt Combat Commander he's kept in his drawer since we were kids."

"He gave that to you?" I asked.

"Sure he did. *And* a box of bullets. Dad said, 'Keep the girls safe, son. And yourself.' 'Yes, sir, I surely will.' But now the girls have put me in a dangerous situation, so I'll probably have to use this to save myself." He brandished the gun to his side and across his front— never pointing it directly at us, but his intent was clear.

Brooke whimpered and pulled my arm.

"I think it's time you two queers go to bed." He stood up and shoved the pistol behind his back.

Brooke ran to the van. By the time I caught up, I found her crying on the bed. I shut the door behind me and held her.

"He's going to kill us," Brooke cried.

"We won't let him," I said. "Besides, the way he's drinking, he'll pass out soon. If the red Cadillac comes here tonight, they'll take care of him."

Her entire body shaking, Brooke stammered, "How do you know they'll leave us alone? We'll be witnesses."

"We'll be gone by then." I poured some wine into our glass and gave it to her.

She downed a few gulps, closed her eyes, and tried to slow her breathing. I drew the curtains, locked the doors, pulled my new key from my boot, and pushed it partially into the ignition.

"We should sleep in what we're wearing tonight."

She nodded quickly and held out her glass. After I filled it, I pulled the bags from the top and piled them on the floor. All we'd have to do before leaving was pull the top down.

"Open the window away from him so we can hear," she said.

I did and tried to peek out the curtains on the table side. I couldn't find him. The ice chest was gone. I checked the other side and saw nothing. Then I heard faint footsteps and peeked out the rear toward the bathrooms. There he was, walking back. He must've run to the facilities as soon as we entered the van.

Another opportunity missed.

We leaned against each other on the bed, our backs propped against the side, passing the glass back and forth.

"Should we set the alarm?" Brooke asked.

"He'll hear it. I'll wake up."

"I'm really scared, Taylor." She leaned into me.

I wrapped my arms around her, trying to ignore my own trembling limbs. "We'll get through this."

A few minutes later, we lay down, facing each other, touching each other's cheeks, and pressing our lips together gently. Soon, her eyes closed, and she slept.

Every one of my senses was on high alert. I knew the shooters would come tonight. The best scenario was they'd wait another hour. I couldn't believe Austin could stay awake that long. After an hour, I'd check the windows, pull the top down, and start the van.

Despite all my efforts, I dozed off. What brought me back to life was the slow movement of tires across the pavement, causing little pops of gravel.

Brooke had turned over, facing the window. I sat up slowly, moved to the end of the bed, wedged my feet between bags until I touched the floor, and tried to see through the tiny gap between the top of the curtain and the windshield.

Austin did not try to hide his tent behind the table structure or a tree. And then I realized he'd positioned it in the open on purpose— an obvious, tempting target while he hid behind the table enclosure.

Without touching any curtains, I tried to see the vehicle moving outside. It was the red Cadillac, pointed straight at the tent. Cigarette smoke wafted out of the driver's window.

Suddenly, the engine roared, and the car lurched toward the tent, crushing it under the tires. The vehicle moved back a few feet before running it over again.

Then thunderous bangs exploded from my left. Austin ran toward the car, gun held straight out, blasting into the windshield and side windows.

Brooke screamed.

"Be quiet," I hissed. "Lay flat."

I yanked the top down, set the latches on both sides, spread the front curtains, and climbed into my seat.

The queen's brother tried to open his door, but Austin shot him at close range.

As soon as I started the van, Austin jerked his face and gun toward me. "Taylor!" he snarled and ran at the van.

I shifted into reverse and cranked the wheel, but he'd tried to open the passenger door before I could push into first and move forward. Finding it locked, he shot through the window, shattering the glass. "The next one goes through your head."

I froze.

He pulled the inside handle, opened the door, and climbed into the seat. "Drive!" He slammed the door as I lurched forward.

Flashes of light and terrified faces filled my vision as I raced out of the rest area and headed for the highway.

"You knew they were coming, didn't you?" He cocked the pistol and shoved it closer to my head. "You were bailing on me!"

"I heard a war outside." I couldn't get enough air into my lungs. "What would *you* do?"

"You *knew* they were coming!" he screeched.

"So did you! They could've killed us too. If you'd been in the tent, they would've come for us. So, yeah, I was ready to get the hell out of there." I jerked the wheel to pass another car.

"Slow down!" he yelled. "You're trying to get a cop after us."

Fear dissolved into anger. "Put your gun away, and I'll slow down." I kept my foot on the pedal until we hit eighty. "Put it down, and I'll go the speed limit."

He uncocked the gun and shoved it behind his back. I slowed to sixty. "Brooke, are you all right?" I looked in my mirror until I saw her sit up with hair all over her puffy face. "Brooke, please open the curtains, so I can see."

She pulled all the curtains back and scooted up to the front of the bed, gulping breaths. "Did you kill them?"

"Yes, I fucking did," he sneered.

She caught my eyes in the mirror before scrunching hers shut, pulled her knees to her chest, held them with her arms, and rocked back and forth.

"We can't drive all night," I said. "We have to stop somewhere."

"Sure. Let's sleep in the nearest parking lot and wait for the sheriff to find us. Fuck that. We're driving."

I checked the fuel gauge. "I have a quarter tank left. We'll have to stop in Kingman. Then we can find a park where we can sleep."

"No!" he screamed.

"A lot of people saw us leave the rest area. Someone has already called the troopers. They know what we're driving."

Austin stomped his feet and slapped the dashboard. "Fuck! Fuck! Fuck!"

Flashing lights appeared far behind us in my mirror. "We have company."

Austin jerked around in his seat. "Shit!"

"There's an exit up here," I said, my heart pounding. "They can't see our van yet. I should get off and find a place—"

"No! Stay on the highway and speed up!" He pulled out his gun and dug bullets from his pocket to reload.

"Are you going to shoot the troopers?" I asked.

"No, I'll shoot you if you don't shut up and drive." He pointed the gun at me.

"Austin!" yelled Brooke. "They might not be after us. If we speed, they'll definitely stop us."

"Fine! Let them try and see what they get." He jerked around to look out the back window. "Faster!" he yelled. He turned back to the front and held the gun to my head. "I said faster."

My sweating hands gripped the wheel. "If you shoot me, we crash." I slowed down a little as my breaths quickened.

He pulled the hammer back. "Faster!"

Every one of my muscles tightened. "Go ahead. Shoot. Then we'll stop for sure." I would not let myself succumb to fear.

He pressed the barrel against my ear.

"Taylor!" shouted Brooke.

Austin bolted from his seat toward Brooke, holding the barrel to her cheek. "I'll shoot your fucking girlfriend."

I glanced back to see Brooke's bulging eyes, then pressed the accelerator until we hit eighty.

"First, I'll shoot her knee." He pushed the barrel into her leg. "Then I'll shoot her tit. How about that, Taylor?" He pushed the gun into Brooke's breast. "Your queer girlfriend will have only one tit." He grabbed her breast as he caught my eyes in the mirror. "Ooh, you have big ones."

I saw Brooke's lips flatten against her teeth as he groped her. I pressed the brake.

"Hey!" He swung the gun toward me.

I pumped the brake again just as Brooke whipped her knife from her boot with a howl.

Austin screamed as the point punctured his forearm, but he grabbed her wrist and beat it with the gun until the knife dropped. Both struggled behind me, Brooke grunting and growling, her hands pushing the gun away from her.

Through the mirror, I saw flashing lights moving closer. I braked hard, forcing them to fall against the passenger seat. Austin back-handed her face with the gun. She shrieked and fell against the side door, pushing down the handle and popping the panel open.

"Brooke! The door!" I braked again, hoping the side panel would stay forward.

Austin stumbled sideways. Brooke reached for her knife on the floor. Just as she lifted it, Austin thrust his foot into her stomach, pushing her hard against the door, forcing it open. She screamed as the door slid backward.

"Taylor! Taylor!"

I pressed the brake as her hands fought to find something to grab onto. I didn't know whether to brake again or keep steady. Her bulging eyes locked onto mine. I leaned back as far as possible while holding the wheel, extending my hand to her. "Grab it!" I screamed.

Austin thrust his foot into her chest. She fell out of the van screaming.

"Brooke!" I slammed on the brakes, trying to keep from fishtailing, forcing Austin into the back of the front seat and against the sink. My tires screeched down the road until the van stopped. Before Austin could get off the floor, I flipped the key to kill the motor, pulled it from the ignition, and leaped out my door.

"Brooke!" I cried as I ran back up the road.

I saw her motionless body a hundred yards back. A trooper's car had pulled onto the shoulder and stopped about twenty yards behind her, its headlight splitting the night to reveal the horror.

My chest was about to burst from running and screaming. I slammed my knees onto the gravel. "Oh, Brooke," I cried. Her body was twisted and broken, her bloodied face and blue eyes looking at nothing as a breeze blew hair across the dirt.

Austin ran up behind me as two troopers emerged from their car with guns drawn. "Drop your weapon!"

Austin thrust his barrel against my head. "Drop yours, or I'll shoot her!"

An overwhelming surge of heat shot up from my stomach and out of my mouth in a scream of rage as I pulled my knife from my right boot and swung my arm behind me, slamming my blade deep into his leg. I rolled to my left and sprang up to a crouch.

The headlight glowered as Austin screamed and dropped to his knees, his hands clutching the knife handle. A trooper grabbed Austin's pistol.

"You fucking bitch!" Austin cried.

"This is Austin Baird," I cried, wiping tears from my face. "He pushed my girlfriend out of our van after holding a gun to her head. He killed two men at a rest area forty miles back. He also beat a man to death in San Antonio three days ago."

"Who are you?" asked the trooper handcuffing Austin.

"I'm that asshole's sister." I moved slowly to Brooke, unable to comprehend her stillness. Her silence. I kneeled and started to weep, forcing hard, wracking spasms throughout my body. I lifted her bloodied hand and pressed it against my wet face. "Oh, Brooke. I'm so sorry."

Grace covered her wet face with her hands. Her throat had squeezed shut, allowing only muffled wails to escape her lips. An arm stretched across her shoulders. She grabbed it and found her friend's tear-streaked face across from hers in the now-empty classroom.

"I'm here, Grace," Taylor said. "Cry as much as you need to."

"How did you survive?" Grace asked.

"I almost didn't. They had to sedate me at the hospital. I so wanted to die that night."

They cried in each other's arms until there were no more tears.

12

CRYING ON SHOULDERS

A few minutes after the lunch bell, Taylor still stroked the girl's head as Grace leaned on her shoulder. Memories of that night twisted Taylor's brain. *Two ambulances. A trooper driving her van as she sat in the backseat of a police car. Alternating between paralysis and wailing. Waking up in a hospital bed.*

A few tears still welled in her eyes. Grace reminded Taylor of her younger self, but unlike Taylor, Grace had her Gram's support and a girlfriend, though they still had to hide their love from others. She wanted to protect Grace from pain and knew Grace wanted the same for Taylor.

"What the hell is going on in here?" Allison bellowed from the doorway.

Grace didn't move. Taylor held her finger to her lips to shush the woman, but Allison stomped over anyway.

"Grace," Taylor whispered as she lifted her arm. "Time for lunch."

Allison scowled down her nose. "Why are you hugging her?"

Grace stirred and groaned.

"She was crying."

Allison scrutinized Taylor's face. "She was, or you were?"

"We both were, you bitch!" Grace barked. "What do you care?" She leaped out of her chair.

"It's not proper for teachers and students to be hugging each other." Allison sucked in her lips. "I need to report this." She turned to leave.

"You know what you need to report?" Grace moved in front of her.

"Grace," Taylor warned as she stood. *Please back away.*

Allison sneered and folded her arms. "And what's that?"

"That you're the meanest so-called teacher in this school. Nobody likes you."

"At least I'm not a *pervert* like *she* is," Allison said, pointing to Taylor. "Like *you* are, Grace Mitchell. You and Maddi."

Grace slammed her hands into Allison's shoulders. "She's my friend. Get the fuck out of here!"

Allison staggered backward, her eyes wide and mouth open, a little fear twitching her mouth that disappeared a second later, replaced by a snarl and a dagger look. She hurled herself toward Grace.

The principal strode into the room.

Taylor stood and shouted, "No!"

"Allison!" Jackson yelled. "Stop!"

Grace just then gripped the woman's shoulders at arm's length, both glaring at the other.

Allison pushed Grace's hands away and turned to Jackson. "Is she going to get away with that?"

"Please wait in my office, Allison," he said firmly with a red face.

"They were hugging each other when I came in here," Allison shouted as she stomped to the door. "Ask them about that!" She exited the room and pounded down the hall.

Jackson leaned against a student desk. "What started this?"

"I'd just finished the chapter when Brooke died," Grace said, her chest heaving.

"Brooke, who?"

"Brooke Skipstone," Grace said. "The real one. I couldn't stop crying. Taylor held me."

Jackson frowned at Taylor. "That's your pen name."

Taylor sighed. "Yes. Brooke and I were best friends until she died in 1974. I wrote a book and gave it to Grace to read. We both cried for several minutes. Grace fell asleep on my shoulder until—"

"That bitch barged in, screaming at us," Grace barked. "Why is she in this school? She's not even a teacher. She's been yelling at kids for years."

Jackson cleared his throat. "She's been with the school since the nineties in some capacity. This is my first year as principal. I can't fire her unless she—"

"Slugs a student?" Grace asked. "You should have let her punch me. A missed . . ." Grace glanced at Taylor.

"A missed opportunity," Taylor said softly, remembering all the times they could have left Austin during that trip. "What would you have done, Grace, if you were me all those years ago?"

"What you did with your knife except sooner and probably wrecked the van." She grabbed Taylor into a hug. "You did what you could. You didn't expect him to push her onto the road."

Taylor squeezed then pushed her back, both women crying. "You should go."

"What am I missing here?" Jackson asked.

Grace wiped her cheeks and grabbed her computer. "Her brother killed Brooke Skipstone. Now he wants to kill Taylor." She looked back. "See you later?"

"Yes." Taylor nodded and wiped her eyes.

As Grace walked past Jackson, he asked, "What did you do to cause Allison to charge you? I heard the yelling, but I missed what you did to set her off."

"Like she needs something to set her off?" Grace scoffed before striding out of the room.

Jackson looked toward Taylor, who decided Grace could not be blamed. She'd suffered enough.

"I'm sorry, Principal Jackson," her eyes averted, "everything's a blur. I can't remember."

He nodded.

Laura and Paige knocked on the doorframe.

"Yes, girls?" Jackson asked.

"We wanted to ask Mrs. MacKenzie something," Laura said with a big smile.

Taylor knew the girls wanted to ask if she was the secret author.

"Maybe another time," Jackson said. "Mrs. MacKenzie has to go home." He exchanged a glance with Taylor. "Something's come up."

The girls frowned and walked away.

Taylor nodded at Jackson, happy to avoid their questions. *My holiday begins early.* "I'll gather my things," Taylor said, walking toward her desk.

Jackson frowned and folded his hands. "Your brother has threatened you?"

"Yes, he wants to kill me too." Taylor dropped her computer into her satchel. "He has for forty-eight years."

"Have you called the troopers?"

"Yes, but they can't do anything unless his threats become more obvious." She held her bag at her waist. "Sometimes they take an hour to get here after they're called. I have guns and some friends."

Jackson frowned. "And your husband."

"Yes, he'd like the opportunity. . . for his own reasons. I'm sorry about this . . . this disturbance today." She breathed deeply, pondering what else to say. "Allison shouldn't work in this school. Grace lost her temper for a good reason." Taylor moved toward Jackson and looked him directly in the eyes. "She demeaned . . . lesbians. There's no room for hate in this school." Taylor held out her hand.

"If there's a meeting on Saturday, I'll be there." He shook her hand. "Megan will deposit your check before she leaves today."

Taylor left the building quickly and climbed into her car, trying to avoid student questions. Grace's truck was gone. Seeing students exit the school, Taylor hurried to back up and leave the parking lot. The original plan was for Grace to meet her at a campground near the river after school, where Taylor would leave her car and move her things into Grace's truck. She stopped near the post office to check her phone.

Shannon texted. *Grace told me about Allison. You're welcome to stop by for lunch. Grace will be at her house for a while. She won't return to school today.*

Taylor replied. *I'm done teaching for the day. Do you know the campground loop near the river?*

Yes, I do.

I'll leave my car behind the snow berm while staying with you. Can you pick me up?

Yes. Be there in 5.

Taylor drove toward the park, passing the road to the gun range, and heading to the river. The open field was crisscrossed with snow machine trails. During the next week, the park would be filled with the roar of engines racing along and jumping over the earthen dike, which protected the town from flooding during breakup in late April.

Channels of the Nenana River had been frozen since November. Two main trails—one going south, the other north—had been formed by trucks and snow machines pulling sleds. Recently they'd been used to find deadfall firewood. But now the place was empty, a snow desert of bare willow and alder trees.

Taylor drove through the ruts and stopped just before the loop. She opened her rear hatch to remove her bag and rifle before setting them on the snow. After driving the car halfway around the loop and stopping when she could no longer see the road, she exited her car and trudged back to her gear. She found the bloody fur of some animal just past the berm away from the river. Her heart skipped beats at the unmourned and unknown slaughter in the wilderness. She could be the same.

Shannon approached in her white Suburban. Taylor hoisted her bag and rifle.

"You got it?" Shannon asked while sticking her head covered by a brightly colored knit cap out the window.

"Sure. I'm only seventy."

Shannon laughed.

Taylor pushed her bag along the rear seat and laid her rifle on the floor. Shannon reached across and unlatched the passenger door before Taylor climbed inside. "Thank you," she said, clutching her satchel. "Can you see my car?"

Shannon leaned forward and searched. "Nope." She wore a bright orange ribbed puffy coat and touched her lips with a neutral gloss.

"I thought about leaving it parked at the school, but then everyone would see me when I wanted to use it."

"What about your garage?"

"Too full of crap to move it inside the door. I sure don't want to return to my house as long as Austin is on the loose."

Shannon backed up on the road and then along the firewood path until she could turn around. "Your brother is a murdering piece of shit. I finished most of your book." She reached over and grabbed Taylor's hand. "That night in Arizona was dreadful. I'm so sorry. Grace told me about you both crying in your room."

"Yes," Taylor said. "She's a wonderful girl. Thank you." She squeezed Shannon's hand before letting go. She'd been touched more in the last two days than many years prior. The contact made her realize how much she'd missed the sensation, how deprived she'd been and how hungry she was for more.

"There's been a lot of chatter on the community Facebook page," Shannon said while driving back through the park.

"Do I want to know?"

"Oh, it's about what you'd expect. There's been some guessing about who Brooke is. Allison swears it's you. Others agree. Do you do Facebook?"

"No. Do you?"

"A little. Mainly just to look at what others are saying. The fastest way to make your new book available to everyone is to join the community Facebook page and give them a link to your website to download it. We can set that up later if you want."

Taylor nodded. "Maybe I should steal some of Levi's thunder. I'm sure he's going to reveal my name tonight. I should come out to the world myself and not be exposed by the likes of him."

"Duck down," Shannon said. "There's a car coming."

Taylor lay on her left side. Shannon lifted her hand in a wave at the driver.

"That was Sammy Lee. He's half blind, so I'm sure he didn't see you. Best you stay down there until I get to my house."

Both their phones vibrated. Taylor pulled hers from her pouch.

"Who's that?" Shannon asked.

"From Maddi. Oh no." Taylor's pulse quickened as she read the text. *There's an older man here at the restaurant I've never seen before. His ears perked up when he heard some men talking about Brooke Skipstone while playing pool. He moved closer and listened to them talk about her writing queer books. Then he said he knew a Brooke Skipstone many years ago, but she'd died young in a car accident. They told him there's an author who lives in Clear using Skipstone as a pen name, that she has a website and everything. For thirty minutes, he's been looking at that site and on Amazon.*

Taylor replied. *What does he look like?*

Tall. Medium build. Shaved head with a tat that's mostly covered by a cap. Mean face. Walks with a limp.

Which leg?

Right.

Which was the leg Taylor stabbed that night. He'd limped during court proceedings, but she hadn't known the limp was permanent. She texted. *That must be Austin. Please be careful. He's dangerous, and I'm sure he's carrying a gun.*

If he's the one who killed Brooke, I'll cut off his balls.

No! Please stay away from him.

I'll take a pic before I leave. See ya later.

Shannon turned into her driveway. "What did she say?"

"Can I sit up yet?"

"Sure."

Taylor lifted herself upright and leaned back in the seat, breathing heavily, trying to calm down. "Austin is at Blue Sky. She said, and I quote, 'If he's the one who killed Brooke, I'll cut off his balls.'"

Shannon laughed. "Maddi's always saying stuff like that. But she's not stupid, and she can take care of herself. She won a trophy in girl's wrestling at the state championship during her sophomore year in Fairbanks before she and her mom moved down here. And her dad taught her self-defense before he passed."

"How did he die?"

Shannon frowned. "Drug overdose. Maddi says it was fentanyl. He thought he'd bought oxys. She went after the dealer. That's when her mom thought they'd better leave town before she hurt someone."

A heaviness settled into Taylor's chest. "So much tragedy in her life, yet she remains resilient and happy."

"Finding Grace changed her life. Both their lives, actually."

Taylor scrunched her brows. "The girl I met last night didn't seem to be a wrestler or tough enough to go after drug dealers. She wears wigs and makeup and false eyelashes. She could be a model."

"Maddi's complicated. She likes to look pretty for Grace, but outside the house, she wears no makeup and spikes her real hair to look tough. I've asked her why, but she clams up. Are you ready?"

"Anything special you want me to do?"

"Like put a bag over your head?" Shannon chuckled. "I'm sorry. I know you're nervous. I'm set back in the trees and out of view of neighbors. So just grab your stuff, and I'll let you in."

Both women exited the Suburban. By the time Taylor pulled her bag and gun out of the seat, Shannon had opened the front door.

"Come on back to my room," Shannon said. "I've got a place ready for your things."

Taylor followed Shannon into a neatly arranged, surprisingly large bedroom with a queen-sized bed—a large wicker basket at the end, a dresser, and a sofa along one wall.

Shannon pulled some empty drawers open. "You can use these on the left side of the dresser and put your bag on the basket. I put the sofa in here to sleep on because those girls stay up late and go back and forth to the kitchen. I'd never get any rest in the living room."

Taylor hadn't expected to be in the same room as Shannon, but the idea didn't bother her as much as forcing the woman out of her room. She smiled. "I can sleep on the sofa. There's no reason for you to give up your bed."

"But you're my guest." Shannon reached for Taylor's hands. "I want you to be comfortable."

Taylor tingled at the touch. "We could take turns."

Shannon tilted her head and smiled. "We could do that. But you sleep in the bed tonight."

Taylor hitched a breath when Shannon's blue eyes twinkled, so much like Brooke's. "You'd think two old ladies could share a bed without raising eyebrows." Taylor pulled her hands away and immediately regretted the loss of warmth and affection.

"If that's what you prefer, I'm fine with that." Shannon grinned. "I promise not to drape myself all over you like Brooke."

The memory warmed Taylor's skin. "I loved that about her. In public, she was a queen, always confident and in charge. But in private, she was often vulnerable and needed to be held."

"She needed *you* to hold her. Did you ever consider the possibility that the stage queen you knew for four years in college depended on you for her confidence?"

Taylor sucked in a quick breath as her heart skipped. "She was amazing long before knowing me."

"Yes, but the accolades meant nothing before she met you. She told you at the campground in Carlsbad about her red swing routine. She liked entertaining but not what came after. I'm sure she felt the same in high school. She only enjoyed the praise when it came from you."

Taylor remembered how Brooke always looked for her smile and nod after she rose from her bow at the end of *Twelfth Night*.

"You were the only audience she cared about," Shannon said. "Brooke was surrounded by fans after her audition at the start of freshman year, yet she wanted to be with you."

Taylor's throat squeezed shut, and she sat back on the bed as her eyes flooded with tears. "And then I let her down. I watched Grace reading that chapter today and relived every time I could have driven away from Austin. Everything I did led to her death." She clasped her face and tried to keep the tears from falling.

Shannon sat next to her and pulled Taylor against her shoulder. "Everything you two did made perfect sense at the time. You didn't realize how evil your brother could be. He held a gun to your head, and you didn't back down."

"No, but then he held it to Brooke's head. Maybe if I . . . maybe . . ." She gasped for breaths.

"Shhh." Shannon kissed Taylor's head and stroked her hair. "You were brave, and Brooke was brave. You both did your best. The only villain is Austin. And now we need to make sure he doesn't harm you again."

Taylor clutched Shannon and buried her face against her chest, finding comfort in the woman's warmth and touch. After a few minutes, Taylor stopped crying but clung to Shannon, inhaling her sweet jasmine and patchouli aroma and feeling her squeezable body, untethered beneath loose clothing. "You don't mind?"

Shannon kissed Taylor's head again. "Not at all, sweet lady. 'We all need to be held and loved,' said Crystal Rose. Even the author who created her."

Taylor sat up and found Shannon's eyes. "I haven't been in so many years, only through my characters. Before I heard about Austin's release, my only emotions were theirs. Then I was overwhelmed with fear and anger and everything I had lost because of him. But I had no one to share my feelings with. I was locked in a prison cell, screaming for someone to listen to me, to help me, but all I heard was Marshall's accusations about secret boyfriends and criticism about my writing." She tried to swallow the lump in her throat. "I saw dogs in the village chained to their houses their entire lives, never spoken to or played with. I wondered if that would be my fate until Austin killed me."

Shannon's hands held Taylor's cheeks, her thumbs lightly stroking her eyebrows. "No, Taylor, that will not be your fate, not as long as Grace, Maddi, and I have any breath and energy left to support you. I would have gone nuts in this town if not for those two girls. I had no idea you existed. We could have been friends all this time."

Taylor held Shannon's wrists, keeping her hands against her cheeks. "I wish . . . Maybe we should take the girls and go to your house in Homer tomorrow."

"We could, but Austin would eventually find out where I lived and come after us. We need to remove his threat to your life."

"How?"

"We'll find a way."

"You shouldn't put yourself in danger. You barely know me."

Shannon shook her head. "That's not true. I've taken a crash course in knowing Taylor Baird. I'm halfway through your first novel and will start *The Moonstone Girls* tomorrow. You've bared your soul to me and shared your deepest desires and fears. What turns you on and off. What makes you laugh and cry." She tightened her eyes. "Besides, Alaskan women do not back down to Outsiders with a grudge. He doesn't know what he's up against. Now that I've found you, I'm not letting go so easily."

Taylor hugged her fiercely. "Thank you." She kissed Shannon's cheek. They locked eyes and shared a warm smile. *I'm not letting go either, Shannon.*

Grace flung open the door to her house, still thinking about what she should have done to Allison before Taylor and Jackson stopped her. How could she go back to that school after Spring Break? Couldn't they leave for Homer and finish her classes there? After tossing her pack onto her bed, she went to the kitchen and made a meatloaf sandwich, hoping the leftover from a week ago hadn't spoiled.

Her eyes roamed the walls as she chewed. She didn't want to stay there any longer. The place reeked of bad memories—arguments, fear for her mother's health, paddlings. She'd take more clothes today and come back tomorrow with Maddi for the rest when Levi held his community meeting.

She turned on her Bluetooth speaker to its highest volume and played "I Got the Juice" by Janelle Monae, an especially sexy hip-hop song, the first one she'd ever danced to in front of her mirror. Four years ago, she'd locked her bedroom door and played the song, trying to imitate the dance moves in the music video. Dad had banged the door and shouted for her to turn it off. He wouldn't have such filthy music in his house.

Later he asked what she was doing in her room. "Just dancing in my mirror. Twerking my butt and juking my hips."

His eyes bulged, but all he said was to keep the music down or play it when everyone was out of the house. He never complained to her again.

She got into the habit of driving home for lunch, turning the music up as loud as she could, and stripping in front of her mirror, all in defiance of him and the world. Her brother never came home with her. He'd rather go to a friend's house and smoke weed.

She'd recorded some of her dances to show Maddi. They'd danced together in their room at Gram's but kept the music down out of respect for her.

Maybe tomorrow, she and Maddi would rock the house and dance naked as they took down her posters. Allison's accusation echoed in her mind. *Perverts! You and Maddi!*

She should have said, "Damn right! We have sex every night and love it." But all she could say was, "We're friends." Her father had pounded the message that queers were filth into her head for years. Why couldn't she shake herself free from caring about his opinions?

She'd asked herself that question many times.

She turned on "WAP" by Cardi B and Megan Thee Stallion, rapping the lyrics as she undulated her nude body. She'd done nasty things to this song in front of the mirror. Exhilarating things that a teenage girl would love to do when no one else could see, when the music thumped the walls and no one could hear how bad her singing was. It was always liberating.

When the song ended, she pulled a suitcase out of her closet and filled it. Still naked, she dragged it into the living room and checked the lock to the basement. The number sequence was the same as yesterday —1489. To be sure, she fetched her phone from the bedroom and checked her photo of the lock from the day before.

The same.

Her stomach flipped as she inhaled a deep breath. *He's getting lazy.* She pushed the 9 to 0. Nothing. She pushed it to 8 and clicked. Her heart leaped into her throat. *1488.* The code was 1488. She removed the lock and opened the door.

Grace flipped the light switch and slowly walked down the stairs, her hands trembling along the handrail as her neck prickled. Soundboard covered the ceiling and corner walls where his computer and microphone stood on a large office desk. She flipped another switch, illuminating the entire room. A Nazi flag stretched between the studs of one wall. A photo of Hitler hung next to it.

She almost laughed. Her father was a white supremacist. Like that was a surprise. A quick check of the rest of the walls revealed a few nude posters of adult women, some newspaper articles, and a locked filing cabinet.

All that time she'd wondered what was down there, and this was it?

She took photos of everything, wondering what was the point. Which of his followers would care?

After shooting a picture of a leather-clad dominatrix poster, another light behind the stairs caught her attention. The studs had been covered by sheetrock, creating an enclosed nook. She found another computer monitor on a small table. Wires from above were connected to a nearby switchbox on a table. She followed each strand. Three were stapled to studs under the bathroom and three traveled to different locations in her room. A ladder leaned against the wall.

Tingles swept up the back of her neck and across her face. She raced back to the monitor and switched it on. She gasped as she saw three images of her room—looking out from the mirror, behind her bed, and the corner above her door. And three images from the bathroom—from the mirror, toward the toilet, and above the shower.

Her chest tightened, forcing her to suck hard to get air into her lungs.

He'd recorded all her dancing, including the one she'd just finished. Memories flooded her mind of all she'd done with the hand-held showerhead, which was installed soon after she'd danced to "I Got the Juice."

When she was fourteen.

Grace screamed in rage. She nearly pulled the wires out of the box but slammed her fist onto the table.

He did have child porn. OF HER!

Her heart raced and she panted with nausea, trying to figure out what to do as she paced around the floor.

She couldn't let him know she knew. Everything would have to stay the same, so he wouldn't suspect before she could get the police out there. Sometimes he came home early on Fridays.

And she couldn't look for the cameras. Or stare at her mirror funny.

She'd have to go back into her bedroom, *naked*, knowing he would see, and casually put on her clothes. Bile filled her throat.

Hell, he'd already seen everything she could possibly do, so what did it matter?

After taking photos of the monitor and the wire locations, she opened the drawers at his main desk, looking for thumb drives. Several lay haphazardly in a bowl in the middle drawer, and three numbered drives were lined up near the front. She pulled the drawer out farther and found three in the back. She grabbed those and shut the drawer.

Grace walked up the stairs and closed the door, fastening the lock, and making sure the numbers were set to 1489.

Why was 1488 the code? She Googled and a hate symbol database was the first listing. The number 14 referred to fourteen words—"We must secure the existence of our people and a future for white children." And since H is the eighth letter in the alphabet, 88 referred to Heil Hitler. It was one of the most common white supremacist symbols.

Why hadn't she thought to check on hate group numbers rather than try over eight thousand of the ten thousand possible combinations? She'd been so stupid, giving him way too much credit. He was simply another aggrieved white racist and homophobe, like so many others. And an absolute—*do as I say, not as I do*—hypocrite.

Grace breathed deeply several times before forcing herself to walk back into her room to dress. She faced the mirror as she pulled up her panties, her cheeks burning. When her chin quivered, she turned around to fasten her bra. Her whole body shook while she slipped on her leggings and sweatshirt. Finally, she left her room.

She needed to pee, but she could wait until Gram's.

Never again at that house.

She collapsed in a chair near the front door and bawled. Her own father. Why hadn't she figured it out? He'd threatened to kick her out about the posters, then said nothing more. Of course, he wouldn't. He had a porn star living in his house, providing free videos. He'd expressed his disapproval of her dancing, which made her want to keep doing it just so he could watch from his basement, doing . . . what? Did he . . . or just make money selling them?

Sometimes he'd complained about how she dressed in public, even calling her a slut at times when she'd dressed no differently than other girls. All the while sending out her nude videos.

She slammed her fists into the chair.

Who'd seen her? Who knew she was the twerking teenager?

Who'd believe she'd been unaware of what her father had done? Would anyone think she'd done all those things entirely on her own? Either way, she'd be condemned as a slut, especially by those who'd watched her videos.

She struggled to get enough air into her lungs.

She longed for hugs from Gram and Maddi.

But did she want them to know? Would they change their opinion of her? How would she tell them?

After one last lock check, she grunted moving her bag and stepped outside. Soon she was driving to Gram's, thinking of the best way to get that fucking son of a bitch father of hers.

13

THE TRUTH SHALL SET YOU FREE

Taylor had sat before her computer, trying to muster the courage to tell everyone her story. She knew the general reaction would be very different than what Shannon, Grace, and Maddi had offered her. Marshall's would be mild in comparison to all of his friends'. But it was time to step up and step out. Come what may.

She took a deep breath and started. *My best friend in college was named Brooke Skipstone. For a few days, we were lovers before my brother Austin killed her in 1974 as we drove to Oregon to start new jobs. After he was arrested and I provided evidence against Austin regarding others he had killed, I finished the journey to Medford alone—heartbroken, shunned by my parents, trying to find some reason to live.*

The hollow pain of those final 850 miles once again squeezed her heart.

I started teaching at a private school where Marshall MacKenzie was a math and science teacher and the son of the Headmaster. I adored my students and the shows we presented to our audiences. After two years, Marshall and I married, but I never told him or anyone else about Brooke or Austin.

Years later, after we'd moved to Alaska, our daughter died after a failed attempt to stop drinking and use drugs. Losing her reopened old wounds about the death of the only person I'd loved with all my heart. I found some solace in writing under Brooke Skipstone's name. As far as anyone in the world knows, Brooke is a prize-winning author who lives in Alaska—through me.

I learned months ago that Austin would be released from prison. I had fought against his parole for years, but his sentence was completed in February. He had sworn to kill me because I would not lie to keep him free. I decided I didn't want to die by his hand without anyone knowing about Brooke and me, so I wrote a book I hope some of you will read. It is free and available on my website at the link below.

If you read this, you may understand that two women can truly love each other. And those who hate queers are a threat to everyone.

She was tempted to add *Including Levi and Allison*, but she didn't.

The photo Maddi had sent of Austin had shaken her. Somehow, she had shot him glaring just to the right of the phone. Cold eyes, deep creases on his forehead, no hint of humor. *Here is a photo of my brother Austin at the Blue Sky Lodge today. He was responsible for killing five human beings forty-eight years ago. The only reason he is here is to kill me. He knows where I live but not where I am staying now. If you see him and wish to help me, please post his location on Facebook. Thank you.*

Shannon brought their tea to the table. "Are you finished?"

"I think so," Taylor said, "but you should read it." She turned the computer toward her as she sat down.

Shannon sipped and read. "You adored your students. Did you ever adore Marshall?"

Taylor hesitated, not because she didn't know the answer, but because she'd never told anyone else. "No. He was kind, and I think he loved me, but I never felt the same for him as I did for Brooke. We both loved our students. He'd help with my shows. I helped his kids write their reports and make presentations for science fairs. He was going to become Headmaster after his father retired. It would've been awkward staying at the school if I hadn't married him, and under the circumstances, I didn't see another option."

The tea dulled against Taylor's tongue, and she struggled to swallow. "I never felt real love again until my children were born. But as they grew older, more distant, and more troubled by their own heartaches, I had to lock my feelings up again because they hurt too much." She reached across the table with her hand, hoping Shannon would extend hers.

Shannon wiped tears from her cheek with one hand and held Taylor's with the other. "Children know just when to throw a dagger, and they rarely miss. Grandkids, on the other hand, can be lifesavers."

"You're very lucky to be with Grace."

"Yes, I am." Shannon extended her other hand to Taylor's. "Don't yours have their own phones and email accounts?"

"Yes."

"Then send them your books and tell them directly what you want them to know."

Taylor shook her head. She'd already tried to connect with her sons, and they had rejected her. "Their fathers would not be pleased."

"They're not pleased now, so who cares?" She let go of Taylor. "If they come around at some point, then fine. But don't give up on your grandchildren."

Taylor nodded as a fresh shot of hope tingled her limbs. "I won't. I'll send them something tonight." She turned her computer back around. "Post this?"

Shannon nodded. "Punch the button and wait for the fireworks."

As soon as Taylor posted, Grace opened the front door and stepped inside with a grunt, dropping her suitcase and day pack onto the vinyl floor. She stared at both women, jaw clenched and eyes narrowed, then flung the door closed behind her.

"What's wrong?" Shannon asked, her body stiffening.

Grace breathed more rapidly, tightening her lips, but her chin began quivering, and she lost all semblance of hiding her pain behind anger. Her hands shot to her face, and she began to cry.

Both women hurried to her.

"Grace, what happened?" Taylor asked, putting her arm around her shoulder.

Shannon did the same from the other side, and both led her to a seat at the table. Shannon sat next to her, Taylor across.

"Tell us," Shannon said quietly, stroking her hair. "We're here to help you."

After a few seconds, Grace sat up and lowered her hands, staring at the table. "Dad turned me into a porn star. He's taken videos of me since I was fourteen and sent them who knows where."

Taylor glanced at Shannon, her chest heavy and cold and barely able to breathe.

"I got into the basement and found a Nazi flag and some posters. But the real killer is all the cameras he's mounted in my room and the bathroom. And what's really cool is, before I opened the lock, I gave him one last naked dance to drool over." She raised a slack face to Taylor and stared at something only she could see. "I found a monitor behind the stairs which shows six viewpoints." She barked a hard laugh. "I'm in 3D in my bedroom, but the bathroom offers three unique shots. I can lie back in the tub, spread my legs, and use—"

Shannon's face lost all color as she squeezed Grace close. "Don't punish yourself," her voice quaked. "You've done nothing wrong." She kissed her head. "You're not to blame for what you do in private. He's the bastard. You're innocent."

"But . . ." Grace whimpered.

"But nothing," Shannon said, hugging her tight. "Just let it go. It's over and done. Leave it behind."

Taylor saw herself in the girl, devastated by guilt so long ago, but having no one to hold or console her. Taylor, because of what she hadn't done; Grace, because of what she had. But Shannon's message was true for both of them—*Let it go. Leave it behind. Austin's the bastard.*

"Will he know you were in the basement?" Taylor asked.

"No." She sat up. "I didn't want him to destroy the evidence. I took photos of the setup and grabbed a few flash drives." She pulled one from her pocket. "Maybe I can see how my dancing has improved. Or not." She wiped her face.

"Who will you call?" Shannon asked.

"No one around here. All the troopers love him. Probably the FBI." Grace's phone dinged. She found a message from Maddi.

Where are you?

At Gram's. Why?

Just overheard Austin talking to Levi on the phone.

"Shit!" Grace blurted. "Austin's here?"

"Maddi texted us earlier that he's at Blue Sky," Taylor said.

Grace thumbed her phone. "Well, now he's talking to the pervert." Grace replied to Maddi—*About what?*

Taylor's Facebook post. Everyone here's talking about Taylor admitting she's Brooke Skipstone and a lesbian. A couple of men spotted Austin and showed him the photo you posted. Austin screamed, "She's a fucking liar!" He's getting ready to leave. Stay at Gram's. I'll be there soon.

Grace lifted her eyes to Taylor. "You told everyone the truth on Facebook?"

Taylor nodded slightly. "Yes, I did." Her chest swelled with pride but quickly emptied. Nothing good was coming.

"Cool," Grace said with a glint in her eye, but her lips still curled back with disgust. "Looks like Austin is going to hook up with the pervert."

"How would Austin know Levi?" Taylor asked.

"Maybe he heard people talking about his podcast."

"Okay, but how would he know his number?"

"They're both racist pigs," Grace said. "Maybe there's a directory we don't know about."

A light switched on in Taylor's head. "Austin joined the Aryan Brotherhood in prison. Levi's a Neo-Nazi. Maybe he's in the same group."

"But what would he want with Levi?" Shannon asked.

"Information about me," Taylor said. "My address, for instance. Maybe he planned to stay at Levi's until he eliminated me. His house is less than two hundred yards from mine."

"Wow," Grace said. "What would've happened if I was there when Austin showed up?"

"Has he ever complained about you being gone every night?" Shannon asked.

"It hasn't been every night until about two weeks ago," Grace said. "Before that, he'd make a snide comment or two, mainly about you. But he's said nothing recently. I've gone to his house for a little while almost every day when he's gone."

"What about yesterday when you brought me the book to sign?" Taylor asked.

"He sent me a text to stop by before I went to school." She snapped her fingers like she'd remembered something. "He told me if I didn't bring it back, he'd change all the locks so I couldn't get inside the house, which bothered me because I still wanted to get into the basement."

"Which he knew," Shannon said. "As long as you couldn't get in, you went home every day to try."

"But now you won't," Taylor said, "because you couldn't stand to look at him." Her pulse quickened to keep up with the rush of ideas in her brain. "On the same day that Austin is meeting Levi. This seems too convenient. What would you have done if Levi had told you to stay away from the house for a few days?"

Grace harrumphed. "Probably gone over just to spite him."

Taylor exchanged a glance with Shannon. "How'd you break the code on that lock?"

"He'd left the numbers in the same position as yesterday—1489. He'd never done that before. I thought he was getting lazy and just forgot to spin all the dials, so I tried moving the nine to zero then to eight, and it opened." Grace stood, her mouth open and eyes bulging. "He did it on purpose! He wanted me to know about the cameras." Grace clenched her fists and snarled. " And stay away from the house while Austin is his guest."

Grace ran to her pack by the door, pulled out her school computer, and hurried back to the table. "Let's see what's on these flash drives." She inserted the one she'd left on the table and double-clicked the image. One jpeg file was visible. She clicked on it and found a typed document with her signature and Levi's at the bottom. The two women looked over Grace's shoulder as she scrolled through *Contract for Video Services.*

"What the fuck is this?" Grace shouted.

Taylor's heart pounded as she skimmed through the words. "According to this, when you turned eighteen, you agreed to the installation of cameras in the house and to engage in nude activities, which would be recorded and distributed by your father, who would deposit half of all proceeds into your college savings account."

"I've never seen this before!" Grace pleaded.

Shannon held her shoulders. "Do you remember him asking you to sign anything after your birthday?"

Grace sucked in breaths. "Some. One had to do with transferring my savings to my own account. Another put the truck in my name. But I never agreed to this contract crap."

"Did you read any of the documents?" Shannon asked. "Or did you just sign where he pointed?"

"Where he'd put an X. God, how stupid can I be?" She yanked out the drive and inserted another, finding the same contract image. She tried the last drive and found the same. "So no matter which drive I took, I'd see this document and do what?"

"Not call the FBI," Taylor said.

"Why not?" Grace blurted. "This signature doesn't mean anything. He's just covering his ass."

"But it would be hard to prove otherwise," Taylor said. "Still, what would he expect you to do?"

"I don't know. Maybe he'll claim he didn't know what he was signing—that I installed the cameras to get him in trouble."

"How do you know there are actual cameras?" Shannon asked. "You saw a box and wires and images on a monitor, which could be a compilation of photos he took for his screensaver image. Was the monitor even connected to a computer? It's like he wants you to accuse him so he can humiliate you."

Grace growled in frustration. "Because that's what woke lefties do —go crazy about stuff that supposedly doesn't matter, like Confederate flags and statues of Robert E. Lee and using the right pronouns." She pounded the table. "Damn it! I know he's got recordings of me."

Taylor stood and paced a few steps. "Maybe he wanted you to go into the basement to see the wires and make assumptions so you'd accuse him. Then he'd counter by claiming you tricked him into signing the document, that *you* planted the flash drives, even strung the wires which aren't connected to cameras at all."

Shannon said, "He wanted you out of the house because Austin would be there."

Taylor placed her hands on the back of a chair. "You said Levi stopped caring whether you spent the night here about two weeks ago?"

Grace nodded.

"Maybe that's when he first heard from Austin. With you gone, he could have installed the cameras or just the wires."

Shannon rose. "In any case, Levi wants to portray you as a liar. No matter what you say about the basement, he'll twist it around and accuse you because you're a liberal, a Black Lives Matter and Antifa supporter—"

"And queer," Grace said.

"Does he know?" Shannon asked.

"If the cameras are real and he started using them years ago, he would know. Maddi and I went home at lunch and even sometimes after school last year." She flattened her lips against her teeth. "I'll bet those videos were best-sellers."

"Another thing," Taylor said, "he knew you wouldn't remove the cameras or do anything to signal to him you were there. But by not doing anything or confronting him soon, he'll claim that's proof you knew all along."

Grace kicked out her feet and leaned back in the chair, staring at the ceiling. "And then I went back in front of the mirror nude and got dressed. Why would any respectable girl do that, knowing her father would see her?" She covered her face with her hands and screamed, "Shit!"

Taylor's phone rang. Marshall's name appeared on the screen. "Hello?"

"I've been getting lots of calls about that Facebook post," Marshall grumbled.

Taylor switched to speaker and sat down. "Are you calling to see if I'm safe or to criticize me?" She glanced at Shannon.

"Why, Taylor?"

"Why did I embarrass you? Or how did I finally summon the courage to out myself?" She paused for a response. When all she heard was his breathing, she continued. "Levi was going to reveal the real Brooke Skipstone tonight. I just beat him to it." She sucked in a breath. "What did you say to your friends? Did you defend me at all?"

"I told them to read your book."

"Like you did?" she said hopefully, a flutter in her belly.

"Most of it." He paused. "That brother of yours was a total asshole."

"Because he hated queers?"

"Because he killed Brooke," he snapped. He lowered his voice. "You two . . . you two seemed to really love each other."

She sighed. Shannon stood and moved toward her. "Yes, we did."

Marshall cleared his throat. "You always seemed so happy at school. I never would have guessed you'd experienced something so traumatic."

"I was an actress, playing a part. I cried every night in my apartment. The kids made me smile and laugh at school." She paused, debating whether she should continue stating the lie she'd told her kids —that he'd always made her laugh. But it was too late for lies. She closed her eyes. "I tried as hard as I could to love you, Marshall." Her throat squeezed shut, and she tried to blink back tears.

Shannon touched her shoulders from behind.

A breath hitched in his chest. "I guess no one could have filled the hole in your heart that Brooke left."

"No." Taylor held Shannon's hand. "I know you tried."

"Are you safe?" he asked with an edge in his voice.

She was surprised by the question. Grace nodded to her. "As much as I can be right now."

"How'd you get a picture of Austin at Blue Sky?" The edge grew sharper. "You weren't there, were you?"

"No." The *safe* question, she realized, was merely to find out where she was and who with. "A friend of mine sent it. But Austin's with Levi now."

"With Levi? How do . . . I just spoke to him."

"Really? Why?"

"I asked him to not talk about you tonight because you'd already confessed." With no tenderness, he said, "I didn't see the point."

She bit her tongue. He didn't see the point in being put through more humiliation. "But Levi said no because I didn't tell the whole story."

"Something like that." He snorted and bit his words. "How did *you* know?"

"Because Austin will tell his side of the story, and he's had forty-eight years to dream up alternative facts." She tried to ignore the bitter taste in her mouth. "You might be interested to hear what he has to say. I know I am."

"He was convicted and sent to jail!" he barked. "How can anyone believe him?"

"Unfairly convicted, he'll say. Besides, almost half the country believes an election was stolen, and the government wants to control us with vaccines. Almost everything Levi says is a lie, yet most of this town agrees with him. As soon as they hear Austin's version of events, and Levi agrees, many will side with my brother."

Shannon opened her iPad and signaled to Taylor they had two minutes.

Taylor nodded. "Maybe Austin will raise some doubt in your mind. I'll post my rebuttals as he speaks on Facebook."

"Since when do you have a Facebook account?" he whined.

"A friend helped me this afternoon."

"The same friend who sent you that photo?"

"No, that's someone else."

His anger rose. "Since when do you have all these friends I don't know about?"

"No need to worry, Marshall. None of them are male." Her muscles tensed. "I need to go. Good-bye." She ended the call.

"I hate to say this," Grace interjected, "but he seems more concerned about himself than you."

Taylor raised her brows and slipped the phone back into her pouch. "You caught that, did you?"

"Wasn't hard."

Taylor could never understand Marshall's jealousy and accusations. He didn't love her. He just wanted to possess her. He'd been the only one to cheat, after which his suspicions and accusations against her only intensified—the very definition of projection.

And as often as she had said he didn't care about her, he had never claimed he did.

Shannon turned up the volume to reveal Levi's theme music—"We the People" by Kid Rock, a hard-driving song full of *fuck you's* and *Let's go, Brandon.*

As the song faded, Levi shouted, "Let's go, Brandon" in sync with Kid Rock as another voice started laughing in the background.

Austin's.

Taylor's pulse raced.

He clapped and laughed then, just before the end, he said, "What a great song! I've never heard it."

"Kid Rock released that in late January," Levi said. "I think it's his best."

"Sums everything up, doesn't it?"

"Yes, it does. Good evening, folks. That other voice you hear is none other than Austin Baird, Taylor Baird MacKenzie's brother, just released from prison for crimes he claims he didn't commit. For those of you who haven't checked Facebook recently, Taylor posted her confession to writing queer books under the name of Brooke Skipstone, who—get this now—was Taylor's lover in college. Bet finding that out didn't sit well with her husband of forty-six years! What do you say, Marshall?"

Shannon looked to the ceiling. "Oh, Lord. This is going to be worse than I thought."

Taylor opened her computer lid, refreshed her Facebook page, and readied her fingers to type. She'd fight back with facts.

After a good laugh, Levi continued, "She also claims that her brother wants to kill her. And she wants all of us to read her newest queer book about how Brooke Skipstone died. But Austin says don't bother because it's full of lies. Is that right, Austin?"

"Damn right."

"So you're telling us you were wrongly imprisoned."

"Yes, I was. For forty-eight years, all because of the lies my sister told."

"Sometimes we hear of a prisoner being released after spending years in jail, but most of those have been black. At least that's what I remember."

"That's exactly right," Austin said. "Over half of released prisoners are black. And guess why that is?"

"You tell me."

"Because the entire legal system is rigged against white people."

. . .

"Oh, my God," blurted Grace. "Half of wrongfully convicted prisoners are black because of the prejudice they experience that puts them into prison in the first place."

"Your sister says you were responsible for five deaths," Levi said. "How does she come to that number?"

"Five, huh?" Austin laughed. "I was only charged with two. A couple of my friends and I went drinking downtown. My friend Tony, drunk by that time, got the hots for a lady singer at a club. So they went to her dressing room to mess around. Except Tony discovered *she* was a *he* in drag. Tony went berserk and beat the queen to death. He ran out of the bar with me and Phillip close behind, only we didn't know what had happened. Later, Tony told us what he'd done, and we all went home. We didn't know that the club was run by the Mexican Mafia. The next day they killed Tony and Phillip. I still don't know why they didn't get me."

Taylor started typing her rebuttals, trying to stifle the screams of frustration climbing up her chest.

Austin continued, "Taylor and Brooke were driving to Oregon because they had jobs waiting for them. They asked me to come along for protection, so I said yes. I'd never met Brooke before, but it was obvious from the get-go that she liked me. She kept smiling and showing off her legs and saying nice things to me. But Taylor wasn't happy about that. At the time, I couldn't understand why she glared at me and always stepped in when Brooke and I got to talking. I had no idea my sister was a predator queer. I don't think Brooke knew either."

"I knew he'd go there," Shannon said.

Grace flung herself out of her chair with a "Jesus!"

"It only gets worse," Taylor said while typing the truth to counter his lies.

"The first night," Austin said, "we stayed in a campground in New Mexico. The two girls had a van to sleep in while I'd brought my tent. We were eating dinner at a picnic table and drinking beer, Brooke laughing and flashing those big blue eyes of hers, and right in the middle of it, Taylor pulls Brooke away and says she wants to walk around. Brooke said, 'C'mon, Austin, go with us.' But Taylor said, 'No, he's got to clean the table and put up his tent.' After an hour, they come back, Taylor's arm hooked on Brooke's, and she gives me a look like, 'Please get me away from this girl.' I tried, but Taylor said they needed to take a shower."

"Oh, my God," Grace said as she paced the floor, "here comes the best part."

"The next morning, I went to the camp store, and some guy tells me what happened that night. Brooke was screaming because Taylor had attacked her. Someone called the sheriff, who talked to them at three in the morning for disturbing the campground. Then later, he filed a report, identifying the van and its location and where the girls were headed, which was all the Mexican Mafia needed to know where I was."

Shannon shook her head. "If Taylor attacked Brooke, then why didn't Brooke tell that to the sheriff? This is such obvious bullshit."

. . .

Austin continued, "The next day, we were followed by two guys in a red Cadillac. At one place we stopped for gas, those guys went inside the store, and I'm positive Taylor talked to them. She told them where we would stop and that I slept in a tent. Sure enough, at a rest stop in Arizona, that car showed up and ran over my fucking tent. I was hiding behind one of those picnic tables, so I came out shooting and got them both. I jumped into the van and drove that sucker out of there. The girls were screaming, 'What happened?' but I didn't tell them anything until we were on the interstate. When I did, Brooke jumped up into the passenger seat, asking if I was hurt and how did those men know where we were, and on and on."

Taylor looked up from her computer and said, "No, Grace, *here* comes the best part."

"So I told Brooke the truth," Austin said. "Taylor wanted those men to kill me because I'm her competition. Then all hell broke loose. Brooke and Taylor got into a huge fight. And then a cop started chasing us. The girls were screaming at each other. Taylor actually pulled Brooke out of the front seat, so then they're wrestling with each other. I told them I needed to stop to see what the cop wanted, and Taylor screamed at me to speed up. Then Taylor pushed Brooke against the side sliding door, which popped open. I was trying to slow down in case she fell out. Brooke was screaming at me for help. Then Taylor kicked her out of the van."

"Are you kidding?" Levi asked. "Taylor kicked her out?"

"Exactly right. I stopped as soon as I could. Taylor got out first and ran back to the police, screaming at them that I had killed Brooke. They arrested me. The only two people I killed were those two Mafia members, and that was self-defense. My parents went broke hiring lawyers to defend me, but nothing could stop Taylor's lies."

"That's quite the story, Austin," Levi said.

"That's the God's honest truth."

"So why did you come to Alaska? Do you intend to kill your sister?"

"Why would I want to kill my sister, even though she stole my entire life from me? I spent forty-eight years in jail for murders I didn't commit. I have no intention of going back to jail because of her again."

"Then what do you want?"

"I want her to admit what she did and apologize to me. That's it. She's already admitted to being queer. Confessing to being a murderer is hardly worse than that."

"I hear you," Levi said.

"Taylor," Austin said, "if you're listening and want to do the right thing, call Levi, and we can set up a meeting."

"Actually," Levi said, "I'm calling a community meeting at my church tomorrow at five o'clock so everyone can air their grievances about the queering that's happening in Clear and the rest of America. Taylor, you're certainly welcome to come and seek forgiveness if you want. Austin, will you join us?"

"If Taylor goes, I'll be there. Thank you, Levi, for giving me this opportunity to share my story. I've wanted to . . ." His voice cracked. "I've wanted to tell my side for forty-eight years. Thank you."

"You're very welcome, Austin. The truth will set you free. Now, folks, we've got much more to get to this evening, so be sure to come back after this message from our sponsors."

As a commercial for diet supplements started, Shannon lowered the volume.

The last thing Taylor typed was, *The troopers arrested Austin after he held his gun to my head while I knelt before Brooke's broken body. Austin's fingerprints were found on the drag queen's body, whose name was Luis. Austin's prints were also found on the sink in the dressing room and other places. One of the men Austin shot that night did not die. Diego said his brother Luis was a beautiful human being who should have been a woman. All the evidence is available in the public record.*

Austin called me last night and said, "I'm sorry I didn't kill you when I had the chance. But karma is a bitch. You'll get yours."

What do you think he meant?

Taylor posted her message and closed her computer—breathless, head pounding, her throat aching as if she'd screamed for several minutes. But it had all been in her mind.

"I'm sure you don't want to hear the rest of his broadcast," Shannon said.

"No," Taylor replied, trying to calm down. "We need to help Grace decide what to do about Levi. The only way to defeat lies is to keep shouting the truth. No matter the consequences. I should have done that years ago."

14

IT'S ALL A LIE

Grace's phone dinged. She pulled it from her back pocket. "Maddi's on her way."

"Good," Taylor said. "She should have a voice in this."

"The pervert," Grace said, "will know that Taylor is hiding with me. And I'm at Gram's."

"I know," Taylor said. "It's time we persuade him not to tell that to Austin. Grace, I want you to describe what you found in the basement today without mentioning your dancing or removing your clothes. Don't make any accusations against Levi. Don't give him something to deny. You went home at lunch like normal and checked the lock like you always do because you've been so curious about what's down there. Keep it dry and simple."

"Okay, but why?" Grace asked.

"Because you're going to tell your father you will post that description to Facebook along with your photos and the document you supposedly signed unless he agrees not to tell Austin where he thinks I am."

A smile spread across Grace's face. "He can't deny facts and photos from his basement. Let the dear citizens of Clear come to their own conclusions. I'm on it." She started typing.

Taylor walked to the refrigerator. "I'm starving, Shannon. Do you have any cheese?" She opened the door.

"Yes, I do. It's in the first pull-out drawer. Kerrygold Reserve Cheddar. You'll love it."

Taylor found an open block in a Ziplock bag. She cut off a chunk with a paring knife on the counter and took a bite. "Mmmm. This is good." Her mouth flooded with saliva and her hunger pangs melted away. "I can't live without cheese. You'll have to bring some to my house when we go there later." She nibbled the piece quickly like a chipmunk.

"We're going to your house?" Shannon asked with wide eyes.

"What?" Grace asked, her fingers still moving along her keyboard.

"Levi will promise not to tell Austin where Gram lives," Taylor said, "but that will be a lie. He'll drop Austin off, or they'll check out this house, but we'll be at my place because everyone knows I'm not there." She pointed to a security camera on top of a kitchen cabinet. "I noticed you have the same security system I do. We can leave a couple of lights on and disconnect the door sensors, so they don't ding when the door is opened. That way, they won't suspect a camera watching them. If Austin shows up, you'll get a notification on your phone, and we can watch him on video. If that happens, Grace will post her note about what she found in the basement."

"Okay," Shannon said, her brows scrunching her forehead. "If he shows up here and doesn't find us, won't he check your house?"

"Most likely," Taylor said, "but we'll have time to prepare for them. We should leave soon. I want Grace to send her note just before we go."

"I'll pack a few things," Shannon said as she went to her room.

"Taylor," Grace said, "do you want to look at this while I grab my stuff?"

"Sure." Taylor sat in the chair Grace had just vacated and skimmed through what she'd written. "This is perfect, Grace."

"Thank you!" she yelled from the other bedroom.

Taylor read through the "contract" more carefully this time. *Such bullshit. How long did it take Levi to come up with this?* She peered at Grace's signature and noticed some specks. She wiped the screen, thinking they were dust, but the dots didn't move. She clicked on the magnifying glass icon until the signature filled the page. "Well, look at that." She dragged her finger over sections of a line through the signature that hadn't been completely erased. "Hey, Grace, you need to see this."

"What?" She entered the room, stuffing clothes into a sports bag.

"You didn't sign this. He took a picture of your signature on something else and did a lousy job of pasting it. See the lines?"

Her mouth fell open. "Yes, I do. Shit! That makes me feel better."

Taylor took a screenshot of the enlarged section. "You should add another sentence or two pointing out this forgery." She moved the image to the left until Levi's signature showed and took another screenshot. "And point out this signature is clean. You never signed this document."

Shannon emerged from her room with a rolling carry-on suitcase and a shotgun. "I'm ready."

"Don't forget the cheese," Taylor said as she darted into Shannon's room to retrieve her bag and rifle. When she returned to the living room, Shannon disconnected the door chimes from her alarm system. "Did you turn off your light, Grace?"

"Yes. What do you want my message to be?"

"I will post everything on Facebook if you so much as hint to Austin where Gram's house is. I'll know if you do."

Grace's thumbs tapped her screen. "Done."

"Tell Maddi to meet us at my house. Are we ready?"

"Let's go," Shannon said. "Grace, we'll follow you."

In another minute, both vehicles backed into F street and headed to Third.

"Should you tell Marshall we're coming?" Shannon asked.

"I guess." She texted. *I'm bringing friends home with me. Two minutes.* Taylor sighed. "I've never brought a friend to my house before. Marshall won't know what to do. He's invited some of his friends for dinner, but that was years ago." Her stomach ached at the confession of her lonely existence, but her chest fluttered with excitement. "We'll have a girls' night in."

Shannon turned left on D Street. "What about Marshall?"

"He sleeps upstairs. We'll be downstairs." Her phone dinged.

From Marshall: *Who?*

Taylor replied. *Grace and her grandmother, Shannon. We're spending the night. Do not tell anyone.*

"How will he react to Grace and Maddi?" Shannon asked.

"He'll be banished upstairs by then. I wasn't expecting guests, so—"

Shannon chuckled. "There's no need to worry, Taylor. We're not here for an inspection."

"I know. I just hope I remembered to flush the toilet before I left this morning."

Shannon barked a laugh. "If it's yellow, let it mellow has always been my philosophy. Everyone's piss looks the same."

Grace turned right onto Fourth Avenue and drove slowly toward Taylor's house. Before the garage, the snow berms rose high and squeezed the driveway. Shannon's Suburban passed through with just a few inches to spare on either side.

The two vehicles parked side by side near the main entrance to Taylor's house. Six-foot tall berms nestled them on three sides. Marshall's snowblower had thrown the white dust just to the top before it slid down the face, broadening the hills after each storm. A narrow gap pointed to steps and the door, which Marshall opened.

"Need any help?" he asked.

Grace popped out of her truck. "Hey, Mr. MacKenzie. I'm good." She pulled her bags from the bed.

"How about you ladies?"

"No ladies here," Shannon said as she hoisted her bag and gun. "Just kick-ass women assigned at birth."

Taylor guffawed. She turned to Marshall, carrying her bag. "Marshall, meet Shannon, my new best friend."

Marshall stood blinking in the doorway, preventing the women from moving into the house.

"Marshall," Taylor said, "you're blocking our way."

"Oh. Sorry." He walked through the mud room and stood by the refrigerator, scratching his ear.

Shannon shut the doors behind her.

"Where do you want me?" Grace asked.

"Down the hall, last bedroom on the left," Taylor replied as she set her satchel on her office chair.

Grace moved out of the kitchen.

"Follow me, Shannon," Taylor said as she walked through the pantry and utility room into the bedrooms on the east side of the house. She glanced around quickly for stray clothes or used tissues. Seeing the panties she'd changed out of that morning on her bed's rumpled sheets, she promptly dropped her bag, covering them. "This is where I sleep. Put your bag on the other bed for now."

"Is this where you want me to sleep?" Shannon asked with a slight grin.

Taylor cocked a brow and fixed her eyes on Shannon's. "We'll decide that later." Then she noticed Marshall standing in the doorway, frowning. Her chest tightened as Shannon turned back and rolled her eyes.

Waving her hand at the man, Taylor said, "Marshall built this extension seventeen years ago all by himself. At first, it was going to be an exercise area and game room, but when our kids' families came up, we turned it into bedrooms. Your room is where I grow my flowers and veggies, but I didn't plant anything this year."

"Why is that?" Marshall asked, folding his arms. "You never told me."

"You never asked. If Austin kills me, you'd have had a big mess to clean back here. I saved you the trouble." She couldn't stand Marshall's accusatory stare. "C'mon, Shannon, I want to show you my office." She moved toward the doorway, but Marshall blocked her.

Lowering his voice, he said, "Can I talk to you for a second?"

"Why?"

"Excuse me," Shannon said as she wedged past the man. "I'll go flush your toilet, Taylor."

"Don't look first," Taylor cried after her with a nervous laugh as Marshall moved into the room and closed the door behind him. Her face burned. "What the hell are you doing?"

"I want to know what's going on between you two." He tightened his eyes. "Are you two sleeping together? In my house?"

"She's my friend. Not my lover. I just met her yesterday."

"Then why did you bring them here? To rub your new relationships in my face?"

Taylor laughed and shook her head. "Yes, Marshall, you're the motivation behind all my actions. I write to humiliate you. I stay by myself to anger you. I find friends to make you jealous. How can you stand living with all my abuse?"

He clenched his jaw. "It's hard. Especially this last week."

She looked at this man, her husband according to some pieces of paper, and couldn't believe she'd stuck with him all these years. "I'm sure this past week has been very difficult for you."

"Yes, it has, so why did you bring your *friends* home with you?"

She tried to maintain her composure. "Because Austin is at Levi's, who knows Grace stays with Gram. Levi knows Grace and I are friends, so where else would I be hiding except at her house? Austin will likely go to Shannon's house tonight, looking for me."

"He said he doesn't want to kill you."

She gasped. "And you believe him?"

His eyes darted everywhere except to hers. "He seems pretty convinced you lied to put him in prison."

Anger heated her chest. "Even after all the facts I posted to refute everything he said, you doubt what he did?"

"I didn't say I doubted, but there are several who do."

"They believe Austin because he lies with such conviction and anger. And he's not queer." She blew out a breath. "Why do you care whether I hug Shannon or sleep in the same bed? You and I haven't touched in years. You don't even like me, yet you stood in that doorway like a spurned teenager. Move on, Marshall. I'll either be dead soon or gone. There is no third option. Please go upstairs." She opened the door and left him behind, trying to shed her anger.

Maddi's squeals filled her ears as Taylor entered the kitchen and found both girls hugging each other.

"Hey!" Maddi ran over and squeezed Taylor. "Your brother is a total asshole. I could have kicked out his knees when he went to the bathroom at Blue Sky, but someone came out just as he pulled the door open." Her eyes widened as she looked over Taylor's shoulder. "Who's this?"

"That is Marshall," Taylor said. "He lives upstairs."

His mouth dropped open as he stared at his wife.

Maddi reached out her hand to him. "I'm Maddi, Grace's girl-friend. Nice to meet you."

Marshall barely nodded to her.

Maddi lunged back to Grace and kissed her lips. "So Grace and I are down the hall. Where are you, Gram?"

Shannon smiled. "You know the room Haley and Crystal cleared for Payton and Bekah?"

"The one where Crystal ate Haley out until she screamed?"

"Yes, that one. There are two rooms through the pantry. Taylor is in one, and I'm in the other."

"Oooh. That should be fun." Maddi winked twice.

Marshall stammered. "Who . . . who are you talking about?"

"Crystal and Haley in *Crystal's House of Queers*," Maddi said. "Taylor's book. You haven't read it?"

Marshall scrunched his brows and scratched his ear.

"We're all fans of Taylor's writing," Shannon said. "She's a brilliant author. Don't you think so?"

Marshall's mouth opened and closed several times, but no words emerged. Finally, he said, "I'll be in my room if you need anything, Taylor." He left the kitchen and plodded up the stairs.

The four women bit their lips and stared at each other with bemused eyes until they heard the upstairs door slam shut.

"What's up with him?" Maddi asked.

Taylor shook her head. "He wants to possess what he doesn't want and accept misery to avoid embarrassment."

Maddi rolled her eyes. "That sounds unhealthy."

"It is," Taylor said as she put her arms around both girls. "Please stay as open and spontaneous as you are now, and don't hide yourselves from the world. People need to see what real joy is."

"Not hiding is the kicker," Grace said. "Teachers are fired because they mention their same-sex spouses to their students. How many states are passing laws against queer rights? Soon they'll banish Pride Month."

"Which is why you have to help them understand they're wrong," Shannon said. "Your happiness with each other is infectious."

"I saw horror on Marshall's face," Maddi said.

"Learn to ignore it," Taylor said.

"Like you ignore your brother's threats?" Maddi asked. "Hate for queers never stopped, but people tried to hide it. Now they hear their leaders say out loud what they thought to themselves, which gives them permission to expose their hate. 'I don't want my kid taught by a queer. I don't want to see movies and TV shows about queers. I don't want a man in a girl's restroom.' And on and on. Get rid of Austin and Levi, and maybe there's a chance, but right now, people can't get enough of what the haters say."

"So we expose them for what they are," Taylor said. "Let's eat something first, then make plans. I've got chicken fajita strips I can heat up with peppers and onions or Mandarin orange chicken on rice or a frozen lasagna, but that will take the longest."

"What's a fajita?" Maddi asked.

"Are you kidding me?" Taylor rolled her eyes. "Spicy chicken in a flour tortilla with queso, refried beans, and guacamole."

"I understood about half that sentence," Maddi said.

"Same here," Grace added.

Taylor shook her head in disbelief. "The only thing I miss about Texas is Mexican food. I will not allow you to be deprived of eating a fajita."

"Fine with me," Shannon said. "I love fajitas. Mind if I help?"

"All you want," Taylor said. "Give us twenty minutes, girls."

Grace flung her arm around Maddi's shoulders. "That's just enough time to bring Maddi up to speed on the pervert."

"What pervert?" Maddi asked.

"Come back here, and I'll tell you." They walked down the hall.

Taylor opened her freezer and found the bag of chicken strips. "A can of refried beans is in the pantry."

"On it," Shannon said.

Soon they were chopping onions and multi-colored peppers, adding cumin and chili powder to the beans, and black truffle hot sauce to sour cream. Shannon heated tortillas in one pan while Taylor sautéed the chicken and veggies with butter in a skillet.

"I like cooking with you," Taylor said. "I hope we can do it more often."

"Anytime you want," Shannon answered.

"How do you think Maddi will respond to Grace's story?"

"She'll be mad as hell and want revenge," Shannon replied, "especially if they discover the cameras are real and have been used for years. I think Levi's counting on them being too embarrassed to go after him." She rolled her eyes. "Only sluts dance nude or have sex in front of mirrors, after all."

"Would they be embarrassed?"

"Not Maddi. She knows the people who would slut shame them are the same ones watching lesbian porn on their computers and phones."

"I think we're ready. Do you want to tell the girls, and I'll set plates?"

"Sure." Shannon walked down the hall.

Taylor arranged all the food on her granite island and stacked plates on a counter. She peeled the top from a guacamole tub and mixed in some onions, chopped tomatoes and jalapeños, salt, and lemon juice.

Cooking for Marshall had become drudgery, but this reminded her of better times with her children and grandkids before the pandemic. She'd always cooked them a hearty breakfast until they moved out and was disappointed to learn their children were often given cereal and protein bars in the morning. But when they visited, they enjoyed omelets, Dutch baby pancakes covered with fruit and whipped cream, and brisket and egg tacos. This summer would have been her grandkids' first visit in three years. Would her food have tasted different to them, knowing she's queer? She'd probably never find out.

"He's a fucking pervert!" Maddi yelled as she stomped through the hall toward the kitchen. "One way or the other, I'm going to get him."

"*We* are going to get him," Grace said, following on Maddi's heels.

Shannon stood behind them, sharing a glance with Taylor. "Let's eat, and then we can decide what to do."

Taylor took a plate and removed a tortilla from the warmer. "Let me show you how it's done." The girls watched as she built her fajita, topping it off with guac and some shredded cabbage.

Maddi ate a chicken strip. "Yum!" She dipped her finger in everything else, sucking off the food with a slurp and another "Yum!" and "This is really good, Taylor."

"Thank you." Little sparks danced across her skin.

"Or you could use a spoon," Grace said as she held out the utensil.

"Why?" Maddi asked. "Then we'd have to wash it. Aren't you supposed to eat this with your hands?"

Taylor grinned. "Exactly right, Maddi."

Maddi sucked her finger again as she hurried to the table to sit.

"What do you want to drink?" Taylor asked.

"Beer," Maddi said.

"White wine if you have it," Grace said.

Taylor glanced at Shannon, who nodded. "I let them have a little at my house. Grace likes Moscato."

Taylor hitched a breath. "Like Brooke." She caught Grace's eyes, and they shared a smile.

Taylor brought glasses and a few beers to the table. She pulled a wine bottle from the wire rack on the refrigerator and unscrewed the top. "My sons' wives said they liked Moscato before they visited years ago but never drank any, so I have several in the rack. I'd love to share this with you." She poured a glass for Grace. "Shannon?"

"Please." She held out a glass.

Taylor poured Shannon's, then one for herself. So many memories filled Taylor's mind of Brooke holding a wine glass, moving gracefully over the wooden floor in their apartment as she practiced scenes. Then the last time they drank wine together in the van . . .

"Taylor," Shannon said softly. "Earth to Taylor."

Her memories blurred and faded, leaving an image of Shannon holding her glass for a clink. "Oh, sorry. Cheers." Taylor smiled and touched her glass to Shannon's.

"You left us for a minute." Shannon smiled.

"Happens all the time."

For the next ten minutes, they cleaned their plates and had seconds. Maddi and Grace ate whatever was left.

Taylor drained her glass and set it down. "What did Levi say?"

"He called me," Grace said. "Just after I told Maddi about dancing in the mirror and the wires in his basement. She heard everything he said."

Maddi added, "He called because he didn't want to see his text posted on Facebook."

"He said if I post what I sent him," Grace said, "he will drive Austin to Gram's himself. I told him, 'Go ahead. Gram and I will likely shoot him, but Maddi will want to bleed him out slowly.' He asked, 'Who's Maddi?' 'My girlfriend,' I said. 'I plan to introduce her to everyone at your meeting tomorrow.' He started screaming, telling me not to come anywhere near his church. And I better not be a queer. I said, 'But Daddy, you've got the videos of me and Maddi having sex in my bedroom. You've known the truth about me all this time and never said a word to me. Never tried to punish me for my transgressions or persuade me to like guys. And why is that? Because your congregation will want to know why you allowed queers to have sex in your house on multiple occasions without telling us to stop once. Why didn't you, Daddy? But they'll understand once they know about your porn videos.' He screamed some more and said, 'If you say one word about being queer, I'll . . .' 'What, Daddy?' I asked. 'What will you do?' 'Austin and I will come after all of you.' Then he hung up."

Taylor's stomach dropped, and a vice squeezed her chest. Now all of her friends were in danger, not just her. Maybe she should have stayed silent and accepted her fate. She caught Shannon's glance and couldn't hide her fear.

Shannon grabbed her hand. "We're here for you."

Maddi finished her beer and sucked in her lips. "He never once denied having videos. Grace and I can't decide whether Levi's worse than Austin or the same, but both need to be exposed for what they are."

Grace leaned toward the women. "I posted the text, photos, and fake contract to Facebook just before we came in here for dinner. What the idiot didn't realize is the contract states he makes porn videos. And the fact that my signature is obviously forged means he wrote it."

Maddi stood. "The only way to this house is down Fourth Avenue. The snow's too deep all the way around for an old man like Austin to get here otherwise. He'd be post-holing the entire way." She leaned over the table. "We should all park our trucks blocking the entrance to the driveway tight against the berms so they'd have a helluva time trying to sneak up on us."

"They'll go to Gram's first," Grace added, "but we'll see them through the security camera. Then they'll probably come here. Or try to."

Shannon stood. "Then let's move our vehicles."

Since Maddi was the last to arrive, she moved her truck to the head of the line, straddling where the road ended and the driveway began. Then came Grace's truck. Shannon left her rig where the snow berms almost touched the side doors. After realizing she couldn't open the door, she backed up.

"Grace, you need to park this. I'm too old and fat to squeeze through." Shannon walked toward Taylor, standing on the deck.

Grace took Shannon's place and drove forward. She climbed over the seats to the back, then pressed the button on the fob to raise the hatch. After exiting, she lowered the door and locked the SUV.

Maddi came over and squeezed her. "You're so flexible."

"I have to be to keep up with you," Grace said.

"The only way they can get in is if they backdoor us. The pussy is plugged."

Grace groaned and threw her arm over Maddi as they walked toward the deck, laughing.

"We heard it," Shannon said.

"Great analogy," Taylor said.

Marshall opened the door to the deck. "What are you all doing?"

Taylor turned toward him. "Your friend, Levi, has teamed up with Austin to come after all of us. We're trying to slow them down."

Marshall cleared his throat and looked away. "I just finished talking to Levi."

"And?" Taylor and the others moved toward him.

"He wanted to know if I'd seen Grace. He said he can't find her."

Taylor's muscles tensed. "And you said?"

"I told him I haven't seen her for years. I asked him if he knew what she had just posted. 'Damn right!' he yelled. 'It's all a lie!'" Marshall looked at them, then away, and breathed a few times quickly. "'Then where'd she get the pictures from the basement?' I asked. 'You've told me no one goes down there except you.' He said she found photos online."

Marshall sucked in his lips and swallowed, then glanced at Taylor. "I said, 'They're exactly what I saw when you showed me your sound booth.'"

Taylor gasped. "You've been down there?" A bitter tang filled her throat.

"Once," Marshall said. "Two weeks ago. But I never saw a monitor connected to cameras. He didn't show me the entire basement. Just his computer and microphone setup."

Taylor glared at him. "The Nazi flag?"

His ears reddened. "I saw it but didn't say anything."

"Then what did Levi say?" Shannon asked.

"He said I'd better not tell that to anyone."

"Or else what?"

"He said, 'Do it and find out.'"

Taylor folded her arms, her whole body on edge. "Did you tell him about me being Brooke Skipstone before or after that visit?"

Marshall licked his lips. "After."

Taylor's head pounded. "You told a Nazi?"

"I . . . uh . . . I didn't think . . ."

"You confided in a fucking Nazi." Taylor stepped closer. "Are you going to post a comment about Grace's photos?"

He glared at Shannon, then at Taylor. "Are you going to sleep with her?"

Taylor's face burned. "Are you going to defend a lying, pedophile Nazi?"

Maddi flipped out the blade of her Spyderco knife and held it close to Marshall's face. "Did he show you videos of me and Grace?"

He shook his head, eyes bulging. "No. I swear."

She lowered her blade to his crotch. "Then use your balls or lose them. Post a comment on Grace's photos."

Panting, Marshall stared at Maddi's hard eyes until she touched the blade tip to his jeans.

"Now," she said.

"Okay." He turned around and opened the door. Maddi followed him inside along with Grace.

Taylor blew out a breath, her mind swirling with rage.

"I told you," Shannon said. "Don't you dare fuck with Maddi."

15

THE GIRL YOU USED TO BE

While Marshall thumbed his phone as Maddi looked over his shoulder, the others read Levi's response to his daughter's post.

Grace has NOT been in my basement. Whatever photos she's posted are easily found on the internet. Here is a copy of my actual signature, which differs from the one on the supposed contract. Grace simply forged mine and made hers look like I'd cut and pasted it. I've never seen that contract, and there are no cameras in her bedroom or bathroom. I don't know why Grace is lying, except she's a leftie and friends with Taylor MacKenzie, who gave Grace a signed copy of Crystal's House of Queers. *Here's a photo of that gem. I don't know where my daughter got the idea of posting nude videos, but I can sure take a guess! Grace has definitely changed since Taylor started teaching at the school. That woman has preyed on my daughter! Turned her against me. Her own loving father. But that's what queers do. Turn everything ass-backward!*

"That man is sick," Grace said, her face reddening. "Yes, he's a pervert, but he's dangerous. He accuses *you* of preying on me. And the videos were *my* idea!"

Taylor touched her arm. "Now we know why he wanted the signed copy."

"Alright," Marshall grumbled. "I've written it. I hope you're satisfied." He started to stand, but Maddi held him down.

"Let them see it before you post," she said while handing his phone to Taylor.

Taylor read it out loud. "I was inside Levi's basement one time two weeks ago. The computer/microphone/sound booth depicted in Grace's photo is exactly what I saw. I also noticed the flag and portrait, like in Grace's photo. I did not see the rest of the basement, so I can't comment on the photos of wires or another monitor. When I told this to Levi, he ordered me to stay silent or else. I am not a neo-Nazi nor do I support their beliefs. I regret staying silent about this and wish I had not told him my wife wrote under the pen name of Brooke Skipstone."

"He should remove that last sentence," Shannon said. "It sounds too much like a forced confession. Levi will pounce on that and claim Marshall is being made to lie."

"I agree," Taylor said as she deleted all the words after *beliefs*. Then she posted his message and handed the phone back to Marshall. "Do you regret telling him about my books?"

He looked down. "Yes. I should have talked to you."

She raised her brows. "Because he's told the world and embarrassed you?"

"Well, he's done that. And embarrassed you."

Taylor shook her head. "I was nervous, but I knew you would tell him. You couldn't help yourself. And then he'd tell everyone, and then maybe something would happen so Austin couldn't drive into town and shoot me with no one caring or knowing."

"I would have protected you," Marshall pleaded.

"Before or after yelling at me about my books and my history with Brooke? I wouldn't have known he was in town if not for Maddi. You played your role, Marshall. Keep watch from your bedroom if you want to protect me."

"Where are your outside lights?" Maddi asked.

Taylor led them to the sunroom. "There's a big light over the driveway, one on the deck, and another on the porch outside my bedroom. The darkest area is east of the deck toward the trees."

"Which is where they'll come," Maddi said as she looked out the windows toward the backyard. "But that snow is at least four feet deep, and the berms around the deck are six feet tall. It would be crazy to attack from there. They'd be exposed for thirty yards as they slogged toward the deck, and then they'd have to climb over the berms."

"Austin is sixty-nine years old with a limp," Taylor said. "I don't see him trying that."

"Levi would," Shannon said. "Just to prove he's a tough guy. He runs a small militia group called the Clear Creek Patriots. They dress in camo and meet at the shooting range on Sunday afternoons in preparation for when the government tries to take their guns." She chuckled.

"Were you ever part of that, Marshall?" Taylor asked.

"No." He fidgeted. "But I've heard of it."

Taylor scrunched her brows. "Has Levi asked you to join?"

"Yes, but I haven't."

"What are those mounds in the back?" Maddi asked as she pointed to three humps like graves across the yard.

"They're raised planters," Taylor said, "for my garden."

"If you were them, Maddi," Grace asked, "how would you sneak up on this house?"

"I'd come out of the trees where it's darkest," Maddi said, "then crouch behind the planters all the way across until I could connect to the trail leading to the stairs to the second story. What's up there?"

"A deck," Marshall said. "It's the fire exit from my bedroom. I just shoveled it two days ago. The trail goes around the house to the driveway."

Maddi pointed to a security camera on top of the entertainment center. "What if you set that on a windowsill upstairs so we can see them come out of the trees?"

Taylor gave Marshall the camera. "Set it above the dresser so I can check the view."

Marshall took the camera and hurried up the stairs.

Maddi turned on all the lights in the living room and sunroom. "Keep these lights on to get as much light on that yard as possible. And remove the window screens, so it's easier to shoot."

Taylor clutched her throat. "We're going to shoot out of the windows?"

"What else?" Maddi asked. "They'll be armed. How else do we stop them?" She and Grace pulled the screens off and set them against a wall.

Taylor turned to Shannon, her heart banging inside her chest. "I'd have no problem shooting Austin, but—"

Shannon held Taylor's cheeks. "We have to prepare. If they come with guns blazing, then we have to shoot back."

Taylor's phone dinged, and both women found an image of the backyard on her phone. She texted Marshall. *Perfect.*

After Taylor switched on all the outdoor lights, she found Marshall at the bottom of the stairs.

"Now what?" he asked.

"Watch TV upstairs or join the commentary on Facebook," Taylor said. "I'm sure they'll wait until well after dark before they come around."

Marshall folded his arms and scrunched his brows. "What are you going to do?"

"I'm going to calm down by cleaning the kitchen while you protect all of us from upstairs." She turned around, ignoring the scowl she knew he threw at her back.

"C'mon, girls," Shannon ordered. "Let's pick up our mess."

Once they were all in the kitchen, they heard Marshall plod up the stairs.

"Maddi," Taylor said, "you were pretty quick with that knife." *Faster than Brooke was.*

"When I need to be," she said. "Guys think girls are weak, so they can do whatever they want. My knife makes them think twice before doing something stupid."

"Have you ever used it?"

"Mom's boyfriend abuses her," she said calmly. "I've tried every-thing to get her to leave him, but nothing's worked." She furrowed her brow. "I cut him a few times after he hit Mom and told him if I ever saw another bruise on her, he wouldn't recognize himself after I was done with him. It's worked so far."

"Good."

"I wasn't going to cut off Marshall's balls, but he didn't know that."

Taylor smiled. "Neither did I. Glad you're on my side, Maddi."

Her face broke into a wide smile. "My pleasure."

They hugged then Taylor said, "Okay, let's put these plates away."

"We'll clean," Shannon said. "You go tend to your grandchildren. Send them your book."

Taylor took a deep breath and nodded before walking to her office. As she pulled out her computer and set it on her desk, she tried to remember when she last spoke with her sons' families. Gene rarely FaceTimed, usually waiting for holidays or birthdays. Gene's eldest daughter, Leslie, a rising senior at seventeen, was a star athlete—soccer, track, and basketball—and a top student. Her fifteen-year-old younger brother, James, claimed she had no social life, but he, on the other hand, had a girlfriend. Both appeared on the staged calls, commenting and occasionally smiling as they sneaked looks at their phones. The last call happened between Christmas and New Year's.

George's kids were a little younger. The plan had been for the cousins to meet in Portland and fly together to Fairbanks in July for camping at Denali Park and fishing and tour boating in Seward. A plan now deemed inappropriate by her sons.

Taylor had tried to start a serious conversation with Leslie and James the last time they'd visited but was unsuccessful. Too many people in the house, always busy with meals and games and going places and coming back. She'd wanted them to know they could confide in her if they ever felt the need, but their conversation never broke through a polite façade.

Their knowledge of each other had remained skin deep. She was merely MawMaw—the cook, Scrabble and piano player, and gardener.

And now she was going to out herself to them. Her muscles quivered under hypersensitive skin. She almost walked out of her office but clenched her jaw and forced her fingers to type.

I sent your father a version of this message yesterday, but he didn't want to discuss it. I'm afraid you may never know the truth about me if the worst happens, so I have decided to share something about my past and present with you tonight before my brother succeeds in killing me.

She told them about Brooke and becoming lovers and her murder by Austin.

He is now in Clear, looking for me.

When your Aunt Heather died, the pain of losing her ripped open my old wound of losing Brooke. I realized I had denied my identity for most of my life and needed to accept my queerness. I wrote books as Brooke Skipstone. She lives on in my soul and mind, but few know who she was. And no one knew who I really am.

Until now. The Life and Death of Brooke Skipstone *tells my story with Brooke. I hope you will read it and then talk with me. What you share with your parents is entirely up to you.*

I know I am dumping a lot onto your young lives. I love you both and hope we can be closer after tonight.

Her stomach clenched as she attached her book and sent the message to their email addresses. Coming out to her sons, Marshall, and the town was so much easier than to her grandkids. But at least she held no more secrets.

Her mind snapped back to the present when Maddi leaned through her doorway. "Is this where you write?"

"Yes, it is."

"Do you play that keyboard?" She inched inside, her eyes fixed on the Korg 88-key sound machine stretched between two massive speakers.

Warmth spread up Taylor's neck as she watched Maddi's face flush with awe, fingers reaching. "Yes. Do you?"

"I want to."

"Go ahead."

"Grace! Come here!" Maddi lunged for the bench and searched for the power button with both hands.

"Back left," Taylor said with a laugh.

Maddi reached over the keyboard and pressed the button.

Grace entered, followed by Shannon. As the screen powered up, Maddi hit random notes with her left hand as she spun a dial with her right. A bluesy, thumping rhythm played in the background as she hit single notes to the beat. "Old School. Awesome!"

Maddi stood and undulated her hips, facing Grace. Both girls danced inches apart to the rhythm while Shannon laughed in the doorway.

"Do you want me to play something along with that beat?" Taylor asked.

"Yes!"

Taylor slid around them and jammed a melody. The girls raised their arms and juked their bodies in mirror images of each other.

When they started kissing, Shannon called out, "Change the song, Taylor, or you and I will need to leave the room."

Taylor stopped with a snort.

"Do that song from the play," Grace said. "The one you and Brooke sang at your house."

Taylor smiled at memories of the first time she played the song for Brooke, then hit some buttons until a rhythm started. She added the piano melody on top. The girls pulled out their phones.

"Chapter Three," Taylor said.

Soon the girls were singing.

> *The power's in the flower*
> *Your eyes will spin around*
> *The magic's in the color*
> *To take resistance down*

After the fourth verse, Taylor stopped. "You girls sound good."

"You should hear Gram," Grace said.

Taylor flashed a big smile at Shannon. "Do you sing?"

Shannon's eyes gleamed. "Sometimes to the songs they put on speaker."

Grace put her arm around her grandmother. "She was in a rock band at my age. Rumor has it she smoked weed and even dropped some acid."

Shannon blushed. "Not even a quarter of a tab. Only once."

Maddi widened her eyes and drifted around the room, saying, "Oh, the colors. They're so pretty. I can hear them."

Grace guffawed.

"And the weed?" Taylor asked with a grin.

Shannon stuck out her chin. "I rolled a few J's in my youth. But it was a hundred times less powerful than the stuff they sell today."

"And you know this how?" Taylor asked, her pulse racing.

"I was curious, so I went to one of the shops in Fairbanks and bought a vape pen and a cannabis cartridge. I tried it at home one afternoon." Her eyes turned to saucers. "And I got so stoned."

Maddi laughed and lifted Shannon's arm opposite where Grace stood and mimed having to help her walk. "We took her to her room, where she slept for ten hours."

Grace said with a straight face, "Maddi and I finished the vape cartridge to make sure Gram wouldn't endanger herself. Then we did other things for ten hours." She and Maddi shared a smile.

"Think I'll stick to whiskey," Shannon said.

"I want to hear you sing," Taylor said, her brown eyes fixed on Shannon's sky-blue irises.

"Okay. Play something you wrote."

Taylor pulled a crate from her bookshelf and flipped through a pile of song sheets. She chose one. "This was one of Brooke's favorites from a one-act musical I wrote. It's called 'The Girl I Used to Know.'" She handed it to Shannon.

Taylor played the melody and sang. Shannon jumped in during the second verse.

I remember when my life was easy
Catching butterflies and trampoline
I could jump in the summer breezes
And play with puppies in my evening dreams

Then at seventeen, I ran away
Chasing every guy who called me babe
Till the parties died, and so did my life
All the dreams I had were tears that dried

And I feel like going home
To find the girl I used to know
The one who had no doubt
What life was all about
When a day in the sun
was all the fun
I'd need
I'll find the girl I used to be
And never leave

"That's pretty," Maddi said.

"I wrote this song in college," Taylor said in a flat voice, "not knowing my daughter Heather would live such a life." A twinge of pain stabbed her chest. "I played it for her after one of her rehabs, and she laughed. 'I sure as hell need more than a day in the sun, Mom.'"

"Let's sing it again," Shannon said, touching Taylor's shoulder. "You want to do harmony?"

"I'd love to." She let the painful memory go and focused on the joy she'd felt when singing with Shannon for the first time.

The two women sang as Grace and Maddi watched them with mouths open and sparkles in their eyes. When they finished, the girls filled the room with applause and whistles.

Taylor and Shannon hugged. It had been years since Taylor had sung out loud. "We sound good together," Taylor said, pulling the woman closer, warmth spreading through her skin. "Before singing just now, I felt like I'd been holding my breath, listening to memories. I'd love to sing more with you."

"Me too."

Marshall cleared his throat from behind them.

Everyone turned toward him, but Taylor and Shannon still held each other's arms.

"I heard the piano from upstairs," Marshall said, looking from Taylor to Shannon, then to the floor. "Levi posted this on Facebook. I figured you hadn't seen it because . . . you were playing and singing." He gave his phone to Taylor.

She read Levi's post out loud. *Austin wanted me to suggest a place he could meet his sister. I thought my daughter's grandmother's house would work. What do you say, Taylor? Let's meet at Gram's house. I can make sure the meeting stays civil.*

Taylor laughed. "I'm sure you can, Levi."

"What are you going to do?" Marshall asked as he took back his phone.

The two women shared a glance and a wry smile.

Taylor pulled out her phone and opened Facebook. "He's fishing, Marshall. He's telling me he knows I'm with Shannon." She wrote, *Who the hell is Gram? And why would I trust a Neo-Nazi, child pornographer, militia leader to guarantee my safety? How about the trooper station in Nenana tomorrow at ten o'clock?* She pushed her phone into her sweatshirt pouch. "Since I denied knowing Shannon, he'll think we're at her house, so he'll go check. Marshall, have you added any more comments?"

He sucked in his lips. "No."

"Have you gotten flack because you confirmed Grace's photos?"

Marshall scratched his neck. "Yeah. Leroy said he didn't know what basement I'd been in, but he hadn't seen anything like what was in those photos. Which is bullshit. Leroy's in the militia, so Levi must have told him to say that." He shook his head. "Seems like the truth doesn't matter. Just what team you're on."

Taylor searched her husband's eyes. "Has anyone said anything about my book?"

He raised his brows and grinned. "Yeah. Allison."

Grace cocked her head and narrowed her eyes. "What did she say?"

"Allison caught you and Taylor in your classroom, holding each other. Taylor said Grace had been crying. Now Allison knows why, because she cried too when Brooke died."

"Really?" Taylor asked, blood rushing to her head. "That's a shock."

"She also said Austin is a lying piece of shit."

Grace laughed. "She always has to be hating on somebody. If your book affected Allison, then it should affect others. Maybe there's hope for queers in this town."

Taylor's phone dinged with a message from Leslie. *Thanks for sending this, MawMaw. I'll start reading your book tonight. For now, this will be just between us. James won't tell because he's afraid of getting into trouble. Are you safe??? Your brother wants to kill you? Can't you call the police?*

A knot grew in Taylor's throat. She bit her lip, trying to keep tears from flooding her eyes, and leaned into Shannon, showing her the screen.

Shannon put her arm around Taylor's shoulders. "Like I said, never give up on your grandchildren."

Taylor texted back. *I'm safe for now with good friends who want to protect me. Message me anytime. I love you, Leslie.*

"What's going on with our grandchildren?" Marshall asked with an edge. "You didn't tell them, did you?"

Taylor hastily wiped her eyes and stood up straight, chin out. "That's none of your business, and don't you dare get involved in my communications with Leslie."

His face reddened as he blurted, "What did you tell her?"

Taylor's phone dinged again with Leslie's message—*Is PawPaw with you?*

She showed the screen to Marshall. "What should I tell her?" Her body tensed. "Yes, he is, but he's about to rat on you to your father? Because he wants me to remain closeted forever, alone and friendless, so he doesn't get embarrassed?"

Marshall glared at her, breathing heavily. He glanced quickly at the girls, finding their hard eyes. "I'll go back upstairs and keep a lookout."

"Good choice," Taylor said. She read her text out loud—*PawPaw is upstairs protecting us all. Don't worry. I'll keep you updated.*

Marshall sucked in his lips and averted his gaze. "If I see anything, I'll let you know." He walked through the kitchen and up the stairs.

"Why do I breathe easier every time he leaves the room?" Grace asked.

"Because he thinks all the air is for him," Taylor answered. "We have over an hour before it's completely dark, so relax and check your guns."

Maddi flung her arm around Grace's neck. "We should take our shower now. We might be busy later."

"Good thinking." Grace kissed her girlfriend's cheek. "What will you two do?" She winked. "I'd love to hear more songs."

"If we survive the night," Shannon said, "we'll practice some tomorrow morning."

"Deal," Grace said as she put her hands on Maddi's hips. "Let's get our clothes."

"Why do we need clothes to take a shower?" Maddi asked as she pulled off Grace's hoodie, revealing a tank top.

Grace widened her eyes in mock shock and looked back at the laughing women as Maddi pulled her into the bathroom. "She really wants to take a shower!"

Maddi ripped off Grace's top just as Grace shut the door with her foot. Their squeals and laughter crescendoed even after the shower started.

"Those girls make me laugh a dozen times each day," Shannon said through panting breaths. "I don't know what I'd do without them."

"Write books and laugh through your characters," Taylor said, massaging the laugh kinks in her cheeks. "That's what I've done for years." She blew out a big, satisfying breath. "But the real thing feels so much better."

Shannon fixed her eyes on Taylor's. "That's true for a lot of activities."

"That's what I hear," Taylor said as her heart danced in her chest. "But all I have is faded memories."

"Then maybe we should make some new ones. Like your song says. Find the girl you used to know." She held out her arms.

Taylor rushed toward Shannon and buried her face in her friend's neck. "I want to." She pressed her body hard against Shannon's.

After a few seconds, Shannon grabbed Taylor's hand, kissed it, and led her to the back bedrooms.

16

AWFUL STRANGE NOISES

Taylor breathed slowly as she nestled against Shannon's breasts, floating in the afterglow of intense love-making. A dam built by years of isolation and an aching need, buried by fear of . . . something . . . had burst so suddenly she thought she had died.

And then she'd died again, only to drift back to consciousness through Shannon's soft humming and delicate kisses on Taylor's forehead and cheek.

No stress, no memories, just the total awareness of now. For a few precious moments, her mind drifted in a tranquil void.

How could nothingness be so fulfilling?

She felt words moving to her tongue and tried to hold them back, not wanting to break the moment. She focused only on her breathing. But one sound pulled her out of herself.

The humming.

So rich and beautiful. Soulful.

Taylor's voice joined Shannon's, a third above. Their harmony grew more expressive until each voice danced around the other, growing in volume and spiraling up the scale until Shannon's voice cracked.

She laughed and coughed. "I'm too old to go that high."

Taylor touched Shannon's plump lip with her thumb. "I thought I heard you whimper in that range."

The skin beneath her neck flushed red. "If you say so. I wasn't focused on my voice at that point."

"Nor was I." Taylor kissed the blush, then locked eyes. "I've never jumped in bed with someone I just met, but I am so glad I made an exception."

"At our age, we need to eat, drink, and be merry when we can."

"For tomorrow we die?"

"Or the day after. Or a month. We never know."

Taylor sighed. "Even before Austin was released, I worried about losing my ability to write." Tremors of her old fear moved up her chest. "I have this urgent need to write a book and finish it as soon as I can before I'm unable to. My greatest worry is being in the middle of a story and forgetting where I'm going. Or worse, not being able to read what I've written. It's crazy, but I think that's why I get so consumed with my books. I'm afraid I'll die before I finish."

Shannon's fingertips meandered down Taylor's neck and to her chest. "It's better to hear time's wingéd chariot at your back than ignore it."

"'To His Coy Mistress.' I used to teach that to my students back in the day. *Let us sport us while we may, like amorous birds of prey.*" She grabbed Shannon's hand and sucked one of her fingers. "I think we did a great job of preying on each other." She twirled her tongue around Shannon's thumb.

Shannon chuckled. "Yes, you seemed to be particularly ravenous."

Taylor playfully bit Shannon's pinky. "I was deprived for over forty years. What did you expect?"

"Exactly what you did. But please don't wait another forty years for a second course."

Taylor cackled and straddled Shannon's thighs with just a little grunt at the effort. "I can't believe I've mounted another naked, seventy-year-old woman in my bedroom and am talking dirty with her."

"If we can't talk dirty at seventy, when can we?"

Taylor lightly stroked Shannon's skin from her ribs to her pubis, feeling a tickle of desire deep inside. "By now, we're supposed to know better."

"I know better than to follow some silly rule men created." Shannon lightly pushed her fingertips up Taylor's thighs. "Besides, men talk dirty at all ages and see nothing wrong. But if we do it, we're sluts."

Taylor leaned forward, planting her palms on the bed on either side of Shannon's stomach. With a sensuous smile and slightly swaying breasts, she said, "We're either helpless princesses or dirty whores."

Shannon cupped Taylor's breasts. "According to men, who can't think beyond either and or."

Taylor peered deeply into Shannon's blue eyes. "And how should they think?"

She gently twisted Taylor's nipples. "Start over. Throw out every preconception about men and women. Think of possibilities without judgment."

Taylor reached for Shannon's breast with her right hand and raised her brows. "I can see several possibilities." She humped Shannon's pubis. "What about you?"

Shannon laughed, released Taylor's breasts, and removed Taylor's fingers from her nipple. "Why are we in our current situation?"

"You mean naked and aroused?" Taylor continued her slow humping.

Shannon rolled her eyes and smiled. "I'm trying to make a point, Taylor. Think of something besides your clit."

"I can't now that you've said that!" Taylor humped faster.

Shannon sucked in her lips, trying to keep from laughing, but she erupted anyway.

"Don't you dare think about your clit, Shannon!" Taylor squealed. "Don't do it!"

They heard pounding on the bedroom door. When Taylor tried to dismount, her foot kicked one of Shannon's breasts, causing them both to grunt then laugh.

"What are you two doing?" Maddi asked, knocking some more.

"We're very worried," Grace said. "We're hearing strange sounds and questionable language. Maddi thought she heard someone say *clit.*"

Both girls laughed.

"Give us a minute," Shannon said, pulling herself to a sitting position.

Both women helped each other off the bed and looked for their clothes, trying to stifle their laughter.

As Shannon pulled on her panties, she said, "We are in this situation because Austin couldn't reject his binary interpretation of sexuality."

Taylor searched for her panties and finally found them in a corner across the room. "Why are these over here?"

"I think I ripped them off and tossed them over my shoulder."

Taylor flashed a leering grin. "Excited, were you?" She sat on the bed and lifted a foot to insert into one hole. "You were talking about Austin."

"Yes." Shannon squirmed into her leggings. "He felt a real attraction to Luis, even had sex with him, but once he realized Luis was male, Austin could either hate him or hate himself. He was trapped in a binary world of gender expectations." She pulled her sweatshirt over her head.

"Weren't you wearing something underneath that?"

"Yes, but I found my sweatshirt first. Besides, it's less to take off later on." She winked at Taylor. "Austin could think only in terms of straight or queer, and everything in his life up to that point had made him fear being queer."

Taylor pulled up her leggings and found her bra. She stopped and frowned just before she put an arm through a strap. "I don't want to wear this."

"I don't blame you."

Taylor tossed it onto the bed and put on a shirt and hoodie, remembering she'd been worried Shannon might see her dirty underwear on her bed a little earlier that day. Now, she could be comfortably naked around this remarkable woman and not feel embarrassed.

Shannon sat on the bed and put on socks and boots. "What if Austin had seen a movie or two about queers, read some LGBTQ books, or discovered that a friend was gay or trans before encountering Luis? Maybe he would have realized that being queer is not a disease but a possibility among many. That gender expression is not a light switch but a dial. Then maybe he talks to Luis or continues to have sex with him. But he doesn't kill. He's not trapped in a world of zeros and ones or right and left. That's the queering Levi fears. Where the gender options are not just stereotypical male and female but offer a whole range of prospects. Because if that happens, he's just one expression of maleness among many. Levi's not the cock of the roost. He's just a human with a cock."

Taylor pulled on her socks. "Did you enjoy sex with your husband?"

Shannon smiled. "Yes, I did. I loved my Pete. He was a good and kind man. Not a back-slapper, loud, or hail-fellow-well-met kind of guy. He always respected me and my opinions. So when I broached the idea of going to a swinger party, he heard me out, and then we did. Tentatively at first, but slowly boundaries disappeared. Pete and I gave each other freedom and more love in our last years than we had shared in all the decades before." She blew out a breath. "Then he died."

She moved to Taylor and held her waist. "You're not dying on me anytime soon. I'm going to make sure of that."

Long-stifled emotions of desire and happiness had done more than fill Taylor's chest with flutters and thumps. They had enlivened all her senses—itching her, demanding to be scratched. She pulled Shannon closer.

"Can we come in yet?" Maddi asked.

"Yes," Shannon said over her shoulder.

Heat flushed Taylor's skin as she clutched Shannon's back and pressed their lips together.

"Whoa," Grace said after opening the door. "Do you want us to leave?"

Taylor didn't flinch or feel embarrassed. She slowly pulled her lips away. "No. What's wrong with two women kissing each other? You two do it all the time."

"Yeah, but I've never seen a woman kiss my Gram before."

"Do you mind?"

"No," Grace answered with a grin. "It makes me happy. Until yesterday, I didn't know any queer adults or didn't think I did."

"When we talk to our online friends," Maddi said, "they always comment about never seeing older queers. And all their grandparents are straight."

"And even if they're supportive," Grace added, "they don't understand what the big deal is when they talk about how hard it is to be queer."

"Well," Taylor said, "now you can tell them you know two seventy-year-old women who kiss in front of you."

Maddi folded her arms. "And other things. What was going on in this room?" she asked with feigned shock. "I'm pretty sure I heard both of you say, 'Don't think about your clit!' Is that some sort of old-school edging technique?"

Grace covered her mouth with her hands and laughed.

Taylor looked at Shannon with a grin. "Do you want to take a stab at that?"

She cleared her throat. "Not really. You two shouldn't be listening through doors."

"We weren't!" Maddi shouted. "We heard you from the kitchen. You guys were loud!"

The two women blushed and tried to keep from laughing. Shannon composed herself and folded her hands at her waist. "Whatever we were doing had nothing to do with . . . edging. At our age, getting to that . . . point . . . is a gift and not to be toyed with."

Both girls erupted in laughter.

"Shhh!" Shannon's voice cut through the laughter. Her security system had sent a signal of movement in her house. She sat on the bed and held her phone out for all to see, making sure the mute button was on. Two men entered through the back door and moved slowly into the kitchen.

Austin and Levi. Each carrying an AR-style rifle, dressed in camo. Shannon took screenshots.

Levi hand-signaled to Austin to check left while he went right.

Austin limped out of view. Taylor had always wondered if she should have thrust her knife over her shoulder rather than around her side. Going up would've taken more time and likely got her killed. She'd dreamed of that scenario many times with different endings.

She hoped whatever decisions she made that night wouldn't haunt her again.

Grace started a screen recording on Shannon's phone. Her eyes tightened. "They came with guns. They want to kill all of us. Shit!"

Maddi squeezed her shoulder. "Not if they die first."

Taylor shuddered. She'd hoped others would help her defeat Austin. Not him, plus a militia leader. She grabbed Shannon's arm. "I'm sorry . . . I didn't expect . . ."

"And they don't expect all four of us," Shannon said with a firm nod.

The two men returned to the kitchen, both shaking their heads. Then Levi stared directly at the camera mounted on top of a cabinet. His lips curled back as he dragged a chair to the counter, stood on it, and ripped the camera down.

Taylor and the girls gasped.

Shannon pressed the screen to unmute herself. "Levi, that is destruction of property, and I have you on video."

He snarled at the camera and threw it into the living room.

"Good move, Shannon," Taylor said. "Should we post this?"

Shannon's hand shook as she gave her phone to Grace. "Here. You do it."

Grace thumbed the screen quickly to post photos and the video with the message, *Austin and Levi just broke into my house with rifles. Maybe Austin lied when he said he didn't want to kill Taylor. And Levi threatened to "come after all of you" if Grace posted her note about his basement and cameras, which explains his carrying a rifle. If you see these dangerous men, please call the troopers.*

"It's done," Grace said and returned the phone to Shannon.

"Will they come here next?" Taylor asked, her pulse racing.

"They don't know about our blockade," Maddi said, "so they might drive down Fourth with their headlights off until they realize it's blocked. It's better to check that out by being outside. I'll get dressed."

"I'll go with you," Grace said.

"Girls," Taylor blurted. "Maybe you should stay here with us."

Grace sucked in her lips. "That's what the pervert would expect. All the women huddled in fear. Fuck that."

Both girls left the bedroom.

Taylor grasped Shannon's hand. "Are we ready for this?" Her stomach turned to stone. This was the moment she'd waited for, had dreamed about. And for the first time, she didn't squirm in fear.

Shannon covered Taylor's hand with hers. "Almost. Turn on your porch light. Get your gun and flip these lights off. Then go to the kitchen."

"Kiss first?"

Shannon leaned to her and sucked Taylor's bottom lip into her mouth. "We'll share lots more later. Don't worry. We'll get through this."

A minute later, they were in the darkened kitchen. Huge flakes of snow fell heavily outside the windows.

"Shit," Shannon said. "Snow will make it harder to see them." She leaned her rifle into the corner of the cabinets.

"And harder for them to see through the windows," Taylor said. "They might get careless, thinking they're invisible." She laid her rifle on top of the counter. "Those flakes are the size of quarters."

Grace and Maddi entered the kitchen carrying two shotguns. They put on their jackets and donned wool caps.

"We're going to the woodshed, Gram," Maddi said. "We'll be able to see and hear them and still have some cover."

"What will you do if you hear a truck?" Taylor asked.

"Nothing if we hear them back up. If they don't, we might fire a shot into the trees to spook 'em."

"Don't do anything crazy," Shannon warned.

Maddi scoffed, "Have you ever known me to act crazy? C'mon, Grace. Let's go hunting." She walked into the mud room.

"Please be careful, Grace," Taylor said.

She turned, her face ashen and tight, her breath quick. "When there's danger, Maddi's blood turns to ice. Which is good because mine doesn't. We'll be all right." Both girls left the house and trotted across the driveway toward the woodshed.

Shannon punched numbers into her phone. "I'm calling 911 and telling them my house was broken into. At least that should get a trooper headed in this direction."

Marshall entered the kitchen, carrying his rifle with one hand, barrel pointed toward the floor. Shannon moved into Taylor's office when a dispatcher answered.

His body and voice tense, he said, "I saw the video. When did that happen?"

"Just a few minutes ago," Taylor replied. "They might be headed this way. The girls are in the woodshed, listening for a truck. You should be upstairs keeping watch."

He sucked in a breath and thrust out his chin. "What will you two do?"

"Stay here and check the windows. Has Levi posted anything?"

"No, but others have. Allison said it's proof Austin is a liar. Tommy said it's awful suspicious that Levi and Austin would go into an empty house and then be caught on camera. He thinks it's a setup. And there's others."

Taylor folded her arms, wary of the edge in his voice. "What do *you* think?"

He averted his gaze. "You knew they'd go to her house and wanted to prove both of them are trying to kill you." He looked toward the office and snapped, "What's she doing?"

"Calling the troopers about the break-in."

He shook his head and gripped his rifle. "This is a helluva mess. How does this end without someone getting shot or killed?"

Her throat burned. *By you or them?* "I don't know, Marshall. Maybe you should wait outside and offer to negotiate. You're good buddies with Levi."

"Oh, you'd like that, wouldn't you?" He sucked in a raspy breath. "Maybe he and the others would take me out."

She hitched a breath. "Others? Who?"

"I meant Austin." His eyes flinched.

What does he know? Every nerve stood on edge. "When's the last time you talked to Levi?"

He stammered. "I already told you. When I called him about Grace's photos."

"And not since?"

"Why would I call him?" he screeched.

"Maybe he called you. Did you talk to Levi again after you called him?"

"I'm trying to protect you!"

"Answer the fucking question, Marshall."

His body shook. "Speaking of fucking, what were you and that bitch doing in your bedroom?"

Her stomach dropped. "When?"

"Half an hour ago," he sneered. "I heard awful strange noises coming from your room when those girls were taking a shower."

The scene in the campground bathroom when the woman scolded her and Brooke flashed through her mind. And like then, she couldn't help herself. "They would be strange to you since you've never heard what great sex sounds like."

He clenched the rifle and glared at her.

Shannon left the office and entered the kitchen. Marshall narrowed his eyes at her and seethed.

Shannon shared a quick look with Taylor, then fixed her eyes on Marshall. Taylor glanced at her rifle five feet from her side and inched toward it.

"What are your plans with my wife?" Marshall shouted, his nostrils flaring.

"To protect her from Austin and Levi," Shannon said firmly. "What are yours?"

Taylor's pulse thrashed in her ears as she slipped sideways slowly.

"Are you a queer?" Marshall demanded.

Shannon folded her arms and lowered her chin. "Asks the jealous homophobe with a death grip on his rifle. It's obvious your only concern is keeping your ego intact."

"Answer the question." He squeezed his rifle, his trigger finger flexing against the magazine well. "We wouldn't be in this situation tonight if not for queers." His lips curled back in disgust. "The drag queen, B&T, all the lesbians and homos in Taylor's books, and probably you!"

With no warning, Shannon strode toward Marshall and clasped the barrel with her right hand as she grabbed his trigger finger and bent it backward. Marshall grunted as his hand released the grip, and his leg buckled.

"What the fuck!" Marshall shouted.

Shannon yanked the rifle away from him and stepped back.

Taylor grabbed her gun. "Stay down, Marshall!" Her stomach boiled.

"Did you know the safety was set to fire?" Shannon asked, eyes tightened into daggers aimed at him.

Kneeling on the floor, holding his trigger finger, trying to catch his breath, he glared at Shannon. "No, I didn't. Why did you do that to me?"

"You were getting too excited for my taste," Shannon answered. "I don't like angry men jerking a Bushmaster toward my face." She looked at Taylor. "I don't trust him."

Marshall stood. "Give that back to me." He started to take a step.

Taylor lifted her barrel toward him. "Don't move, Marshall. You can't control your anger. You could've killed her."

He snarled as he glowered at both women. "I should have." He charged toward Shannon until she swung the rifle butt against the side of his head. He groaned and collapsed onto the floor.

Taylor fell back against the counter, gulping breaths. She had pulled the trigger while aiming for Marshall's chest, but she'd never flipped off the safety. She would have killed him. Tremors spread throughout her body.

She'd pulled the trigger.

"We need to restrain him," Shannon said.

"There's duct tape . . . in the drawer behind you."

Taylor laid her rifle on the counter and stared out the window—breathless. She had seen Marshall as Austin, rushing to hurt Brooke. But this time, she wasn't clinging to a steering wheel, unable to stop him.

Marshall would have hurt Shannon. She had no doubt. But she didn't want to kill him.

The snow fell hard against the drifts and berms. The fire escape steps were already covered by two inches. The porch light shone against the nearby flakes, making them glow, but darkness lurked close behind. It would be hard to see anyone outside.

Or hear anyone.

A scene began to unfold in her mind of men carrying rifles around the house. Heavy snow, dim light. She watched it play like a lucid daydream, heard the kicks and grunts and thuds. Then the swoosh of bound limbs dragged in the snow.

They didn't need targets to shoot at from a distance.

They needed trees to hide behind, shadows to lunge from, rope to trip, and shovels to swing.

Austin had not expected Taylor's knife nearly fifty years ago. Or

Brooke's. If they had done nothing and allowed themselves to be controlled by his pistol, he might have escaped—shot them both and taken the van. What saved Taylor was her unexpected counter-attack.

That night, they had to employ the same.

Taylor turned and saw Shannon taping Marshall's wrists together behind his back. "Is he breathing?"

"Yes."

"Here, I'll do his feet."

Shannon handed her the tape. Taylor pulled off a strip and began wrapping his ankles. "We can't fire at these men as they come for us. That's what they want us to do. Levi and his militia surely have body armor and helmets. If we shoot at them, they'll know where we are and will shoot back. I pulled my trigger when Marshall lunged for you. If I hadn't forgotten to flip the safety, he'd be dead, and I'd go to jail. None of us is going to jail for them." She ripped off a foot-long piece of tape and handed it to Shannon. "Over his mouth, then we'll drag him to the closet down the hall."

After Shannon affixed the tape, she said, "I think he's been talking to Levi. He was determined to do something with that gun. And he said he'd protect us from *others*."

Just as they'd pushed his feet inside the door before closing it, both their phones dinged with a message from Maddi. *Vehicle approaching.*

Taylor texted back. *Do NOT shoot unless fired upon.*

"What's your plan?" Shannon asked.

"We're going to do the same to them as we did to Marshall. Then call the troopers." She entered her office and found a box behind a row of books. Taylor set it on her desk and revealed two black leather boot sheaths holding double-edged, five-inch knives. Taylor handed one to Shannon. "This is Brooke's. There's a clip for your boot. We're going to need them tonight."

17

ACE IN THE HOLE

Grace huddled with Maddi, peering over a pile of firewood about three feet tall, covered by a steel roof. They sat on railroad ties, keeping the split logs off the ground. During the five months of the year when snow didn't cover the roads, tires rolling on gravel could be heard a half mile away. But through the thickening snowfall, the only sounds were thunks, a rusty hinge-like noise, and rattles as a truck moved slowly toward them over the uneven road.

Grace placed her palm on Maddi's back, noting her slow, steady breathing, a lifeline for Grace, whose heart was pounding in her ears. She shivered, despite the temperature of twenty degrees that would hardly faze her under normal conditions.

A squeal of brakes slapped their ears. The driver must have just realized he was about to hit the front end of Maddi's truck. The squeaks of the truck body settling down after the quick stop were replaced by the distinctive rumble of an idling diesel engine.

A door opened. The girls could not see the truck or the man, but they did hear the muttered, "Shit." Then a few seconds later, "Just like Marshall said. There's no way to get around."

Like Marshall said?

"Get in," blurted Levi. "Troopers can't get by either."

The door closed with a muffled thud. Then maybe opened and closed again—Grace couldn't be sure. Soon she could no longer hear the engine. The sound of her father's voice made her skin crawl. "Was that Austin?" she whispered.

"No," Maddi answered. "That sounded like Leroy."

"Did you hear?"

"Yeah. The bastard's on their side. Let's go."

They ran back to the house, bending low. Once inside, Maddi blurted, "Where's Marshall? Levi knew about our trucks blocking the driveway."

"He's knocked out and bound in a closet," Taylor said. "Levi knew?"

"Yeah." Grace's chest heaved. "We heard Leroy and Levi. We couldn't see anyone else, so there could have been more than two."

Shannon harrumphed. "That bastard planned to shoot me!"

"Marshall?" Grace gasped and jerked her head toward Taylor. "Why?"

"He must've made a deal with the devil," Taylor said. "He said others were coming."

"Who?" Maddi asked.

"I don't know," Taylor said. "But he'd obviously talked to Levi. Maybe Marshall was supposed to let them in. Girls, there's a change in plans. We are not going to shoot them unless we have no choice. We'll surprise them, knock them out, and call the troopers. Got it?"

Maddi flipped out her knife. "Can we cut them?"

"Cutting, yes. Killing, no. I need you both to get some things from the garage. Turn on the light to find the items, then flip it off when you leave."

"What do you need?" Maddi asked as she closed her knife and returned it to her back pocket.

"Just inside the door on the right are coils of rope. Bring three and a long piece of PVC tubing. Behind you are shovels, an axe handle, and even a baseball bat. Pick which ones you feel most comfortable swinging. Go! They have to get back to Levi's house and make their way through the snow before they can enter my yard. We have maybe fifteen minutes."

The girls ran out of the house, across the driveway, and into the garage. Grace pushed her arm through three coils of rope and grabbed the tubing. Maddi hefted the bat in one hand and a short shovel in the other.

"I think I like the shovel," Maddi said. "You want the bat? It's a Louisville Slugger."

"My favorite."

They flipped the lights off and ran back to the house, where they were met by Taylor.

"Follow me." Through the rapidly falling snow, they moved onto the trail Marshall had shoveled around the house until they reached the back entrance to Taylor's bedroom. "Maddi, you can hide in this clump of trees. The only light will come around the front corner of the house, so no one will see you. Swing your shovel—"

"Into his nuts," Maddi said. "Then tie him up."

"Right," Taylor said. "Grace will be around the corner under the fire escape steps. If you hear someone falling down the stairs and no one's come your way, run to help her because she'll have two to deal with. Shannon will be in the screen room with her shotgun, just in case. Nobody can see her in there from outside."

"Got it," Maddi said.

"Grace," Taylor said, "follow me." Taylor led her to the stairs. "I figure at least part of Marshall's plan was for Levi and Leroy to come upstairs, where Marshall would let them inside. Except no one will open the door, so they'll have to come back down the stairs. That's when Shannon will pull the rope from the screen room and trip the bastard. Can you climb up this pile of snow without touching the rail and tie one end of this rope to the post on the landing?"

"Sure." After a brief scramble to the top, Grace tied the rope. "Done."

"Take this tube," Taylor said, "tie the other end of the rope and push it toward Shannon behind the screen."

After a few seconds, Grace maneuvered the tube to the screen.

Shannon said, "Hold it there, Grace, until I cut a hole." A moment later, she added, "Okay, push it through."

Grace did until she could feel Shannon removing the rope.

"You can pull the tube back now," Shannon said.

"Grace," Taylor said, "carefully lay the rope against the back corner of the step and hold it there, so Shannon knows how much slack she has to work with."

Grace did as asked. "Okay, Gram."

Shannon pulled in a few feet of rope until the span between the stairs and the screen room was hidden behind the five-foot wall of snow piled up between the stairs and the screen. No one would see the rope when first climbing the stairs. Someone might as they descended and looked straight down to the right, but Grace figured the person coming back down after being denied entry into the house would be in a hurry and not checking for tripping ropes.

Taylor handed Grace the bat and shotgun. "Hide under the stairs. If the rope works and someone trips, he might take out the rail as he falls to the bottom. If he's still conscious, you've got your bat. If the rope doesn't work, use the bat through the side rails to trip him. Shannon will have you covered with her shotgun. Got it?"

Grace smiled and said, "Yes, ma'am. I want to be on your team if we ever play capture the flag."

"I loved that game, but all I can do at my age is make the plans. If you see two men head toward Maddi and no one comes up the stairs, go help her. Take care of yourself, Grace. I'm going back inside."

Taylor disappeared through the curtains of snow. Soon, all the inside lights turned off. A slightly yellow halo glowed far to Grace's right over the deck, stopping at the crest of the berms. She could not see the planters or the woods behind.

Grace leaned her shotgun against one of the 4x4 posts supporting the landing and held her bat in her right hand. If need be, she had enough space on one side of the stairs to lean out and ram the bat through the rails above the fifth step. The rope waited on the seventh step.

The ripping whine of a snow machine drew close, then stopped.

Maddi was right. They'd move through the trees until they came to the yard.

Her pulse quickened, and she held her breath, fearing they'd see it emerge from the stairs and give her away. She was eager to strike back at him—the pervert who dared to condemn others.

Dark figures moved toward her between a planter box and a shed, visible only because they eclipsed the snow. Once they hit the trail, their movements quickened without hesitation toward the steps. They wore no helmets, just black wool caps above faces streaked with white and black paint. Their breathing was ragged and strained as they kept their rifles shoulder high.

Her heart pounded against her chest. *They'll hear me!* Their boots thumped up the steps to the landing, where they stopped inches above her.

"Damn, I'm tired," Leroy said.

"No shit," Levi said, then coughed.

They took the next steps slowly, gulping breaths.

Two for her, none for Maddi. Would Shannon trip the first or second coming down? If the second, he'd fall into the first, and they'd both crash to the bottom.

She dared not move or breathe as she squeezed the bat.

Levi grasped the door knob and tried to twist it. "Damn," he muttered. "It's locked." He gently tapped on the door. "Marshall. Open up."

"Where is he?" Leroy asked.

"Maybe he copped out on us."

"What do we do?"

"Go around to the front."

"What if he didn't get their guns?"

"Then he didn't."

Leroy whined, "We could get shot."

"Two old women and two teenage girls? Give me a break."

Levi headed down the stairs, Leroy following close behind. Grace moved to the fifth step, ready to lean out and shove her bat through the rail. As soon as Levi's boots passed the rope, Grace knew what Gram would do.

"What's that?" Leroy asked, pulling his foot back onto the landing.

Grace froze.

Levi stopped and turned. "What's what?"

Leroy leaned over the rail and pointed. "That's a rope."

"Fuck." Just as he reached the seventh step, the rope snapped taut, slapping his hand.

Why did Gram pull it? Grace gripped her bat.

Levi grabbed the rope with both hands and pulled hard.

But the rope came free, forcing Levi to stumble backward against the rail.

Snap!

"Shoot them, Leroy!" screamed Levi as he fell toward the hill of snow.

Leroy shot twice toward the screen room, then stomped down the stairs.

Grace screamed and swung her bat against the back of his head just as he lifted his rifle toward a blur, racing around the corner of the house to the stairs.

Leroy grunted when the bat hit home, then screamed when Maddi slammed the shovel into his groin.

Wood snapped to Grace's left. Levi had gathered himself and pointed his rifle toward Maddi, standing at the foot of the stairs. "Put down your weapons, or I'll—"

Grace swung her bat against his nose. Bones cracked.

He fired as he fell backward, unconscious.

Rage boiling her gut, Grace bent over her father and screamed, "You fucking pervert!" then lifted the bat to slam his face again.

"Grace!" Shannon yelled from the screen room. "No more!"

Grace panted breaths as her ears pounded. She raised the bat higher, then Maddi's hands covered hers.

"No more, Grace," Maddi said. "Let's tie them up and bring 'em inside."

The sight of his blood pouring from his flattened nose fed Grace's hatred. She would have pulverized his face if Maddie hadn't stopped her.

Maddi cut two lengths of rope and tossed them to Grace. "Tie his feet and then his hands."

Soon, the girls were grunting and sweating, pulling their loads of overweight, middle-aged-soldier-wannabes around the house. Grace dropped Levi and helped Maddi lift Leroy through the mud room into the now-lit house.

Taylor had just finished taping gauze on Shannon's forearm.

Wide-eyed, Grace asked, "Are you hurt?"

"I'm fine," Shannon answered. "Just a scratch."

"From Leroy's bullet?"

"One of them. I'm fine." Shannon stood up and helped the girls set Leroy into her chair. "I called the troopers. They're on their way. We'll tie him up while you get Levi," Shannon said.

The girls struggled more with Levi, whose head banged on the steps and threshold a few times. All four had to help lift him into a chair.

Taylor looked at Levi's wound. "I'll get bandages. Keep his head back." She went to her bathroom.

"Go get their guns," Shannon said as she wrapped the rope around Levi's chest and the chair back.

The girls headed back toward the stairs. "Where's Austin?" Maddi asked.

"Maybe he was supposed to come in later," Grace answered. "Those two barely made it across the yard. No way Austin could follow."

"It would be easier now, using their steps."

They gazed into the trees as snowflakes drifted around them.

"Naw, I think he's waiting for a phone call," Grace said.

They found the men's rifles and retrieved their shotguns from the porch.

"Would you have killed Levi?" Maddi asked.

"Probably. But I'm glad I didn't," Grace said. "He needs to confess."

When they entered the house, Taylor was wiping blood off Levi's face. His eyes met Grace's. "Bet you enjoyed that, didn't you?"

Grace smiled and moved closer. "It's about the funnest thing I've ever done. Then Maddi had to stop me before I smashed your face and brains into the snow."

She glanced at Leroy, who struggled to open his eyes. "Did he show you my latest video?"

Leroy stammered and cleared his throat. "I . . . didn't see it."

Acid burned her throat. "Compared to the others you've seen, I think this one was the best. You should watch it."

"I . . . only saw . . ."

"Shut up!" Levi shouted.

"Which ones, Leroy?" Grace moved her face inches from his, blood pounding in her ears. "How about me and Maddi? You must've liked those."

Leroy strained the ropes around his chest, trying to suck in air. "Look, I didn't want to watch them—"

"Shut the fuck up!" Levi pulled against his chair.

Grace stepped backward and whipped the back of her hand against Levi's nose. He screamed. "Damn, I'm so clumsy."

Taylor pushed a towel against his face. "You are one disgusting piece of shit, Levi." He screamed through the cloth. "Am I pushing too hard?" She pulled the towel away with a twist. He cried out in agony.

Maddi flipped out her knife and put the point inside Leroy's nose. "You didn't want to watch?"

Leroy tilted his head back, trying to avoid the blade. "Please. I didn't want to."

"Then why did you?" Maddi pushed the point deeper into the nostril.

His entire body vibrated in fear. "Because he forced us to."

"Us? Who's us?"

"The militia."

"I'll kill you, Leroy, if it's the last thing I do!" Levi shouted.

Maddi pushed her knife until a bit of blood oozed onto her blade. "Did you and your buddies watch me and Grace?"

Leroy started to cry. "We didn't want to."

Maddi flicked her wrist to remove her knife. Leroy screamed as he jerked his head, tipping his chair back against the table. Blood dripped out of the half-inch slice in his left nostril.

"Maddi," Shannon warned. "Was that necessary?"

"Very." She placed her foot on the chair, hard against his crotch, and slammed the front legs onto the floor. She looked directly into Leroy's twitching eyes. "That little cut will heal, but you'll always see the scar. Every time you look at your fucking face, you'll remember how you got it. And why."

"I'm sorry," Leroy cried. "I'm so sorry."

"Not enough," Maddi sneered. Her lips curled back from her teeth as she moved toward Levi and held her knife close to his eye. "How much has this eye seen, Levi? It would be a shame if it never saw anything again."

Levi strained against the ropes and moved his face as far from her blade as possible.

"Maddi," Shannon snapped.

Maddi smiled at the woman as she moved her blade closer to his eye. "Where's Austin?"

Levi blinked rapidly. "He's back at my house, waiting to hear from us. If I . . . if I don't call him soon, he'll b-blow up my basement."

"That's total bullshit," Maddi scoffed.

Levi sucked in breaths. "He's old and can barely walk. He's at my house, I swear to God. Let me call him, and he'll drive on over here. You can be waiting for him."

"All you do is lie." Grace's voice shook, her lips curled back in a snarl. "I should have bashed your fucking face in. Maddi, let me borrow your knife."

Levi's muscles tensed as he jerked his face away.

"Girls," Taylor said. "The troopers will be here soon. Let them deal with him."

"Maddi," Shannon said, "why don't you move the vehicles so they can get through?"

She blew out a big breath and shook her head. "Sure."

Grace threw her arm around Maddi's shoulder and handed over Shannon's fob and her truck key.

"You coming?" Maddi asked.

"No." Grace put her mouth to Maddi's ear. "I want to record a confession."

The girls kissed quickly before Maddi went outside. She trotted toward the Suburban across the brightly-lit driveway.

"Where's Marshall?" Grace asked.

"Come help me," Shannon said, then walked down the hall. When she opened the closet door, they found Marshall sitting up, his eyes bulging.

"Do you want to do the honors?" Shannon asked Grace.

"Sure." She gripped one end of the tape and yanked it off his face.

He yelped and struggled to fill his lungs. "I need my inhaler."

Shannon pulled the knife from her boot. "Tough shit."

Marshal pushed back in fear.

She stared at the man with a stern look as she cut through the tape around his ankles. They lifted him to standing.

Grace found his eyes as heat flushed her skin. "Levi and Leroy ran up the back steps and knocked on your door. They weren't happy you wouldn't let them in. What was the plan?"

He looked away. "Where are they?"

"Tied up, nursing their injuries in the kitchen," Grace answered. "The troopers are on their way. Your friends said you were supposed to get our guns. Is that true?"

He swallowed. "That's what they wanted me to do."

"Why?"

"Because Levi said otherwise, he'd have the whole militia storm the house. I was trying to avoid a war."

Shannon harrumphed. "But instead, you got knocked out by an old woman. It must be awfully embarrassing for you men to be bested by us." She grabbed his shirt and pulled him toward the kitchen. "We need another chair, Taylor."

Marshall stopped in the doorway and looked at his two friends, bound and bloodied.

Grace pulled out her phone and started recording a video over Shannon's shoulder. She had to have proof of what had happened to show the troopers.

"Is that you, Marshall?" Levi asked, craning his neck to see him. "Where the hell were you?"

"He took a nap in the closet," Shannon said.

Taylor glanced at Grace as she held a chair. "Sit down, Marshall."

"You're going to tie me up?" he asked.

"You're damn right I am," Taylor answered. "We don't trust you."

He sat slowly. "I just did what I thought would be best."

Taylor wrapped the rope around his chest and through the back rails. "For you or me?"

"Both."

She tied his feet to the chair legs. "And what was the plan?"

"Levi called me—"

"Shut the fuck up," Levi yelled. "You don't have to tell them anything."

The phone shook in Grace's trembling hands. She was afraid someone would notice.

"This whole plan was yours," Leroy said. "Marshall and I won't go down to protect you."

"What did he tell you, Leroy?" Taylor asked as she tied Marshall's taped wrists to the chairback.

"That we'd be let into Marshall's room and come downstairs to find all four of you under control."

"How was Marshall supposed to do that?" Taylor asked.

"He'd threaten to shoot Shannon. He figured you'd do anything to protect her. And the girls would do the same."

"And then what?"

Leroy glared at Levi. "You and Grace would say what Austin and Levi wanted you to say to protect Shannon and Maddi."

Marshall jerked his face toward Taylor. "I planned to shoot Austin as soon as he came into the house. I played along with Levi's plan so I'd get the chance. There would've been no confessions. Just one dead asshole."

Taylor held his shoulders from behind. "You should have told us, Marshall," she said with mock concern. "Then we wouldn't have put you in the closet after you almost killed Shannon."

"I didn't almost kill her!"

"Your finger was awful close to pulling the trigger, and you kept jerking the barrel toward her. Maybe you wanted to give her a flesh wound to make me cooperate? Was that how you were going to control all four of us?"

"She seems to be the queen bee around here," he grumbled. "A shot in the arm probably wouldn't faze her at all."

Shannon pointed to her bandage. "How'd I get this, Leroy?"

"Levi told me to shoot!"

"Goddamnit, Leroy!" Levi screamed.

Grace slipped her phone to Shannon and moved toward Levi. "Why did you shoot at Maddi instead of me?" She smirked. "Just couldn't suppress your fatherly affection?"

He sneered. "I wanted to hear you squeal."

Grace smiled. *Thanks for the confession, idiot.* She turned to Leroy. "How'd you get involved in this crazy plan?"

He shook his head and sucked in his lips. "By being stupid. Levi said he'd promote me to Lieutenant Commander. And he threatened me."

"With what?"

Leroy shot a glance at Levi, who glowered back at him. "He has secrets about lots of people in town."

"But you know his secret of making porn videos. Why can't you threaten him?"

Leroy coughed and whined. "Because once a file is on your phone or computer, you can never erase it. I mean, you can, but the file is still recoverable. He airdrops stuff onto everybody's phone, then records you watching."

Without any apparent anger, Grace asked quietly, "Is that how you watched Maddi and me when we were still minors?" She kneeled in front of him.

He sighed and closed his eyes. "Yeah."

Grace wanted to both puke and gouge out his eyes, but she controlled her voice. She wanted a clear confession. "And he's given you lots of videos of me dancing and showering?"

He whimpered, his chin quivering. "I'm sorry, Grace."

"Are they still on your phone?"

"Yeah." He cried.

Levi barked a bitter laugh. "Leroy, you're such a fucking liar."

Leroy strained against his ropes, glaring at Levi. "And what will you be once all this comes out? Nothing!"

Levi smirked. "Nothing's coming out. We still have our ace in the hole."

Movement outside the window caught Grace's eye. Maddi's hair was gripped in someone's hand while the other held a gun to her head.

Austin!

Adrenaline surged through Grace's body. "Maddi's in trouble!" She ran to the mud room door and yanked it open.

"Grace!" Taylor yelled behind her.

Grace opened the outside door. "Maddi!"

"Get down!" Maddi screamed. She whipped her legs around, trying to sweep Austin's feet, but he still held her hair and slammed the gun butt into her head. She dropped face-first onto the snow.

Grace growled and moved toward Austin. He limped a step and stomped his foot onto Maddi's back, his pistol pointed toward her head.

"Stop!" He shot a round into the snow, inches from Maddi. "When I fire again, you'll see her head explode."

Grace stopped about thirty feet from him, clenching her fists, staring at Maddi for any hint of movement.

Austin laughed. "Tell Taylor to come outside."

When Grace rushed outside, Taylor stepped toward her rifle on the counter, but the shot jerked her attention back to the window. She would not allow him to harm the girls. After sharing a quick glance with Shannon, she rushed through the doors and stopped in front of Grace, fear and anger churning her gut. "I'm here, Austin. Leave the girls alone. This is between you and me."

Grace screamed, "No! What are you doing?"

Taylor pulled a knife from her boot. "Stay behind me." She turned toward Austin, pointing the knife at him.

Austin cackled. "Are you going to throw it at me?" He took his foot off Maddi's back and lifted his gun toward his sister. "Ever heard the one about bringing a knife to a gunfight?"

Maddi's right hand moved slowly toward her back pocket.

Taylor smiled, ignoring the roaring hatred in her ears. "But this isn't any old knife, Austin. It's already tasted your blood. Do you recognize it? It's the same as the one Brooke pulled on you. You know, the girl who had the hots for you."

Austin barked a laugh. "I knew you'd like that version of events."

"*You* wanted to believe that version. For forty-eight years, you fantasized about her. But the truth is Brooke pulled her knife as soon as you touched her."

Austin's face stretched into a snarl.

Unable to keep the pain from her voice, she cried, "Why did you kick her out of the van? Surely you knew I'd stop, and the police would catch you."

"I hated her," he snapped. "She kept flirting and smiling at me, but it was all a lie. She was a total queer for you."

Maddi flipped out the blade with her thumb.

Taylor pulled her eyes back to her brother. "Austin, I see you still have the limp my knife caused." She took two steps toward him. "I should have swung over my head and skewered your fucking heart! But now I have another opportunity!" She screamed and ran toward him.

"Taylor!" Grace shrieked.

Austin laughed and pulled the hammer back. "Promises made. Promises—"

Shannon burst through the doorway and swung a rifle toward Austin.

In a blur of motion, Maddi whipped her body and right arm around and up, thrusting her knife into Austin's groin. He screamed, then grunted as Shannon shot him in the chest. He dropped onto his side.

"Maddi!" Grace screamed as she ran toward her girlfriend. Maddi stood, revealing blood oozing from her hairline. The girls clutched each other.

Taylor bent over, gasping for breath, the shot still echoing in her brain.

Shannon came from behind and held her. "Why the hell did you run at him?"

"I wanted to kill him before you did."

"What a wonderful, crazy fool you are." They hugged.

Sirens wailed in the distance.

Taylor approached Austin slowly, dropped to her knees, and touched his neck. "You are finally out of my life. Fucking good riddance." Her mind swirled until Brooke's hand touched her shoulder. Clutching it, Taylor struggled to stand, fighting back a wave of dizziness. They stood for a moment, staring at the body until Brooke's lips brushed against her cheek and then murmured, "Thank you."

Taylor tried to grasp Brooke's hand but it slipped away. Tears welling in her eyes, she turned to the others and announced, "He's dead."

She walked over to Maddi, pulled gauze from her pocket, and dabbed blood from the girl's head. "Let's get you inside and take care of that."

"Austin jumped me when I was getting into my truck," Maddi said. "I think he was waiting there the whole time."

"Ace in the hole," Grace said. "That's what Levi called him. I thought I heard two doors open and close before Levi's truck left."

The sirens grew louder.

"I never moved my truck," Maddi said. "They can't get through." She quick-walked to her vehicle, started it, and backed straight toward the deck.

Flashing lights and sirens moved down the road toward the house.

"Get rid of the gun, Shannon," Taylor said. "I don't want them thinking we're a danger to them."

"Oh yeah." Shannon opened the front door of her Suburban and laid the gun inside.

A trooper car pulled forward, turning left, tight against the garage. An ambulance followed.

"Show your hands," Taylor said.

Two troopers wearing dark blue Stratton hats emerged from the front seat and walked toward them. An EMT grabbed a kit from the ambulance and hurried to Austin.

"I'm Officer Barnes, and this is Officer Grady," Barnes said. He had a barrel chest and thick neck.

Grady kneeled near the body.

"We're not armed, officers," Taylor called. "This is my house. That's my brother, Austin Baird, dead in the snow. That's his pistol. I called you about him yesterday. We have a video of him carrying a rifle into Shannon's house."

Barnes moved closer to the women. "What the hell happened here?"

"My brother wanted to kill me," Taylor said. "Two others in cahoots with my husband tried to invade my house and shot at us. They all met their match and are now tied up in my kitchen. Two are injured. This is my good friend, Shannon. Her granddaughter, Grace, and her girlfriend, Maddi. We have some videos and photos to show you that prove what I'm saying is true."

His head cocked and eyes wide open, Barnes said, "You four women killed this man and tied up three others inside?"

"That is correct, Officer," Taylor said. "Do you want to stand outside, or can we explain everything in the living room?"

Barnes blew out a breath. "We can go inside. Is anyone armed in the house?"

"No," Taylor said. "All our guns are leaning against the kitchen counter."

The other EMT joined Barnes.

They started walking toward the porch until Taylor stopped and pulled out her phone.

"A message from Leslie," Taylor said with a little catch in her voice. She showed the screen to Shannon.

Hey, MawMaw. I love your book. I need to talk to you. Can I call? Are you safe?

Taylor replied. *I am finally safe. The troopers are here, so I need to talk to them. When I'm done, I'll let you know. I can't wait to talk to you.*

"Never give up on your grandkids." Shannon draped her arms over Taylor and Grace, who held Maddi against her side.

Taylor leaned into Shannon's shoulder. "I'll never give up on them, or on us, or me ever again. I finally have something to live for."

18

ARRESTED THE WRONG PEOPLE

For two hours, Barnes and Grady viewed the video and questioned everyone. Leroy and Levi were picked up by another officer and taken to Nenana.

"Are we done?" Taylor asked Barnes. "It's been a long night." The adrenaline had worn off an hour ago, and the boost from the coffee she'd just finished was short-lived.

"I think we are." He stood from the table in the sunroom.

Maddi and Grace lay in tangles on the sofa, sleeping, while Marshall loudly complained to Officer Grady in the kitchen. A bandage had been placed on Maddi's forehead along her hairline.

"This is my house," Marshall insisted. "That woman slammed a rifle butt into my head. Why isn't she in handcuffs? I demand to be released. I've been taped up, tied up, and handcuffed for several hours."

"Are you taking him?" Taylor asked Barnes. "You've seen the video where he talks about shooting Shannon in the arm."

"Yes, but his lawyer will argue he was stating a hypothetical. We can keep him overnight, but he'll probably be released tomorrow."

Marshall's voice became shrill. "If you take me away from my house, all four of them will have a queer orgy. What would you do if your wife brought home her girlfriend and had sex with her?"

"Let's go, Mr. MacKenzie," Grady said.

"You're taking me to jail?" he screeched.

"If I don't, I'll have to come back here in ten minutes to break up a fight or worse. Let's go."

"I'll sue you!" Marshall shouted as Grady led him outside.

Barnes stood. "Maybe you should go back to Shannon's house."

"We'll do that," Taylor said, "but it's too late to move everything now."

"Besides," Shannon said with a flat voice and straight face, "we have a queer orgy planned."

The officer rolled his eyes.

Grace pulled Maddi closer in her sleep. Barnes cleared his throat and turned away.

Taylor harrumphed. "Do they sicken you? Those girls truly love each other. Many men would grimace in disgust if they saw them hugging or kissing in public. But they'd gladly watch their porn videos. Like Leroy and Levi and several other men in town." She locked eyes with him until he flinched and turned away. "When will you secure warrants for Levi's basement and his militia members' phones?"

"Hopefully, tomorrow."

Shannon stood and approached the officer. "Have you ever watched lesbian porn, Officer?"

Barnes kept any emotion from his face and tipped his hat. "I'll be in touch tomorrow." He strode into the kitchen and out of the house.

Once his tail lights disappeared behind the garage, Taylor clutched Shannon with trembling hands. "Is it over? Is it finally over?" she asked, her eyes welling with tears.

Shannon patted the back of Taylor's head. "Yes, sweet Taylor. You are no longer hunted. Austin is behind you. But I don't trust Marshall."

"I can't live with him. It would be worse than ever."

"Come to Homer," Shannon said. "The girls can't stay here."

Taylor moved to the sofa where Grace and Maddi slept. "They were so brave tonight. They will not hide who they are. I wish I could have been like them."

"They're brave because they have each other like you had Brooke." Shannon sat beside her.

"But we still planned to hide," Taylor said. "Times were different back then."

"They haven't changed in this town or in thousands of others. But queers won't go back to the closet. There are too many of us." Shannon leaned over and touched her granddaughter's face. "Grace, dear. All the men are gone." She stroked Maddi's hair. "Maddi, wake up."

They both stretched like cats until Grace sat up with a jolt. "Did you fart?" She grimaced and waved her hand in front of her nose.

"Maybe," Maddi said with a grin, still stretching. "Here's another." The sound of slow, lazy raspberries seeped out of her butt. She giggled as the others laughed. "It's those fajitas." She stood. "I think they're dancing in my intestines." She wiggled her hips, took a few steps, and farted with a smile before running to the bathroom.

Shannon laughed. "She goes from knife-wielding man-slayer to giggling teenager in under a minute."

"Because she has to," Grace said. "She gets hit on at Blue Sky all the time even without her makeup and wigs. When she acts like normal Maddi—cute, bubbly, sweet, silly—some dude thinks she's an easy score, makes a move, and she has to back him off. She can't be herself around most guys without them thinking she's flirting. Something guys don't have to worry about. Like hidden cameras." She leaned back on the sofa and looked at the ceiling. "When are they going to search the basement?"

"Barnes hoped for tomorrow," Shannon said. "The officers confiscated their phones."

"What's going to happen?"

"Several will go to prison."

"You sure?" Grace asked. "The pervert will think of something. He's the king of gaslighting."

"Levi still owns their secrets," Taylor said. "Marshall's not free of Levi, nor is Leroy, nor maybe half the men in this town. They have even more incentive to help him now."

"Then we need to expose the bastard," Grace said. "I want to post my video and tell everyone what happened here tonight."

"I think Levi believes you won't because you'd be too embarrassed," Shannon said.

Grace scoffed. "Half the town already knows I'm a porn star. I think back to a comment someone said I thought was weird, but now it makes sense. Or a look I couldn't understand at the time." She scrubbed both hands over her face. "Unless you have objections, I'll post right now."

"It's your video," Shannon said. "Do what you want with it."

She nodded and stood. "I'll see what Maddi wants to do." She left the room and soon could be heard knocking on the bathroom door. "Are you finished?"

"The door's open," Maddi said, then giggled.

"I'm not that gullible. I need your help, so come to the kitchen after you've flushed."

Taylor's phone dinged with a message from Leslie. *Can you talk?*

Breathless, Taylor texted back. *Yes, but it's so late for you.*

Can I call? I snuck outside. Please.

Yes.

Taylor sucked in breaths as she waited for the ring.

"Do you want me to leave while you talk?" Shannon asked.

"No. Sit here with me." She grabbed Shannon's hand and swiped to accept the call. She punched the speaker icon as her stomach seemed to flip. "Hello, Leslie."

"MawMaw," Leslie said in a nervous, breathy voice. "Are you alone?"

Taylor hesitated. Shannon moved to get up, but Taylor squeezed her hand. "No. I'm with a very good friend who saved my life tonight. I trust her entirely."

"*Her?* Where's PawPaw?"

Taylor hitched a breath and glanced at Shannon.

"Is he okay?" Leslie asked.

"He's fine. He made poor decisions tonight and had to leave the house, but he should be back tomorrow." Taylor listened to Leslie's quick breathing. "You can tell me anything, Leslie. Don't be afraid."

"That time with Julie in your room. The scene in your book. Is that when you knew?"

Taylor's heart fluttered. *Did Leslie have a Julie of her own?* "I wasn't sure. I had barely kissed a boy by then, so that was my first sexual encounter. If a boy had done that, I'd probably have racked him. But with Julie, I remember wanting more."

Leslie remained silent.

"You can trust me, Leslie," Taylor said.

"When did you know for sure?"

"Not until that night with Brooke. Chapter One in the book I sent you. I should have known sooner, but I was scared of my parents finding out and my friends." She paused, debating whether to make the obvious connection to Leslie's situation. "I'm sure I felt the same as you're feeling now."

Leslie cleared her throat and hitched a few breaths. "I'm really scared. Prom is coming in May, and a boy has already asked me, but I've never been on a date. I can't even imagine having to talk to him and dance . . . My parents want me to go. We've . . . been fighting."

"About the prom?"

"Some, but also about book bans and other issues."

Taylor hesitated. "Have you had a Julie experience?"

After a long pause, Leslie said, "Kinda. But no one knows. It just happened when I stayed in a hotel for my club team tournament. We text, but she lives in another city."

Taylor leaned forward and held Shannon's hand to her cheek. "How can I help?" She would do anything to give Leslie the support she needed.

"Let me visit you. Like tomorrow. Please. I don't know what to do, and I can't talk to anyone here." Leslie paused, then gasped. "Shit!" she muttered.

Taylor's stomach froze at the sound of a man's voice and hurried steps. *Gene!*

"What are you doing?" her father blurted.

Leslie whined, "Nothing."

"Leslie?" Taylor stood, her heart racing. "Leslie?"

"Who are you talking to?"

"Just MawMaw."

"At this time of night? Give me the phone," he barked. "Now!" After lots of jostling and background noise, Gene hissed, "Mom?"

Taylor's body shook. "It's me. Please be kind to Leslie."

"Why are you talking to her at almost four in the morning? She snuck out of the house for this."

"And how many times did you sneak out at her age?"

"Why does that matter?" he growled. "Leslie has never done it before now."

"She wanted to know if I'm safe. My brother, Austin, tried to kill me tonight, but he was killed instead. She was worried—"

"How did she even know about Austin?" he bellowed. "Did you send her your book?"

Taylor's throat ached. "Yes, I did. I didn't want to die without—"

"You had no right!" He ended the call.

Taylor flinched at his words.

"You had every right," Shannon said, holding her shoulders. "Call him back. If he doesn't answer, leave a voicemail."

"Yes." Her body tensed as she focused her glare on his contact information. She pressed his number. His phone rang twice before he must have punched the end button. She called again. This time it rang three times before stopping. The next time she called, his phone went directly to voicemail. "Gene, you must listen to your daughter. She called me for a reason. You will drive her away if all you give her is disapproval. She needs love, not anger." Taylor closed her eyes and tried to slow her breathing as she ended her message.

She called Leslie's number and left another voicemail. "You can call me any time. If he takes your phone, use a friend's or buy a prepaid phone. Hang in there, Leslie. I love you." Taylor pressed *End.* As she sucked in her lips, she tapped her temple with her fist. *Stupid. What have I done?* "She wouldn't be in trouble if I hadn't sent her my book."

"You threw her a lifeline," Shannon said, touching Taylor's cheeks. "Now she knows she has someone she can talk to."

Grace and Maddi entered the living room. "What was that about?" Grace asked.

Taylor pushed her phone into the hoodie pouch. "My granddaughter, Leslie, needed to talk to me, but her father caught her on the phone. Now he's screaming mad at her and me."

"Why at her?" Maddi asked.

"She's always been the perfect daughter and student. The best at everything she does. Now, this happens, so he blames me for sending her my book."

Grace raised her brow. "Did she call because she's queer and needed to tell you?"

"Yes."

Grace draped an arm around Maddi. "Did you suspect her like you did me?"

"More you than her. She never talked about boys or hanging out with friends. I always felt she hid a different version of herself behind her public image."

"Her father will ground her," Maddi said, "take her phone, forbid her from contacting you, basically put her in jail to stop any queer influence. She'll either cave, hide behind a thicker shell, or run away."

"She wanted to visit me tomorrow."

Maddi smiled. "Then be ready to buy her ticket when she calls you from the airport."

Taylor pushed her fingers through her hair and breathed deeply. "A few days ago, I wouldn't have considered flying her here without permission. But now I would without hesitation because I know how you both need your Gram. I'd give anything to be needed like that."

Shannon held Taylor's shoulders and squeezed. "We all need you."

"Sure." Taylor wiped tears from her cheeks. "You need me to hide you in trees and under stairs. I can't believe how much danger I've put you in."

"You had nothing to do with the pervert's behavior," Grace said. "You put yourself in danger because of me, so I think we're even. And why the fuck did you run at Austin? He had a gun and you had a knife."

She shuddered, remembering the rage she'd felt when she charged. "I saw Maddi's hand reach for her knife, so I thought she would stab Austin if I could distract him. And I knew Shannon would come out the door with a gun any second. Besides, just like he'd regretted not shooting me for forty-eight years, I'd regretted not killing him that night. I wanted him dead one way or the other."

Maddi kissed Taylor's forehead. "You're my idol."

"Did you post?" Shannon asked.

"Yes, we did and outed ourselves to this worthless town. We're not hiding from anyone ever again." Grace scrolled through her phone. "And the shitstorm has started. I'm surprised so many people are up this late and online."

Sirens wailed. Then a few blasts of an air horn.

"That sounds like a fire truck," Maddi said.

They moved to the sunroom and looked down the driveway onto Fourth Avenue.

The siren and horn grew louder. They opened the door to the deck and stepped outside.

"That truck is coming down D Street," Taylor said.

Grace and Maddi went to the other side of the deck and looked for flames.

"Shit!" Grace yelled. "My house is on fire. Maddi, let's go." She started to move off the deck, her face tense and fists clenched.

Shannon held out her arms to stop her. "Hold on, Grace."

"Why? I've got stuff I want to get out." She squirmed against her grandmother's arms.

"They won't let you inside. Let the fire department do its job. Think. Why is your house burning?"

Grace breathed quickly.

"Because one of Levi's friends set it on fire," Maddi announced. She moved toward Grace. "Someone who'd like to get rid of us. We should all go inside." She took Grace's hand and led her back into the house.

Taylor and Shannon followed.

They gathered in the kitchen, where Grace opened her computer on the table.

"Any comments about the fire?" Taylor asked.

Grace held her face in her hands. "Yes. We've been accused of setting it to hide the fact there are no cameras or videos."

"Wow," Taylor said. "Surely some think the obvious arsonist is one of Levi's friends."

"Yes, but then militia members like Tommy berate them for being stupid."

Taylor frowned. "Then how do they explain Leroy's confessions?"

"According to them, Leroy blamed Levi to hide his own guilt."

"But their phones—"

Grace shook her head. "All hearsay now until the police get warrants. And even then, they can't force the owner to unlock them."

"There are other ways to get the data," Taylor said.

"Maybe, but that takes time, which allows Levi and his friends to build an alternative story. Remember, we're the queers, the groomers, the pedophiles. And certainly liars."

Taylor's stomach hardened as she sat stiffly in a chair. "Even without the videos, two men in camo paint, carrying assault weapons, tried to enter my house—"

"At the invitation of your husband, they point out," Maddi said.

"But they fired shots!"

Grace pointed at the screen. "Tommy says, 'Who wouldn't shoot after being ambushed on the stairs in the dark?' He claims the troopers arrested the wrong people. We killed Austin when all he wanted was his sister's confession."

Taylor closed her eyes as her head pounded. "It's like they live on a different planet." Maybe Barnes and Grady would soon return to arrest them for assaulting three men, burning Levi's house, and killing her brother.

Just when she thought she could finally rejoice in her freedom, she'd found a new prison. Her chin dropped against her tightening chest. She'd never live in Homer with Shannon. Never see Leslie. Tears welled in her eyes.

"Hey, look at this post from Jackson," Grace said. "He asks if anyone listened to the entire video like he did. Everything that Tommy is ranting about is bullshit."

Taylor lifted her head and wiped her eyes. "What's he talking about?"

"There are several minutes of a dark screen at the end. When we played it for Barnes, we cut it off when it turned black." Grace scrolled past all the recent posts until she found her video. She fast-forwarded until she found the last image of herself screaming for Maddi as she raced out of the house. "Gram, you must have put the phone down and never stopped the recording."

Shannon closed her eyes and scrunched her forehead. "I didn't! I tossed it onto the counter."

They all gathered around the computer to watch.

Grace maxed out the volume and hit *Play*.

The phone banged and slid onto the counter. Taylor yelled, "Grace!"

"It's Austin!" Levi yelled. "Get 'em, Austin!"

"What's he doing?" Leroy asked.

Levi laughed. "He's holding Maddi's hair and pointing his pistol at her head."

A door opened and banged against the wall.

Grace yelled, "Maddi!"

A muffled Maddi said, "Get down," then she screamed.

"Austin just clocked Maddi," Levi said. "She's down!"

"Did he kill her?" Leroy asked.

A muffled Austin shouted, "Stop!" Then a loud bang.

"Shit!" Leroy yelled. "Did he shoot her?"

"When I fire again," Austin said, "you'll see her head explode."

"Taylor!" shouted Marshall. "What are you doing?"

Levi whooped. "She's going to meet her Maker."

"Is she outside?" Leroy asked.

"Yeah." Levi chuckled.

"I'm here, Austin," Taylor said faintly. "Leave the girls alone. This is between you and me."

"Taylor!" Marshall screamed.

"No!" shouted Grace. "What are you doing?"

"Shut up, Marshall," Levi said. "If she lives, we're all going to jail. Let him kill all of them. That's the only way out of this."

"Yeah, Marshall," Leroy said, "you've got videos too."

"Do it, Austin," Levi said. "Goddamn! Why does he have to talk? God, they're both talking."

"Shoot them, Austin!" Leroy yelled.

Taylor screamed.

Heavy, quick footsteps started loud, then moved away.

"Oh, shit!" yelled Levi. "Shannon's got a rifle. Watch out!"

Austin screamed. A loud bang roared.

Grace yelled, "Maddi!"

"Fuck!" Levi screamed. "Austin's down. Damnit!" He muttered, "Let me think, let me think."

"What's happening now?" Leroy asked.

"They're out there hugging each other," Levi said.

The sound of sirens rose in the background.

"We are fucked!" Leroy cried.

"What are you going to do now, Levi?" Marshall asked.

"You'd better hope I think of something," Levi said. "You're going down as hard as the rest of us."

"Really? Why?"

"What's the name of that kid you fathered but nobody knows

about?" Levi laughed. "Hey, I got it. You called Leroy and me because the four women were having an orgy downstairs, and you couldn't get them to stop."

"That's crazy," Leroy said. "What about the videos, Levi? They're going to search your house. You know they will."

"By the time they try, it'll be nothing but ashes."

"How?"

"Don't worry. All the evidence will be burned."

The sirens grew louder.

"Everyone be cool," Levi said. "The troopers are almost here."

They listened for a few more minutes, but the men said nothing more until the women and officers entered the house.

Taylor's head hurt with the irony. Marshall had another child and videos of Grace and Maddi on his phone. And he shut up after Levi urged Austin to kill every one of them. All his suspicions of her, all of his judgmental comments about her and others, and yet . . . her stomach didn't churn. Her pulse didn't race.

The others looked at her with wide eyes, waiting for her reaction.

She smiled. "Well, that clarified everything, didn't it? Thank you, Principal Jackson." She stumbled to a chair and sank into it. All her limbs tingled as blood rushed to her extremities. Sucking in breaths, she smiled. *Freedom, once again. Even Tommy can't twist Levi and Austin out of this.*

Grace and Maddi stared at her. "You didn't know about Marshall's other child?" Grace asked.

"No, I didn't. Seems like we were both keeping secrets." She walked into the living room and gazed at the photos of her time in the village, camping in Denali, her grandkids, and family visits to Alaska. All showing happy people and great memories.

All lies.

She and Marshall had pretended. The truth emerged as soon as the visitors left, and the cameras were shoved into pockets. They argued and accused and did not touch. For years neither of them had laughed together unless family was around.

Shannon followed her. "How are you doing?"

Taylor sighed. "How did I live this way for so long? How did he?" She stood before two multi-photo frames showing babies and toddlers in one and their current versions in the other—her grandkids. "I barely know them, and they certainly don't know me. The only one who wants to connect is now cut off."

She bit her lip and tried to blink back tears. "And though so many strangers have loved my books, they embarrass my family, causing anger or shame. Well, from now on, that's their problem. I'm not hiding who I am anymore."

She blew out a long breath. "The only things I want to take from this house are some clothes, my computer, copies of my books and the medals they've won, photos of Brooke, my keyboard, and my songs. I have most of these pictures on my phone." She turned to Shannon. "Do you have room?"

"I know exactly where they'll go." Shannon held Taylor's hands.

"Would you be embarrassed to sit with me when I sign copies of my books?"

"I'd be proud. And I know just where you'll do it—the Homer Bookstore." She cocked an eyebrow. "I know the owners."

"Oooh, a woman with connections. I love it." Taylor touched Shannon's cheeks and kissed her lips.

Grace and Maddi entered the living room. "Either you two kiss a lot," Grace said, "or we have great timing. Or bad, depending on your perspective."

"Not enough," Shannon said with a smile. "And neither of us cares about your timing." The two women kissed again.

Afterward, Taylor texted a message to Barnes. *Please listen to the ENTIRE video. You will hear what the men say as they watch Austin's attack.*

"Let's check the fire," Maddi said, pulling on Grace's hand.

Soon, they were all standing on the deck, looking toward Grace's house. The firetruck's lights swirled against the still-falling snow as orange flames and sparks danced in the sky. In another context, the scene could have been festive.

"Wouldn't it be amazing," Grace said, "if they put out the fire before it burned everything?"

"I don't think that's a possibility," Taylor said. "It's a volunteer fire department. How many of those men would rather the place burn to the ground?"

Maddi hugged Grace from behind. "Maybe Levi had his basement rigged, so all he'd have to do is call a number, and a bomb would explode."

"I'll bet no one else knew that number," Grace said, "or he'd have died long ago."

Taylor's phone rang.

Maddi yelled, "Kablooey!"

Grace screamed and nearly jumped out of her skin as Maddi squealed in laughter.

"Damnit! I will so get you back!" Grace complained as Maddi hugged her, giggling.

James' number showed on Taylor's screen. She swiped. "James? Where—"

"MawMaw," Leslie whispered, her voice hoarse from crying and shouting, "James let me use his phone. I can't stay here. Will you buy me a ticket to see you?"

Taylor's mind spun. "I'll do anything to help you, Leslie. Try to sleep and talk to your parents in the morning. Maybe your father will be calmer—"

"He slapped me." Her breaths hitched repeatedly.

Taylor grabbed Shannon's arm as her stomach clenched. "I'm so sorry, Leslie. Please try talking to them in the morning. Call me if you still want to leave, and I'll get you out of there."

Leslie gasped, then softly whimpered. "Thank you, MawMaw. I love you."

Taylor's eyes flooded with tears. "I love you too. Call me any time."

Leslie ended the call. Taylor buried her face into Shannon's neck. That was the first time any of her grandkids had said *I love you* like they'd meant it. Not a throwaway line at the end of a call but a genuine, heartfelt statement of fact. Her heart drummed in her chest.

"Who was that?" Grace asked.

"My granddaughter," Taylor replied, wiping her cheek. "She needed support and love, but all she's getting right now are anger and hate. How many others in this town are like Leslie? Grace, Maddi, do you have any idea?"

Grace sighed and sucked in her lips. "More than people think."

Maddi hooked her girlfriend's arm. "I overheard Donna, the owner of Blue Sky, talking to one of her friends. A granddaughter told her she should have been a boy."

Taylor dreaded the response. "And?"

"Her friend told the girl, 'God doesn't make mistakes.'"

"Nope, *she* doesn't," Grace said with an ironic grin. "Except maybe with Austin."

"And possibly Levi and Leroy," Maddi added.

"The mistake is believing male and female are absolute," Shannon said.

The big flakes returned, plummeting in droves. The girls stuck out their tongues to catch them.

Shannon held out her hands. "Which of these is male? And which female?"

"If it's on my tongue," Maddi said, "it'd better be female."

"There is no gender in snowflakes," Grace said. "Each one is unique."

Shannon smiled. "Exactly. Then why wouldn't *she* do the same with people?"

They lifted their faces to the sky for a few seconds as the flakes kissed their skin.

"This old woman needs to go to bed," Taylor said. "It's been a long day, and tomorrow we need to pack."

"To go back to Gram's?" Grace asked.

Taylor opened the door. "To go to Homer."

"Fuck yeah!" Maddi shouted.

The girls ran inside.

Shannon shouted after them, "Don't hog the bathroom! Some of us need to pee."

19

A CONTAGION WORSE THAN COVID

For the first time in years, Taylor had not drunk four shots of liquor before climbing into bed. Shannon had spooned her and lightly stroked her skin until Taylor had drifted away to a soft, dark place without dreams. When the vibrations woke her up, she and Shannon lay in the same positions where they had fallen asleep.

Taylor scooted toward her nightstand and grabbed her phone. Gene's name appeared on the screen. She stood and quickly moved to the other bedroom, closing the door behind her. "Gene?"

"Where is she?" he growled.

Taylor's stomach dropped. "Leslie's gone?" She checked for missed calls and voicemails. Nothing. *Why hasn't she called me?* "Have you contacted the police and checked with her friends?"

"Of course."

"Did you listen to her this morning, or just pepper her with questions?"

He sucked in a breath like he was trying to restrain himself. "What did she tell you last night? I know she used James' phone to call you. What's going on between you two?"

"She called about my book. Did you read any of it?"

"I started . . . but it's pretty racy. I'm surprised you think it's appropriate to send to Leslie and James."

"They both have phones, Gene. What do they watch on Netflix or HBO or YouTube? My book is mild compared to what they can see every day."

"But you're their grandmother."

Her muscles tensed. "So now they'll know what I was like in college. When did Leslie leave?" *Maybe she had a wreck.*

"I don't know. Damnit, Mom! She was perfect before you sent her that book. I hope you're happy you destroyed my family."

She gripped the phone harder. "My book didn't destroy anything. What did she tell you?"

"That she understood how nervous you and Brooke were about your relationship."

"And you said?"

"I told her, 'That's great, but they have nothing to do with you.'"

Her throat tightened. "You knew what she was trying to tell you. Why couldn't you show some sympathy?"

His voice turned dismissive. "Every teen in America is being forced to wonder if they're queer or not. It's a contagion, worse than Covid."

"You sound like Levi."

"Who's he?"

"A local who wanted to kill his daughter and help my brother kill me." She balled her hands into fists. "Austin is dead, by the way. Thanks for asking."

"I don't know what you're talking about. Or want to know. Where's Dad? I tried to call him, but it went straight to voicemail."

"He's in jail right now and doesn't have access to his phone. He'll be home later."

Gene paused, then said quietly, "Dad's in jail? Why?"

She massaged her pounding temples. "It would take too long to explain, and I don't have the time. How do you think this ends with Leslie?"

"We'll get her home and talk this out."

Her skin heated as she gripped a pillow. "You slapped her last night and made it clear this morning you don't want to consider her feelings. Nothing changes between you two until you drop your authoritarian attitude. How did you turn into a bigot?"

"I am her father, not her enabler. We've already seen what happens when a parent refuses to discipline a child and wants to be her friend."

Gene had thrown this punch at her many times, and it still hurt. "Maybe if Heather had known a loving grandmother she could confide in, she wouldn't have chased abusive men all her life."

"Don't get involved, Mom."

"I already have." She ended the call. She knew Gene lashed out at her partly because of his guilt in Heather's death, but the pain in her throat was still real. The throbbing in her head came from her frustration with him. How could he not see he was driving Leslie away?

Shannon knocked gently and opened the door behind Taylor. "Leslie's father?"

"Yes. I didn't want to wake you."

"I heard most of your end. Has Leslie called?"

Acid gurgled beneath her throat. "No. I'm worried. I hope she hasn't hurt herself."

Shannon stroked Taylor's hair. "She'll call as soon as she buys or borrows another phone. Why don't we get dressed, and I'll make coffee and breakfast?"

Taylor stood and pulled Shannon to her. "Thank you." All her muscles relaxed. "I've never slept so peacefully before without booze."

"It's been a while for me too. Did I snore?"

She touched Shannon's cheek. "You purred. Did I?"

"Just some soft moaning when I stroked your skin."

Taylor raised her brows. "You must not have been too serious if all I did was moan."

"You needed to sleep. And so did I."

Taylor's phone rang, displaying an unknown number. She swiped quickly as her heart pounded. "Leslie?"

"MawMaw! This is my new number. I'm driving to the airport."

Shannon grabbed some clothes from the suitcase on the bed near Taylor and dressed.

"Your father called. He ordered me not to get involved. Then told me about your conversation this morning."

"Whatever he told you is a lie," she snapped.

"He wouldn't listen?"

"He wouldn't stop yelling at me. I tried staying calm and talked about your book. I gave him every clue I could that I was in a similar situation. All he did was blast you for butting in. He ordered me to not get involved in any LGBTQ business, that I was just going through a phase."

"Yes, something he now blames on me and the media."

Shannon whispered, "How do you like your coffee?"

"Cream, no sugar."

"I'll bring it to you."

Taylor smiled and mouthed, "Thank you."

She left the room, closing the door behind her.

"Was that Shannon?" Leslie asked.

"Yes."

"Is she your girlfriend?"

Is she? Her head seemed to drift. "We haven't discussed that, but she is a very good friend. I'm going to stay with her in Homer."

"But . . . what about PawPaw?"

"I can't live here, Leslie." She didn't want the girl to turn against her grandfather, but she could no longer pretend. "PawPaw is very similar to your father. We . . . we haven't been close for many years. What did your mother say?"

Her voice tensed. "She defers to Dad, as always. I tried to talk to her, but all she said was why can't I wait until I'm in college when I'm out of the house."

Taylor asked gently, "Why can't you?"

"I'm lonely," she whined. "I have *teammates*, not friends. A week ago, some girls I didn't know were handing out rainbow bracelets. I asked why. They said to show support for the LGBTQ community in

Florida because their governor signed a *Don't Say Gay* bill. I put one on. James saw me with it and joked about my being gay to our parents. I tried to explain, but Dad said to stay away from that crowd, and Mom looked so afraid. I knew then what would happen if I ever tried to talk to them about . . . my problem."

"You don't have a problem, Leslie. Your parents do."

"James gave me some money before I left. We talked some. He's sorry for ratting on me about the bracelet."

"Good for him." Her chest warmed. *There is hope in that family.* "If you want to see me, I'll fly you to Anchorage, then take you to Homer."

She hitched a breath. "Would that be okay with Shannon?"

"She'd love to have you. And so would Grace and Maddi—that's Shannon's granddaughter and her girlfriend. You'll love them." The possibility of welcoming Leslie into her life warmed her heart. "If you come to Alaska, your whole life changes. You'd have friends, and you'd have adults you could talk about anything with. Are you sure you want to come here?"

"Yes, but what if Dad flies up?"

"He won't have any idea where we are. Maybe it would be easier to talk to your parents from up here. Maybe they'd be more willing to listen and understand if they see the consequences of their rejection."

"Okay. When would I fly?"

"I'll have to check what's available, but sometime today." The implications of such a move then twisted Taylor's stomach. She'd allowed herself to become excited without thinking this through. "Leslie, you've worked hard to be a top student and athlete. If you stay up here—"

"I know, but for now, I'm just visiting my grandmother over spring break."

Taylor closed her eyes and bowed her head in relief. "You're off next week?"

"Yes."

"Well then, you and your parents will have several days to figure this out. I'll text you when I have the flight information."

"Thank you. I can't wait to see you."

"I can't wait to hug you. Bye for now." Taylor blew out a breath. Not a life-changing move. Just a vacation, though she worried a week was not enough time for Gene to come to his senses.

Shannon opened the door with a mug of coffee in her hand. "How did that go?"

"Wonderful. I need to check flights." She stood, intending to go to her office.

Shannon laughed. "You're naked, Taylor. Even the girls wear t-shirts and boxers outside their room."

Taylor's face flushed with heat. "I'm sorry. I'm excited to see Leslie again. I mean, it's horrible her father has driven her to this, but I am so happy she wants to see me. A week ago, I was afraid of anyone knowing I wrote lesbian romances or that I'm queer. I thought everyone in my family would disown me. And now Leslie can't wait to see me." She kissed Shannon's lips. "Pardon my morning breath."

"I don't think it's stronger than my coffee breath." She gave the cup to Taylor. "We'll see you in a few minutes. The girls are raring to go." She closed the door behind her.

Taylor took a few sips, pulled clothes out of her bag, and got dressed.

She found the girls devouring pancakes at the table and Shannon stacking two plates with another batch she had brought. Before Taylor sat down, Grace said, "Tell us what you want from your office, and we'll load it into Gram's car."

Taylor followed them to the room and pointed to two boxes of music, her book medals, copies of her novels, and the keyboard set-up. She grabbed her computer and went back to the table where she found her pancakes buttered.

"Do you want syrup?" Shannon asked.

"Yes, thank you. Do you think we can be in Anchorage by nine tonight, or would ten be better? I can get Leslie onto a flight leaving DFW at 2:30."

"Ten might be safer," Shannon replied. "It's a five to six-hour drive to Anchorage, maybe more, depending on the weather and the roads."

The girls carried the keyboard into the kitchen. "This thing weighs a ton," Maddi said.

"It weighs more when you're walking backward," Grace said with a grunt.

Shannon held the doors open until the girls exited the house.

Taylor bought the ticket, typed in all of Leslie's information, then forwarded the flight info to Leslie's phone. Soon after, she received a text. *Thank you! I just parked my car. Will text you when I'm at the gate.*

For the next hour, they packed their vehicles.

"We need to get your car before we leave town," Shannon said to Taylor.

"I'm not taking it. Marshall's truck is dead. He can dig my Subaru out of the snow. I'd rather drive with you to my new home."

"Good," Shannon said. "I hate driving by myself. I texted my neighbor to plow my driveway and shovel the walkways. He'll make sure the house is warm and the water pump works."

The girls burst in from the mud room.

"We have shit coming," Maddi said, scrolling through her phone. "Tommy's gone crazy and is trying to get people to come over here."

"Crazy about what?" Taylor asked.

"He ranted all night on Facebook about the fire and how we doctored the video. 'There's a reason that part is dark,' he said. But what really set him off was a friend of his saw two people duck into an abandoned house and then lights shining through a window. He thought someone was robbing the place, so he checked it out. And found his daughter Laura and Paige 'going at it.'"

Taylor clasped her hands. *Please let them be safe.*

"Where are the girls?" Shannon asked.

Grace locked eyes with her grandmother. "At your place. They'd seen the video of Austin and Levi and knew our door was unlocked and the camera disabled. Laura texted me a few minutes ago about her father threatening Taylor."

"Tommy blames you for turning the girls queer," Maddi said.

"You know," Taylor said, "I wish I could claim the credit. The more queers are visible, the better the world is. But most stay in the closet like I did for forty-plus years. Hiding takes its toll."

"So does hatred," Grace added. "What will Laura and Paige do now? They'll never know any peace here."

A green Ford Explorer drove into the driveway, followed by a black jeep. Each backed up, completing a 180 with their fronts facing toward D Street, blocking the entrance for any other cars. Principal Jackson and Allison emerged and trudged through the eight inches of new snow toward the mud room entrance.

Her pulse racing, Taylor led the others to the porch. "Hello, Allison. Principal Jackson."

Allison stomped her boots to rid them of snow and looked at Grace and Maddi. "I'm sorry Levi did that to you two. No girl deserves that."

"Even queers?" Grace asked.

Allison cocked her head and tightened her eyes. "I said *no* girl, and I meant it."

Grace nodded at her.

Jackson grabbed the snow shovel leaning against the porch railing and began to cut a trail between them and his and Allison's cars.

"You cried when Brooke died?" Grace asked.

The two locked eyes. "Maybe more than you." She looked at Taylor. "I'm sorry you had to go through that, Taylor. Your own brother, no less. But y'all took care of him."

"Thank you, Allison," Taylor said. "Brooke's death must've reminded you of your own loss."

Allison sucked in a breath and nodded.

Grace scrunched her brows. "What loss . . . ?" Then the memory slapped her head, and she looked toward Allison. "Your son died in a car accident. I'd forgotten. I'm sorry."

Allison pursed her lips. "Five years ago. A drunk driver."

Grace nodded and reached out her hand. Allison grabbed it for a few seconds, then let go.

"What brings you here?" Taylor asked.

"Crazy Tommy is on his way. Laura and Paige aren't here, are they?"

"No," Taylor replied. "We didn't hear about them until Maddi checked Facebook this morning. Is that why he's coming?"

"Partly," Allison said. "We were afraid the girls were here and came to warn you."

Maddi flipped out her knife and grinned. "Didn't you watch the video? We're batting four for four just by ourselves."

"Who's the fourth?" Allison asked.

"Well, actually, Marshall was the first," Shannon said. "I had to hit him upside the head for getting too frisky with his rifle."

"Marshall decided to be jealous about someone he's disliked for years," Taylor said.

Allison squinted. "Jealous?"

Taylor hooked arms with her friend. "Of Shannon and me."

"Oh, Lord," Allison muttered, then harrumphed. "Maybe I'm missing out on something."

"Find yourself a good woman," Grace said with a smile. "You'd be much happier with life."

Allison shook her head. "Couldn't get much worse with my husband, so I'll think about it."

Grace barked a laugh. "I'd pay lots to see that, Allison. Send me pictures when you find her."

Jackson returned the shovel to the porch.

Horns blared behind the garage. People shouted, "Move your fucking cars!"

Jackson rolled his eyes. "The crazies have arrived." He trotted toward the noise.

Allison raised her brows at Taylor. "You might need a gun."

Maddi closed her knife and slipped it into her pocket. "Tommy and his brothers are serious nut cases. You never know what they'll do." She left the porch. "C'mon, Grace."

The girls followed Jackson.

"Where's yours?" Taylor asked Shannon.

"In the front seat. I'll just hang back in case we need it." Shannon opened her front door and pulled her shotgun closer.

Taylor hooked Allison's arm while she walked toward the girls. "Come on, let's see what the ruckus is about."

Tommy, his wife Betty, and his brothers were yelling in Jackson's face. Tommy's belly hung over his belt. Stocky with an enormous square head and beady eyes, he had an unusually high-pitched voice that shrilled when he was angry.

Maddi lurked near the garage, close but not noticeable. Grace stood a few steps behind Jackson, who held up his palms and said, "The girls aren't here, Tommy, so turn around and go home."

Tommy noticed Allison and Taylor approaching and broke away from Jackson.

"Have you hooked up with the queers, Allison?" Tommy sneered.

The shouting stopped.

Allison released Taylor's arm and planted her fists on her hips. "If you and your brothers were the only alternatives, I'd sure consider it. You boys get uglier every year. Betty, how do you stand it?"

Betty raised her brows slightly as a tiny grin formed on her face.

Taylor folded her arms and realized she wasn't nervous. "After all your clamoring on Facebook, this is all you could get to follow you here? Why are you making so much noise in my driveway, Tommy?"

"Where are you hiding my daughter?" he shrieked.

"I'm not hiding Laura or Paige, but I understand why they'd stay away from *you*."

"You turned my daughter into a queer."

Taylor smiled. "If reading my books gives some the courage to accept who they are and tell others, I'll write more. Why do you hate queers?"

Tommy spit. "It's not natural. God created Adam and Eve, not Adam and Steve." One of his brothers laughed.

Shannon groaned. "How old is that joke, and you still laugh like it's the first time you heard it?" She shook her head. "Men."

Tommy's face reddened as he stomped toward Taylor, his finger stabbing the air between them. "We are searching your house, and if I find Laura and Paige, I—"

Maddi covered the distance to him in two quick leaps and kicked his left knee. He gasped and crumpled onto the powdery snow. Before his brothers could move more than a foot toward her, she'd flipped out her blade and crouched. "You do not want to take another step. Back off. His knee still works."

Tommy groaned as he grasped his leg, barely visible in the snow. Neither of his brothers moved toward Maddi. They took a looping path toward Tommy and helped him up, slapping the flakes off his clothes.

"Next time, I'll break it," Maddi said.

His breathing labored, Tommy said, "All of you queers need to leave this town."

"I agree," Taylor said. "We are heading out today."

Grace spit out her words. "Did you burn my house, Tommy?"

His nostrils flared as he shot her a fevered stare. "Word has it that you and your whore did it. Now you'll have to find some other mirror to dance in front of."

Grace clenched her fist and charged toward him. Jackson stepped in front of her. "Don't, Grace." He held her arms. "That's what he wants you to do."

A siren yelped once, then twice more as a trooper car drove slowly down Fourth Avenue. Through a loudspeaker, Officer Barnes said, "Return to your cars and unblock this road."

Jackson and Allison backed their cars toward the deck.

Tommy shot a glare at Taylor, then spit on the snow. His brothers helped him back to their truck. After Barnes had parked, Tommy spun his tires as one of his brothers flipped off everyone behind them.

Jackson emerged from his car and found Grace standing with Maddi and Taylor. "Will you be in school after the break?"

"I'm never coming back to this town," she answered.

Jackson blew out a breath, then nodded. "I understand. Call the school a week from Monday so we can arrange to finish your courses online."

Grace nodded. "Okay. What about Laura and Paige? I don't think they're coming back."

"Tell them the same thing."

Jackson held his hand out to Taylor. "Thanks for holding down the fort this past quarter. The kids enjoyed your classes. And I enjoyed *The Moonstone Girls*. I've never read a book that made me laugh and cry so many times."

Taylor shook his hand as a tingling warmth spread in her limbs. "Thank you, Mr.—"

"Ralph. Just Ralph. Make sure Grace calls me."

"We will," Shannon said, joining the group.

He nodded and walked back to his Jeep.

Allison approached Grace with a grin and hands on her hips. "Are you going to push me down?"

Grace smiled. "I haven't decided."

Allison cocked a brow. "You've got some spunk, girl. Reminds me of a certain teenager I used to know about thirty-five years ago." She opened her arms, and Grace leaned in for a hug.

"Seriously," Grace said, "send me pictures when you find her."

Allison laughed. "You'll be the first to know, but don't hold your breath." She released Grace and looked at Taylor and Shannon. "You two take care of yourselves and these young'uns. And Maddi, damn, you're a devil with that knife. Keep everyone safe."

Maddi nodded.

Jackson drove out the driveway, followed by Allison.

Officer Barnes stood with a glaring Marshall by the trooper's car. Taylor's eyes fixed on her husband's, her mind swirling with scenes of anger and hurt and regret.

Shannon spoke quietly to Taylor. "We can leave anytime you're ready. Do you want us to give you some privacy?"

"No. Come with me." Taylor moved toward the men, the others following close behind.

Barnes tipped his hat. "I hope we didn't ruin your gathering."

"No, you came at a good time," Taylor said as she stared into Marshall's eyes. Once they flinched, she knew he'd seen the entire video they'd posted.

"Why were they here?" Marshall asked.

Holding Maddi's hand, Grace said, "Tommy thought we were hiding his daughter and Paige after we turned them into queers."

Marshall scrunched his forehead. "They're queers now?"

Maddi grinned. "Yeah. Taylor has unleashed a plague on this town. Good thing we're leaving before it infects you and Barnesy."

The officer tucked in his chin and scolded her with his eyes.

"Officer," Shannon said, "you know what Tommy's likely to do when he finds Laura. What are her options?"

"How old is she?" Barnes asked.

"They're both eighteen," Grace replied. "Seniors like me. Paige lives with her grandparents. She's supposed to move out when she graduates."

"Considering their age, they should find another place to live. Tommy doesn't have to provide anything for Laura. Same for Paige's grandparents. Do they have friends they can stay with?"

Shannon glanced at Taylor. "I think they might."

Barnes listened to an alert from his radio, sighed, and faced the women. "There's a wreck on the Parks Highway just north of the Fireweed Roadhouse, so I have to leave. Where can I find you?"

"Nowhere close by," Taylor replied. "You have our phone numbers."

"Well, I need to run. Marshall, make sure you behave."

As soon as Barnes left the driveway, Marshall said, "Gene called a little while ago. He thinks you know where Leslie is."

"She's where she needs to be," Taylor said.

He tightened his lips and thrust out his chin. "Why'd you have to interfere with his family?"

"I'm helping his family whether he knows it or not. He just doesn't understand that yet." She sucked in a breath and sighed it out. "Marshall, I'm sorry I wasn't honest with you or myself so many years ago. As a result, we've spent a lifetime hiding things from each other. I thought maybe something would change if I let you read my books, but they just caused you more anger and heartache. I'm leaving now with my friends."

He frowned. "Where are you going?"

"Far away. My car is parked on the backside of the loop at the campground by the river. I left my fob and house key on the kitchen table."

She turned and walked toward Shannon's car. The others moved toward their vehicles.

He threw his arms above his head and shrieked, "Just like that, you're going to leave?"

"Just like this, I'm going to live." She climbed into the Suburban and shut the door. The seat hugged her as she glanced at the woodshed one last time, its logs trapped inside, frozen and cold, waiting to burn. She knew that feeling too well.

Shannon started the engine and drove past Marshall—his hands clasping his head—for the last time. Taylor's stomach fluttered with excitement as a future full of friends and laughter and love seemed within reach.

20

CARAVAN OF QUEERS

Taylor remembered the first time she rode in Shannon's car through the park, worried about being seen, diving to the seat before Sammy Lee could spot her. Now, she sat upright, looking for people to greet.

Leslie texted. *I'm boarding the plane!*

Taylor replied. *Great. Get some sleep during the flight. Will see you in eleven hours. Love you!*

Shannon turned into her parking lot and stepped out of her car. When Grace pulled in, she said, "Text Laura and Paige. I'm sure they've been worried about Tommy checking on this place." Shannon gazed at her duplex. "I'm going to be so happy to get out of here. This house has no character. It's just a vinyl box in the woods."

"Someone else has been here," Maddi said. She froze and pointed to tire tracks next to her truck.

"Maybe our neighbor?" Shannon asked.

Maddi looked at the unblemished snow outside the other duplex. "No." She turned back toward their front door and whipped out her blade. "Grace, did they answer?"

Grace checked her phone, then shook her head. "Shit."

Shannon pulled out her shotgun.

Sweat dripped from Taylor's armpits. *Please no.* She shivered as she approached the door.

Shannon unlocked the deadbolt and turned the knob. As she pushed open the door, the others groaned. Spasms surged through Taylor's gut.

Ketchup, mustard, and syrup dripped down from the letters of "Queers Live Here," and "Groomers," and "Pedophiles" on a wall. Possibly the entire contents of the refrigerator had been dumped on floors and furniture. Flour and sugar had been tossed everywhere.

"Laura? Paige?" Grace called.

Shannon moved forward, trying to avoid stepping on food or garbage. "Whoever it was broke through the back door."

"It was Tommy and his crew," Maddi said as she slipped down the hall toward Grace's bedroom.

Shannon and Grace moved gingerly toward the other bedroom.

Taylor took photos, her stomach tight.

"Laura? Paige?" Grace called again. "You're safe now. If you're here, come on out."

A muffled voice said, "Grace?"

Taylor jerked her head toward Shannon's room. *Please, don't let them be hurt.*

Shannon leaned her shotgun against a wall and walked toward the sound.

Grace shouted, "I'm here, Laura."

Her heart thumping, Taylor entered the room and found clothes strewn over most of the carpet, some wet with yellow stains. The smell of urine soured the air.

Something pushed up the quilt hanging off the end of the bed.

"They're in the basket," Shannon said, then pulled off the cover.

Panting, Grace opened the lid. "I'm here," she said softly. "Laura, Paige, come on out."

Shannon pulled out pillows and blankets, revealing Laura's back.

Taylor grabbed the bedpost and took a deep breath.

Grace helped Laura stand and step out. Her braids loose and

frayed, she grabbed Grace in a fierce hug. Shannon reached down for Paige. Her face was wet with tears, and her curly mop lay limp on her head. She panted through a slack mouth as Shannon helped her out.

Paige's eyes widened at seeing Taylor. Before the girl could fully extend her arms, Taylor rushed to pull her close. "I'm so sorry, Paige. You're safe. We'll get you out of here."

"It was my father and uncles," Laura said, pushing her loose hair out of her face. "We heard a truck pull up and thought maybe it was you. Then I heard him banging on the front door, calling my name. We pulled the quilt over the basket, grabbed pillows, and got inside. They called our names as they looked around the house. When he couldn't find us, he told them to trash the place. They screamed and laughed like crazy men. We were so scared. After ten minutes, they left, but we thought they might still be outside." She looked around the room. "I'm so sorry, Shannon."

"It doesn't matter, Laura," Shannon said as she patted the girl's back. "Now we don't need to pack."

"Where are you going?" Laura asked.

"To my house in Homer." Shannon smiled. "And yes, you can come with us if you want."

Laura hugged the woman. "Thank you!"

Taylor touched Paige's face. "Are you better?"

She hitched a breath and nodded. "Mrs. MacKenzie, can I come with you?"

"Certainly. And please call me Taylor."

Paige squeezed her again.

Maddi stood in the doorway with a small duffle bag, her eyes moist and puffy. "I collected what they didn't ruin. Everything else was tossed in a full bathtub where they dumped my hair dye and all my makeup. And there was piss around the tub, so I'm sure it's in the water. Oh, and they used my lipstick to write 'Smile for the camera' on the mirror. Those are some sick dudes. I took photos for Barnesy." Her lips quivered. "All my wigs are ruined." Her body shook as she wept.

Grace held her and pressed her forehead against Maddi's. "Gram will buy you new ones and replace all your makeup."

"You sure?"

"Yes, she's sure," Shannon said, hugging them both.

The girl with ice in her veins had finally been hurt, but her friends would make sure she wasn't broken. Taylor kissed Maddi's cheek. "We'll stay in Anchorage tonight and shop in the mall tomorrow before driving to Homer. If you see a dress you like, I'll buy it for you."

Maddi wiped her tears. "Something short?"

Taylor laughed. "As short as you want."

"With cut-outs," Grace said, grabbing Maddi's hands. "You'll be the sexiest girl in Homer."

Maddi sniffed and stretched her lips into a smile. "Glammed up and hot as hell. Nobody knows me there. I can dress however I want."

Taylor smiled and looked at Shannon. "We should hurry before Tommy realizes his mistake and comes back."

Shannon nodded. "Grace, help find anything we can salvage."

"I'm calling Barnes." Taylor pressed his number and waited for several rings before he answered.

"Taylor. What's up?"

"Tommy and his brothers trashed Shannon's house on F Street. Laura and Paige hid in a basket while they pissed everywhere and made the nastiest mess they could. I'll send you photos in a few minutes. We're going to leave before they return. The front door will be unlocked."

"Jesus Christ! What's wrong with those fellas?"

"I don't have time to go through the list," Taylor said. "Laura and Paige are going with us. Please don't tell anyone."

"Okay. I won't be able to get there for another hour. Drive safe." He ended the call.

Shannon and Grace had partially filled a suitcase.

"Are we ready?" Taylor asked.

"Let's go," Shannon said. As she walked into the living room, she grabbed the photo of Pete from the wall.

By the time they reached the Parks Highway, Laura and Paige were asleep in Shannon's back seat.

"They couldn't make a sound," Taylor said, "while those crazy men yelled all kinds of things. One of them may have opened the basket and seen the pillows. And yet the girls couldn't flinch." She turned toward Shannon. "Would Tommy have hurt them?"

Shannon entered the highway. "How crazy does a man have to be to do what he did to my house? Crazy enough to kill his daughter and her lover. He had to have burned Levi's house. Surely, he'll go to jail."

"Even if he does, he'll always believe I turned his daughter queer."

"As will many others. More than a few people will interpret our story of the past few days as an obvious attempt to spread the queer agenda."

"True," Taylor said. "No one but you knew Grace and Maddi were a couple before I gave Grace my books. So they'll say I turned them queer. You lived in Clear for two years before outing yourself to the girls and succumbing to my advances. Laura and Paige snuck out to be with their boyfriends before they read my book. And now this caravan of queers is heading to Anchorage to pick up my granddaughter who turned lesbian after reading my book. They'll see a common thread— my novels. Which is why they want all LGBTQ literature to be banned because look what happens if you don't."

Shannon shook her head. "Levi and his ilk will certainly make that case."

Taylor sighed. "Seems like for every step forward, we're forced to take two back. How many people in this country want to reinstate sodomy laws and ban same-sex marriages?"

"More than will admit in public," Shannon answered.

"So what do we do?"

"Tell the truth. Your book originally ended with Austin sneaking into Levi's community meeting and shooting you, or not, depending on the crowd's reaction. Tell what really happened, including two girls terrified in a basket while grown men pissed everywhere."

A chill crept into Taylor's chest. "And now those girls have nothing but the clothes on their backs. Grace and Maddi have just a little more."

Shannon glanced at Taylor with a smile. "They have us and all the love we can give them."

Taylor sighed. "And, I hear, a beautiful house on a hill, like a ship on stilts floating above a sea of rhubarb. Sounds wonderful."

Shannon laughed. "Which is suddenly very crowded."

They stopped for a few minutes at Maddi's house, where she left her truck and packed the few things she'd kept at her mother's. Then the caravan of queers returned to the highway.

Taylor fed her playlist from the early 70s through the car's speakers so she and Shannon could sing, to the great delight of the girls in the back seat, who joined in occasionally. Paige sat on her knees behind Laura, redoing her loosened braids.

Before Trapper Creek, they stopped for gas, snacks, drinks, and bathrooms.

"Are these all yours?" the smiling, middle-aged cashier with bright pink lipstick asked.

The four girls turned their heads and smiled at the two women who chuckled.

"Yes, they are," Shannon answered. "One grandchild and her friends. I'm Gram and this is MawMaw."

"And we'll pick up my granddaughter in Anchorage," Taylor said with a smile.

"All girls?" the cashier asked while bagging the snacks.

"No guys allowed in this family," Maddi said as she flung her arm around Grace's neck, kissed her temple, and headed outside. Laura and Paige shared an ice cream cone, not caring if their tongues touched, as they walked through the door held open by Grace.

The cashier pursed her lips as she handed the last bag to Shannon.

"Aren't they a hoot?" Shannon asked. "Thank you."

Taylor sipped her coffee as the woman's face followed Shannon, who was now laughing with the girls outside her car.

"Disapprove?" Taylor asked the cashier.

The woman snapped her head back to Taylor, looking exactly like her mother the second-to-last time they'd talked face-to-face.

The cashier smiled at the customer behind Taylor. "Did you find everything?"

The memory of that meeting with her parents fought its way into Taylor's mind as she walked to the Suburban. She tried talking to the girls and eating some of Maddi's fudge M&Ms, but when she shut the door and buckled up, that day slammed into her head with a vengeance. Her stomach churned as she stared out the windshield, watching the movie in her mind.

Her parents had flown to Las Vegas the day after Austin was arrested and driven to Kingman. At the time, Taylor had no thoughts of hiring a lawyer. What had she done? But Pat and Ken knew their son needed the best they could afford.

Her parents met first with Austin in the hospital. Taylor waited in the main lobby. When they emerged from the elevator, Taylor stood and approached them. They offered no hugs, just hard, disappointed faces.

"You stabbed your brother?" Dad asked.

"He held a gun to my head and told the police he would shoot me." Their eyes didn't flinch, lips tight against their teeth. "He killed Brooke."

"He denies that," her mother said.

Taylor's stomach boiled. "He killed the drag queen, then called Diego's family so they'd know where to find and kill Tony and Phillip."

Her father's jaw muscles bulged repeatedly. "Why are you trying to ruin him?"

"Because he kicked Brooke out of the van when I was driving fifty on the highway."

"She'd pulled a knife on him!"

"Yes, because he held his gun to her chest and threatened to kill her if I didn't drive faster."

"That's not what he says."

Her face burned. "Why would I make this up?"

Her father's lips curled back from his teeth. "Because you and Brooke were homosexual lovers." He shook his head slowly. "How long was that going on?"

"Two days."

He barked a laugh. "You were best friends for four years, roommates for three, and you want us to believe you decided to have sex just three days ago?"

Mom's stare was intense; her beady brown eyes narrowed and cold as a vein beat in her neck—the same look she'd seen on the cashier's face—sharp and hateful.

Taylor's throat throbbed with pain; her legs wobbled. "Can we go somewhere and talk through this?" The fact they'd offered no sympathy, no comfort for the loss of Brooke, punched her gut. She couldn't get enough air into her lungs.

"No," her father said, "we need to hire a lawyer, which will cost us a fortune." They stomped away.

She collapsed into a chair and wept.

Taylor knew the police had called Brooke's parents early that morning when she was sedated. She'd tried calling their home later, but no one had answered, so they were probably on a plane.

She drove the van to the police station and waited inside. She expected to see them enter the building, so when she heard Francis say, "Taylor?" from behind, she almost fell out of her chair. Taylor jumped up, saw them, and approached them with her arms out for a hug.

When Brooke's father grabbed one of her arms and took her across the lobby, her stomach dropped. "How'd you get here so fast?" Taylor asked as Wyatt turned chairs around to face the corner.

"We flew in my plane," he growled. His tanned face reddened as he leaned toward her. "My daughter is dead because of you and your brother."

The world stopped. "Me?"

Francis dabbed her eyes with a tissue as her chin quivered under a beehive hairdo.

"Why did you allow Austin to go with you?" he demanded.

"We didn't know what he'd done. Brooke wanted—"

"You're blaming Brooke?"

Taylor couldn't breathe. "No, but—"

"And why were you camping like hippies in a van?"

"I thought she'd . . . told you that's . . . what we—"

"If you had stayed in hotels without your brother, none of this would've happened. Besides the fact that our only child died on the side of a road in nowhere Arizona, her reputation will be ruined over and over again during the trial because you had to tell the police you were both fucking dykes!"

Francis grasped his arm. "Wyatt, you have to lower your voice."

He jerked his head around to see if others had heard him.

Heat surged up Taylor's neck as she clenched her fists. "I loved Brooke more than myself. I would gladly have traded places and died in her place. We made every decision together. I'm sorry many of them turned out to be wrong, but we thought they were the best at the time. I will never forgive myself for her death, and I will never stop loving her." She stood and stared at the couple who had been like a second set of parents to her, always full of joy and happiness whenever they visited her and Brooke.

Taylor sighed and knew their relationship was over. "I loved you both and thought you loved me, but that was before you knew I was gay."

She left the building. She never spoke to Francis or Wyatt again.

The next day, Taylor went to the station, intending to provide more detail to the police. She found her parents sitting beside a gray-haired man in a dark suit.

He stood and approached. "Hello, I'm Dustin Blakely, attorney for your brother. Are you represented by counsel?"

She nearly gagged from his cologne. "No."

He smiled, revealing his exceptionally white teeth. "Your parents would like to speak to you privately. We can walk to my office."

A few minutes later, Taylor sat across a table from her mother and father in a cold room with plush leather furniture.

Her father cleared his throat. "According to Mr. Blakely, Austin's shooting of the two at the rest stop was self-defense. The prosecutor will have a hard time proving Austin killed the drag queen, but even if he does, the lawyer could spin it as temporary insanity caused by the total shock of . . . Austin's discovery."

Taylor stared at him and realized he couldn't admit his son had sex with a man.

He continued, "And it would be tough to prove that Austin was the one who called the bar to identify Philip and Tony."

She knew what was coming.

"The shock of Brooke's death made you say and do crazy things that night," her father continued, squinting his eyes like he was trying to hypnotize her. "You were angry at Austin for not preventing Brooke from falling out of the van."

Her chest burned. "Falling?"

"You were driving fast on the highway because you feared Diego's gang was chasing you. Austin said he saw another car leave the rest area right after you did. Brooke got scared because you were driving so fast. She yelled at you to stop, but Austin said the car was gaining on them. Brooke freaked out and pulled a knife on Austin. They struggled, and you slowed down. Brooke yelled again at you. She opened the side door and threatened to jump if you didn't stop—"

Taylor's head pounded. "Brooke killed herself."

"No," her father said. "It was an accident. She fell."

"Yeah," Taylor sneered, "and maybe I jerked the wheel accidentally during all the drama or drifted off onto the shoulder to make the *fall* more likely?" When she glared at him, she could only see Austin's boot kicking Brooke out the door. Her gut twisted.

"Something like that. Whatever you want to say that makes sense." He swallowed. "The other charges might put him in jail for maybe five years." Her mother's chest heaved. "But charging him with Brooke's murder can put him in for life. We can't bring her back, but you can help your family put this behind us with less turmoil."

They both looked at her with pleading eyes.

"Please, Taylor," her mother whimpered.

She stood, every muscle twitching as her pulse raced. She spoke slowly. "I will go back to the station and tell the lieutenant about this conversation. Then I will give them a recorded account of what happened, under oath. Austin is a homophobic, racist murderer who killed the woman I loved most in the world. Whatever I can do to put him in jail for life, I will do."

Her father slammed his fist onto the table as his face turned purple. "Damn you, Taylor!"

She stormed out of the room and then the building.

The memory faded, and Taylor again saw spruce forests and snowy mountains. The rejections from both sets of parents that day shaped the rest of her life. Being queer was dangerous and had to be hidden. What followed was crushing loneliness in private and a continuous stage performance everywhere else. She had buried her true self and lived inside her new character for a never-ending show.

Until last night.

"Taylor," Laura said, "would you and Shannon sing again?"

Shannon reached over and held Taylor's hand. "You're as pale as a ghost. And your skin is clammy. Are you sick?"

Taylor calmed her breathing. "No, just a bad memory." She grasped Shannon's hand and looked back at the girls. "I know exactly how horrible you feel about your parents' rejection. I felt the same many years ago, and it burned my heart and mind for years. Shannon and I will do everything we can to give you love and support." Tears dripped from her eyes. "So you will not have to hide who you are or love."

Shannon handed her a tissue.

"Thank you," Laura said, leaning forward to touch Taylor's shoulder.

"You're the best," Paige said as she hugged Taylor's neck.

A little later, the two women sang again, and Taylor's mind filled with happy memories of Brooke and her harmonizing in the van. She watched Shannon's joyous face belting out "Up Up and Away" by The Fifth Dimension and knew a very special person had entered her life. If Taylor had raised her dyke flag months ago, she and Shannon might have found each other sooner.

But now they felt a higher calling than just enjoying life with each other. They had five lost girls who needed them.

After a few more stops and hours on the road, they finally pulled into the parking area for the South Concourse at the Ted Stevens International Airport. Maddi emerged from Grace's truck wearing a clinging, low-cut, sheer golden dress and tennis shoes. Her red thong was clearly visible through the material. Her natural hair was gelled and combed back, revealing siren eyes with glitter eyeshadow. Her full lips were bright red.

Laura and Paige stared with mouths wide open. Shannon clapped her hands and smiled. Taylor stood breathless.

Grace walked around her truck, grinning, then hooked Maddi's arm. "Shall we?"

Maddi nodded.

Taylor gushed, "You are gorgeous. How?"

"I took some of Mom's makeup and found my prom dress from three years ago."

Grace squeezed Maddi's hand. "I had to force myself to keep my eyes on the road while she turned into a goddess."

"The last time I wore a dress and glammed up, the guys called me 'skank' and 'ho.' I ran outside, and Grace and I snuck away. Since then, nobody's seen me like this except for Grace and Gram."

"Well," Taylor said, "let's show the world what they've been missing. Are you nervous?"

"Not anymore. The people I care about the most love me. Who cares what everyone else thinks?"

Taylor nodded. "Exactly." She hooked Maddi's other arm. "May I?"

Maddi nodded.

They walked from the garage to the escalator, turning heads at every step. Maddi kept her smile as hundreds of eyes popped around her.

Once inside the terminal, Taylor's phone dinged with a message from Leslie. *I landed fifteen minutes ago and am just now leaving the plane. Meet me at Baggage Claim 5.*

Taylor replied, *On our way. We have two more girls with us—Laura and Paige. Will explain later.*

"What's Leslie like?" Laura asked.

"Wavy blonde hair, light blue eyes, about 5' 6", very athletic and smart. And she can sing."

"So she's perfect?" Paige asked.

"No, she's queer," Laura said. "Otherwise, she'd be home instead of sneaking off to Alaska."

Taylor turned, her stomach tightening. "Being queer makes her more perfect."

Laura and Paige scrunched their eyebrows and said, "Huh?"

Grace smiled, and Maddi nodded her head and clapped.

Taylor locked eyes with each of the girls as she spoke. "We need to eliminate the mindset that being straight is normal, and we're abnormal. I've lived most of my life believing that shit, and I won't allow you to do the same. You girls are better human beings because you've broken free from the continual pressure to fit into stereotypes."

"Compulsory heterosexuality," Shannon said.

"Exactly," Taylor agreed with a firm nod. "Girls are socialized from babies to adults to believe women have a natural preference for relationships with men. And guess why?"

"So they'll believe they need men," Grace said.

Maddi nodded. "Like Taylor and Brooke supposedly needed Austin to drive to Oregon. When all he did was fuck up their lives."

"Not anymore," Taylor said, blowing out a satisfying breath. "I am thrilled being with all of you, especially Shannon." She gave her a tender kiss.

"Oh, thank you, dear," Shannon said, hugging Taylor.

"People are staring," Laura said.

"Tough shit," Maddi said before kissing Grace.

"Maybe they're jealous," Paige said, then kissed an amazed Laura, who smiled, looked around quickly, and kissed her back.

The group hurried across the gleaming granite floor to a shiny escalator to access Level One, then went left to wait, all eyes looking back toward people descending from the upper level.

"Is that her?" Paige asked, pointing to a girl wearing sweatpants and a long sleeve t-shirt with tight, colored braids scattered around her blonde head. "She's pretty."

Taylor's heart jumped. "Yes!" Taylor waved. "Leslie!"

The girl's eyes widened in recognition, and she blushed, her lips twitching into a smile.

Taylor stepped quickly to close the distance and threw her arms around Leslie, squeezing extra hard to make up for the years without touching her. "Oh, I'm so glad you're here."

Leslie clutched her hard, then pulled one hand back to quickly wipe her face.

Taylor stroked her back. "You're safe, and you're with friends. They're all good girls and have such stories to tell." She leaned back to look at her granddaughter. "Did you sleep on the plane?"

"A little."

Taylor wiped a tear from Leslie's cheek as her stomach fluttered. "I know you're nervous, but you'll feel much better in a few minutes. Just let them pass without overthinking. They want you to be happy as much as I do." Taylor kissed her forehead. "You ready?"

Leslie blew out a couple of breaths and nodded. Taylor clasped her hand and led her to the others, who stood as couples on either side of Shannon.

Taylor stopped about two feet away, feeling taller than she was, and pointed. "That's Maddi and Grace."

Her eyes fixed on Maddi, Leslie asked, "Did you come from a party?"

"No, *this* is my coming-out party. The Maddi I always wanted to be."

Both girls gave Leslie hugs. "Your MawMaw is the best, tied with my Gram," Grace said.

"She's a badass," Maddi said with a wry grin.

Leslie snorted a laugh and glanced at Taylor. "Really?"

Taylor pursed her lips. "So they say. This is Laura and Paige."

The girls smiled and stepped forward to hug Leslie.

"I love your braids," Laura said.

Leslie touched one of Laura's box braids, her eyes wide with awe. "Did you do these?"

"Paige did. She'll do yours if you want."

Paige nodded and smiled.

"Cool." Leslie smiled. "And you must be MawMaw's girlfriend, Shannon. Who saved her life."

The woman grinned and held the girl's hand in both of hers as her eyes twinkled. "We all saved each other. I'm so happy to meet you."

"I love your buzz cut," Leslie said then laughed. "MawMaw, why don't you get one?"

Taylor chuckled. "Great idea! Shannon can do it after we get to Homer."

Grace grabbed a small red suitcase after Leslie pointed, and the girls walked in a pack, talking non-stop, punctuated with Maddi's squeals and Paige's giggles. Taylor and Shannon followed, holding hands.

Her chest light and her skin flushed with warmth, Taylor sighed. "I'm so happy to be with them and you. My heart has grown three sizes."

"That's impossible. It was always huge."

"But it had no one to love." Her insides shimmered with happiness. "Each time I finished a book, my heart hurt because I had to leave my characters. But these girls are real, and they're not leaving. I'll love them forever. Even if Leslie goes home after the holidays, we'll still stay connected. And you." She stopped and faced her friend, holding both hands, tears welling in her eyes and a lump of joy forming in her throat. "I love you, Shannon. I truly love you."

Shannon's eyes reddened, and she smiled. "I love you, Taylor Baird."

Taylor's hands moved up the woman's arms and around her neck. She leaned forward for a kiss, then stopped. "I don't even know your last name." She gasped. "What the fuck is it?"

Shannon wiped her nose and chuckled. "It's Wolfe. Shannon Wolfe."

"Cool. I like that." Their noses touched. "An intoxicating wolf, if ever I saw one." Taylor pressed her lips to Shannon's for a deep, lingering kiss.

After a few seconds, applause and whoops of "Go Gram!" and "Go, MawMaw!" filled the air. Their girls had come back to cheer them. Several others joined the young women with smiles and clapping and even a few pats on the back.

Blushing, the two women looked around them, offering happy nods to hundreds of strangers who now knew the secret Taylor had spent most of her life hiding.

Her chest expanded with pride as it filled with deep, satisfying breaths.

Taylor hooked arms with Shannon and walked forward, surrounded by a new generation of out and proud queer girls.

EPILOGUE
THE LIFE AND DEATH OF BROOKE SKIPSTONE

July 1, 2022

I sit now with Shannon, swinging on a bench on our deck, over-looking a lush green yard lined in rhubarb and delphiniums. The cedar shiplap house juts out from a grassy slope like a boat, supported by thick wooden posts, waiting for a super tide to launch on a new adventure. A long Pride banner stretches across the prow-shaped railing, visible to anyone who cares to look up to the hills from Kachemak Bay and the Homer Spit, a five-mile stretch of land jutting into the ocean—home to shops, boat harbors, restaurants, and hotels. And several display areas to announce special events and services, including the girls' first live edition of *The Queering* podcast. Call-ins welcome!

For years, queers have defended themselves by stating facts—sexual identity is not a product of social influence, queers don't seduce others into becoming queer, fear of the queer child has no logical basis. But Grace wants to try another approach. Why should governments and schools have any role in encouraging or discouraging straightness *or* queerness? Just like public schools can't promote religion, they shouldn't be able to promote heterosexuality. The question is not whether the queering of America *can* be stopped but whether it *should* be stopped.

The girls scamper onto the deck, bubbling with excitement.

"Wish us luck," Maddi says, wearing a purple wig, fishnet hose, Daisy Duke shorts, and a sports bra with the slogan *Love is Love* in rainbow colors.

"You don't need luck," Shannon says. "You've worked too hard to screw up now. Give 'em hell."

We both stand and share a group hug.

Their exuberance heats the air. I look from face to face and see passion and confidence. "Take a deep breath, then say *Showtime.* That always worked for me. Now go! The world is waiting."

Grace leans in to give Shannon and me a kiss on our cheeks. "Love you guys."

The others do the same before their footsteps thunder across the deck.

Shannon once said there is nothing more dangerous than a man with a podcast, except for queers who have the same. The girls have been developing their show for weeks, joined recently by Leslie, who brokered a deal with her parents. She went home after spring break only if she could spend half the summer in Alaska. Leslie missed our Juneteenth Pride March, but she was here for the Women's March and the celebration we hosted at our house. She stays in Laura and Paige's room and is a cherished member of our family.

Grace changed her last name to Wolfe and has cut all ties to the pervert, who remains in jail pending trial. Leroy, Tommy, and even Marshall struck deals with the prosecutor to provide information about Levi. Though the fire destroyed all his equipment and the house, two flash drives survived, containing videos of Grace and Maddi.

So much has happened in the world since we left Clear in March—more attacks on the LGBTQ+ community and against women's reproductive rights, mass shootings, and now Monkeypox, already being stigmatized as a gay disease.

Though it is easy to fall into despair over such events, living in a family like ours fosters hope and determination to call out wrong and do whatever we can to correct it.

I no longer hide behind my memories of Brooke or the new stories I created because of her. She is everywhere in my life—books with her name line shelves in this house and local bookstores, and her photos hang next to Shannon's beloved Pete on our walls.

But I have laid her to rest.

She no longer haunts my dreams or squeezes my heart. She is a glorious memory from a distant past.

Shannon is my soulmate and lover as we co-parent our girls who walk the beaches, holding hands and kissing freely. I call all my grandchildren, and they've grown to know me and my new family. My sons and their wives know where I live and are always welcome here. In a month, when *The Life and Death of Brooke Skipstone* is available in paperback, I will send them copies, authored and signed by Taylor Baird.

I don't need to hide behind Brooke's name any longer.

For now, we enjoy a sunny day in the upper fifties as we gaze across the bay at the Grewingk Glacier, which calves into a lake as it retreats, exposing fractured rock cliffs. A slide and tsunami have happened before in the 60s, but the danger threatening Homer increases as the globe warms.

So many possible threats endanger our lives, but we remain optimistic. We are embraced by love, enlivened by daily laughter, and thoroughly engaged in life.

Besides, if the flood comes, we'll all gather on the deck and ride this boat of a house over troubled water until we can build a better world.

Rainbow-colored and hate free.

It is five o'clock. Shannon clicks *Play*, and Grace's voice fills the air.

"Hello, Homer and all the communities around Kachemak Bay. If you're listening from anywhere else in the world, we welcome all of you to the first edition of *The Queering*."

Shannon grasps my hand as our chests swell with pride. We face the incoming breeze with joy and strength and love.

THE END

by
Taylor Baird

ACKNOWLEDGMENTS

NO ONE in the world is *actually* named Brooke Skipstone. Such a hard sentence to write and harsh truth to admit. The question before me now is what to do with her. She has possessed my mind for five books, and I'm unsure about her future.

I am convinced more than ever that reality and truth are constructs. I can see no difference between my life memories and those I've described in my books. If anything, the ones I've *created* are more real to me.

I could share so many more stories with you about Crystal Rose or Tracy Moonstone or Jazz or Laney or Grace and Maddi, but like most lives, they're often mundane and uneventful—not the stuff of high drama fiction. Nevertheless, they remain some of my most cherished friends. When the inevitable mind decay begins, I'm sure they will continue in my consciousness and outlive my family, who will claim I have lost it as I speak to invisible beings.

But we'll know I have joined a reunion of my peeps on Shannon's deck, where we toast the past with wine and whiskey, smiles, and tears. And hold hands to face what comes next.

Taylor said, "There's always a little truth in what I write, even if it's hidden on the edges." Through my eyes, that truth pervades every phrase and paragraph. The words within Brooke's covers are more real than any I utter or hear.

Maybe she'll come back for another saga. Or perhaps she'll evolve into someone else. I'm already feeling the rumblings in my soul of another story, more epic and archetypal than anything I've written so far.

I'm a pantser, so I will have to go with the flow before deciding. But I do feel a change in the air.

As I write this, most of the leaves—yellow, orange, and more red than usual, beautiful in death—have fallen, soon to be covered by feet of snow and frozen until May, when a new book will emerge.

Authored by? Wait and see.

As I write, I depend on beta readers and editors to help me understand what I've created and discover where I'm going. One of the best at this task has been Lili Bokan. I sent Ruth Torrence a description of my original idea. Her enthusiasm and approval gave me the go-ahead to proceed. She has helped me write four books now. And Emily Wright, an excellent author herself, was in on this one from the beginning and made so many parts better.

Additionally, I once again welcomed the great comments and suggestions from Bianca Lice and Oskar Leonard. New readers—Kaycee Racer, Tessa Hatfield, Abyjane Richards, Jordan Devine—helped fine-tune my story and writing.

Most special thanks go to Lily May Morris, an outstanding editor at both the microscopic and macroscopic levels. She is absolutely focused on how to make a character arc, chapter, paragraph, sentence, and single word the best they can be. I depend on her expertise.

Cherie Chapman has designed all my covers, each perfect for the book's themes and catching a reader's eye. She is the best. Check her out at ccbookdesign.com.

Without the help of all the above, I would have to wrestle with my multiple selves and ghosts alone. Deep and sincere thanks to all.

Many of them wondered whether this story was true. Otherwise, why would I use my name as Taylor's pen name? Did Brooke Skipstone die on the side of a road in 1974?

The more I think about it, the more I realize something very special and significant did. Or maybe my imagination has twisted things once again from event to symbol, or vice versa.

I do envy Taylor's liberation and finding love and purpose late in life—so different than many can hope for.

An ending found only in fiction? Perhaps not.

ABOUT THE AUTHOR

Brooke Skipstone is a multi-award-winning author who lives in Alaska where she watches the mountains change colors with the seasons from her balcony. Where she feels the constant rush toward winter as the sunlight wanes for six months of the year, seven minutes each day, bringing crushing cold that lingers even as the sun climbs again. Where the burst of life during summer is urgent under twenty-four-hour daylight, lush and decadent. Where fish swim hundreds of miles up rivers past bear claws and nets and wheels and lines of rubber-clad combat fishers, arriving humped and ragged, dying as they spawn. Where danger from the land and its animals exhilarates the senses, forcing her to appreciate the difference between life and death. Where the edge between is sometimes too alluring.

The Queering is her fifth novel. Visit her website at https://www.brookeskipstone.com for information about her first four novels—*The Moonstone Girls, Crystal's House of Queers, Some Laneys Died,* and *Someone To Kiss My Scars.*

Made in United States
Troutdale, OR
12/23/2023

16389877R00195